GETTING EVEN

Judy is an innocent 16-year-old when she is raped by her older brother—a drunken, vicious rape. It leaves her emotionally scarred, bitter and resentful, broken inside. She turns to alcohol to deaden her pain, but that only leads to a second rape. Judy begins to hate men. And as time goes on, she moves into a cabin on the California coast, and leads a solitary life. But life continues to deal her some cruel blows, and eventually her hatred of men takes a new turn. She begins to excise the pain by killing it. And now Judy is on her third murder. It gets a little easier each time.

EASY MONEY

Charley doesn't expect more than a cheap meal when he stops at the roadhouse, so finding Janie is a real bonus. She is exactly the kind of girl he is looking for to run a blackmail scam down in Miami Beach. Janie is 23 but looks like she could easily pass as a teenager, and Charley figures that the two of them can clean up running the underage-sex gambit on the lonely tourists. Janie agrees. The first guy they run the ruse on is a middle-aged widower. After seducing him, Janie changes into her teenage outfit, and Charley threatens him with the cops for seducing his sister. And so the cruel con begins.

Getting Even
Easy Money

ROBERT SILVERBERG

Stark House Press • Eureka California

GETTING EVEN / EASY MONEY

Published by Stark House Press
1315 H Street
Eureka, CA 95501, USA
griffinskye3@sbcglobal.net
www.starkhousepress.com

GETTING EVEN

EASY MONEY

ISBN: 979-8-88601-128-9

Cover design by Jeff Vorzimmer, ¡caliente!design, Austin, Texas
Text design by Mark Shepard, shepgraphics.com

PUBLISHER'S NOTE

First Stark House Press Edition: February 2025

7
Foreward
by Robert Silverberg

9
Getting Even
By Robert Silverberg

111
Easy Money
By Robert Silverberg

228
Robert Silverberg
Bibliography

FOREWORD

You will note from the copyright notice that these books were written more than sixty years ago. The world has changed quite a bit in the past sixty years, and I ask you not to hold me to account for having failed, in 1964 and 1966, to have my characters live up to the moral standards now being set forth by the inhabitants of 2025, who were not even born when I wrote these stories. I have written, among other things, a great deal of science fiction, but these two were not science fiction books and I made no attempt to predict the future in them. They are novels of their time. Please read them as that.

Robert Silverberg

Getting Even
ROBERT SILVERBERG

CHAPTER ONE

Carter was driving from San Francisco to Los Angeles via the coast route, Highway One, when he saw the totally naked girl sprawled out shamelessly on the beach. The time was just a little after dawn when he came upon her down there.

The coast route is not the quickest, nor is it the safest way to get to Southern California from the Bay Area. But it is by far the loveliest route, and in the summertime, the coolest. It hugs the Pacific shore for hundreds of miles, winding spectacularly through fog-swept redwood country. At some points, the road travels along cliffs hundreds of feet above the ocean; elsewhere on the route, it rides at sea-level.

There are long stretches of endless hairpin curves, and a man not fully alert at the wheel can easily go tumbling over an embankment and down a dizzying three-hundred-foot drop. But the chief inland route, U.S. 101, is swelteringly hot in the summertime, and so, despite all the hazards of fog and heights, Carter had chosen to travel via the coast route this time.

The road was practically deserted at this hour. Carter had to be in Los Angeles for business reasons by early afternoon, and just to play it absolutely safe, he had set out in the early hours of morning. He figured that he had to allow himself at least eight hours in which to make the trip down the California coast.

Now it was just past dawn, and Carter was nearing Monterey, with hours of solitary driving yet ahead of him. That was when he saw the nude girl.

The road curved in such a way that if he looked straight ahead and down, he had a good view of the beach from the seat of his car. Glancing down, he spied the bare-bodied figure on the beach, and his eyes widened a little in surprise. She was no bigger than a lizard, from this height, but Carter had unusually sharp eyes.

Naked! Yes!

The figure was that of a girl stretched out casually on a blanket. She lay on her back, stark naked, waiting for the embrace of the sun—or, perhaps, for someone else's embrace. He could see her bare breasts and even the tiny dots of her nipples. There could be no mistake about it. She was as bare as a newborn babe.

Carter slowed down.

He had always considered himself a keen and enthusiastic appreciator of womanly beauty, and something like this would be too good to miss.

The only thing he liked better than looking at a woman's nude body was touching a woman's nude body. And he had made good time so far on his trip, thanks to the emptiness of the road at this hour. He could well afford to take a little time out here for some entertainment, he decided.

Guiding his car over to the shoulder of the road, Carter parked it there, very carefully, by the embankment at the edge of the cliff. When he looked down, he was able to see the fringe of white beach a few hundred feet straight below the road, and then the blue Pacific.

The girl was about thirty feet from the edge of the beach on the ocean side. The morning sun was creeping slowly up the beach toward her. Now an arm of sunlight bisected her across the hips. Before long, all of her nude body would be in the direct light of the sun.

Carter kept a pair of field glasses in the trunk of his automobile. He went around back to fetch them, and, leaning over the side of the embankment, focused them with care on the girl.

She was blonde, and she was deeply tanned all over her body, with none of the white bikini strips at breasts and hips that are so common these days. Apparently, thought Carter, the girl was in the pleasant habit of taking regular nude sun baths. That was how her skin had acquired that all-over honey-tan color.

Her body was compact and muscular. She was extremely athletic-looking but there was nothing at all masculine about her appearance: she had full, ripe breasts tipped with little dark nipples, strong thighs, a flat belly, lean attractive legs. As Carter watched her, she stretched restlessly, drew her legs up, wriggled in sheer voluptuous motion.

Muscles flickered into view under the even brownness of her skin. The nude girl rolled over onto her belly, revealing luscious, mounded buttocks. Then, as though not caring for that position, she flipped back again to resume her supine position.

Carter felt his pulse-rate increasing at a furious pace. Perspiration plastered his thin, white shirt to his back. The morning was still cool, but there was sea moisture in the air, generating sweat. He began to breathe raggedly.

The girl was splendid.

In one wild instant of desire, Carter told himself emphatically that a view through field glasses was not enough. He had to see her close-up, to feel those high-peaked breasts, to touch those taut buttocks, to know her intimately, as she deserved to be known. There was something magnetic about the sight of this magnificent creature this superb female animal, lying so unashamedly on the beach, naked, waiting for the kiss of the sun.

He glanced at his watch.

It was only a little past six in the morning. The traffic would not start to get heavy for another few hours. If he got back on the road by seven or even half-past-seven, he still would be able to reach Los Angeles in plenty of time for his appointment.

But right now, Los Angeles and his business engagement there did not matter in the slightest. All that mattered in the entire universe was this naked girl sunbathing down there on the lonely beach.

I'll go to her, Carter thought.

I'll get me a little action. Yes!

He looked around. Someone had cut steps into the side of the cliff, leading down to the beach. Carter put the field glasses back in the trunk of his car, locked everything up, combed his hair in the reflection in his windshield, and started down the steps.

It was a long trip.

There must have been a hundred steps or more, and Carter was completely soaked with sweat before he had gone half way. But every step, he knew, took him that much closer to the full-breasted, wantonly nude girl who was sprawled out on the beach.

She still had not moved. She lay stretched out gracefully, one hand resting across her eyes to shield them from the sun, the other toying with little handfuls of the white sand. Her breasts rose and fell gently, the pointed nipples stabbing into the sky.

Carter took extra care to make his approach a silent one. He was certain that when the girl saw him creeping up on her, she would jump to her feet in panic, quickly wrap herself in the beachrobe that lay discarded a few feet from her blanket. Perhaps she would scream— certainly she would run away from him in terror, thinking that he was a rapist.

But perhaps not. A girl who sunbathes nude on an open beach might not panic so easily. In any event, he would get a close look at her before she fled, and that was what he wanted at the moment.

He continued the descent. Three steps from the bottom, Carter missed a step, lost his footing, and went flailing downward to fall noisily the rest of the way. He landed unhurt, with a dull thump, in the sand.

He rose immediately. You clumsy idiot, he cursed himself angrily. The girl was probably fleeing in fright by now after that entrance—

No.

She was still there. She had rolled over onto her stomach and lay there looking at him, grinning pleasantly. Sunlight sparkled on the ripe mounds of her bare buttocks. She was lying with her chin propped up by her fists, with her elbows in the sand, and as she lay in that position, Carter could clearly see the upper hemispheres of her breasts all the way down to the place where the rosy aureoles began. They were lovely breasts. They were not quite the same shade of tan as the rest of her, Carter noticed now, but a lighter creamier more delicate color.

She did not seem at all embarrassed by her nudity. She lay there fully exposed without making any attempt to cover herself.

"Hello," she said. Her voice was husky and musical. "You've got to be careful coming down those steps, you know. They're pretty tricky. You came damned close to having yourself a nasty spill."

Carter smiled awkwardly. Her dazzling beauty, clothed only by the sun, left him dumbfounded. He stared at the sumptuousness of her. After a moment, he said lamely, "I—I didn't mean to disturb you—"

"You aren't disturbing me. This beach isn't private, you know."

"But you're—you're—"

"Naked? What of it? It's the best way to sunbathe, isn't it? And I'm not embarrassed about it if you aren't. Come here. There's room on the blanket for the two of us."

She beckoned to him. Carter walked hesitantly toward her. The girl rolled over and sat up cross-legged, revealing the entire front of her body to him for the first time. Her breasts drew his eyes like magnets. They were big, heavy globes of flesh, but set high on her chest and close together, the way breasts ought to be. The nipples were dark and oddly small, almost virginal.

The rest of her was first-rate, too: the firm thighs, the taut belly, the hips and all the rest.

She said, "Usually there's nobody else on the beach till at least eight o'clock. Are you from around here? No, you aren't. I see that."

"I'm from San Francisco," Carter said. He felt like a sleepwalker, moving around in some unearthly dream, as he looked down at the ripe hills and valleys of her sumptuous, nude body. "I was driving down to L.A., but then I saw you on the beach—"

"I heard your car stop, and I figured it was something like that." Her blue eyes shot him a provocative glance. "Well? Aren't you going to take your clothes off and sunbathe too? We've got the whole beach here to ourselves, you know."

It was working out much too well, Carter thought. Things like this never happened so smoothly except in dreams, and he was still was pretty damned sure he was awake. He had never been frightened of a woman before. Ordinarily, he was a healthily aggressive male who took his women where he found them and gave them as good a loving as he got from them, with no complications. But he found himself almost frightened of this bold, beautiful, eerie girl with the sleekly shining nude limbs and the tapering, supple, athletic body.

"Is it—safe here? I mean, without clothes?" he asked, haltingly.

"Of course. In this part of the woods you do as you please. Anyway, I told you nobody ever comes along at this hour."

"I did," he objected.

"You were different. You saw me from the road." She shrugged. "Look, if you don't want to sunbathe, just forget the whole idea."

"No—if you say it's all right."

"Sure it is."

Hesitantly at first, then quickly Carter stripped off his clothes and deposited them in a little heap on the sand near the blanket. The girl did not look away as he undressed, even when he got down to his shorts. Instead, she appraised his nakedness frankly and without a show of modesty. And she seemed to approve of what she saw. Carter believed in keeping his body in trim, and women found him attractive. Take a good look, girlie, he thought, exposing himself fully to her keen gaze.

"I can't stay long," he explained to her as he lay down beside her on the blanket. The sun was very warm, even this early in the morning. "I have to be in L.A. by this afternoon."

"You can leave whenever you like," the girl told him blandly.

Carter was uncomfortably aware of the warmth of the girl's naked thigh only inches from his own. He wanted to reach out, to grab her, to throw his body on top of hers and take her. But she remained cool, and in a sense distant from him emotionally, though right up against him physically. He did not touch her. Like her, he shielded his eyes from the sun. He glanced sideways at her, noting the jutting profile of her breasts. She was no older than twenty-five, he decided. He couldn't make up his mind whether he had found a kook or a treasure.

There was a long moment of silence. Then the girl said, "What's your name?"

"Joe Carter. You?"

"My name is Judy," she said. She didn't offer a last name. He didn't inquire.

"You go sunbathing every day?" he asked.

"Every day that the sun shines. I get up at five in the morning and come out here."

"And you never meet anyone else?"

"Sometimes I do," she said enigmatically. "I don't mind company. I sunbathe for a while, and then I take a swim, and then I go back home and eat breakfast around eight o'clock."

"You live by yourself?"

"Most of the time."

"What do you do?"

She shrugged, and the shrug made the deep bowls of her breasts dance voluptuously. "All sorts of things," she said. "I support myself by selling little pottery things to the tourists."

They fell silent again. The girl stretched out on her back and covered her face with the back of her arm. The conversation seemed to be at its end.

After a few moments, Carter turned his head toward her and let his eyes travel over the elegant nudity of the blonde girl.

God, she was beautiful!

Her eyes were closed, and her face was serene, and her skin seemed to gleam in the dancing sunlight. Her big breasts rose and fell evenly in rhythm with her breathing. Carter had never seen such round, perfect breasts before, and he had seen plenty of breasts. These were incredible. He was obsessed with the desire to clasp his hands to them and caress them.

But he did not. Five minutes passed, and Carter still hesitated.

Unfulfilled lust made him tense and edgy. He held a debate with himself about whether he ought to reach out to touch the girl. She ignored him. She seemed to be sleeping soundly, bathed in the warmth of the sunlight. A fantastic girl, he thought. To be able to lie here stark naked next to a complete and utter stranger, sleeping calmly in the sun....

He couldn't stand it any more.

Carter turned toward her. He let his hand reach out and hover tentatively over the steep mound of her right breast. Then he lowered the hand to cup the warm, vibrantly firm flesh.

He expected her to brush the hand away. Instead, the girl moved toward him, still keeping her eyes closed and her face expressionless, and pressed her body tightly against his.

Carter's lips automatically went to hers. They kissed violently, a torrid, lingering kiss. She kept pressing her rich, warm lips against his until he thought he would scream from the tension of wanting her as much as he did. His free hand dove down the front of her body, over the satin of her skin, and found the warmth of her thighs.

Carter was a well-bred man. He believed in asking, not taking, when he was with a woman. So he said, "Do you want to make love?"

Her eyes opened, slit-wide.

"Yes," she said huskily.

It was almost eerie to make love on that empty beach, with the surf booming only a few yards away, and the sand pipers squeaking shrilly, the gulls wheeling and cawing overhead. They did not speak after that one interchange of question and answer. Carter touched her thighs, and they moved for him, and he rolled over onto her, feeling the sand under the blanket moving against his knees and his elbows as he positioned himself.

He took her, and she took him.

They affected their union almost roughly, in quick, hungry movements. The girl moved beneath him with the easy grace of a leopard or some other big jungle cat. Carter was uncomfortably aware of the bowl of the sky above him. His back and buttocks, rising and falling above the girl, were exposed to the view of anybody who came down the road— as he had come down the road. Nothing would be visible of her except her legs, sticking out on either side of his body, and her arms, clasped around his back and the golden crown of her head. But anybody who came down that road would know that there was a couple writhing on the beach blanket.

As the frenzy of passion mounted, though, Carter stopped worrying about exposure. From the road, they would seem too tiny to matter to anybody passing by, unless that somebody were equipped, as he had been with a pair of field glasses. Besides, the girl's passions were so intense that he had no time to worry about irrelevant things like being watched from the road.

She was agile, powerful, vigorous. Her muscular legs came up and held him, and he lunged again and again to her. He shivered with pleasure at the feel of the big globes of her breasts against his chest, the rock-hard nipples drilling into his skin.

She was gasping now. Moaning. Spasming with ecstasy. Carter stayed with her as long as he could. Then the supreme moment came in a blaze of fulfillment, first for her, then for him.

And it was over.

Carter continued to cover her nakedness for a long moment until enough strength had flooded back into his sweat-flecked, wearied body to allow him to roll free. His heart was still pounding, and in his mind he was still enacting that steady movement.

Then he pulled away from her and opened his eyes.

He half expected to find that they had had an audience while making love, but the beach was still as deserted as always. The girl lay half on her side, her breasts rising and falling slowly, now, her nipples soft. He could see the marks on her golden skin where his fingers had gripped the firmness of her in the paroxysms of his lust, but the marks were quickly fading.

The girl had a mysterious half-smile of contentment on her face. And Carter noticed, for the first time, a definite appearance of cruelty about her nostrils and her slightly pouting lower lip.

They looked at each other in silence.

He studied the globes of her breasts, the firm pillars of her thighs, the flat drum of her belly. He wanted to imprint the look of this girl's nakedness on his mind, because he doubted that he was ever going to see her again, and this was something worth remembering.

After a long silence the girl said, "Let's go for a swim."

Carter frowned. The suggestion didn't enthrall him. He was tired; he had had only a few hours sleep during the night. The driving had taken something out of him, and now the interlude of passionate lovemaking had left him further depleted of energy. Besides, it was nearly seven in the morning by now. He would have to be getting back on the road again soon if he wanted to get down to Los Angeles on schedule.

But there had been something oddly commanding about the girl's tone as she said it—as though going for a swim with him was of the utmost importance for her. And in a strange way, Carter felt that he owed her the favor of his company in a swim, in return for the totally unexpected morning's pleasure that she had just given him. She hadn't had to invite him to join her here. Or to give her body to him when he reached for her.

"All right," Carter said. "But I can't stay in the water long. I have to be getting on the road again pretty soon."

"It won't be a long swim."

Carter rose, and reached down to give the girl a helping hand. But she declined the lift and came to her feet in one quick, lithe bound. Planting her feet in the sand with her legs slightly apart, she stretched, making muscles ripple on her tanned body. Her breasts quivered. Standing up, she was even more spectacular than before. Her breasts stood up and out and away from her body in a fantastic way. Her buttocks were tight, ripe globes of sensuality. She drew every muscle in her lovely body taut, and relaxed it.

Then she turned and ran toward the water.

Carter stood where he was, watching her fascinated by the motions of her nudity. She ran gracefully and swiftly, her breasts jiggling up and down, her buttocks rippling with hidden muscles. She hit the crystal water with high running strides and dove instantly, her body striking the water flatly and slipping under the surface. She swam out beyond the breakers and surfaced looking back expectantly at him as he stood gazing out from the shore.

"Well? The water's wonderful!"

"I'm coming," he called.

Carter trotted down to the water's edge, uncomfortably conscious now of his nudity, and let the little waves swirl up around his ankles. The water was icy. It was never very pleasant to swim in the Pacific, he remembered. Especially at this hour of the morning.

The girl waved impatiently to him.

Carter advanced slowly into the water. Bigger waves splashed against his knees. When the frigid water reached his loins, he shivered and flung himself recklessly forward into it.

Once he was completely submerged, he found that the cold was not so bothersome. Carter made his way through the rough water and swam easily out to where the girl waited. But by the time he had drawn near to her, he realized that he was winded. Ordinarily, Carter was a good swimmer, but he was fatigued now by the many things he had done this morning. As for the girl, she frolicked like a dolphin.

"Chase me!" she called mockingly.

She did a surface dive, and for an instant the bare gleaming mounds of her buttocks were visible above the water. Then she began to swim even farther out from shore, pausing every few moments to shout a challenge for him to come and follow her. She swam with superb skill, cutting knife-like through the cold water.

Putting on a burst of speed, Carter swam after her, only to find that she was matching his pace. By so doing, she was keeping the same distance ahead of him all the time, never letting him close the gap.

Carter began to get angry.

He saw that she was toying with him, mocking him with her skill and swiftness. She was virtually attacking his manhood by this game. What's the matter, he wondered? Didn't I love you good enough? You were thrashing around with me like you enjoyed it all right.

He wondered if perhaps in some obscure way he had failed her in the lovemaking, and so had provoked this display of scorn from her. But she had seemed to respond to him warmly enough when he was taking her, Carter told himself.

She was getting farther ahead of him all the time. Carter sucked air into his lungs and doubled his efforts. He was able to narrow the distance that separated them. Looking ahead, he saw her, not too far away now, her body shining through the water, back and buttocks momentarily visible as she swam.

His heart thundered. Suddenly he gasped for breath, pulling in a mouthful of salt water that almost choked him. Carter heard the tinkling sound of her laughter coming from just ahead of him.

Treading water until he recovered his poise, Carter glanced back and saw that they were quite far out from shore now, as far as he had ever cared to go in ocean swimming. But he knew that something basic was at stake in this contest. He could turn and swim back to shore, sure, but that would be an admission of defeat that could burn in his breast forever.

No, he thought. I'll catch her! I'll show the naked little witch!

He raced furiously after her. It seemed that he was gaining on her again, but she was only toying with him. She let him come within a few yards, and then streaked ahead of him again.

Carter longed to catch her, to hold her water-sleeked body prisoner in his arms here in the water, perhaps even to make love again as they swam. Yes! That would show her who was virile! Seize her, pull her body up against his, wrap her legs around his own. And then a lunge, a quick movement, again and again as they bobbed on the waves, crushing her close, her breasts drilling into him even as he drilled into her ... the searing moment of mutual ecstasy....

But his strength was leaving him. Now Carter began to panic, and he realized that he no longer could afford to worry about his masculine pride. He was completely exhausted. He hardly had the strength to kick or to lift one arm above his shoulders. And they were very far from shore in the rough, chilly sea.

The girl seemed to sense this, too, because she had stopped retreating from him. Now she swam back in his direction while he treaded water and tried to catch his breath. Turning, he saw the shore a vast distance away. There was a hot band of pain across the middle of his chest, and nausea in his guts.

"Tired?" she asked as she drew near him.

"Yes," Carter gasped. "Not—not used to this much swimming, I guess."

She put her arms around him as though to support him. He felt the tips of her full round breasts grazing his skin. Her thighs twined about his body, gripping him firmly in what could have been the position of love, if only he had had the strength to love her just now. Her lips were only inches from his own. He stared into her cool blue eyes.

She smiled sweetly, "I hate men. I loathe them. I was raped when I was sixteen. I never forgot it. Men disgust me. Especially when they make love to me. That's when they make me really sick."

"Huh? What—"

"I take my revenge, though. All alone, out here, where no one can see. You're the third one so far, and you won't be the last. All men are fools. Bestial, selfish, ugly fools."

Gripping him tightly, she dragged his head below the surface. Carter flailed out wildly, but his tired body could not fight her pantherish strength. He felt her flat muscles tightening about his body, shoving him down. Her breasts pressed into him, taut globes of flesh.

He got his head above water for a moment and gulped air into his lungs.

"I didn't rape anybody!" he protested.

"All men are the same!" she hissed at him.

Her hands were on his shoulders. She pushed him down under the surface again. He felt her lithe, naked body snake around him, and he could not break her grip on him. She was holding him down. Her breasts were practically in his face.

There was a bursting sensation in his lungs. He could hear her laughing somewhere above him. He gasped for breath and drew in only water, and she laughed again and shoved him down deeper.

His brain was numb now. He had no strength left to defend himself. Her nakedness was like a cage around him.

He realized he was being punished for another man's crime long ago, and sadly wondered why. In another moment he was past the point of no return; his lungs filled with water and he began to sink, still vaguely conscious, bewildered by her sudden treachery, no longer hearing her silver laughter as he dropped down and down and down through the beckoning depths.

Judy Domanig remained where she was, treading water staring downward at the sea. There was no sign of him. She waited, her breasts heaving. There were goosepimples breaking out on her nude flesh. She put her hands on her breasts and held them, squeezed them as he had squeezed them, the one who was dead now.

She waited in case he might come floating up above the surface.

He didn't show. The water was fifty, sixty feet deep here, maybe deeper. He had plenty of room to descend. Of course, he wouldn't stay down there forever. It wasn't in the nature of human bodies to remain submerged unless they were weighted down. But there were fast currents down there, and they would take his body and whip it along the coast, sixty miles, seventy miles, far from the place where this had happened. He would be washed up on shore a few days from now, a naked, unknown man that nobody could connect with what had occurred here.

When fifteen minutes went by and there was still no sign that he was going to come to the surface, Judy began to swim toward the shore.

She was tired. Even though she took care to keep herself in magnificent physical shape, it was always a strenuous effort to drown a man. And she had done some pretty fancy swimming just before the final act. Besides, swimming in the frosty Pacific took a heavy toll on your body's energy. So she was glad to get out of the water at last.

She stroked into the shallow water and waded up out of the sea. Standing naked at the edge of the beach, she shook herself like a wet puppy dog. Her breasts jounced and jiggled, twin globes of sensuous flesh. She looked out at the ocean while the sunlight caressed her nude buttocks and back, drying her and warming her.

No sign of him. Good. Good. He had probably already been swept far down the cape and out of range. That was the one thing that worried her: that the men she killed would pop up accusingly right under her, soggy and swollen with water.

Judy turned. She presented the front of her body to the sunlight now as it came over the cliffs from the east. The warm beams stroked her breasts, fingered her nipples, explored the taut drum of her belly with its golden silken skin, then touched herself below.

Slowly, she walked up the beach toward the place where she had left her blanket and beachrobe. A great joy possessed her. The joy of killing, of knowing that another one was dead.

And first she had let him love her. Why not? She had needs, just like everybody else. Of course, it was degrading to admit it. Degrading to let a man cover your body with his and move in violent, rapid lunging. But yet it brought you pleasure, and you could wipe out the humiliation by taking his life afterward.

Basking in the sunlight, Judy stretched, smiled, presented her nakedness to the world. It was still early in the morning. She reached her arms toward the horizon. She put her hands on her bare breasts.

It felt so good to stand naked in the open air, under the sky and the sun, she thought.

But she couldn't remain much longer. There was a great deal to do, now. She ran her hands over her bare skin, brushing away the flecks of sand that had clung to her, and the salt that was drying on her. Then she picked up beachrobe and put it on. A pity to cover her nakedness with the sun so nice and warm, but this was, after all, a public beach, and the morning was moving along. Judy didn't want to attract any more attention today. She had already had all she wanted.

She belted the robe closed. Her breasts jiggled around nicely inside it. She picked up her blanket—the blanket on which she and the dead man had celebrated the rites of love only half an hour before—and shook the sand out of it. Then she folded it.

His clothing, now.

He had left everything in a neatly folded heap. Judy scooped it all up and wrapped the blanket around it. She didn't fool with the wallet that she could feel in his trousers, or with the expensive-looking wristwatch that he had tucked into one of his shoes just before running down to the water. Robbery wasn't one of her motives.

She looked around. There was no sign of him on the beach anywhere. Now she started up the stairs.

Up, up, up, the hundred-odd steps to the top of the cliff. She took them at a half-trot. Her vigorous young body enjoyed physical challenges of that sort. She was hardly even winded when she reached the top, although her full, firm breasts were moving fast within her beachrobe, and her forehead was dappled with sweat.

His car sat by the edge of the embankment.

Judy got in. Using his undershirt as a glove to keep her fingerprints shielded, she fumbled in his trouser pockets until she found his car keys. She turned on the ignition and started the engine. Then, glancing back, she saw that the highway was clear, and she began to drive. Her robe opened below her waist, baring her firm, pink thighs and the golden wonder of her hips, but there was nobody else in the car to see.

She drove south on the coast road for about twenty miles, and turned off by the parking lot of a roadhouse that sat perched high over a windswept cape. She put the car in the lot, carefully wiping off the steering wheel with his undershirt. Nobody was ever going to trace her to this car, she thought.

The place was deserted. Judy crossed the paved expanse of the parking lot, her sandals slapping against the asphalt, and took the little underpass that led the patrons of the roadhouse to the beach. Above her was the highway. Here, instead of steps cut into the rock, they had built a metal staircase, winding round and round as it went down the hundred and fifty feet to the beach.

Judy hurried down it, her breasts bouncing under her one garment. She kicked off her sandals at the bottom and ran across the empty beach. Near the shoreline, there was a scrambled heap of big black boulders, forming a kind of natural cave. She clambered over it and quickly thrust the dead man's bundle of clothing between two rocks, on the ocean side.

There. That would do it.

When the naked corpse drifted to shore a few days from now, and the police began their investigation, they would discover the abandoned car in the roadhouse parking lot. They would probably also find the rolled-up bundle of clothes between the two rocks. And they would conclude that this lonely wayfarer, bent on suicide, had parked his car, gone down to the beach, stripped, carefully stowed his clothing, and swam out to sea until his strength failed him. There would be no bruises on his body to indicate that he had been forced under the waves.

A clear case of suicide. And who would ever connect it with Judy Domanig, who lived by herself many miles up the road?

No one. No one at all.

Judy smiled in triumph. She opened her beach-robe and gave the ocean a good look at the front of her naked body, let the spume flick against her breasts and belly and thighs. She laughed.

Then she turned and trudged happily up the beach toward the staircase, her work accomplished.

CHAPTER TWO

Now, of course, she had to get home. Home was twenty miles away, and she wasn't carrying any money. All she had besides her own nakedness was the beachrobe that covered her, and the folded blanket over her arm. But she wasn't worried. This part of California was an informal place. She'd manage. She always had.

The one thing she didn't want to do, of course, was create any link between herself and the roadhouse where she had parked the dead man's automobile. So that meant she'd have to leg it a little. She didn't mind. She circled past the roadhouse, which would not open for business for another three and a half hours, and cut across to the eastbound road leading away from the shore. She walked for fifteen minutes. The sun grew higher and hotter in the sky. But she was naked under her robe, and that made the walking more comfortable.

When she was more than a mile from the roadhouse, she put up her thumb at a passing car.

Very few men will fail to stop to pick up a beautiful young blonde female hitchhiker who is alone and apparently wearing nothing but a short terrycloth robe. The car came to a grinding halt twenty yards up the road from her. Judy trotted toward it, breast-globes jiggling. The robe blew open, showing a lot of thigh below the belt, and the driver noticed it.

He was a man in his forties, going gray at the temples, dressed in khaki trousers and a plaid shirt. He wasn't bad-looking. He grinned at her and said, "Which way are you heading?"

"South," Judy said, though her cottage was twenty miles to the north. "I'm heading toward Redwood Canyon."

"You aren't dressed very much for traveling."

She laughed. "I was out for a morning swim, and somebody gave me a hitch up this far. But now I've got the problem of getting back."

"Well, happens I was heading north, myself. But I guess I can take you down to Redwood. Not so far out of my way. Hop in."

Judy joined him. She was fully prepared for him to make a pass at her, and if he did she knew exactly what she was going to do: a quick jab with stiffened fingers, right into his groin, to leave him gasping and writhing with pain—and then she'd make a hasty exit.

But he behaved himself. He couldn't help stealing sideways glances at her, though. He peeked at her thighs as the flapping robe exposed them. She kept the upper part of the robe in place with her hands. If he realized that she was actually naked under the robe, and not simply wearing a bathing suit, it would lead to trouble. She didn't want to provoke an incident. She had already had her incident for the day, and she was satisfied.

His jaws worked. She saw the muscles bunching. She knew that he longed to get his hands on her. But he drove along with restraint. After fifteen minutes, Judy said, "You can let me off here, thanks."

He slowed. "My pleasure."

She got out of the car and walked a couple of paces away from it. Reluctantly, he began to drive away.

"Hey," Judy called after him.

He braked and looked around. "What is it?"

"I just wanted to show you the latest model in bathing suits," she said. "Here. Take a look."

She yanked at the belt of her robe. It came open, and she drew the sides of the robe apart to give him a brief, dazzling, incandescent look at her nudity. He gaped at the splendors of breasts and belly and thighs, so golden, so naked.

Then she laughed and pulled the robe shut again.

"So long," she yelled, and ran off down the narrow dirt road and out of sight before he could get any ideas about following her.

It was about a hundred fifty yards to the cabin of Annie Caldwell and Marni Holland, two of Judy's friends. They lived in a little shack by the edge of the woods. They happened to be Lesbians, which Judy didn't hold against them, and they were also interesting and talented girls. Annie, the older one, did wood sculpture. Some of her stuff was exhibited each year in big galleries in San Francisco and New York. Marni was a writer. She didn't earn much from her short stories, because they weren't the commercial kind, but she got published in a lot of important magazines and had a good reputation.

Though they lived simply, Annie and Marni had two cars. Which was why Judy had taken this roundabout way of getting home, rather than to risk hitching all the way back up to her own cottage.

Their place was a ramshackle, unpainted cabin in a small clearing surrounded by towering Douglas firs. The two cars were parked near the front porch—a paint-flaking 1955 Oldsmobile and a dilapidated Volkswagen of uncertain vintage, maybe even older than the Olds. Judy stepped between the cars and up onto the front porch.

She looked in.

The cabin was secluded, and the girls didn't believe in excess modesty. Judy could see them in bed from where she stood peering through the dirty window. They were asleep, and the covers were thrown back enough so that she could see that they were naked. Annie was a big, masculine girl in her late thirties, with enormous breasts and a body like a wrestler's. Judy stared at those two vast globes of flesh rising and falling evenly. Marni looked dwarfed next to her, though actually she was not a particularly small girl. She was dark-haired and about thirty, with delicate features, sensitive, moody eyes and a taut firm little bosom that was now exposed to the view of anybody who cared to peer through the window.

Judy knocked on the window pane. Nothing happened. She knocked again, a little louder, and this time Marni yawned and opened her eyes and sat up. She squinted to see who was there, and smiled when she recognized Judy. Slipping out of bed, she padded to the door.

"Hi," Marni said. Nude, she stepped through the door and emerged on the porch. Her hard, little breasts rose to greet the morning sunlight. Her lithe, naked body was slim and agile. "What are you doing around here so early?"

"I've been up for hours," Judy said. "Swimming, sunbathing. I thought I'd come down for a visit."

"I don't see any car."

"I didn't drive. I hitched."

"Like that?"

"Why not?"

"I bet you're naked under that robe," Marni said.

Judy laughed. "That's a bet you'd win. But if you think you're going to get me—"

"Who wants you?" Marni asked, and they both roared with laughter.

Judy had slept with Marni several times. She had also slept with Annie, and with the two of them at once. Although she didn't think of herself particularly as a Lesbian, Judy was willing to get her sexual pleasure in any handy way.

The noise of their laughter woke Annie. She came rumbling out of bed and joined them on the porch, also nude, her vast breasts and firm round belly glistening in the sunlight.

Marni explained why Judy was there. Judy stood between the two naked Lesbians, smiling pleasantly. They didn't ask her very many questions. They didn't wonder why she had gone hitching more than thirty miles down the coast at dawn with no clothes on but a beachrobe, to arrive uninvited and not knowing if anyone would be there to receive her. That was the good thing about Bohemian-type people, Judy thought. They weren't forever nagging you with logical questions. They let you alone.

And so there was no need to explain that she had murdered a strange man this morning, and had come this far to establish an alibi.

Marni said, "Come in and have breakfast with us."

"I don't want to intrude."

"Intrude all you like," Annie boomed. "We're glad to have you."

She followed the naked Lesbians into their cabin. Marni gestured to a rough bench and said, "Make yourself comfortable."

"You mind if I take off my robe?"

"Why should I mind a thing like that?"

Judy was glad to get the bulky, terrycloth garment off. She was not at all self-conscious about her nakedness, anyway. Even in front of the Lesbians. She knew that they desired her. Well, right now she didn't feel in the mood to make love with them, not after her earlier session of passion on the beach. But she might as well give them the treat of looking at her body, anyway.

Annie was getting some bacon into the pan. Her big-buttocked form lumbered around in the kitchen. Neither of the two Lesbians made any move to put anything on. With three naked women in the cabin, it had the look of a nudist camp.

Marni said, "We haven't seen you for a while."

"I've been too busy to see anybody."

"Making lots of pottery?"

"It's the tourist season," Judy said. "I've been sweating over the kiln. How's the writing going?"

"I'm working on my novel again," said Marni. "I've done another hundred pages."

"Think you'll finish this summer?"

"I hope so," Marni said. "The publisher's very eager to read it."

"I'm eager to read it too," snorted Annie from the kitchen. "It's all about me, you know! But I haven't seen a word of it."

Judy smiled. She felt very cheerful, very relaxed. She had almost forgotten about the drowned man by now. All that remained was the thrill, the secret knowledge of her deed, but the tension, the anticipation, the nervous edge before the act—all those things were gone.

She filled her nostrils with the smell of frying bacon, filled her eyes with the bare bodies of her nude friends, and let contentment steal over her.

It was a good life, she thought. Living in these little cabins along the still-wild coast of mid-California. A handful of friends up and down the coast, sculptors, artists, poets—people who were interested in creating things, not in making money or cheating other people. Of course, no matter how comfortable her life was, how many friends she had, Judy couldn't forget the aching wounds within her ... the wounds that had driven her to murder three men in the last year and a half....

Breakfast was a treat. Judy was ravenously hungry. It was to be expected; she had been up since dawn, she had had a lot of swimming and some sex, she had killed a man, and she had hitchhiked and walked, and all that was enough to build an appetite. She shoveled the food down, and the girls provided more.

After she ate, Judy said, "I'd like to borrow your Volks to get home."

"You have to leave now?" Annie asked.

"I ought to. I've fooled around enough for the morning. Now I've got to get back and get to work."

Annie reached out and let her hand rest on Judy's nude thighs, only inches from their apex. The big hand slid up and down along Judy's silken flesh. Annie's breasts began to heave with passion. The nipples turned hard. Beside her, Marni also began to show sensual arousement.

"Stay with us," Annie whispered. "Stick around for a couple of hours and we'll drive you home later."

"Three of us in bed," said Marni, gloating over the erotic voluptuousness of it. "One of us on each side of you, Judy."

Her hand clamped itself on Judy's thighs next to Annie's. Both hands moved inward.

Judy shook her head. "No. I don't mean to be a tease, but I've got to get going. I really shouldn't have stayed this long."

The hands that had been groping toward the apex of her being removed themselves. That was another good thing about people like Marni and Annie: they had respect for the wishes of other people. When you said no, they understood what you meant and didn't try to wheedle you into changing your mind.

"Okay," Marni said. "Here are the keys."

Judy said, "Why don't the two of you drive up to my place tonight? You can both stay over and in the morning you can take the car back."

The eyes of the Lesbians glistened with anticipation. "Sure," Annie said. "Great idea."

Judy stood up. They watched her keenly as she hid her rounded breasts and succulent buttocks within the shapeless folds of her robe again. Then she waved affectionately to them and left the cabin, taking a last glance at the two nude figures as she went out.

They were dolls, Judy thought. They made no demands, and they were always ready to do a friend a favor. If it ever came down to it, they'd certainly testify that she had spent the entire night with them, while a man named Joe Carter was drowning in the Pacific. Not that Judy thought it would ever get to that point. Neither of her two earlier killings had involved her with the police.

She got into the Volkswagen and started it. The elderly car sputtered into life. Judy frowned for a moment, trying to remember the H-pattern of the stick shift. It came to her, and she stepped on the clutch and put the car into gear.

As it rolled slowly away from the cabin, Marni appeared on the porch. Sunlight picked up the highlights of her small, high breasts, her deep-set navel, her sharply jutting hip-bones.

"See you tonight!" Marni called.

"So long," Judy said.

She swung the car around and headed up the bumpy dirt road in second gear. A few minutes later she was at the highway. She turned onto it and headed north at fifty miles an hour.

Going north on the coast road wasn't so bad. You were on the inside, with the cliffs against you. The southbound lane was the hellish one. That was where your wheels were sometimes within a couple of inches of hanging out over the abyss.

As she drove, her morning unrolled in reverse for her. She came to the roadhouse where she had parked the dead man's automobile and stashed his clothes. From here, she couldn't see into the parking lot, but she knew that no one had discovered the car yet. It might be a couple of days before anybody realized that the car had been abandoned in the lot.

Then, about half an hour later, Judy began coming to her own section of the highway. From the northbound lane she couldn't see the beach. But it was down there, and at dawn this morning she had been sprawled out in shameless wanton nudity on the sand, using her bare body as bait. And someone had taken that bait. It had worked out perfectly, she thought. Perfectly!

Now, passing that point, she went to the next exit and swung the Volkswagen around. A narrow road took her inland from the highway exit, and in a couple of minutes she was pulling up at her own cottage.

Her place was set back a few hundred feet from the highway. But it was a short walk down to the road, and then the climb to the beach level. She did it every day when the weather permitted.

Judy parked the Volkswagen next to her own rusty little Corvair and went into her cottage. It was a three-room place, far more attractive than the shack where Marni and Annie lived. There was a real fireplace, not just an oil stove, and a picture window, and electricity, and even a telephone—all the comforts of civilization. The nearest house was half a mile away.

That was how Judy liked it. Solitary.

When she wanted company, she knew how to find it. But she had arranged her life so that unwanted company wasn't very likely to find her.

It was ten in the morning now. She had been awake since five o'clock. As she entered the cottage, her cats began to uncoil and pad toward her. Judy had three cats: a big orange tom, a skinny tiger female, and a plump female Siamese. The tom yawned at her, then told her with a surly growl that he was interested in getting fed.

"You had your breakfast hours ago," she told him. "You moocher, you don't get anything until sundown, you know the rides."

He growled at her again. Judy knelt down and gave him a playful caress. The two female cats came over to be tickled, too.

Judy loved the cats more than she had ever loved any human being. Which was a pretty sad statement to make about a girl who was twenty-four years old.

It was time to get to work, she told herself.

She shrugged off her beachrobe. Though she sometimes worked in the nude, she decided that she had enough nudity for one morning, and she took out of a closet a pair of tight blue dungaree shorts and an old-clay stained white polo shirt. She slipped them on without bothering about underwear. The nipples of her breasts made dark little bulges against the taut white fabric.

She made a pretty fair living with her pottery. No fortune, but enough to keep afloat. Judy turned out small ceramic objects, vases and statuettes, brightly painted and highly glazed. As art, they were pretty worthless, but they were the best she could do, and the sort of things that the tourists loved to buy. She sold them to half a dozen souvenir shops between Carmel and Sausalito. The six stores between them bought her entire output, which gave her a steady income of about $350 a month. The souvenir stores then marked the prices up around 100 per cent and sold them to the visitors from Kansas and Wisconsin who wanted to take home the handicrafts of a genuine California artist. If Judy cared to, she could have opened her own store to sell her work and that of others like her who lived along the coast. But she wasn't interested in becoming a businesswoman. She just wanted to live her own life—as far away as possible from the civilization that she hated.

She knew that she was a bitter, twisted person. She knew that a girl of her beauty and age and health ought to be in love with the world, not retreating from it in hatred and sullen resentment. But she couldn't help herself. That was how she was.

That was what the world had made her.

There was one thing more to do before she settled down with her clay for the morning. She went into the bedroom and pulled open the bottom drawer of her dresser. Inside, underneath a heap of panties, was a notebook with a black cardboard cover, the kind children use in school. She picked up a pen and opened the notebook.

It was her murder diary.

She had recorded the other two killings in it. Now, turning to a fresh page, she began to write an entry under the heading of July 7:

"At five in the morning I went down to the beach and sunbathed nude for a while. Then I had a swim and sunbathed again. A little after six I heard a car stop on the highway. A man came down the stone steps. He was about thirty-five years old, lean, rather good-looking, with dark hair and brown eyes. He saw me naked. He seemed a little unsure of himself because I was naked in front of him. I invited him to come sit down and sunbathe with me...."

Clamping her full lips tightly together in concentration, Judy wrote out a complete description of her morning's activity. The lovemaking on the blanket, the swim, the challenge to his virility in the water. And then the drowning, when his strength began to ebb. And then, coming ashore, hiding his clothes, disposing of his car.

As she wrote she relived the whole scene. Once again she was sleek and naked in the cold water with him. She had her hands on his shoulders and she was pushing him down. His face was wedged between the abundant globes of her bare, quivering breasts, and she was gasping from her exertions as he was making strange spluttering sounds— and then he was going down, down....

Oh, the keen pleasure of that! A greater delight than the explosion of sex within her! A fierce, intense ecstasy of murder!

Judy knew that she was asking for trouble by keeping the murder diary. It was a risk, having something like that in the house. But it was a risk to commit the murders, too. This was part of the thrill—the knowledge that if the police ever came, they would certainly find her detailed confession stashed away under her panties.

She needed to keep the diary. She didn't want any of the details to blur or fade. These murders were the foundations on which Judy Domanig was rebuilding her shattered life.

She finished the entry and put the diary away. Then, accompanied by her cats, she took out a fresh mound of clay and set out to do her morning's work.

She thought once again about the episode on the beach.

And remembered other episodes, darker ones, the torments that had set her on her path....

Nobody who had known Judy Domanig, age fifteen, would have ever predicted that she would turn into a human monster. She was a gentle, playful, lovable girl at that age. She seemed to have everything in the world going for her.

She was good-looking, for one thing. Her body had ripened early, before she was thirteen, and at fifteen she had a woman's easy grace and poise. Her breasts were high and full, and she was long since past the filly stage where she was ashamed of having breasts at all. She was proud of her body.

She was lively and intelligent. Her father was a professor of sociology at the University of California, and, growing up in the stimulating community at Berkeley, Judy couldn't help turning out to be an interesting and alert girl.

She had a good family life, too. Everybody about her was kind and loving.

At fifteen, she could look forward to nothing but the best in life. After high school, she'd undoubtedly go to college, right here in Berkeley. She was talking about studying biology and working in a laboratory, doing research. And no doubt she'd meet some attractive young man, perhaps a young university teacher, and they'd get married and have two or three attractive children. Life was a fine prospect for Judy at fifteen.

By the time she was sixteen, everything had changed. And life was hell.

What happened in between was very simple. Her brother Ned came home to live with the family.

Judy had never really known her oldest brother very well. He was nine years her senior, and he was a stranger to her. When she had been a little girl, Ned was always the center of attention in the family, a rangy, handsome boy with a shock of long, glossy black hair. Ned was the first child, and the other three were just afterthoughts, it sometimes seemed.

When he was fifteen, Ned got into some kind of trouble. Judy, who was only six, naturally was not given the details. But Ned left home at that point. He was sent to a boarding school in Oregon, and he returned to Berkeley only at Christmastime. He even stayed away in the summers.

When Judy was ten, she learned that her brother Ned—who now was going to college in Idaho—had gotten married. And at Christmas that year, Judy met her sister-in-law Irene, a tall, gentle, dark-haired girl who seemed already wrapped up in some mysterious inner sorrow.

Ned's comings and goings over the next few years were rarely discussed in the family. Judy was old enough now to realize that he was a black sheep, a wound to her father's soul. He had flunked out of several colleges, Judy knew. Then he went into the army, but from what she gathered he wasn't much of a success there either.

At Thanksgiving time, four months short of Judy's sixteenth birthday, Ned came home again—this time not on a visit.

"I'm divorced," he said. "And broke. I'm going to stay here for a while and rest up and figure out what the hell I want out of life."

To Judy, her brother Ned was a fascinating, romantic figure. Suffering was written in deep lines on his face. It was obvious that in his twenty-five years he had been through a great deal of torment.

Her adolescent heart went out to him. She wanted to comfort him, to give him sisterly warmth, to make him feel as though the world held at least one person who cared about him. Washed up at twenty-five, jobless, his marriage shattered, his life a succession of empty incidents, Ned really seemed to be in a bad way, and Judy was eager to help him.

The trouble was, Ned didn't seem to want to be helped.

His attitude toward Judy at first was one of irritated contempt. He fended off all attempts she made to talk to him, giving her a kind of "Go away, little girl, you bother me" scowl. Judy was depressed about that. She couldn't break through the shell of bitterness that her brother had encased himself in. He sat in his room all day, coming out only for meals. He did a lot of drinking. Mainly, he read dog-eared paperbacked books. Now and then, a friend visited him, some other man his age, bringing a bottle of liquor, and Judy would hear loud laughter coming from the room. There were never any girls.

Judy's father was openly upset about the whole thing. He couldn't very well turn Ned away from his door, but he certainly wasn't happy to have him around an untidy, unruly, embittered man-who-was-still-a-boy, lounging around his room all day and using up the family liquor supply. There were a couple of loud quarrels between father and son; then the elder Domanig simply shrugged and slipped into a mood of toleration, ignoring his son's presence.

Judy continued to try reach her brother. In her naive, girlish way, she was convinced that she could be his salvation—that she would be able to help him straighten out his messed-up life, if he would only let her spend some time talking to him.

"Go away," he said, morosely.

"Why don't we talk for a while?"

"I don't want to talk, kid. Just be a smart chick and go away."

But Ned's attitude toward his sister changed abruptly one Saturday afternoon early in December. He had been living in the house for two or three weeks, then, and his sullen mood hadn't lifted for a moment. He continued to regard his sister as nothing more than an annoying little girl who happened to live under the same roof with him. Then he got a view of her nude body, and after that everything was different.

Judy had taken a shower in the bathroom at the end of the second floor. She hadn't bothered to lock the door, because it was generally understood that this bathroom was used only by Judy, her mother, and her nine-year-old sister. The family didn't believe in locking bathroom doors, since if you slipped and broke a leg or something while taking a shower it was better to have the door unlocked so help could get to you.

After her shower, Judy started to get herself ready for her evening date. She was going to the movies with a boy named Tony Madison, the son of one of the other professors at the university. Judy was still a virgin, of course. She was curious about sex, but not curious enough to make any actual experiments with a boy named Tony Madison, the son of one of her innocence later on—say, when she was seventeen or eighteen. She was sensible enough to realize that including in sex when she was still this young could be biting off more than she was ready to chew.

Still, she was a normal, healthy girl, which meant she petted and necked a little. She had allowed Tony Madison to open her brassiere and play with her bare breasts. That was as far as she had ever gone with any boy, and she considered it pretty daring. But it felt nice to have someone fondling her breasts, and Judy knew that she had a good pair of boobs, anyway. She didn't see any harm in letting Tony stroke them if it gave them both pleasure.

Now, nude and pink from her shower, Judy was shaving her legs in the bathroom.

And the bathroom door opened suddenly.

Her brother Ned stood there, staring hungrily at her youthful but womanly body.

He was a mess. He hadn't shaved in two or three days, and his hair was rumpled, and his eyes were bloodshot and bleary, and his shirttail was hanging out. He looked forty years old, not twenty-five. Judy could smell the liquor on his breath ten feet away.

He stood lurching in the doorway, his eyes glassy as they fixed on the ripe, pink young breasts of his sister, on her smooth belly, her flaring hips her solid columnar thighs, her firm, jutting buttocks.

Color flared in Judy's face. She didn't know what to say or do. She didn't feel ashamed of her body, but it was the understanding in the Domanig family that the male members of the family and the female members were supposed to respect each other's privacy.

Ned wasn't respecting anything, right now. He was getting a good eyeful. And Judy stood there with everything she had hanging out. There was no place to hide.

After what seemed like half an hour had gone by—it was actually no more than fifteen seconds—Judy found her tongue and said, "This bathroom's in use, Ned."

"Yeah. So I see."

"Will you excuse me?"

"You got quite a build on you, sis." He grinned at her. "I never guessed you were stacked like that. You ought to buy yourself better bras."

"Come on, Ned. Go away."

"What's a matter? Ashamed in front of your poor old brother? Hey, you're a pretty one."

"Ned!"

"Gimme a sisterly little kiss," he mumbled, stepping into the bathroom. His hands clutched at her. One of them grazed the ripe, hot mound of Judy's bare, left breast.

She looked at him in shock as she jumped back. "You must be drunk, Ned. Come on, get out of here. You've got no right—"

He pawed her again. This time he got a good grab of both her breasts. When she pushed one of his hands away from her firm, resilient flesh, he moved it down and grabbed one of her buttocks.

Judy began to get frightened. This was no way for a brother to behave toward his sister. But they hadn't grown up together; they were practically strangers. And Ned was drunk. She realized that to him at this moment, she was just a good-looking naked broad who happened to be within grabbing reach.

She pushed him, hard, away from her. He thumped against the bathroom wall. Judy grabbed up a bath towel and wrapped it around herself from breasts to thighs.

"Go on, now," she said. "You ought to be ashamed of yourself, Ned!"

"I never knew—that you were built like that, sis—I never knew—"

"Will you be a good guy and get out of here?" she asked, in a calmer tone now that her nudity was shielded from his bloodshot gaze. "You don't want me to yell and raise a fuss, do you? I'm sure Dad wouldn't like it if he knew what you've been doing in here."

That got to him. He shrugged and lumbered out of the bathroom.

Trembling, Judy slammed the door and locked it. She dropped her towel. Then she huddled down in a little, frightened, nude heap as the pent-up tension went shivering through her.

Nobody had ever seen her whole body naked before—nobody male, anyhow, since she had grown up. Now Ned had. He had taken a good look. And she could still feel the touch of his hands against her breasts, her buttocks. Though she had just had a shower, she felt filthy again. Virgins of not-quite-sixteen don't like the private places of their bodies handled like that.

Even so, Judy felt more sorrow than hatred toward her brother. She pitied him. He was such a wreck! To sink that low, to be reduced to getting drunk and feeling up your own sister—

She still wished she could help him.

But the bathroom episode had altered things in the house. Only Judy and her brother were aware of what had happened since she didn't want to tell her parents about it, and Ned certainly wasn't going to. But now Ned realized that his sister was a woman.

And Ned was woman-hungry.

Judy found him staring at her now instead of ignoring her. She could catch a glimpse of him, studying her profile, as though trying to match the outward appearance of her clothed body with the voluptuous reality of her bare breasts, as he remembered them. There was a curious intensity about his expression as he ogled her. It made Judy uncomfortable, because it seemed so abnormal. She had wanted to get to know her unhappy brother, yes. But she hadn't bargained for anything like this.

The tension mounted for six days.

Judy now locked the bathroom door when she took showers, and hoped that her mother wouldn't notice and ask her to explain. When she dressed and undressed in her bedroom, she nervously watched the door in case Ned should unexpectedly barge in. She avoided wearing tight-fitting sweaters around the house, because she couldn't stand the weird, intense gaze Ned turned on her.

Saturday arrived—one week since he had seen her body. Judy had another date with Tony Madison. They went to see a French film at an art theater at Telegraph and Bancroft, and then he took her for a drive up into the Berkeley hills. Tony was a good-looking, attractive boy of eighteen; he would be starting college next fall. Judy was very fond of him. She could easily see herself married to someone like Tony Madison.

Tony was tactful with her. In his parked car, he kissed her and put his hands under her sweater and cupped and caressed her bosom, unsnapping her brassiere so he could fondle the silken-smooth mounds of her bare young breasts. He made her nipples go hard and her body go hot with desire. But Tony didn't try to rush anything. He never tried to slip his hands under her skirt and grope for forbidden territory. He was a level-headed young man who knew that if he moved at a reasonable pace, Judy would eventually give him everything, without any remorse afterward.

He took her home about midnight. She was in a pleasantly excited mood, warm with desire and love. When they kissed good night outside her house, Judy was rather more passionate than she generally was. She slipped her tongue into his mouth, and pressed her body flat up against his, letting him feel the firm globes of her breasts. She was able to feel too, as they embraced, the manhood of him. It excited and frightened and fascinated her.

As she went into the house, Judy thought, maybe in another six months or so I'll let him Do It with me.

The thought delighted her. She had no fears of sex. But when she lost her virginity, she wanted it to be a beautiful and meaningful experience, something that she would remember happily for the rest of her life.

She went upstairs to her bedroom. The house was quiet. Her parents were out at a faculty party at the other end of town. Her younger sister and brother were asleep in their rooms. A light was on in Ned's room. Judy thought briefly of stopping by, saying hello to him. She had never really given up her dream of winning Ned's confidence and getting him to allow her to help him untangle the twisted strands of his life.

But she decided against visiting him now. She was in a wonderful mood after her delightful evening with Tony Madison. She didn't want to spoil it. Ned would only be surly and impolite to her.

She went straight to her bedroom, closed the door, and got undressed quickly. She glanced at her bare body in the mirror. Her nipples were still swollen. They hurt, a little, from being erect. But it was a pleasant kind of pain. She closed her eyes, and relived for a moment the happiness she had felt as Tony's hands wandered tenderly over those twin mounds of ripe, young flesh.

Then she got into her pajamas, washed up for bed, and turned out the light.

Usually Judy fell asleep the moment her head hit the pillow. But not tonight. She was too full of joy, of plans and dreams.

And so she was still awake, ten minutes later, when her brother Ned came tiptoeing into her room.

She heard the door creak open. She sat up, blinking in the darkness.

"Who's there? Ned, is that you?"

"Shhh," came his hoarse voice. "Don't make any noise, you hear?"

"What do you want? I've gone to sleep."

"Just be quiet." He was advancing across the room in the darkness. Judy could smell the by-now familiar scent of him, that repelling mixture of stale, sweat, cigarette smoke, and whiskey fumes. Suddenly terrified, she trembled in the darkness.

Then she felt his weight on her bed.

He pulled back the covers and dropped down heavily beside her.

"Gonna have some fun now," he muttered thickly.

"Ned, no! You're drunk, Ned!"

"Keep your mouth shut."

"Ned, I'm your sister!"

"Shut!"

"Ned—"

Suddenly his hand was at her throat. Judy froze. The words that were about to leave her mouth died back of her lips. She shivered and gasped for breath as the big, strong hand tightened.

What's he going to do, she asked herself? Oh, no, he's cracked up. He's going to kill me. This is going to be one of those cases you read about in the newspapers. Brother goes berserk, slays family....

His harsh breathing sent nauseating fumes into her face. The hand still gripped her by the throat, though not so tightly, now. But she was afraid to cry out. What good would it do? Her parents weren't home. Nobody was here to help her. And that choking hand might tighten again.

She heard Ned panting. His other hand was busy now, unbuttoning the top of her pajamas. The fingers slid onto her bare flesh, fondled the firm, up-jutting young mounds of her breasts, toyed with them, pinched the tender, little nipples.

No, she thought, quietly going crazy inside her skull. No, no, no!

The hand moved downward from her breasts after a moment, found the snap that held her pajama bottoms shut, and tugged at it.

He began to pull the garment off her.

CHAPTER THREE

Even now, eight years later, Judy could not help feeling a shiver of revulsion as she returned in memory to that shattering episode. Her flesh crawled whenever she thought about it. And she could not help thinking about it. Hardly a day passed without her reliving it. It lodged in her past like a thorn, cutting into her soul.

Sweat rolled down her smooth skin as she shared once again the plight of that virginal, adolescent girl, alone in a dark house with her drunken, half-insane older brother, unable to cry out, unable to defend herself against his bestial lusts.

With one hand remaining at her throat, Ned efficiently stripped away Judy's pajamas with the other. First, the pajama bottoms came off. She felt his hand intimately stroking her flesh, touching her thighs, moving upward and inward to her purity, exploring her in a shocking way.

Then he maneuvered her out of her already-open pajama-top, so that she was totally nude in the bed. The sheets felt cold against her bare buttocks.

He muttered, "You ever tell anybody a word of what's happening and I'll fix you good, you hear me? I'll fix you plenty good!"

Her eyes stared upward at him in mute appeal. She was adjusted to the darkness, now, and she could make out his features, twisted, rigid, the features of a madman. Or of a hopeless drunk.

He doesn't know what he's doing, Judy told herself, still trying to make excuses for her shameless brother. He's too drunk to think. He—

It didn't matter. Whatever the excuse, the fact remained that he had stripped her naked. And his hands were moving over her previously untouched body in a lasciviously lustful way.

Now he was gripping her breasts ... digging in hard ... trapping the nipples ... tickling her thighs ... rubbing against her belly. Then, reaching underneath, grasping the firm, bouncy flesh of her buttocks.

Judy felt soiled, stained, polluted.

But the real soiling was still to come.

She heard a zipper working. She did not look down to see, but she did not need to.

"No," she whimpered. "For God's sake, Ned, you can't—"

He slapped her across the mouth, so hard that she felt her lip began to puff up instantly. "I told you to shut up," he grated. "I don't want any sounds out of you, you little witch. Just lie there."

"Ned, I beg you—"

He slapped her again. Not across the mouth this time, but across the breasts. He hit the delicate globes of soft flesh with all his strength. Judy had never known such pain before. It was like getting slammed in the chest by a swinging baseball bat. She hissed in agony and doubled up, and after that she was silent.

Her brother's body was above hers, now, a dark, bulky shape in the blackness of the room. His breathing was loud and ragged. The stink of his breath made her want to throw up. She quivered with terror.

She couldn't believe that this was really happening to her.

She felt his rough, powerful hands on her thighs, now digging deep into the tender, yielding flesh, forcing her legs—

He was pressing against her.

Closer... closer....

Then he grunted and plunged at her.

Judy thought she would go out of her mind from the pain of it. It hit her suddenly, all at once, like a firebrand being plunged against her. There was a quick, red haze of agony blazing outward from her body, so keen and so intense that she could not even think. In the moment that it happened, she did not pause to reflect that she had just lost her virginity. Her mind was blanking out under the impact of that ruthless treatment of her unready body, that demonic violation of unprepared tissues.

Her head lolled back. Her figure went limp.

Then consciousness returned, a fraction of a second later—and the waves of horror came rolling in to engulf her.

Ned was on top of her, riding her, lunging again and again, diving at her tender body. She could hear her own voice howling for mercy, as he ravished her. In the wild frenzy of the moment, Ned did not even bother to shut her up. He simply went on with the rape.

His body crushed down against the soft globes of Judy's breasts. Her legs were flung wide, straining the muscles of her thighs. And there was that red-hot pain in the most sensitive part of her body as he smashed against her.

Again!

Again!

Again!

Each new lunge brought fresh agony. Would he never finish? The rape seemingly had lasted for hours already. How long would it take? When would the pain end? When would he leave her?

Suddenly, he made a fierce grunting sound. Judy felt him clutch at her flesh, grab her buttocks and push himself down even more strenuously against her. And then there was most revolting moment of all, as his body shook with the hammer-blow jolts of his fulfillment, and she felt him quiver with her, felt the shuddering force of his ecstasy, felt herself spinning in a foul wave of lust....

And then the rape ended. But the real nightmare was only beginning.

His weight lifted from her. Judy lay like a corpse in her bed, limp, her legs still askew, her eyes closed. She made no attempt to cover her violated body. The pain was still fearful, a hot, throbbing ache, a stinging sensation, and above all the inner pain, the mental anguish of knowing that she had been raped....

... by her own brother....

He stood by the side of the bed. "If you ever say a word about this to anybody, I'll murder you," he told her. "Don't think I'm joking."

She wanted to struggle back to sanity, wanted to sit up and ask him why he had done such a terrible thing to her. But the old Judy, the calm, poised, rational, curious Judy was gone. Forever. He had murdered her with his brutal act of lust. She could not speak to him now. She could only lie there in a state of shock, her numbed brain refusing to accept the enormity of what had been done to her.

Ned went out of the room, carefully closing the door behind him.

Perhaps fifteen minutes passed. Slowly, Judy fought her way out of the thickets of hysteria. She rolled over and lay curled up tightly, sobbing furiously to herself, her knees drawn up until they practically touched the tips of her aching breasts. Then she realized that her parents might be coming home from their party at any minute. Sometimes they looked in her room to make sure that she had come home safely from her date. If they looked now, and found her lying in this telltale predicament, it would be impossible to hide from them what had taken place tonight.

And she wanted to hide it. She didn't want to brand her brother as a rapist. She didn't want to advertise herself as a girl who had been violated. The only way she could survive this horror without being forced to divulge it to the world was by swallowing it and forgetting it.

Or so she thought.

So she got up from the bed. It wasn't easy. She was shaky-legged and at the verge of collapse. The bed was a mess. She ripped the sheets off and carried them into the bathroom. She put them in the laundry hamper. Then she washed showered, still in terror.

The pain was subsiding now—the physical pain, that is. She still ached, and she knew that she would continue to, for a while. But that part of it wasn't so serious. It was the other part, the psychological part of it, going through the rest of her life as someone who has suffered an incestuous rape—that was what terrified her now.

She dried herself off. She found her pajamas and put them on. She put fresh sheets on the bed. If her mother asked any questions, she would simply say that she had spilled something on the bed, and that would explain changing the sheets.

Shaking, Judy got back into bed. She hugged her pillow. Terror still throbbed in her.

I'm not a virgin any more, she told herself.

She could still feel his weight on her, that savage treatment of a body that was not prepared for such an act, the shattering impact as her innocence was overthrown by brutal force.

It wouldn't have been so bad, Judy thought, if a stranger had raped her on the street—dragged her into an alley, pulled her panties off, taken her, and then fled. But this way—

To have Ned be the one to do it—that was the worst part of all. How could she ever face him again? Or he face her? A wedge had been driven through the family that could never be removed. The unspoken fact of his treacherous violation of her purity would always remain, the deepest stain on a soul already blemished again and again.

Judy didn't sleep much that night. Somewhere toward morning, she slipped into a light, uneasy doze, but when dawn came she was awake again.

She looked at herself in the mirror. She looked like a wreck. Pale, bloodshot, tense. But she hadn't felt much more pain during the night, and the earlier hurt had dwindled to a dull, inconvenient ache. She dressed to go down for breakfast, wondering what was going to happen when she and Ned encountered each other.

She could have saved herself the speculation. Ned didn't show up for breakfast.

Judy faked things at the family table. She did the best acting job she possibly could, pretending that last night had been a perfectly normal Saturday night for her. She made conversation, ate a reasonably substantial meal, and passed the butter when asked.

Ned didn't appear all morning. About one in the afternoon, Judy's mother came down from his room and said, "Has anyone seen Ned today?"

"Not I, mother."

"Not I."

"Me neither."

Nobody had seen Ned. Ned was gone. He had packed his things and vanished in the night.

Judy was profoundly glad he had left, of course. And she knew why he was gone. It was good to know that even he had a conscience that there were some deeds that were too monstrous to face the next day.

A few days later, they got a postcard from him. He was in Mexico. No explanation of his sudden departure. No word that he'd be coming back.

Judy knew why.

She was faced now with the task of putting back together the ruins of her life. That wasn't so easy, and in fact it got harder and harder as the days passed. She had thought that the shock of the rape would wear off after a little while. Instead, the inner sense of outrage became stronger and stronger.

She looked at the girls she knew, and felt sour envy because they still had their innocence and she had been stained by rape. Some day soon they would give themselves to boys they loved, and it would be a thrilling and wonderful experience. But she had nothing to look forward to except the memories of agony.

She looked at herself, and wondered if the signs of her experience had started to show. Did she look depraved, now? Was the golden glow of virgin purity gone from her face? Was it obvious to everybody who looked at her that she had unwillingly crossed the borderline into the realm of womanhood?

She had a hard time sleeping. No night was complete without its nightmare re-enactment of the rape. She felt the hands clutching her breasts, the fingers digging into her thighs as they drew at her legs, the fiery lunge of violation ... and she woke up, drenched with sweat, trembling with real terror.

The emotional effects of the rape began to become evident to her only gradually, like a bunch of boobytraps cleverly planted in her soul. She discovered, for instance, that her relationship with Tony Madison had been forever altered by what Ned had done to her.

She and Tony went out on another date the week after the rape. Judy had recovered her surface calmness, and as far as anybody else knew, all was perfectly as it should be with her. Yet inwardly, she was imprisoned in a cage of grief and bitterness.

When Tony took her up into the hills and parked the car, Judy realized that it could never be the same with him. The happy yielding of her virginity to Tony that she had dreamed about would now never take place.

They settled onto the back seat. Tony drew her close. He tried to kiss her, but Judy twisted at the last minute so that he received not her lips, but only her cheek.

She couldn't help remembering her brother's slobbering mouth pressed against hers.

Tony's hand went to her sweater, cupped her breasts from outside. It wakened memories of pain, of a drunken hand violating squeezing the twin tender mounds of sensual young flesh. Involuntarily, Judy winced.

"No, Tony. Please."

"What's the matter?"

"I just don't feel very affectionate tonight."

"You've been kind of distant all week, Judy. What's wrong? You sick or something?"

"I'm fine."

"You look so pale, so moody."

She shrugged. "Just one of those spells, I guess. I'm sorry."

"If something's troubling you, you can tell me about it, Judy."

"There's nothing!" she snapped.

"If it's about me—"

"There's nothing!" she snapped.

The fact that she had lost her temper was a dead giveaway that she was lying to him, and both of them knew it. She felt abashed. It wasn't his fault she had been raped, after all. So she tried to relax.

"I'm sorry," she said, gently. "I've been awfully edgy all week. I didn't mean to yell at you. Put your arm around me and hold me close."

They sat quietly for a little while, staring out at the lights of Berkeley below them. Judy tried to force herself to relax. When he put his hand hesitantly on her sweater a second time, she did not push it away. She attempted to unbend, to get into a receptive mood.

I'll let him play with me, she thought. And then maybe if he wants to go a little farther than before, I'll let him. Maybe I'll even....

No. No, she couldn't do that.

There was no reason in the world why she shouldn't let Tony Madison have sex with her now. After all, she had no virginity left to lose, so why not make him happy? But yet she knew what she was afraid of. If he made love to her, he would find out that he wasn't the first. He'd be able to tell that her virginity was gone. He'd feel cheated and angry. It would be the end of their tender, blossoming love affair ... the end of her dream of marrying him someday.

And as she considered it, she saw that that dream was ruined anyway, no matter what she did.

If she gave herself to Tony, whether now or six months from now, or even three years from now on a wedding night, he'd discover that someone else had had her ahead of him. Which would sadden and disillusion and anger him. On the other hand, if she never gave herself to him, what kind of relationship would they have had?

She saw that she had no hope of marrying Tony. If she slept with him at all, he'd find out the shameful truth about her. And the only way she could keep that truth from him was to deny herself to him ... forever.

Round and round and round.

He gripped her breasts. He was breathing hard, full of sincere passion. His body pressed against hers, Judy remembered their good-night kiss, the night of the rape, and how excited she had been to feel his taught body against the front of her. And how soon afterward had she felt another man's body in a much more intimate way!

She shivered and pulled away, shocked and dazed by the abrupt explosion into her mind of all her rape memories, as vivid as ever.

"No," she gasped. "Let go of me, Tony. I—I don't feel well. Take me home."

Looking back at her sixteen-year-old, newly de-virginized self from the age of twenty-four, Judy could see how the rape had destroyed her. It cost her a sense of her own completeness, first. Then it cost her her love for Tony, for she had to draw away from him in order to preserve her shameful secret of violation.

Poor Tony. He never did understand why we had to break up. And he was my only chance for happiness, too. Damn Ned! Damn him!

The fact that Ned had died in Mexico a year and a half after the rape, killed in some drunken barroom brawl, did not ease the weight that pressed on Judy's soul. The damage was done. The death of the miserable, tortured man who had raped her did not undo the crime. He was at peace, now. But she was condemned to go through life wearing the scars of his deed.

And so, this morning, a stranger had paid for her sufferings. Not the first to pay, either. Nor the last Judy vowed.

She busied herself at her work. Shape the ceramic pieces, apply the glaze, fire up the kiln. A busy day, a quiet day, nobody to bother her in the silence of her cottage. That was how she liked it. Just the cats padding around, minding their own business.

After she had everything in the kiln and blazing away, she fixed lunch for herself. Then she went down to the beach again to sunbathe and swim. Not nude, this time. She didn't dare. She could romp around nude on the beach only in the hours just after dawn. If she tried it here in the early afternoon, the state troopers would pounce upon her, pronto. But she had a good swim, anyway. And the sun was warm. She wondered how long it would be before the dead man's body washed up on shore. And where.

Back to her cabin, now. She took another sun-bath, this time a nude one, in the clearing behind the cottage. She sprawled out deliciously, tanning her breasts and buttocks, while her body dried in the sun. Her bikini dangled from a nearby bush, drying off also.

Still nude, Judy went back into her cottage. She took a short nap. Then she emptied out the kiln and packed up the new merchandise. She read for a while. She gave the cats dinner.

About eight o'clock, there was the sound of a car outside. Her company was arriving.

Marni and Annie, her Lesbian pals.

CHAPTER FOUR

They got out of the battered, ancient Oldsmobile and came trooping into her cottage. Annie yelled, "Hey, Judy, you here or aren't you?"

"I'm here. In back, packing up some stuff."

They came around to see her. Marni was wearing tight green pedal-pushers and a maroon sweater. Annie's fleshy body was encased in a pair of faded dungarees and a loose flannel shirt. Judy looked up from her task of wrapping up parcels of pottery.

"Hi," she said. "What's new?"

"Another suicide," said Marni. "We saw the skin-divers going to work as we drove up here."

"Where?" Judy asked.

Annie said, "Down near the roadhouse, it seems. They found some guy's clothing hidden in some rocks. And his car was parked in the roadhouse lot. They're dragging for his body right now."

Judy felt a pang of fear. Why were they telling her this? Were they playing some kind of game? Did they know that before her visit to their shack this morning she had murdered a man and made it seem like suicide?

No, she realized. They didn't suspect a thing. They were just relaying the latest bit of neighborhood gossip, that was all. It wasn't like Marni and Annie to play games of that sort.

Marni said, "It's about the fourth one this year. There's something about the coast that makes people want to drown themselves, I guess."

Annie laughed. "I tell you something, that's a tough way to die, swimming out until you sink. Takes too long. You got all that suspense wondering when you're finally gonna go under. Me, if I was killing myself, I'd just jump off that big cliff. Quick."

"Too messy," Judy said.

"And what if it doesn't kill you?" Marni wanted to know. "You fall three hundred feet, you smash your face to a pulp, you twist your neck so you head's looking the back way, and you're still alive. And you spend the rest of your life in a wheel chair screaming with pain."

Annie said, "Well, you know what the odds are? You jump three hundred feet and smash yourself up and live? It isn't very likely. Anyhow, if it does happen, all you do is take poison when you get the chance."

"Seems to me it's simpler—"

"Hey, cut it!" Judy yelled. "What kind of talk is all this, anyway?"

Marni shrugged. "Well, there was that guy who drowned himself, and—"

"Let's talk about some other subject," Judy said.

"How about the subject of booze?" Annie asked. She produced a paper bag. "We brought some wine, just in case you were running low."

"I'm not running low," Judy said. "I'm out completely. So thanks."

She took the bottle—it was a gallon of Chilean red wine, cheap and tangy—and opened it in a hurry. Five minutes later, they were sitting around in Judy's living room downing the wine and listening to the faint sounds of a San Francisco FM station trying to waft Mozart through the forest to them.

Judy felt queasy about the suicide discussion. They had found the clothes awfully fast. If they found the body too, it might still show some marks of the death struggle—bruises around the neck, where she had shoved him under the water.

To hell with worrying about that. Let them find the body. How were they possibly going to connect it with her, anyway?

She sipped her wine. The three women talked. The evening trickled away.

And then it was ten o'clock. Bedtime. Judy believed in going to sleep early, getting up early. You economized on your electricity bills that way. And you had the use of the beach in the early hours of the morning before anybody could come along and object to your nudity.

She had invited Marni and Annie up here to have sex with her, not because she was particularly inclined toward Lesbianism, but because she owed them a favor. They had let her borrow their car. In return, she was letting them borrow her body.

Judy could take the dyke stuff or leave it alone. She had had some good times in bed with other girls, true, but it didn't mean all that much to her. She still rather would have loving from a man—even though she despised men.

Her first Lesbian experience had come three years ago, when she was twenty-one and still living in San Francisco. She had gone to a coffee shop in North Beach and a beatnik chick had picked her up and taken her to her pad. And Judy had been just drunk enough not to object when the beatnik chick took Judy's sweater off and unfastened her brassiere and started kissing the tips of her breasts.

The rest had followed swiftly and pleasantly.

Since then, Judy had made it in the butch way with perhaps a dozen different girls. Some of her best friends were gay, and she enjoyed their company. And, from time to time, she let her company enjoy her.

She stood up and yawned. "How about the sack?" she suggested.

"We still got a little wine left," Annie said.

"So finish it," Judy told her. "Marni and I will meet you in the bedroom whenever you're finished boozing. Come on, Marni."

The slender girl got up and went with Judy. Annie, a big chuckle booming around in her massive body, shrugged and poured herself another glass of wine.

Of the two Lesbians, Marni was the one that Judy preferred. Annie was too big, too butch, too coarse. Almost like a man, except for her anatomy. She was a superb sculptor, but she didn't happen to be very bright.

Marni on the other hand, was delicate, sensitive moody. Very much like Judy in many ways, except that Judy had great physical strength, and Marni was softly feminine. Judy could wrestle a man to the ground if she had to. She could outswim most men, outrun them, and outdrown them, too. She had built her body painstakingly, knowing that was her only security in strength. Somehow, she managed to be muscular without looking it. But Marni was girlish in her strength.

They entered the bedroom together. Judy's bedroom was a long, practically empty room. She had no bed, only a king-sized mattress that rested directly on the floor. A couple of chairs, a painting, one of Annie's wood sculptures—that was all. Simple. Judy hated clutter.

Marni said, "I wish I could have left Annie home tonight, you know."

"That's no way to talk about your lover." Marni shrugged. "I'd rather have you all to myself, Judy."

"You already have."

"And I loved it. If I didn't have to share you—"

"You do," Judy said. "That's the way it works. I don't intend to get mixed up in any quarrel between you and Annie. You want me, you both have to have me."

Marni nodded. "Yes. You're right." She crossed the room and reached her arms toward Judy. "Kiss me," she whispered. "While we're still alone in here."

Judy accepted the slim, dark-haired Lesbian's embrace. Their bodies pressed together. Judy could feel the hard, little mounds of Marni's breasts jutting into her own. Their lips met. Marni kissed hungrily, greedily, trying to devour Judy. Her tongue plunged deep.

They clung tight for a long moment.

When they parted, Marni looked flushed and dazed with desire. Judy was calmer, although the torrid kiss had certainly awakened her own longings. Her breasts felt hot; her nipples swelled.

"Let me undress you," Marni whispered passionately.

Judy had dressed about six that evening, for the nights get cold along the coast, even in summertime. She was wearing a loose-fitting cashmere sweater and a pair of gray slacks. She hadn't bothered with a brassiere, because she hated the feel of a useless garment confining the tender hills of her breasts, but she had put a pair of bikini panties on under the slacks.

Marni pulled the sweater off and uttered a little gasp of surprise at finding Judy bare-breasted beneath—not because Judy's breasts were any mystery to her, but simply because she had expected to have to work a little harder than that to see them tonight.

"You're so lovely," Marni whispered. "How I wish you were really one of us!"

Judy smiled. The dark-haired girl moved close to her, and delicately cupped the rising mounds of Judy's breasts. Judy closed her eyes. She enjoyed Marni's feather-light caress, the fingers enveloping her nipples, trapping them, gently stimulating them....

Panting, flushed, Marni tugged at the zipper of Judy's slacks. Down it came, and the slacks followed, revealing the nearly nude body beneath, hidden only by the pink, gauzy bikini panties that rode low and provocatively on Judy's hips.

Marni reached for the panties. Judy shook her off.

"First, let's undress you," she said.

Marni grinned, and Judy went to work, peeling the garments away. In moments, Marni's breasts were bare; then her pedal-pushers followed, and at last her panties, revealing the slender nudity of her. Marni body was agile, always poised like a doe's for immediate flight. But flight was the one thing she didn't have in mind now.

She moved close again. Her bare breasts touched the warm tips of Judy's. Her hands slid under the elastic waistband of Judy's panties, drew the flimsy little garment down, down, down....

Off.

Now both girls were nude. They tumbled down together onto the mattress, already locked in a sensual embrace of deep passion.

Lips went to lips. Breasts rubbed against breasts. Ivory-smooth bellies slid against each other in wanton urgency. Legs slipped between cool, elegant thighs, which clamped tight on them.

At first, Judy had been shy and self-conscious about Lesbian loving. Not any more. It was a route to pleasure; an unconventional route, but not an unpleasant one. She could give herself up freely to people like Marni and Annie. More freely, in fact, than she could with a man. For though the sensations a man had to offer were more intense, he also tended to awaken those bitter racking memories, memories of anguish and shame and violation. Nothing about Marni linked her to the crudest moment of Judy's life.

Marni was kissing Judy's breasts now, stroking her buttocks her thighs.

Judy shivered with ecstasy. That was the wonderful thing about making love with another woman: she knew your body as though it were her own, knew where to touch you and what kind of force to exert. Men were clumsy bunglers, most of them, when it came to that sort of caress.

Judy closed her eyes. She lay back on the mattress, adjusting her legs, letting Marni run riot over the treasures of her body. A kiss here, a caress there, the brush lips, the light flick of a tongue—

Passion mounting, gasp after gasp.

"Hey, you two, wait for me!" Annie bellowed.

Judy opened her eyes. She saw the big bull-dyke, her lips and cheeks stained purple by the cheap wine, standing over the bed, hurriedly pulling off her clothes. Annie flung garment after garment aside. Now her breasts were nude, hanging out like two basketballs somebody had glued to her chest. She was climbing out of her dungarees, now, and her panties.

Annie wasn't really a fat woman. She was just big. She didn't have puckered dimples of flab all over her hips and thighs and buttocks, the way a really fat woman would. Nor were her breasts huge, revolting, swaying slabs of dangling meat. Annie was an attractive woman. But nature had been generous in designing her. She was close to six feet tall and weighed at least two hundred pounds. Her thighs were like marble pillars, her buttocks were as big as continents, her belly was soft and rounded. All the flesh was solid and none of it was superfluous. But there was an awful lot of her.

Looking at Annie's nakedness, Judy understood why she had become a Lesbian. It would take a Paul Bunyan of a man to satisfy Annie, and Paul Bunyans just weren't easily available. Unable to find a man who could give her the kingsize kind of loving she needed, Annie did the next best thing—turned herself into a man, essentially, and played a masculine role in sex.

With a colossal roar of delight, Annie flopped down on the mattress, landing right on top of Marni and Judy.

"Gung ho!" she roared.

"I'm smothering! Marni cried. "Help! Help! I'm choking in her boobs!"

Annie laughed. She was lying with her bosom on top of Marni's face, and those two enormous swells of flesh hid Marni's nose and mouth entirely. Marni made muffled sounds of anguish and thrashed her feet around. Still laughing, Annie reached down and put her hands on Marni's legs, giving her an intimate caress even while she flattened her face.

Suddenly Annie yelped and leaped away from Marni, clutching one hand to her enormous left breast.

Marni sat up. She was laughing now.

"You bit my knocker off!" Annie boomed.

"Just a little nibble," Marni said. "It was pure self-defense. I couldn't breathe."

"Let's get Judy," Annie suggested.

Judy had been watching the byplay between the two Lesbians with some amusement. But she stopped being amused when the two of them leaped at her at once.

Annie caught her by the shoulders, Marni by the legs. Judy struggled, half seriously, half in fun. But for all her wiry strength, she couldn't begin to budge Annie. The big woman was pressing down on the upper half of her body. Her huge breasts were soft and heavy against Judy's bosom and her lips covered Judy's.

Meanwhile Marni was busy, too. She had pulled Judy's legs around. Now she was drawing a trail of kisses down the inside of Judy's thigh ... closer and closer....

Her tongue flicked out and found the area of ecstasy.

Buried under two nude girls, stimulated at top and bottom, Judy went into a wild paroxysm of lust. Her body writhed and rippled as though a high-voltage current had been sent through it.

Yes, she thought, yes, yes ... love me, love me!

It was fantastic. She yielded utterly to the mischievous expertness of the Lesbian pair. They knew the magic places of her body, and they worked on them, driving her closer and closer to the sunburst of lustful fulfillment. Wild laughter ricocheted through the cottage.

It was a shameful three-way orgy, and Judy felt no qualms of conscience at all. Maybe respectable, conventional people would be shocked by such goings-on. But Judy felt that she had a license to engage in such wanton exploits. She had tried to be respectable and conventional, and the good people of the world had kicked her in the teeth. They had forced her away.

Forced her into unnatural lust.

Into murder, even.

So her conscience was at ease. She lay there, sweating and throbbing, letting Annie kiss her bare breasts and Marni put her mouth to the territory below. She opened her own mouth wide, filling it with the incredible abundance of Annie's breast. Her tongue flicked against a nipple of huge size, a big, jutting knob of flesh. Her lips compressed into the swollen globe of flesh.

Now the positions shifted, and Judy buried her head to Annie's lap while Annie burrowed toward the warmth of Marni, and Marni embraced them both.

Harsh passion-sounds could be heard in the room. There was the slap of flesh against bare, sweating flesh.

Breasts, buttocks, thighs, bellies, hips, haunches, flanks—all mixed up in a gyrating, endlessly reshaping kaleidoscope of lustful, female flesh. Body against body, sweat dripping, desires aflame, breasts heaving, nipples like rock—

Ecstasy!

Marni on top of Judy, driving hard, pressing toward the goal of fulfillment—

Judy with Annie, now. And then Annie with Marni. And all three, entangled, entwined, defying anatomy, bodies twisting, writhing, a devil-dance of lust, Lesbian desires maddening and inflaming them—

Somebody's breast in her mouth. Somebody's buttocks in her hands. Somebody's hips grinding against hers in sublime friction.

Judy soared higher, higher, higher.

For the second time since daybreak that day, she knew the searing fulfillment of passion. That other time, lying naked on the beach at dawn, she had given herself to a man who was in his final minutes of life, and she had taken a savage pleasure from that knowledge. Now, coupling like a maniac in this three-way Lesbian orgy, Judy derived different pleasure from knowing that here, too, she was violating all the commandments of orthodox society.

Pleasure shot through her in bolt after blazing bolt of radiant delight.

Then it was over. Gasping, moaning in exhaustion, one girl after another toppled limply to the mattress and lay still, bathed in mingled sweat, groggy from the exertion of total voluptuousness.

"Oh, God," Marni moaned. "Oh, oh, what a wild one that was!"

Annie laughed. "I wish somebody took movies of us. We could make a fortune."

Judy lay silent, her head pillowed against the steep globes of Annie's mammoth breasts. She felt strangely calm with all passion burned away. In the silence of the night, she could hear the dull booming of the surf, just to the west of the cottage.

A body was tossing on that surf ... a naked man, bloated and limp, his features already unrecognizable, a man who had been alive at this time last night, and who now was so much carrion, so much garbage drifting on the chilly tide....

Judy smiled. It had been a very rewarding day.

I wish I could kill them all, she thought, and reached out to touch the silkiness of Marni's lovely body as a shiver of triumph ran through her soul.

CHAPTER FIVE

When morning came, Judy was the first to awaken. She got up right at dawn, as though a switch had been turned inside her mind. It was an old habit of hers, waking up early. No matter how few hours of sleep she had had—and she had not had many, this night of Lesbian lust—she found herself awakening with the sun.

She liked those early hours of the day. The world was hers, then. Everyone else was still asleep. She could come and go as she pleased, safe in the illusion that there was no one else alive.

Slipping up from the mattress, Judy smiled down at the nude figures of Marni and Annie. They were fast asleep in each other's arms. Marni looked small and weak, cradled against the gigantic breasts of Annie.

Judy didn't have the heart to wake them so early. She gathered up her beach-robe and towel and slipped out of the cottage, nude. The dew still glistened on the grass, and patches of fog kissed the rounded tops of the hills that bordered her part of the clearing. Judy took a deep breath, making the globes of her breasts rise steeply. She stretched out in the grass, enjoying the sensual feel of the cool moisture against her bare buttocks.

Her tomcat appeared and meowed at her. Judy meowed right back. Then, slipping her beach robe on, she went down the path toward the beach. The little underpass took her to the cliff, and she scrambled down the familiar rock steps to the sand.

Throwing off her robe, Judy reveled nudely in the privacy of the beach at five in the morning. It could have been the first day of the world's creation. Sandpipers skittered along the beach, and the gray surf pounded down against the sand, but there was no sign of another human being. The sun had not yet climbed high enough in the east to get over the cliff and reach the beach.

She walked toward the water, as angry crabs scrambled out of her path. Then she began to trot, her large, firm, bare breasts jiggling nudely up and down with every step she took.

She hit the water on a dead run.

It felt great. Judy hissed in pleasure and pain as the icy chill smashed into her, numbing her, caressing with frigid fingers her nipples, her thighs, her buttocks. She shivered, but she continued to swim outward from shore, and in another few moments, she began to adapt to the severe cold. She had made herself into a tough little girl with such disciplines.

You had to be tough, Judy thought. Otherwise the world walked all over you.

Out, out, out she swam, as though bound for far Hawaii beyond the horizon. The sun was reaching her now, turning the gray sea into morning blue. The cold water was cleansing her of all of last night's sins, washing away the sweat, the Lesbian kisses, purifying her. It was her morning ritual.

Finally, she halted when she was far from land. She turned and looked inward at the sleeping shore. Treading water, she put her hands to the steep cones of her breasts, kneading them, massaging them. She spread her legs wide in the water as though yielding herself to some lover of the merman tribe. She laughed out loud, and listened to the sound of her silvery laughter echoing across the surface of the sea.

Yesterday she had done exactly these things. And an hour later, a car had appeared, a man had halted and come down to the beach to see what her nude body had to offer him....

It had offered him death.

Where are you now, Judy wondered?

Still down there? Buffeted by the currents? Nibbled by the sharks?

Washed up by the tide, lying in a broken bloated heap somewhere along the shore? Or on your way to Mexico, perhaps? Where are you? Who were you?

Whoever you are, I feel no grief for you.

She floated on her back, her breast-tips jutting up above the water, and relieved in her memory her three murders. Three dead men, paying the highest price of all for the cruelties that life had handed Judy Domanig. And there would be more, she vowed. It was a game for her. Take as many as you can, send them to the bottom of the sea ... even the score....

She was shivering now. Even she had her limits in this ice-cold sea. She began to breast-stroke rapidly toward the shore.

She scrambled up out of the water and shook herself dry. Then she ran to her blanket and stretched out, wantonly abandoning herself to the kiss of the warming sun.

It felt so good. Those fingers of flame stroking her body, probing her. Yes! Love me! she begged. Take me! And the sun invaded her nude form, bringing warmth to it.

Occasionally, Judy heard the hum of an automobile speeding by on the highway far overhead. But no one stopped, this morning. Few drivers would risk taking their eyes from the road long enough to spy a naked girl on the beach below. And so there were no interruptions.

After a while, she rolled over and presented the firm, bare cheeks of her buttocks to the sun. Then she rose, gathered up her things, and headed back toward the cottage. She remained nude as long as she dared, but as she reached the steps leading up the face of the cliff, she slipped her beachrobe on.

It gave Judy great pleasure to exhibit her naked body. Even when there was no one around to see it but the cliff and the sky and the sea. Here, she was saying. See what I am! See how beautiful! See what I could have been, if I had had a fair deal!

The terrycloth robe bundled close against the tender, sensitive dots of her nude nipples. She walked quickly to her cottage. It was half past six in the morning now. Marni and Annia were still asleep. Judy shrugged off her robe and read for a while. She fed the cats. She packed up some more of yesterday's pottery.

At a quarter to eight, she woke them.

"Come on, lazybones, up, up, up! I've been awake wake for hours already!'"

The two Lesbians yawned and stretched into wakefulness. Judy, laughing, prodded them into the shower with boisterous slaps on their bare buttocks. Then she got breakfast on the way.

"I bet you've been down for a swim already," Marni said accusingly, as they ate.

"Damn right I have," Judy said. "I was tempted to wake the two of you and bring you along. Would have done you some good."

"The Iron Maiden," Marni shuddered. "How can you be so masochistic? It's rough enough to swim in that water at any time of day—but to go down at dawn—"

"I enjoy it."

"You enjoy punishing yourself then."

"Maybe so. But at least there's something that makes me happy," Judy said.

The Lesbians left about ten o'clock that morning, Marni driving the

Oldsmobile, and Annie fitting her big body behind the wheel of the Volkswagen that Judy had borrowed. Alone again, Judy settled down for her routine of the day.

She turned the radio on and got the morning news. After the usual business about Russia and China and civil rights and the San Francisco Giants, the announcer said, "Troopers are still searching the Pacific below Monterey for the body of Joseph Carter, a presumed suicide. Carter's clothing and abandoned automobile were discovered yesterday afternoon at—"

Judy smiled. Let them keep searching, she thought. Let them search all month! And then they could give the dead man a decent funeral.

Whoever he was.

She got out her clay and got started on her morning modeling. This was the middle of her busy season, while California was thronged with tourists. From November to March, Judy hardly worked at all. She lived on the proceeds of what she had earned in the summer, and spent her time reading, visiting, or just loafing. But in July, she was at the kilns every day.

And as she worked, she couldn't help letting her mind rove backward. Remembering....

Remembering how it had been just after the rape. Judy had made a determined effort to paste the fragments of her life back together. But it hadn't worked. She couldn't do it. The rape had had too powerful an effect on her developing young personality.

The breakup with Tony Madison was inevitable. Whenever she was with him, she found herself obsessed with memories of her brother's foul deed. She couldn't let Tony touch her, kiss her, caress her in any way, for fear that it would lead to sex. And sex was the thing that she feared most of all at least it was, just then.

Such a relationship couldn't survive for long. Tony wasn't necessarily out to make her in a hurry, but he enjoyed kissing Judy, fondling her bare breasts, getting some awareness of passion. He couldn't adapt to a relationship that now wasn't allowed to go beyond the hand-holding stage any more. So he stopped seeing her.

Judy at seventeen was an emotional and psychological mess. She rarely went out with boys any more. She stayed home, reading and brooding. She went through books about sex, hoping to find one that would help her snap out of her tailspin. She read hundreds of novels, too, looking for one that could shed light on her own position.

Her parents were mystified by her transformation from a cheerful, outgoing, confident girl to a dark-souled, miserable, introverted sufferer. "What's wrong?" they kept asking. "What's troubling you?"

Judy couldn't tell them. She couldn't bring herself to blurt out the truth about what had happened to her that night when her brother invaded her bedroom. It was too shameful to tell anybody ... especially her parents.

Like many people who are clutching an ugly secret inside themselves, Judy sought and found a remedy that she thought would help her come to terms with the pain.

Drinking.

She had never been a drinker before the rape. An occasional sip of wine, yes, but nothing more than that. She hated the taste of beer, and she didn't like the fuzziness that hard liquor induced in her brain. Now, though, she turned deliberately toward the bottle, hoping to wash away the anguished throb of shame in her violated body.

She was seventeen and a half when she became a drinker in a serious way. More than a year and a half had gone by since the rape, and Judy had not yet shaken off the effects at all. She still had nightmares in which Ned was on top of her, lunging himself brutally at her. She still woke up in cold sweats. She still maintained a dread of sex, with any one, in any form.

In California, as in most other states, you are supposed to be twenty-one years old before you can legally be served liquor in a bar. The chief victims of that law though, are teen-age boys. Girls are rarely challenged about their ages if they look respectable and capable of holding their liquor, and are not too conspicuously youthful. So Judy didn't find it a very difficult matter to be served in bars. The rape had aged her, anyway. She was solemn and unsmiling, now, with dark rings under her eyes, and she looked two or three years older than her actual age.

She didn't do her drinking in Berkeley, though. That neat, proper university town frowned on teenage alcoholism, and there were frequent crackdowns in the bars, aimed at keeping the kids from the university from getting publicly crocked. Judy took the bus into neighboring Oakland to tank up. Oakland adjoined Berkeley and the streets had continuous names from one town to the other, but Oakland was very different from its egghead neighbor. You could tell instantly the moment you had passed from spruced-up, lively Berkeley to seedy, rundown Oakland. There were plenty of bars in downtown Oakland that were happy to sell Judy, or anyone else, all the booze they could put away.

After a while, she began going to one particular place, just off Broadway. Some random sampling had taught her that what she liked best to drink was rye and ginger ale, and needless to say, that was what she usually ordered.

The bartenders there were a little puzzled when she first began to come in. They thought she might be a prostitute, and that scared them. But when she ignored the approaches of a couple of men, that indicated that she had simply come to drink, and they served her without question. She was an ornament to the place, one of the regulars, that moody, good-looking blonde who stopped in two or three nights a week, had a few drinks, and left alone, without ever saying a friendly word to anybody.

Judy noticed some of the other regulars too. Most of them were broken-down old men or blowsy, disreputable-looking middle-aged women. But there was one man in particular that she noticed with some interest. And he noticed her, too.

He was about forty years old, well-dressed, a good-size man whose hair was just starting to thin. He was usually sitting by himself in the bar, reading a paperback book—not a cheap novel, but generally one of the high-priced works of philosophy or history or literature that you could buy in a university book store. Judy, watching him on the sly, got the impression that he must be a writer, newspaperman or a teacher; some sort of intellectual. And he seemed a lonely man, never entering the bar with anybody else.

After the second week, he began to smile at her. Judy didn't smile back. He didn't make any other overtures, though. Sometimes she would look up from her drink and see him studying her. He had soft brown eyes that seemed to be saying, "Can't we get to know each other? Maybe we can help each other in our loneliness."

She was afraid to encourage him. She sensed that he was a gentle and kindly person, perhaps somebody she could confide in, but she couldn't bring herself to make a move in his direction. She had tried that with her brother Ned, tried to help him conquer his brooding loneliness—and look what her reward for that had been.

So she kept to herself, despite the feeling that this man might give her the warmth and encouragement that she desperately needed.

Until one night, when she had very much too much to drink.

Judy wasn't sure how she happened to get drunk that night. Usually, she was very careful, drinking just enough to get mildly high, then quitting in time. All she wanted was to melt the knot of misery inside her, not to get potted. She had to go home to her parents' house at the end of the evening, after it was all over.

But this time she failed to pace herself. When she finished one drink, she ordered another. When she finished that, the third one was on its way.

It was her brother Ned's birthday, and she realized afterward that that had probably set her going. All the years that Ned had been away from home, in boarding school, in his various college, in the army, in married life, the family had carefully celebrated his birthday just as though he were at home. They weren't celebrating it this year. Ned was dead. The news of his death had come out of Mexico a few months ago and Judy's father had flown down to Juarez to claim the body. Tonight, unable to forget the date, Judy was deep in memories ... of her unhappy brother, and of the misery he had introduced into her own life. And so she drank.

She drank heavily.

And suddenly, she realized that she was getting drunk.

In fact, she was drunk.

She began to giggle. She got up from the bar stool and burst into wild laughter. She had a sudden urge to pull her clothes off, to bare her firm, young flesh to this audience of bored bartenders and soggy boozers. She clawed at her blouse, but couldn't get the buttons open. Then she staggered and dropped to her knees and fell over, her skirt flapping up around her thighs to reveal the tops of her stockings. She made a couple of efforts to get up.

The bartenders got scared. "Get her out of here fast," they said to each other. "She's crocked to the gills! We could lose our license!"

Judy laughed some more. They picked her up. Dimly, she realized that they were going to give her the heave-ho, right out into the grimy street. And there was nothing she could do about it. She'd lie there sprawled out on the sidewalk like the most disgusting sort of tramp.

Then Sir Galahad came to her rescue.

The soft-eyed man with the paperback philosophy books got up and came over as the bartenders were hustling Judy toward the door.

"Wait a second," he said. "Don't do that. She doesn't deserve to be tossed out."

"She's sloshing with the stuff, bud. We can't let her stay here. Law says, you're not supposed to serve an intoxicated person."

"But you can't just leave her on the street! She's so young—"

"That makes it worse. All we know, maybe she's underage too. Come on miss. Out with you!"

"Wait," the man said. "I'll take care of her ... Here—let me have her."

Judy was vaguely aware of an arm around her shoulders. Then she felt fresh air with raindrops slicing through it. She dragged her feet and tried to lie down on the sidewalk, but the man held her firmly and wouldn't let her stop walking.

He said, "I live right here at the corner. I'll let you lie down at my place until you feel all right again."

"Thash—very kind of you—"

She was too drunk to feel any fear. She just wanted to stretch out somewhere. Without any sensation of the passage of time, Judy found herself inside an apartment. There were books everywhere, newspapers, a typewriter. She plopped down on a bed.

Her head was beginning to clear a little, now. She realized that she had been spared a very unpleasant experience, and she was grateful to the gentle-faced man who had rescued her. She opened her eyes and looked up at him, but she had trouble focusing on him. He stood above her, all four of him.

Sweat ran in rivers down her body. Her mind was spinning.

She heard him say, "Here, let's get those shoes off you. Make you comfortable. That's better. Look at you perspire! You must have some sort of fever. I'll take that jacket off you. Easy. That's it And maybe we could button your blouse—"

Suddenly, she felt his hands where his hands had no business to be.

"Hey, cut that out," Judy mumbled.

"Forgive me," he said, and abruptly he was on top of her on the bed.

CHAPTER SIX

Looking back on the scene, Judy still tingled with bitterness at the way he had cheated her. She had been vulnerable, helpless. And he had posed as her noble and chivalrous rescuer, valiantly coming to the aid of a lady in distress. All phony. All he wanted to do was get her to the privacy of his apartment. Well, what could you expect of a man? But the shock of it was overpowering. Judy had been filled with a warm sense of gratitude toward this kindly stranger for taking the trouble to help her. And then, with virtually no warning, his act of generosity turned into an act of erotic greed.

The liquor still held her mind wrapped in a befuddled haze. She was sober enough to know what was happening to her, but too drunk to prevent it.

He opened her blouse, first to cool her off, so he said. But then his hands were fumbling nervously at the catch of her brassiere. He tugged the twin cups away from the luxurious mounds of her pale, young breasts. Judy felt his hands on them, kneading, squeezing, gripping them tensely.

"No—no—no—" she moaned, lying limp and dizzy on the bed in a welter of her own drunken perspiration. "Please—don't—"

"Forgive me," he kept whispering gently over and again. "You're so beautiful ... I want you so much, so very much...."

He was pulling her skirt up, now bunching it around her hips, drawing her panties down.

Judy stirred, trying to hold her legs together. But she had no power to command her body. She was as limp as spaghetti, boneless, nerveless. She lay there with her clothing heaped around her, her breasts exposed, her belly revealed, her thighs askew.

He didn't undress her further. There was no need to bother. He crouched above her, staring with glittering eyes at the treasures of her nudity.

Then he descended onto her.

In soft, moaning tones, Judy protested, and in equally soft tones, he begged her forgiveness, and all the while the rape proceeded to its conclusion. It wasn't a brutal rape, as the first one had been. It was, strangely enough, a tender rape.

He didn't try to force himself to her. Instead, he went to her thighs stroked her, touched her in secret places of desire, caressed her, explored her. He wasn't violating her. He was making love to her.

And Judy, though she was numb with shock, found herself responding.

Her booze-blearied nervous system awakened to his gentle touch. He stroked her where a woman most likes to be stroked and he kissed the tips of her breasts, and covered her body lovingly with his. And her nipples grew hard, and there was sudden warmth in her body. Her body was betraying her. Though she loathed him with all her soul, and wished that she could somehow resist his advances, she found herself throbbing strangely with desire.

"Don't be afraid," he crooned. "Oh, you're so beautiful, I love you so much...."

And he slipped to her, easily, without causing her any pain. It was altogether different from that other time. Now she was warm and ready to receive him, and when she felt him begin to take her, a curious quiver of emotion went through her, and an instant later she realized that he was with her, the union had been made.

Judy sighed. She drew her legs up in a kind of reflex action, cooperating with him, making his role more easy. His fully clothed body pressed down on hers.

He moved. Again, again, again. Judy felt a sensation within herself that she had never known before. A spasming of the muscles, an eerie contraction inside. It was unnerving, and yet pleasant. And it happened again as he moved once more. And again.

She gasped and churned beneath him. Her nipples felt red hot and hard as rock. Her entire body shook with the strange spasms of passion. Dizzy as she was from her drinking, she became even dizzier now.

Abruptly, the man on top of her grunted and gripped her with sudden fierceness. His body moved ... faster, ever faster....

Passion blazed in her. And at the highest moment, she felt the fulfillment of him.

It ended.

He lay on top of her a long moment. Judy was sobering rapidly now, the liquor burned out of her brain by the fire of sensuality. A great anger welled up in her. She knew that she had been violated again, that a man who had promised help had shamefully used her.

A rape is still a rape, no matter how tenderly the raping is done.

"Get off me," she said coldly.

He pulled away and got to his feet. Judy sat up, trembling all over. She knew that she had nothing to fear from this man, that he had already done his worst to her and would not harm her. But she wanted to get away from him quickly.

She moved to hide her nudity from his eyes. She pulled her blouse closed over her bare breasts and drew her skirt down to hide the rest of her body. He stepped back, his face flushed, his eyes bright, and adjusted his clothing.

"I'm—sorry," he whispered. "I got carried away. If you only knew how long I've been watching you—dreaming about you—"

"You make me sick," she told him. "Taking advantage of a girl who's had too much to drink!"

"I didn't mean it. I just wanted to help you. They were going to throw you out on the street. I was going to let you rest here, I wasn't going to lay a finger on you. But then ... when I saw you on my bed ... I've been so alone for so long...."

Judy got to her feet. She felt light-headed, as though she had just risen from a sickbed. She found her brassiere and, turning her back on him, quickly pulled it into place over her breasts. Her panties lay on the floor beside the bed. She snatched them up and popped them into her purse. She didn't want to have to lift her skirt to put them on in front of him.

She said, "I could have you put away in jail for this. It's rape, you know. And I'm underage, besides. You'd rot for it!"

He shook violently. He was really a coward, Judy saw. The kind of man who was afraid to approach a woman unless she was so dead drunk she couldn't resist him.

Judy swept past him and out into the street.

It was raining furiously out there. And she discovered that she was not as sober as she thought, either. Her stomach gave a lurch and the next thing she knew there was a yellow pool of vomit all over the street.

I've got to get out of her, she thought....

She ran. Cold, rainy winds swept at her, reached up underneath her skirt to touch her bare thighs. The warm tingle of her violated body sickened her. She reached the bus stop.

Oh, God, she thought, why did this have to happen to me? Why, why, why?

Somehow, she got into the house without having to face her parents. She undressed and flung herself under a scalding hot shower, hoping to scrub away the taint of this second rape. She could still see the sad-eyed man standing over her in his book-lined apartment, the poor creep, the fumbling, gentle rapist.

Happy birthday, Ned, she thought. Happy happy, birthday!

The episode had taught Judy a great many things, she realized, as she looked back on it.

It had taught her that men were never to be trusted—that even the ones who pretended to want to help you were really just out for what they could get.

It had taught her to be careful about liquor, because it could make her vulnerable to more advantage-taking.

It had taught her that she must make herself strong, physically as well as all other ways, so that she could fend off this world full of greedy rapists.

It had taught her, too, that sex itself could be pleasurable. For in the midst oi her humiliation and shame, she had felt spasms of ecstasy. The trick was, she thought, to control the situation yourself. Never let a man force you, and keep the upper hand ... take your pleasure from him, but don't let him trample you.

It had been a useful lesson. But, like all really useful lessons learning it had been a bitter, sorrowful experience.

The second rape hadn't demolished her the way the first one had. You can only get demolished once. But it had reinforced all the conclusions about the ugliness of life that her incident with Ned had led her to draw. She was a hater, now. She seethed with bitterness. She erected a wall between herself and the world. Nobody, not even the members of her family, could get over that wall and reach the girl inside.

Judy finished high school and went to college. But after two years, she quit. She moved across the bay to San Francisco and took a little room. Her grandfather had set up a small trust fund for her long ago, and the income from that was enough to cover her rent expenses. She made a little money doing odd jobs. She sold some of her pottery. She got along.

She was toughening herself, building that wall ever higher and higher.

She learned judo. She learned karate. No man was ever going to rape her again! She could hike twenty miles without strain. She could swim like a shark.

She dabbled in sex ... all kinds of sex....

But Judy chose her lovers carefully. Now that she had discovered that sex could be something thrilling, she let herself go to bed with men, but only men she could handle, men who were in love with her and unwilling to take advantage of her. She gave herself to them sexually, but not emotionally.

She made them see who was boss, too. She would sleep with them and then throw them out.

"All right. I've had my kicks. You're dismissed," she would tell them.

"But—Judy—"

"Out."

"I love you, Judy."

"Tell it to the Marines."

"Marry me, Judy."

"You've got a case."

"I love you!"

"Tough."

Tough. She got a reputation as being tough, tough as leather, tough as iron. How could they know that within the tough outer shell was a wounded, miserably lonely girl, who had walled herself away from a world that she feared and mistrusted?

She chewed men up and spat them out. And still, they kept on coming, because she was fantastically beautiful, and she fascinated them. Her breezy blonde good looks, her independent spirit, her lithe, athletic body, her full breasts and supple thighs—they drove men wild.

"Crawl," she told them. "Kiss my toes. Get down and grovel in the filth." Men crawled for her.

They kissed her toes ... and other things. They groveled in the filth.

Still, it was not enough for Judy. No matter how cruelly she treated the men who flocked around her, no matter what indignities she inflicted on them, she never had the feeling that she was evening the score for what had been done to her. How could she? How would it ever be possible for her to get back the stolen promise of her youth, her innocence her tenderness her life itself?

That had been taken from her in an instant of monstrous, selfish brutality. And it could never be restored. She would never again be that golden, virginal girl of sixteen with a glowing future ahead of her.

She was stained, marked, scarred.

Yet the thirst for revenge remained unslaked in her. Revenge! Revenge against the entire male sex! She ached for it!

She amused herself by letting men sleep with her and fall in love with her, and then thrusting them aside. She used their bodies the way two men had used hers. She gave her thighs to them, but not her heart.

They came to her. They reached her bed full of hope and love. They caressed the satiny globes of her breasts and the silken-smooth coolness of her thighs. They slept with her and strained themselves to the breaking point to give her pleasure.

They gave her pleasure, all right. Double pleasure, at that.

First, the simple, steamy pleasure of sex the gasping, moaning, panting, spasming pleasure of her erotic fulfillment.

And then, the more complicated pleasure of spurning them-a sadistic pleasure.

"Clear out, pal. I've had what I wanted, now you can go."

How it wounded them!

She slept with other girls, too. She drifted casually into her first Lesbian relationship, found that she enjoyed it, and had others. It was fun, in an easygoing kind of way. She liked going to bed with a soft, breasty wench who was hot for her body. It made for variety, and variety was the spice of life.

Judy tried all sorts of adventures. She sampled drugs, though not the really addictive ones. She made love in combination groups. She experimented with anything that amused her. But it was a cold kind of experimentation. She had made the world her laboratory.

When she was twenty-one years old, Judy made a serious mistake. She let herself fall in love with somebody.

She hadn't intended to do any such thing. When she met Charley Donoway, she intended simply to use him the way she had used dozens of other men ... as a tool to scratch the itch of her lusts, nothing more. He was a lanky, good-looking guy in his middle twenties, who had been through an early marriage and a quick divorce, and now he ran a little bookshop in North Beach, writing poetry on the side. Pretty good poetry, too.

When he first met Judy he said, "I hear you eat men alive. I hear you're a real hellion."

"What if I am?"

"Want to try me on for size?"

"You're asking for trouble, friend."

Donoway shrugged. "Trouble is what keeps you from dying of

boredom."

She went home with him. He poured some wine for her, and put a record on, some African tribal chants. Judy figured she'd let him have her, and then she'd pull him apart with scathing words, the way she did with other men. She was looking forward to the treat.

He stood over her with his hands on his hips, eyeing her. "You want something else to drink, or you want some sex?" he asked straightforwardly.

"You're pretty blunt, aren't you?"

"We didn't come here to play backgammon," he said. "At least, I didn't. Want to go to bed with me?"

"Matter of fact, I do," she drawled.

"Stand up, then. Peel. Let me get a look at that fabulous body I've heard so much about."

"People gossip about me, huh?"

"They say you're stacked as good as Sophia," he told her. "They also say you're a holy terror, a real cast-iron witch."

"One thing at a time," Judy said. "Let's see if I live up to my reputation."

She pulled her sweater off. She unhooked her brassiere and let the cups slide down. The white hills of her breasts came into view, round and high and close together, two magnificent swells of firm, vibrantly sensual flesh tipped with lust-hardened nipples.

"Well?" she said. "Were you expecting more?"

"No," he breathed. "They said you were built like that, but I didn't believe it."

"As good as Sophia?"

"I've never been this close to Sophia. And right now I don't give a damn if I never am. Come on, Judy. Oh, yes, come on!"

He whipped the rest of the clothing off her in a flash. He stripped himself a moment later, revealing a lean, hard, virile body.

They moved toward the bed.

He wasn't gentle with her, but he wasn't rough, either. He was simply masculine. He made it perfectly clear that he was running the show. Easily, confidently, he readied Judy for love. His big strong hands roved her body, arousing her, exciting her. His lips found her nipples and pressed down on them, and his tongue flicked back and forth, and his fingertips brought shivers of delight to her skin in a dozen places.

She was hot and eager for him within five minutes.

And when he took her, she could practically hear the crash of cymbals, the blare of the symphony orchestra, at the sublime moment of consummation.

Their bodies moved in perfect rhythm. He was an elegant, superlatively good lover, and every heave of his lunging body brought Judy closer and closer to a fulfillment such as she had rarely had before. Gasping and panting, her body churning beneath his, she clung to him, yielded herself to him, wrapped her legs around him, dug her heels into his calves.

Higher and higher she soared, toward the absolute summit of ecstasy. Finally, she reached a point that she thought was the limit, only to find to her amazement that Donoway was still with her and ready to take her still higher yet.

Up, up, up into the stratosphere of passion. Up where the air was thin and the mind reeled. Up into a dazzling new realm of desire.

"Oh, God," she cried. "I'm going out of my mind! I can't stand it any more!"

He laughed.

And sent her whirling into a fresh tizzy of erotic excitement.

He wasn't human. He was the most fantastically gifted lover Judy had ever known. Her body throbbed and trembled in his arms. Sweat oiled her body as she lunged at him again and again. Her breasts crushed into the shield of his chest, she cried out in frenzy. At last he joined her at the summit, reaching his pleasure in quick, powerful spasms that drove her into an oblivion of ecstasy.

Afterward, she lay quietly in his arms, trying to understand what had happened to her.

She was dazed. She was a different person. She was in love. She saw a chance to repair the wounds of her soul, to begin life again after nearly five years of hell. He could help her. He was a miracle.

He said, "This is the time when you're supposed to start cutting me apart, isn't it, Judy?"

Her eyes fluttered open. She stared at him as though she had never seen him before.

'I don't want to," she said softly. "I don't see a reason in the world to insult you, Charley. I don't think I've ever been so happy before."

It was the biggest mistake she had made in her whole life.

CHAPTER SEVEN

Judy's fingers dug almost savagely into the clay. She sat cross-legged at the workbench, turning out little knicknacks for tourists, while her mind roved backward in time to that hellish time three years ago....

The only time in her life she had ever been really in love.

Charley Donoway seemed to be everything she wanted. He was handsome, clever, sophisticated, virile, and strong. He was terrific in bed, and he was a real personality with force and vigor, neither a tyrant nor a sponge. With a kind of wonder, Judy realized that she had at last met the person who could help her tear down the wall she had built around herself.

"You want to move in with me?" he asked.

"That's silly question," she said.

They began keeping house together. Night after night, they rang the changes on the act of passion. She throbbed and writhed in his hands as he drove her to the ultimate in ecstasy. During the day, he was at his bookstore, and she worked at her ceramics ... and dreamed of the night that awaited her.

He didn't say anything about marriage. But Judy knew that she wanted to spend the rest of her life with this man. He stood apart from all the others, all those faceless nobodies whom she had bedded with and then spurned. She was willing to crawl to him just as she had forced other men to crawl to her.

It was the happiest time she had ever known. But it didn't last.

The rude awakening came about three months after she had started living with him.

They had made love that night, and it had been as wonderful as always. Afterward, he sat up in the bed and reached across her to get his cigarettes. His arm pressed into the yielding globes of her breasts as he picked up the pack. Playful, Judy wiggled her body from side to side so her breasts rubbed against him. But he took no notice of the gesture.

He selected a cigarette from the pack and started to light it. Judy said, "Light one for me too, will you?"

Wordlessly, he put a second cigarette in his mouth. He struck the match, puffed them into glowing life, and handed one of the cigarettes to her.

Then he said, "You can start packing tomorrow morning, Judy."

She didn't understand. "Are we taking a trip?"

"You are. I'm not."

"Huh?"

"You're moving out. I've got another girl coming in here tomorrow, and there isn't room for two of you. I'm not a harem-keeper."

Judy swung around and stared at him, the big mounds of her breasts swaying and slapping together as her body pivoted suddenly. "Is this a joke of some kind?" she asked him.

"No joke. It's over, kid. That's all."

"Over—"

"Three months. Time for you to be moving along. What did you think, that this was some kind of lifetime lease you had?"

Judy felt herself crumbling apart. She sat there, naked, trembling, her body chilling after the warmth of his love. "No," she said dully. "You don't mean any of this. It was so good, five minutes ago. The two of us making it, like it was for lifetime. And now you say—no. I just don't believe it."

"You better start believing it," Donaway told her, tonelessly. "On account of it's true."

"But I love you, Charley!"

He smiled mirthlessly. "I understand a lot of guys told you they loved you, too. A lot of good it did them. You tossed them out. I'm tossing you out, Judy."

She gaped at him. "You can't do this to me. Please, Charley. Don't do this to me. You're everything I've got in the world. You're my whole life."

"It's a mistake to let yourself get that involved with another person," he said calmly.

"That's what I used to think too. Until you came along and I found out what love really meant. You can't throw me away, Charley. You can't!"

"I can."

She leaped from the bed and flung her arms wide, displaying her naked body to him, all of it.

"Look at me," she yelled. "You ever see a girl built like me? I'm not something you throw away. You told me yourself, you thought I was the most beautiful girl in the world."

"Cover yourself, honey. You'll catch cold. I've seen all that flesh before. Just meat, that's all it is. Big, round swinging things of meat. Come back in bed, now. You got one more night here."

"Charley, I never dreamed you'd do this to me."

He looked at her somberly. "I had a wife, once. I was nineteen years old and I thought she was the greatest girl in the world. I worshipped her. She laid six of my friends one afternoon, just because she was bored. She broke me in half, Judy. And I made up my mind, I'd never let another woman get that kind of hold on my life. Find 'em, feel 'em— you know the rest. But never love 'em. Love is dangerous. You've been fun, Judy, but now it's time for you to go. Just on general principles, I'm tossing you out. It's a hobby of mine to treat women that way. Just as you used to torture men."

"But don't you see, Charley, we're two of a kind! We've both been kicked around by life, we've been wounded by people we've trusted. We belong together. We ought to stay with each other. We—"

"No," he said. "I can't help it if you've had a tough time in life. So have I, and this is the way I make it up to myself. You go out on your pretty pink rear. Now you want to get back into bed with me, or you want to start packing right now?"

She left that night, still not believing that this was happening to her. She couldn't stay with him after what had taken place.

She packed and left at two in the morning, and found a place to sleep with one of her Lesbian friends. The next morning, she thought she might commit suicide. But she changed her mind.

She had never felt so depressed before. Not even after Ned had raped her.

She had crawled back out of five years of misery, had learned how to love a man at last, had given herself fully to Charley Donoway. And, because he bore the wounds of love too, he had kicked her in the teeth.

He couldn't see that she had suffered what he had suffered. He could only see that there was pleasure in making a girl fall in love with you and then throwing her out of your life.

There was poetic justice in that, Judy realized. It was the same trick she had worked on dozens of men in the last few years. Build up their expectations, get them frothing at the mouth with love for you—then give them the knife. But she had never dreamed that Charley Donoway would do that to her.

He had, though. He had played her own game on her. Maybe he had picked her out deliberately, knowing of her reputation as a heartbreaker. Maybe he had decided to teach her a little lesson.

Once more, Judy plumbed the depths of despair. She was utterly shattered, now, for she had risked her emotions, she had come out from behind her wall, and all it had gained her was the most crushing defeat.

She didn't stay with the Lesbian friend for long. She found herself a one-room place in a mangy old hotel on Market Street, and stayed there for a month, seeing nobody and trying to think things out. She laid in a stock of liquor, rarely left her room, and spent most of her time sprawled out nude in bed, drinking and thinking. She didn't take a bath for three weeks. Her flesh crawled, her silken, golden hair turned into a frizzy horror. She ate hardly anything. Her ribs began to show through, and her magnificent breasts started to droop.

Then she made up her mind what she was going to do, if she didn't simply kill herself.

Withdraw from society. Live like a hermit. Get herself a cabin somewhere in the woods near the Pacific, down below Monterey, and keep away. The world can hurt you too easily. The world can wound. Withdraw, live a quiet life, rid herself of the need for money, swim in the ocean, sunbathe ... that was the ticket.

And here I am, Judy thought.

She had occupied her cottage for two and a half years, now. She had friends up and down the coast, cabin-dwellers like herself. They were all part-time hermits and they respected each other's privacy. If you wanted to be alone for a week or a month or a year, they left you alone. If you needed help, they gave you help.

It was the ideal arrangement.

But it left Judy with plenty of time to think. She could think as she lay nude on the beach at dawn, or as she cut through the icy waters, or as she worked at her clay, or as she sprawled in her cabin on winter nights. She could think of all the miserable things the world had done to her to drive her into such solitude.

The first rape....

The "kindly" man in the bar....

Charley Donoway, who had trifled with her heart and then stabbed it in cold blood....

The more Judy brooded about these things, the more vivid her hatreds became. Withdrawing from the world wasn't enough. She wanted vengeance on it.

In her life in San Francisco, she had exacted that vengeance in a psychological way, by letting men fall in love with her and then spurning them. But even that wasn't sufficient. Now, living alone at the edge of the continent, turning into a lonely, twisted, bitter woman, Judy began to tell herself that there was nothing at all wrong with committing murder. Through the taking of life, she could repay herself for the living death that had been inflicted on her.

She nursed the idea for more than a year, toying with it, fondling it in her mind. Then she decided to put it into action.

She couldn't kill her brother Ned, because he was dead already.

She couldn't kill the soft-eyed man who had taken her home from the bar, because she didn't know his name or where to find him.

But she could kill Charley Donoway.

She hated him more than the other two. Her brother Ned had been drunk when he raped her. The man in the bar had just been a lonely, weak individual giving way to sudden temptation. But Charley Donoway had acted in cold blood, deliberately setting her up for the torment he gave her.

She'd get even with him for that.

It was all down in her little black notebook. From time to time, Judy got the book out from its hiding place under her panties, and relived the experience of that first murderous thrill.

November 8: "I went into San Francisco and looked for Charley Donoway. I would rather have written to him, but I didn't think that was a good idea...."

Donoway looked at her evenly as she walked into his North Beach bookstore. It was one of those flawless days that San Francisco sometimes gets in November, the sky incredibly blue, the city's pastel hues sun-washed and brilliant, the air clear and warm.

She looked him in the eye. "Hello, Charley. Long time no see. How have you been?"

"Getting along, Judy."

"It's been better than two years. You've probably run through six more women by this time."

"Four," he said. "Is there any particular book you're looking for?"

"I didn't come here for a book," she told him. "I wanted to give you an invitation."

"Oh?"

"I'm living down on the coast, now. I've got a little cottage in a pretty secluded part of the world. A hermit kind of life, you know."

"Sounds attractive."

"It is," Judy said. "But occasionally, a girl likes company. I was wondering if you'd like to come out there for a weekend, Charley. I promise not to fall in love with you again. I won't even have sex with you if you don't want to. I'm just offering hospitality."

"You hate my guts," he said. "What's the catch?"

"No catch," she replied, smiling. She took a deep breath and let him have a good view of the jutting hillocks of her bosom. "I'm mellowing in my old age, Charley. I don't hate anybody any more. And I thought you'd like the scenery out there. You can walk along the beach ... watch the sunrise and the sunset ... it'll give you some ideas for poetry. We can talk, a little. Like old friends who have something in common. And then on Sunday night, I'll drive you back to San Francisco. I'm not angling for anything. I'm just trying to get to know myself a little better by strolling back through my past. Will you come?"

He considered her for a long moment.

"All right," he said. "I'll come."

She knew that she had to be very cautious about the way she did things. She didn't want him to spread the word around that he was going out to Judy Domanig's place for the weekend. So she saw to it that he didn't have a chance to tell anybody. She drove him home when the bookstore closed a little later in the day, and he picked up some things for the weekend, and then she drove toward her cottage.

He hadn't had a chance to tell a soul where he was heading. He feels guilty about what he did to me, Judy thought, and so he's letting me have my way.

It was twilight when they reached the cottage. Nature was putting on a spectacular display, just as though she knew that Judy was having a poet as a weekend guest. The sun had dipped into the Pacific a little while ago. The sky was stained with pink and blue and gold. There was something dark and menacing about the gray November sea.

"Let's have a look at the water before we eat," Judy suggested. "Okay?"

"Sure," Donoway said.

She led him down the stone steps to the beach. They were all alone there. Plenty of cars were buzzing by on the coast highway, but Judy knew of places she could take him where they wouldn't be visible from up there. She would be able to kill him without being seen. But this wasn't the right moment. Not yet....

They walked along the beach. Donoway was silent, awed by the turbulent beauty of the Pacific as night approached. He stood for a long while right at the edge of the water, staring out at six thousand miles of emptiness.

Then he said, "You've got the right idea, coming out and living in a place like this. It cleanses the soul, living here."

"I wouldn't be here but for you."

"I don't know how to interpret that, Judy. You're still bitter because I threw you out?"

"I told you. I've mellowed. Let's not talk about the past, Charley. Let's just be good friends and share a quiet weekend together. Yes?"

"Yes," he agreed.

So they returned to the cottage and Judy put up dinner. Nothing fancy, because nothing fancy was called for: meatballs and spaghetti, and a salad of crisp fresh greens in oil and vinegar, and a bottle of strong red wine. They ate by dim light, with the cats prowling around on the table. Not much was said.

It was a late dinner, and it was well after nine o'clock by the time everything was cleared away. Judy turned the radio on. Soft music filtered into the cottage. Donoway walked out front and stared at the stars and the moon for a while.

Judy came up to him. "I go to bed early and get up early here. I swim every morning."

"Sounds great."

"I'd like to go to bed now."

He nodded.

"Charley, come to bed with me."

He turned to face her. "You don't have to if you don't want to, Judy. I told you, I'm not expecting any favors this weekend."

"It isn't a favor. If I didn't want to have sex with you, I wouldn't have asked. Let's, Charley. For old times' sake. We were always so good with each other, weren't we?"

"We were terrific," he said.

Until I messed up the deal by falling in love with you, Judy thought.

They went into the cottage. He undressed her, running his hands excitingly over the firm mounds of her breasts, the taut globes of her buttocks. He had lost none of his ability to thrill her. He removed his own clothes, and they dropped down together on the mattress.

This was a man she hated with an all-consuming hatred. Yet she was able to push that hatred off into a dim compartment of her mind. All that mattered now was physical satisfaction which Charley Donoway could give her more intensely than any other man alive.

He readied her body for their love. Then he took her.

He seemed just a little unsure of himself this time. She knew why. He felt guilt for having thrown her out so brutally back then, and he wasn't sure what kind of a reception his embraces were going to get this time. Judy left no doubt on that score, though.

Writhing, churning, gasping, she accepted him with passionate eagerness.

"Charley—" she gasped. "Oh, Charley, split me in half, split me, Charley!"

He dove at her. She arched her back, rising high away from the mattress, forcing herself upward against him.

His hard, lean, agile body propelled her toward the summit of bliss. She gripped him firmly with her strong thighs, as her breasts heaved and her nipples throbbed, and pleasure went ripping through her like the blade of a knife.

Later in the night, they made love again. But this time it was Judy who was in command.

She reached out and touched Donoway. He was awake, or at least he awakened the moment her hand encountered him. Some quick motions of her fingers, and he was ready to make love.

Judy slid her leg across his body until she was over him. Then she sat up, pinning him with her nakedness. She seized him, guided him to her, lowered herself until her buttocks pressed against his thighs.

Then they began to move.

She set the rhythm. Slowly at first, then more vehemently, her body rocking up and down, the cushions of her buttocks slap-slap-slapping on him. She leaned back, making the sensation more intense, and for an instant she lost control of the situation in the fierceness of her feelings, closing her eyes and beginning to moan with pleasure. He tried to swing her over so that he would be on top. He hated this position, with the woman astride the man. Judy knew that.

That was why she had chosen it as Charley Donoway's farewell to sex.

She was quick and strong, and she kept him from overturning her. "No," she said huskily. "Stay down there. Let me do the work."

Her plunging body rose and fell, rose and fell. He reached up, grabbed her breasts, hung onto the twin globes of full fleshy voluptuousness firmly, trapping her rockhard nipples between his fingers.

Pleasure arrived. In upward jolts for him, in spasming quivers for her. Sweat oiled their bodies. In the darkness, Judy slumped down him, making herself into a blanket of flesh. His arms tightened around her and he whispered soft words.

Then they slept again.

At dawn, Judy woke. She looked at him. He was sleeping on his back, with his mouth open a little way. It was the only time she had ever seen him look defenseless.

She nudged him with a fingertip, and he opened his eyes and blinked at her.

"The sun's rising," she told him. "Let's go down to the beach and watch it."

It could have been the first morning after the creation of the world.

The beach was empty. During the night, there had been an unusually high tide, and the encroaching water had washed the sand smooth well up the beach. Now the splayed footprints of the beach birds were the only marks that marred that smoothness.

It was too cold for swimming, too dark at this hour for sunbathing. Judy and Donoway took off their shoes and walked up the beach. They did not hold hands. There was something about the solemn majesty of the ocean this morning that did not encourage conversation.

Judy was wearing a polo shirt and a pair of frayed pedal-pushers. She had not bothered with underwear, and the pink hills of her breasts bobbled and jiggled freely inside the tight polo shirt. The brisk November wind did not bother her. She had trained herself not to pay attention to the weather.

Donoway had put on a shirt, shorts, and his slacks. He walked with his hands in his pockets, squinting his eyes against the breeze, hunching slightly forward.

They walked about two hundred yards south along the beach in silence. It was a fine morning for beachcombing at dawn. Judy thought.

A fine morning for revenge.

Here she was with the man who had done the worst injury off all to her life, in a life studded with injury. Not even Ned, cruelly stealing his sister's virginity, had been as malevolent. For Judy had been in the process of recovering from Ned's shattering deed when she met and fell in love with Charley Donoway. And Donoway, by trifling with her affections, had made certain that she would never in her life trust her emotions again. Before him, she had had a chance. Now she was sunk.

And, though he thought she had forgiven him for it, he was going to pay.

Judy felt very calm. She did not doubt that everything would go properly. So far everything had. She had brought him out here without another soul knowing where he had gone; she had had sex with him twice, in rewarding fashion, now he was down here on the beach where his life would end. It was an exhilarating feeling to know that at any moment of her choice, she could have her vengeance.

He said, "This is the most incredibly beautiful place in the world, Judy. I'm grateful to you for inviting me out here. You know, I feel that I could spend the rest of my life on this beach."

"You will," Judy said.

She came up behind him and brought the edge of her hand down against the back of his neck in a swift chopping motion. It was a perfectly timed, perfectly delivered blow. Judy had studied it with care. She knew exactly where to strike, and exactly how to pivot her body to make full use of every one of her hundred twenty pounds.

At the very least, a chop like that would stun a man into unconsciousness. At most, it would snap his spine and paralyze him. Judy's blow had an effect somewhere in between. Donoway uttered a grunting sound and fell forward on the sand.

He didn't move. But he was still breathing.

He was out cold.

Judy glanced warily around. The beach was still deserted, the highway clear. She bent forward and hooked her hands under Charley Donoway's arms. Then she dragged him fifteen feet westward across the beach toward the edge of the water, and kept on going until she was out in a depth of about a foot of surf.

The water was so fiercely cold that it seemed to be hot. It blazed like flame against her legs. But Judy didn't mind that. She held Donoway suspended, face down in the water. His body was still limp, frozen by that single deadly blow. But she was prepared to take swift action if he happened to recover consciousness.

She pushed his head under the water.

She held him there, one hand on the back of his head to keep his face covered. When the waves rolled in, the water was about two feet deep. When they rolled out again, it was no more than eight or ten inches. But that was all right. It didn't require more than a few inches of water to drown a man, provided you kept his face submerged all the time. She held him down. She pushed his mouth and nose right into the sand when the water was low.

How long did it take for a man to drown?

Judy didn't know. So she decided not to take any chances. She held him under the water for ten minutes. He wasn't moving at all, now. She figured his lungs must be full of water. She straightened up and released him.

He stayed put, floating face down, drifting like a log on the water. He swirled round and round, now moving some twenty-five feet out from shore, now swinging inland again with the inrushing waves. But he did not move at all. He just hung there.

Judy smiled. She waded to the shore and stepped up on the beach. Again she looked around. Still all clear. She pulled her polo shirt over her head and let it fall to the sand. The brisk breeze whipped against the high, out-thrusting white mounds of her bare breasts. Judy unzipped her pedal-pushers, drew them down over her hips and thighs and buttocks, stepped out of them, laid them on the sand next to the polo shirt.

Stark naked, she walked toward the water.

It was a cruelly cold morning to go swimming, nude or otherwise. The air temperature was somewhere in the high forties, and the water couldn't have been much warmer than that. But this was something that Judy had to do, and she had trained herself for it, swimming in all kinds of bitter weather.

She waded out, hissing a little as the water swirled up around her. Cold tongues of ocean licked at the white globes of her nude buttocks, lewdly caressing the soft firm flesh. Water flicked against her belly. A splashing wave struck her breasts.

She didn't care.

She waded out to where Charley Donoway's body was drifting, and dug her fingers firmly into his hair. Then she slid forward into a swimming position and began crawling toward the deeper water in a one-armed stroke.

Out ... out ... out into the quiet world beyond the breakers....

A naked nymph, cutting through the gray dawn sea, towing human cargo behind her. Kick … kick … kick.…

Her teeth were chattering. Her breasts seemed frozen. Goose pimples sprang up like extra nipples on the big swells of her body. Her buttocks were corrugated by the cold. But still she swam. No bathing suit would have protected her against the chill. This was a journey that had to be made in the nude.

Grimly, she forced herself onward, growing used to the cold with each stroke.

After a while she decided she was out far enough. She pulled the body up against her and examined it. Yes, he was dead, no doubt of it. His face was not the face of a living man. He had taken on the bloated water-logged look of a corpse.

With mock tenderness, Judy hugged the corpse up against her for the last time. Take a good feel, Charley, she thought. Rub against my boobs. That's it. You could have had them in your bed every night forever, you know. Only you didn't want to.

Charley … I loved you, Charley.…

She turned him around in the water, so his head was aimed downward. Then she shoved. His soggy, water-soaked clothes weighed down, overcoming the natural buoyancy of the human body. And his chest cavity was full of water too, helping to carry him down.

Down and out of sight.

Judy knew that he wouldn't stay there. He'd come to the surface eventually, but not here. She had studied the reports of the suicides and accidental drownings along this coast, and she knew that the ocean currents would carry a body for many miles before they finally coughed it up on shore.

The job was done. Judy turned and swam for land as fast as she could, a nude sprite cutting furiously through the freezing water.

Coming up on land again was the roughest part of all. The air temperature was lower than the water temperature, and the wind blowing against her wet skin would make things even worse. She had no towel to dry herself with, either.

Naked, she sprinted up out of the water and gasped with shock as the frigid breeze enfolded her.

She fell to the sand, huddling herself up in a fetal ball, knees pressed against the lush globes of her breasts. She rolled over and over, agonized by the pain of the cold, flopping like a beached fish on the shore. Sand stuck to her wet skin. She jerked uncontrollably, trying to warm herself.

The wild spasm of chill passed after a few moments. Judy sat up, breathing hard, her breasts heaving. She was almost dry; the sharp wind had seen to that. She put her hands to the bare mounds of her breasts, cupping them, warming them. Exertion had left a spike of pain wedged into her breastbone.

Slowly, shakily, she got to her feet. She brushed the crusted sand from her naked body. She flicked it off her breasts, her belly, her buttocks. The sun was hitting the beach, now. Judy looked out toward the water, toward the empty sea, and felt the first warm rays on her buttocks and back.

No sign of the dead man out there. Good. Let him rot out there. Let the minnows eat him.

She turned and allowed the sunlight to kiss her breasts, her thighs. Then she picked up her polo shirt and slipped it on. Chastely, she found her pedal-pushers and covered her nakedness.

She trudged up the beach, clambered wearily up the hundred-odd stairs, took the underpass to her cottage. She gave the cats their breakfast. She looked around for the rest of Charley's Donoway's belongings, and found his wallet, his watch, and some keys. She would get rid of those later, driving thirty or forty miles down the road to dump them into the sea.

Stripping again, Judy took a hot shower to wash away the salt water and the sand that formed a scummy surface on her skin. The warmth of the shower melted the chill that had entered her.

After that, she prepared a hearty breakfast for herself. And then she took out the notebook she had purchased, the one she intended as her murder notebook. She turned to the first page.

Carefully she violated the innocence of the notebook with its first entry:

November 8: I went into San Francisco and looked for Charley Donoway. I would rather have written to him, but I didn't think that was a good idea....

Judy put the book away, burying it under its heap of lingerie once more and closing the drawer. As always, when she relived the killing of Charley Donoway, a tremor of satisfaction ran through her. The words in the notebook brought the event to life every time. She could feel once again the tang of the icy water against her nude body, the sting of her hand where she had chopped it into the back of his neck, the whiplash impact of the breeze on her skin after she came dripping and nude from the water.

That had been almost nine months ago. His body hadn't come to light until the spring. He had washed up on the beach somewhere around December or January, lodging in a rock crevice more than fifty miles south of the place where Judy had drowned him. But nobody found him until March, and by then there wasn't much left of his body.

They identified him by his dental work as Charley Donoway, the San Francisco bookstore owner who had disappeared the previous fall. Apparent suicide, that was the verdict that was recorded. What else could you call it, when a body washes up on the shore out of the sea after so many months?

So Judy had gotten away with it.

There was a thrill in that. The knowledge that she had repaid him for a crime against her soul, and had escaped punishment for her deed. She took a savage pleasure in thinking about it.

And, on the day they found Charley Donoway's body, Judy knew that she was going to kill again. She couldn't be content just with Donoway. The fever was in her blood, now.

Kill! Avenge.

She was like a spider, waiting in her seashore lair for the victims to come along. A beautiful spider. A passionate spider.

Thinking about it, about her three murders, Judy smiled. She felt no remorse. Those deaths she regarded as her due. One for each of the three calamities that had wrecked her life.

One for Ned and his rape.

One for the man in the bar.

One for Charley Donoway, who had spurned her heartfelt love.

Judy grinned in satisfaction. She gathered up the clay pieces she had fashioned, and fired the kiln. Once it was blazing away, she went down to the beach for her afternoon swim.

The weather never got really warm here, the way it did down in Los Angeles, but this was a fine, summery day anyway, with the temperature close to seventy degrees and the sun bright and hot. Clad in a skimpy bikini, Judy stepped out onto the beach.

She regretted that she couldn't swim and sunbathe nude in the afternoons. But it was too risky. The highway was busy, and sometimes—though not often—there were even other people roaming around on the beach.

Judy compromised with convention by wearing the most absolutely skimpy bikini imaginable. She had made it herself, by cutting down a standard model she had bought one day in Carmel. It was nothing more than two strips of cloth that covered the bare minimum.

The halter covered the middle and lower part of her breasts, from the nipples down. The bottom part of the bikini hid her in front and about half of her backside. But her hips were bare, and her belly down to the first golden wisps, and the hind cheeks of her buttocks. It was the kind of bikini that probably would have been banned on any public beach this side of the French Riviera. But at least Judy could say, in the not-very likely chance that anybody would complain, that she was at least covering the essentials.

She took a good, energetic swim, then sprawled out to sunbathe. The beach remained empty. She liked it that way. It was amazing how she had come to get along without the company of other people so entirely—she, who had been such a friendly, gregarious girl in her high school days.

B.R., that is.

Before Rape.

But it was true. Sometimes, she went three or four days without seeing another human being, and didn't mind it a bit. She had her cats, and her beach, and her work. And her notebook. Those things were enough for her, these days.

Judy serenely permitted the sun to bathe her. Its wonderful warmth enfolded her.

After a while, she decided that she ought to get back to her kiln. She leaped lithely to her feet and flung her beachrobe over her bikini. Then she headed back the long path to her cottage.

There was someone waiting for her.

Judy saw the automobile before she saw its owner. She didn't recognize it. It was parked outside the cottage, next to her own car, and it wasn't a car that belonged to any of her friends in the coast colony.

It was a long, sleek, late-model Buick, deep maroon in color, reeking of expensiveness.

Her heart leaped. The police, she wondered? That was what she was always afraid of ... the police descending on her out of the blue one day, saying, "We are putting you under arrest for the murder of Charles Donoway...."

But this wasn't a police car. It might belong to a plainclothes detective, of course. She couldn't be sure. Uneasily, she came around to the porch side of her cottage to see who her visitor was.

He was waiting for her on the porch.

He was about thirty years old, a tall man, good-looking, with a deep tan and a lean face with deep-cut vertical lines in the cheeks. His hair was cut in a close brush. His eyes were black and bright. He was wearing a costly-looking suit cut in what Judy guessed was the sharpest up-to-date style. He looked powerful.

He was dressed too well to be a detective, she decided. But her alarm didn't subside. Had he been inside the house? Prowling around?

Reading her notebook, maybe?

"Yes?" she said. "Are you looking for me?"

He shrugged affably and flashed a row of movie-star teeth. "That all depends," he said.

"On what?"

"On whether you can help me. My car's on the fritz and I need a mechanic. Is it all right if I use your telephone?"

Judy felt herself going wobbly-legged with relief.

"Sure," she said. "Come inside." She tried extremely hard to keep her reaction from showing.

CHAPTER EIGHT

She pushed open the door of the cottage and led him in. He laughed and said, "I never even thought to see if the door was open. Or I might have just gone inside and made my phone call without waiting for you to get back."

"Been waiting long?"

"About fifteen minutes," he said. "Sitting here on the porch, playing with your cats. I knocked on your door, but there was no answer, and then I saw that furnace lit in back so I figured you'd be coming back pretty soon."

"That's not exactly a furnace," Judy said. "It's a kiln. I make ceramic pieces for a living."

"Really, now? That's interesting. I'd like to see a few of your things."

"They aren't worth bothering about. Tourist junk, that's all." She took off her beachrobe. As she dropped it on a chair she said, "You're lucky you picked my place to stop off at. Most of the cabins down this way don't have telephones. But—is something wrong?"

He was staring at her in a strangely intense way, his lips clamped tight shut.

After a moment, he snapped out of it. He said, "No, nothing's wrong. Except that's a mighty scanty bikini you've got on, miss."

She laughed, "I forgot about that. If it upsets you I'll put my robe back on."

"No. Don't do that." His eyes traveled unashamedly over her, taking in the contours of her breasts, hidden only partly by the band of cloth over her nipples, and studying the shapely lines of her thighs and buttocks. It was a frankly appraising look, a purely sexual look.

He shook his head. "That's some outfit. They let you wear it on the beach here?"

"There's nobody to say no. Actually, I think it's rather conservative. Every morning at sunrise I take a swim and I don't wear anything at all."

"I wish I had come by at sunrise, then."

"You can try again sometime," she said. "I'm always there. Practically twelve months a year.

"I'll keep that in mind." He flashed the movie-star grin again, and his glittering eyes leaped avidly from her breasts to her thighs and back again. "My name's Jim Norton, by the way."

"Judy Domanig."

"Hello, Judy."

"Hello, Jim. What's the matter with your car, anyway?"

"Generator trouble. I felt it conking out on me as I got past Monterey, and I figured I'd better not risk being on the highway when it conked out altogether. A man sitting in a stalled car can get killed on that crazy highway you got here."

A man can get killed off the highway too, Judy, thought, amiably.

He went on, "So I took the first likely-looking exit and hunted around for a house. I found yours. Wasn't anybody home, so I sat down to wait until you came back. You live here all alone, Judy?"

"All alone. Me and my cats."

"Seems like an awful waste. Girl like you, ought to be out in the world doing things, seeing people, mixing a little. It's kind of like being a hermit, living in a place like this."

"I like it," Judy said. "I tried being out in the world doing things, once. I didn't like it much. That's why I'm here."

"Not a neighbor within yelling distance, though."

"That's right."

"Seems to me it's an awfully lonely life."

"It has its advantages," Judy said evenly. "There are times when a girl likes to be by herself."

"Lived here long?"

"Coming up on three years," she said.

His eyes were still on her body. Judy wondered if it had been a mistake to take her beachrobe off and show herself to him in her bikini. After all, as he had been quick to point out, there wasn't a neighbor within yelling distance. If he got carried away by the sight of all that bare voluptuous flesh that was sticking out around the edges of those two strips of cloth—

No. She wasn't worried. He had a clean-cut, affable look. Not the dangerous type.

Besides, she could handle herself. Nobody was going to start trouble with her and come out of it all in one piece. She knew the techniques of self-defense, and she didn't necessarily fight fair. She had been raped twice in her life, and she meant to see to it that she was never raped again.

So she stood there in her bikini and pointed to the telephone. "You'd better make your call. Jim. You'll find mechanics listed in the directory. The nearest one is about twenty miles down the road. Man name of Gonzalez—he's pretty good with cars."

"What if he doesn't answer?"

"Try Sam Armistead, then. He's farther away, but maybe he's still open this late in the afternoon. You ought to reach one or the other of them. I'm going to get out of this wet bathing suit while you're phoning."

He picked up the directory. Judy went into her bedroom and closed the door. She unclipped the halter of her bikini, took it off, rolled the bottom down. Nude, she toweled the last ocean dampness away from her body. She could hear the man in the next room talking in a quiet voice to one of the garage men.

She debated what to wear, and decided on one of her shifts—a purple and blue muu-muu that she was fond of wearing. She slipped it over her head without bothering to don any underwear. Judy liked the feeling of freedom it gave her to let her breasts bobble free under her shift, to let the fresh air get up around her buttocks and her thighs.

She went back into the other room just as her visitor was hanging up the telephone.

"Well?" she said.

"Complications."

"Such as?"

"Gonzalez isn't answering his phone this month, it seems. So I phoned Armistead, and he says he can't do anything until tomorrow morning. He doesn't have the equipment handy, or something."

"Looks like you're stuck," Judy said.

Norton shrugged. "I notice you've got a car outside. If you could drive me to the nearest motel, I'd be much obliged. And then tomorrow Armistead can come and fix up my car and away I'll go."

Judy regarded him steadily. She took a deep breath, though she knew that that made the points of her breasts protrude against the thin fabric of her shift.

She said, "The nearest motel is about forty-five miles from here, Jim. It's late in the afternoon. If I drove you, it would mean a ninety-mile round trip, and that would be a strain not only on me, but on my car. So why don't you just spend the night here, and to hell with all this fencing around?"

He grinned. "I appreciate the invitation, Judy. And I won't waste any time accepting it."

"You knew I'd offer, didn't you?"

"Well—let's say I hoped you would."

"There's only one bed here," she said evenly. "And it's not even a bed, you'll notice, just sort of a mattress on the floor. I sleep there. If you happen to be a pansy and the idea of sharing a bed with a woman gives you the sickies in your gut, well, you can sleep on the couch over here. Otherwise you're welcome to share my bed."

"With or without a sword between us?"

"Without."

"You're a pretty straightforward girl, Judy. You don't kid around."

"I like living alone," she said, "but that doesn't mean I'm entirely antisocial. I happen to enjoy a good roll in the hay every now and then. You look like you're the kind of guy who can provide one. As long as luck dumped you at my place today, why not take advantage of it?"

"Why not?"

"There's one other thing you ought to be warned about, though. I get up early. Come dawn I'm going to be down on the beach."

"Taking a nude sunbath?"

"Yes."

"Then I'll be there with you," he said. "You think I'm afraid of getting up early in the morning?"

She dropped down into the chair opposite him. Her muu-muu rode a couple of feet up her leg, showing him a considerable length of firm, tanned thigh. She didn't mind that. Neither did he, apparently. She eyed him with interest.

Handsome. Self-assured. Prosperous-looking.

She wondered what he had told the garage men. Normally, Sam Armistead was willing to drop everything and come any distance to be of service. And his well-equipped garage wouldn't be stumped by generator trouble on a new Buick. So Jim Norton had probably said, "Can you come up to Judy Domanig's place first thing in the morning to fix my car?" and Sam Armistead had said, "Sure," and that was all that had taken place. Norton looked like a clever man. And he had obviously been maneuvering from the start to get to spend the night here. Otherwise, he wouldn't have waited around for her to return from the beach, in the first place. He would have tried the door, and used the telephone, and gotten his car repaired and hit the road again.

But here he was. A guest for the night.

"Where are you from?" she asked. "What do you do, anyway?"

His face was a flawless mask, letting nothing through that he didn't want to come through. He said, "I'm from Seattle. I run a night club there."

"I didn't know Seattle had any night clubs."

"A few. A few. I'm a half-partner in one."

"On vacation?"

"You might say that," he said. "I'm driving south. I've been traveling for a couple of days now."

"Heading for L.A.?"

"Further south than that."

"San Diego?" she asked.

"Mexico," he said. "First stop, Tijuana. Then down to Acapulco for a little while. And over to Cuernavaca. After that, quien sabe? I've got some friends, they live on an island off the coast of Yucatan, Cozumel, it's called. Maybe I'll go over there. Or spend some time in Mexico City. I don't know. I'll play it by ear."

"Sounds like you'll have a ball. How long are you planning to be down there?"

"Two months, three, maybe on through the winter. I don't know that yet."

"What about your night club?"

"That's what I've got a partner for." He flicked a quick glance at her leg. It seemed to travel right up her exposed thigh to the zone of hidden splendors beneath the shift. It was the most penetrating glance Judy had ever received. She didn't draw the shift down toward her knees, though. He said, "You ever been in Mexico?"

"No. My brother went there once, though. He got killed in a bar brawl in Juarez."

"Too bad."

"I didn't think so. He was a louse."

"He was still your brother, though."

She smiled thinly. "If he had remembered that he was my brother all the time, I wouldn't have been so glad when I heard he was dead. You can figure that one any way you care to."

"I don't care to," Norton said. "It sounds too complicated. Would you like to go to Mexico?"

"Is that an invitation to go with you?"

"It could be."

"Save it," Judy said. "Things are moving too fast. You don't know a thing about me, yet. Ask me again when you're ready to leave and then we'll see."

"It wasn't a definite invitation," he said. "Just something for you to think about."

"I'll think about it." She laughed. "The way things are going here, you'll be asking me to marry you in another hour."

"That wouldn't be wise," he said. "I've already got one wife."

"Oh. In Seattle?"

"In New York. But we're still legally tied, as of the time I set out yesterday. Does that disappoint you any, Judy?"

"Not at all. I wouldn't marry anybody. Nothing personal in it."

"You're an odd one."

"I sure am," she agreed pleasantly. "But I've got my reasons for being the way I am."

"Want to tell me about them?"

"No," she said. She stood up. In an easy, flowing motion she bent forward, caught the hem of the muu-muu and straightened up. The muu-muu traveled up the length of her body, baring her shins, her knees, her thighs, her belly. Her breasts were revealed. Then she pulled the garment over her head and tossed it away from her, letting it flutter to the floor like an autumn leaf.

She stood nude before him.

He was very still. A muscle flickered in his right cheek. He had lighted a cigarette only a moment before, but now he crushed it out, barely touched, with a quick, short gesture of his wrist. His eyes roamed her body, from the lightly tanned breasts with their erect nipples down to the broadly feminine hips.

"Nice," he said. "Very nice. Why'd you do it?"

"The conversation was starting to bore me. I've discovered that it's a good conversation-stopper when a girl takes her clothes off all of a sudden."

"You're so right, honey."

He rose smoothly to his feet and went toward her. Judy waited calmly. He was a slick operator, she knew, and she wanted to find out what he was like in bed. This was the most direct way of finding out.

He walked forward until he was about a foot and a half away from her naked form. Then he reached out. His hands were sensitive-looking, well manicured, with long, tapering fingers. They closed around the lush globes of her breasts. He stood there for an instant, gripping her breasts as though they were handles.

Then he moved still closer, and his lips crushed down on hers.

It was a violent kiss. She knew there was violence in the man, too, locked up but not hidden very far from the surface. His lips were hard against hers, and his tongue lanced into her mouth with no hesitation. His right hand remained clinging to her breast, and the other hand slipped down her body and clapped firmly against the satiny mounds of her buttocks.

His suit was rough against her bare skin, but she didn't mind that. She kissed back, equally intensely, matching his fervor.

He let go of her. They stepped apart. His lean face was flushed, his nostrils flaring.

"Get undressed," she said.

"Just what I was planning to do."

She watched impassively, without helping, as he removed his clothing. She meant to stay cool, detached, as she gave herself to him. She was not sure yet whether she wanted to kill him or not. Probably not. It was only a couple of days since she had dragged the last lonely wayfarer under the surface of the water, and her killer instinct was not so fierce that she cared to repeat the act again so soon. It had been six months between the first murder and the second ... three months between the second one and the third....

No, she doubted that she would kill him. But it was still a possibility, if he gave her reason to do it. He was an arrogant man. Charley Donoway had been arrogant, too. Judy might find it necessary to punish this stranger's arrogance, if he treated her badly—

He was almost out of his garments, now. His body was impressive. Judy had seen a lot of men, but not many like this. He had enormously broad shoulders—that hadn't been padding in his suit that gave him that V-shaped physique—and strong, muscular thighs. His chest was covered with a thick, coarse mat of black hair. His belly was flat, and Judy suspected that she could ram her fist into it with all her might and not get much more than a grunt out of him.

And he was very, very male.

He stood there, not exactly smiling, but obviously in a smug, complacent mood, fully aware that he had the sort of body that would excite any woman. Judy didn't resent his smugness, because she shared it, having a body of irresistible beauty herself.

They were well matched, she thought. They deserved each other.

"Come here," she said.

"Uh-uh. You come to me."

"Tough guy?"

"Sort of," he said. He pointed to his body. "I call the shots."

"You proud of it?"

"I've got every reason to be," he said. "I like a woman with spirit, you understand. But she's got to remember that so long as I'm the one with her, I'm the one who's in charge."

"Okay," Judy said. "You're the one in charge."

CHAPTER NINE

She crossed the room and stood in front of him. She pressed herself close, but did not kiss him. Instead, she sank slowly to her knees before him, allowing the tips of her breasts to graze his skin enticingly on the way down.

When she was kneeling in front of him, she put her hand on him. There was more of him than one hand could contain. Instead of putting her other hand next to her first, though, she kissed.

He smiled. He stood straight and tall in front of her, letting her pay homage to him.

He enjoys this, she thought—

Abruptly, she brought her teeth into play. She had kept her lips over them while she was caressing him, but now she pulled her lips back and let her sharp, white little teeth close in on him. Slowly, she brought her jaws together, a fraction of an inch at a time. She knew that it must be painful to him. But he didn't say a word, not even a murmur.

Judy took her mouth away from him. She looked up and saw him studying her with interest.

She said, "I've got very strong jaws. One good snap—who'd be boss then?"

"I didn't think you'd do it."

"Pretty sure of yourself, aren't you?"

"It would be a messy bit. I'd probably bleed like a pig, and there'd be no doctor within miles. So I'd bleed to death right here."

"A pity."

"You sound pretty cool about it. Somehow I don't think you've got murder in your heart, Judy."

"You don't know me yet."

"It wouldn't add up," he said. "When they found me, they'd arrest you on a manslaughter charge. It might be the first case in California history of a man bleeding to death because a woman had bitten him there. Think of the headlines, Judy. Your nice peaceful life ruined by nosy reporters. You'd get a special chapter to yourself in the next edition of Krafft-Ebing."

She laughed. "Nobody would ever have to find you, Jim. I'd take your body down to the beach and dump you in and you'd drift away."

"But there'd be the blood all over your place," he pointed out. "And the trail of blood all the way down to the beach. Uh-uh, Judy. It wouldn't be smart."

"We'll see," she said.

And she put her mouth to him again.

He didn't flinch. For the second time, her lips engulfed him and her head moved, bringing the sweetest of sensation to him, and then, as she had done before, she bared her teeth and pressed them against his skin.

He stood calmly. Another man might have panicked after that cool discussion of murder, but not him. With folded arms, he waited for her to finish playing her games.

He's daring me to bite him, Judy thought in wonder. Daring me!

A wild impulse swept through her, and she nearly gave him the surprise of his life. It was a temptation, she knew. What better revenge could she take on the whole male sex than to deprive this confident arrogant stranger of his masculinity itself?

A snap of the jaws—

She had to get a steady grip on herself to keep from performing the grisly deed without pausing to think. But she kept control over herself. She moved her head back and released him. Then she stood up again.

"You're pretty cool," she said.

"I didn't think you'd do it."

"I almost did, though. I came closer than you want to imagine."

He laughed. "But you didn't do it. You want to know how I knew?"

"How?"

"Because it wouldn't make sense to ruin me like that before I had been to bed with you. Afterward, maybe. But not before. You'd be cheating yourself."

Judy laughed. "You sure are sure of yourself, aren't you?"

"I sure am," he said.

Then he slapped her in the face.

It wasn't a love-tap. It was an open-handed wallop across the cheek and mouth that sent Judy's head spinning backward and almost knocked her off her pins. She reeled away, a step or two.

Then she got control of herself and said, "What was that for?"

"To show you that I can kid around too."

"Some joke."

"Yeah. I thought so too," he said.

He stepped toward her and brought his hand up again. Judy thought he was going to slap her in the face, and she ducked her head, but he crossed her up by hitting her across the breasts.

Wham! Wham! Two quick slaps, forehand and backhand, one for each boob. The two quivering mounds of flesh jiggled and leaped around. The pain went through her with blazing intensity.

He smiled at her. Judy leaped at him.

She was ready to break his neck. She started to chop at him, but he moved with stunning swiftness. He caught her right arm by the wrist and brought it up and around, and the next thing she knew her arm was folded neatly behind her back and he was forcing her to her knees.

"Down ... down...."

"Let go."

"You get down. Or I'll break that arm right off you, honey."

Judy hesitated. He gave the arm a little twinge, just to show her that he meant business. She wouldn't be able to swim very well with a broken arm, and she didn't feel like calling his bluff. He had called her bluff, before, when her teeth were sinking into him, but she couldn't take the chance that he would be equally polite about it all.

She dropped to her knees.

He was right behind her, still keeping his iron grip on her twisted arm. He brought his other hand around and cupped it over the soft mounds of her breasts. He played with one breast, then the other, fondling the ripe white hillocks, toying with the nipples. Despite herself, Judy was getting hot for him. Her nipples were rigid and throbbing hard.

His hand slipped lower, to the sleekness of her belly, and then even lower than that. He probed a realm of warmth, caressing her in an intimate way.

"You're a cutey, all right," he told her. "Lots of fire—that's what I like in a woman. You don't mind if I get rough with you, do you?"

"You're hurting my arm."

"If I let go, what will you do?"

"Let go and see," she said.

He laughed. He put his lips to the nape of her neck and kissed her lightly. His breath was hot against her skin. He nibbled her earlobes. He drew a line of kisses along her cheek.

Then he let go of her arm.

He did it so suddenly that Judy toppled forward and had to brace herself on her hands and knees. She spun around, ready to throw herself at him and work him over with any weapon handy, fingernails included.

But he was grinning at her. "Damn you!" she said.

"Come on. Let's fight. Let's wrestle, huh? It's a good way of warming up."

"No fair. You're bigger than I am."

"But you fight dirtier," he said. "So it all evens up. Come on!"

He seized her. She squirmed in his arm, and managed to break his grip. They writhed on the floor in what could have been an embrace of passion, except that they were locked in furious combat.

She gave it all she had. She was an unusually strong girl, and she could see that he was aware of her strength and impressed by it. Several times, he tried to force her shoulder against the floor, and each time she resisted him and managed to squirm free.

Her breasts were heaving wildly. Sweat had burst from every pore of her skin, so that she had an oiled, gleaming look. Her eyes were glazed with excitement. They locked limbs again.

Body twisted against naked body. They thumped around on the floor, while the cats circled them, puzzled. Judy grunted with strain. She knew how she could win the contest: by grabbing him in a most vulnerable place. But he knew that too. A naked man is always very much aware, when he fights, of what's exposed. And he was taking good care that she didn't reach him there.

Her muscles corded and tensed as she struggled with him. But he was too much for her. She had fought well, as well perhaps as any woman could have done. Yet slowly but surely, he was mastering her.

He got his arm around her waist. He held her tightly, practically cutting her in two. Inexorably, he pivoted her body, twisting her around so that her forehead was pressed against the floor and her bare, tender buttocks were upturned and exposed.

Judy sensed what he was going to do, a moment before he did it. And her face crimsoned from shame and embarrassment at the realization.

He was going to humiliate her.

He was going to celebrate his victory over her by—spanking her.

"No," she yelped.

He laughed. And then the flat of his hand descended on those two, smooth, firm cheeks. The impact was a stunning one. The solid flesh leaped and shook. He hit her buttocks again. Judy kicked her legs, but only thrashed the air. And he spanked her a third time.

Her buttocks were growing hot. They tingled with the pain of his short, sharp, powerful blows. He wasn't easing up on her, either. In a coldly dispassionate way he was spanking her with all his might.

Whack!

Whack!

Whack!

And Judy discovered a very odd and surprising thing. She was enjoying the sensation of being spanked.

She didn't like the idea of being spanked. That was humiliating to her personality. But the actual physical response, the messages being carried not through her mind but through her automatic nervous system, were pleasurable ones. There was something fiercely exciting about lying naked in the arms of a naked man, getting her buttocks tanned this way.

She was hot and throbbing. Her nipples were mounds of rock. Her throat was dry with desire. Her ears rang. Her face was flushed. And her buttocks were red, alive with pain, blazing with heat.

And still the hand descended.

"Enough!" Judy husked. "Take me now, damn you! Take me! I'm ready! Take me!"

Jim Norton laughed. Then he released her, and let her roll over, and fell on top of her.

And he lunged at her and took her. She was as ready to be had as she had ever been in her life, and when he took her she felt turned on in every molecule of her body. She knotted her legs around him and dug her fingers, into the ridged muscles of his back and held on tight, hips churning and heaving.

Higher ... higher ... the erotic frenzy threatened to consume her entirely....

Then came the sunburst of passion. For her, but not for him. She was at the absolute peak of her ecstasy, and yet she realized in awe and in wonder that he had somehow managed to contain himself. It was the most fantastic demonstration of masculine self-control that Judy had ever witnessed. It was almost like a miracle.

But she had no time to ponder it. Because through her mind there flooded fulfillment of such radiant power that all rational thought was blotted out. Time stood still. She soared into the outer reaches of the universe, lost among the stars.

When she snapped back into the right time and the right space, he was still with her, ready to take her on another adventure.

She lay limp and sweat-soaked beneath him, staring up in disbelief. He was smiling full of well-deserved pride at his own masculine powers. They were still joined.

"How did you do that?" she asked.

"Practice makes perfect," he said. "You ready for the next one?"

"I'm still a little groggy from the last round."

"Fine," he said. "I love to ball a groggy woman. Turn over."

"Huh?"

"Over."

"But—I don't—"

"Like this," he said, and seized her body by the hips and gave her a quick flip so that she lay face down on the floor. Judy thought that he was going to spank her once again.

But that wasn't what he had in mind. Not at all.

This time Judy was unprepared for his move. She felt his body pressing down on hers, and then an instant later his hands were on her buttocks, gripping the soft mounds of flesh that so recently he had been punishing with cruel blows. His fingertips dug in firmly.

And then he was against her. Pressing.

"No," she gasped in pain and sudden terror. "Don't! Don't!"

He paid no attention. His body whip-lashed forward against her, and there was an instant of almost incredible agony, like the loss of a second virginity, and then the pain was gone and in its place was pleasure of a kind that Judy had never known before.

He covered her with his body, his chest against her back, his thighs pressing to her buttocks, and he surged and surged again, and each motion brought a new pang of ecstasy to her. She trembled with the intensity of it. She shook. Torrents of perspiration rolled down her lust-dizzied body, making her bare skin gleam.

Norton reached underneath her and cupped each of his hands over one of her breasts. He filled his fingers with the overflowing generosity of her abundant bosom, digging tight, trapping the red, swollen nipples. Then his left hand withdrew from her breast and began to slide down the front of her body.

To make things a little easier for him, Judy rose on her knees in a kind of half crouch. That served a double purpose. It allowed Norton's hand to move freely underneath her body, and it also thrust her buttocks backward against him to make the sensations all the greater, all the more thrilling.

His hand found the tops of her thighs and grasped her there. All the while, he continued to assert himself in a frenzied assault on this new temple of her ecstatic sensations.

Judy thought she would go out of her mind.

She had never known a man like this before, with such incredible, demonic powers of sensuality. He hardly seemed human. Here in the space of a single hour, he had loved her right to the brink of madness, and then, with scarcely a pause, he had turned her over to attack her from another direction, all without showing any seeming signs of strain himself.

She hated him for his cold arrogance, for the serenely confident way that he had taken possession of her.

And yet—and yet—

Within the core of her hatred for him was a strange fascination that bordered on worship. In this man who had entered her life so unexpectedly, Judy sensed her own stronger self, her masculine counterpart, someone who stood apart from the world as she did.

This was a man whose slave she could let herself be.

Right now, gasping and softly moaning in the throes of her second ecstasy, Judy pushed the softness of her body against him, and shivered as he stimulated her in three places at once.

The ultimate surge of ecstasy was arriving now.

Yes ... yes....

NOW!

All of Judy's pent-up erotic fervor erupted in a wild, spasming, furious blaze of fulfillment. And this time, Norton joined her. He held nothing back. At the height of her own sensation, Judy was aware of his sudden, final body-splitting lunge at her, and then of the cataclysmic concluding of his passions.

She fell forward onto the floor. He slumped down on top of her.

For a long time, neither of them moved, as the afterglow of ecstasy slowly ebbed.

CHAPTER TEN

A long time afterward, Judy rose from his embrace and said. "Are you hungry?"

"It's eight hours since I had lunch."

"I'm not much of a cook. But if you'll settle for hamburgers—"

"Anything, love. Anything." He sat up and reached into his discarded jacket for his pack of cigarettes. "Just so long as it's food."

"Let me take a shower first," Judy said. "Then I'll get the eating organized. Okay?"

"Sure," he said.

She padded nude into the bathroom and turned the shower on. She was sweaty from the double session of lovemaking. She got under the needle-sharp spray and let the water cascade down over her breasts and belly.

As she soaped herself, Judy thought back over the events of the afternoon, trying to come to some terms with the upheaval in her life that this man's presence promised to cause.

Who was he? Where bound, and why? He had told her a few things about himself, speaking in an oddly offhand tone. He could just as easily have been making everything up on the spur of the moment. Judy realized that she didn't actually know a thing about him—except that he was handsome, somewhat sinister, fantastically virile, and totally without fear.

He fascinated and repelled her all at once.

Suppose, she thought, as she ran the bar of soap over the smooth, wet mounds of her jutting breasts—suppose, just suppose he asks me to go to Mexico with him. It's a possibility. He likes me. He knows that I speak his language, that I'm his kind of woman. That wrestling match we had—I gave him a damned good fight. I impressed him. I know I did.

Okay, then. Suppose he says, "Come to Tijuana with me, babe."

Do I go? Or do I pass?

Judy didn't know. Again and again, she had resolved not to have anything to do with men except on a casual basis, never to let herself get involved. Here she was, ready to make the old mistake again, ready to give herself to this stranger who said he was Jim Norton the same way that she had given herself to Charley Donoway.

And what if the same thing happened? What if he used her, and threw her away when he got weary of her, just as Charley Donoway had done?

Judy pondered it. And decided that this time she'd be armored against such an event. She was older, wiser, tougher, schooled now in the various ways that a man can injure a woman. So long as she kept her wits about her, she'd make out all right. So long as she looked out for Number One, and never let herself get too emotionally dependent on this man, she'd avoid getting wounded.

Sure. If he says come along go with him. Why not? He's exciting. He's full of power. He's dynamic. He's sexy. He'll give you a good time.

Just remember that it won't be for keeps. That the breaking point is bound to come, sooner or later. Just be prepared for it. If you see it coming, maybe you can break with him before he breaks with you. It's easier that way.

And, Judy added, "If he treats you like dirt, kill him."

Killing him wouldn't be a snap, she knew. A man like this was wary, strong, ferocious. Even so, he wasn't invulnerable. He had to sleep sometimes. He had to turn his back on you. She knew that she could take him, if she had to. With three murders under her belt already, she qualified as an expert.

She laughed. Here she was, not even knowing the man three hours, and already she was simultaneously figuring out a way of life that made her his mistress and a way of life that made her his executioner.

Things move fast around me, she thought. But maybe I ought to go a little slower. Be prepared for the eventualities, but don't force anything.

Judy turned the water taps off and got out of the shower. She toweled herself dry, watching with pleasure as her bare breasts bounced around when she pulled the towel back and forth over her skin.

Draping the towel around her shoulders, but otherwise remaining nude, she went out into the adjoining room, where Jim Norton had been sprawled out on the floor smoking a cigarette. She didn't see him. Or his clothing, either. Nor was he in the kitchen or the bedroom. For one puzzled moment, Judy thought that he had taken her car and disappeared, but a glance out the window told her otherwise. Her battered car and his big sleek one still stood side by side where they had been.

Then she saw him. He had walked about twenty feet away from the house and was standing with his back to it, admiring the view.

She went out to him.

"Getting some fresh air?" she asked.

"Yes," he said. He turned, and laughed when he saw that she was nude. "You walk around out here like that all the time?"

"Why not?" she said. "Nobody's to see. I told you, this is a secluded neighborhood!"

"People sometimes wander by."

"Not often."

"I did."

Judy shrugged. "You had an emergency. Anyway, if anybody wants to wander by and see my skin, let them look. I don't give a damn. It doesn't upset me to be seen. If it upsets them to see me, let them close their eyes."

"Aren't you cold like that, though? The temperature must be fifty degrees."

"I'm used to running around naked in cold weather," she told him. "I don't like wearing clothes."

"So I see. How's dinner doing?"

"It isn't doing at all. I just got out of my shower and I didn't know where you were. So I came out to see if you were still around."

"Just surveying the view," he said. "Studying the lay of the land, so to speak."

"Okay. I'll get the hamburgers cooking. You going to stay out here?"

"For a little while."

"I'll call you when dinner's ready, then."

"Come here, first."

She went to him. He caught her by the end of her towel and pulled her up close to him. Quickly, he fondled her breasts, her buttocks, her thighs. He kissed her, a quick, hard kiss. There was nothing very passionate in what he did. It was as though he were simply testing his memory of the feel of her flesh against the real thing, as long as she happened to be standing there. Judy smiled at him, and he smiled back, not really a smile so much as a fast on-off smirk.

She went back into the house to see after dinner.

Somehow, for once, she didn't feel like remaining nude just now. She tossed down the towel, picked up the muu-muu that she had worn before. Then she went into the kitchen.

It was almost time for the hourly news broadcast. Judy switched the radio on as she began to fix dinner. Maybe they'd have another bulletin about the Joseph Carter suicide case. Maybe they'd have found the dead man's body by now, or something like that.

There wasn't any news about Carter. What Judy heard on the radio was this:

"Sacramento police report no success in the manhunt for 34-year old Lloyd Holbrook, who evidently slipped out of town early this morning after taking two lives. Holbrook, the manager of a finance agency in the capital city, reportedly slew his wife Delores, aged 27, and a man identified as Paul Kremer, 26. No apparent motive for the slaying was disclosed. Holbrook is believed to have headed south in a maroon Buick, and may be in the San Francisco area at this time. Police speculate that he is heading for Mexico, and the border patrols have been alerted. He may be armed and is considered dangerous. Holbrook is described as white, six feet, two inches tall, weight 190 pounds, dark eyes, brown hair, crew-cut, no unusual scars...."

Judy grabbed the edge of the sink for support as shock and amazement burned through her.

There was no doubt about it. Her guest was the wanted murderer!

There couldn't be any room for mistake. The man she had made love with and was now fixing dinner for, fit the description perfectly. And the maroon Buick ... yes, that fit too. It couldn't be a coincidence. There weren't two men of the same appearance driving the same kind of car—and the man who called himself Jim Norton had been so mysterious about his background, so deliberately hazy—

Of course. A double murderer, heading away from the scene of his crime. Stopping by a lonely ocean-side cottage on top of a dark cliff to have a place to hide out for the night, while the heat was on.

Everything he had told her had been lies. The night club in Seattle, the wife in New York, all the rest—fantasies designed to still her curiosity. "He may be armed and is considered dangerous," the newscast had said. Well, he was certainly dangerous; Judy had sensed that just from making love with him. There was a power in him, a demonic force, that meant danger for anybody who got in this man's way. Armed? Well, maybe yes, maybe no. He had been pretty casual about leaving his clothes around the living room. Certainly he wasn't carrying a gun on him; she would have felt that when she embraced him. But he might have a knife somewhere in his suit. Or a gun in the glove compartment of his automobile. The newscast hadn't said how he had committed those murders. Only that two people were dead.

Judy looked uneasily toward the other room. He was still outside, evidently.

What am I going to do?

Panic hit her for a moment. But only for a moment, and then she felt calm again, and even amused at the situation.

There was nothing to be afraid of, simply because she was playing hostess to a killer. In fact, she realized it might be the best thing that had happened to her in a long while.

He's a murderer, she thought. Okay. So am I. I'm ahead of him in kills, as a matter-of-fact. Three to two. So why worry? He isn't a wild beast—or if he is, he's the same kind of beast I am.

We're two of a kind.

We belong with each other.

Judy smiled. A surge of triumph filled her, as she saw the new shape of her future unroll before her. It was a future joined to this strange man, this Lloyd Holbrook. She needed him, and he needed her. They were alike, two dark souls marked for apartness.

She could be invaluable to him. She was his only way of getting safely out of California. All roads leading out of the state would certainly be monitored, with troops watching for a maroon Buick. The airports would be under surveillance. Everything.

But she had a car. Not much of a car, but it could get them to Mexico. She'd drive him. Let him hunker down in the trunk, and she'd get him through all the roadblocks safely. And after they were safe on the far side of the border, down in the land of the sun, they'd make a new life together, the two of them, both of them hard as iron, meant for each other, a perfect match....

Yes!

The more she thought about it, the more perfect it appeared to her. It thrilled her. Her body tingled, remembering the savage ferocity of Holbrook's embrace, remembering the incredible virility of the man. To have a lover like that every night—

Yes! Yes! Yes!

She moved quickly about the kitchen, getting the meal ready. The cats sat quietly, watching her. Judy felt a stab of pain as she thought about them. How would they fit into her new life? Would Holbrook want to take three cats along with him on their flight to Mexico?

Probably not. There might even be difficulties, taking a cat across an international border. He might insist on leaving the animals behind.

What the devil, though. She couldn't shape her life around little animals no matter how fond she was of them. They could be given away. Her destiny was that of a free spirit, unfettered by cats.

When the hamburgers were sizzling, Judy went outside and called to him.

"Dinner's on!"

He came in. She was setting the table. He didn't attempt to help her. He just stood to one side, motionless in his masculine superiority. Judy didn't mind. She scarcely looked up at him.

"I see you decided to put some clothes on," he observed. "To be formal at dinnertime?"

"I didn't put much on," she said. "If you'll notice, I'm naked underneath the muu-muu."

"I notice. I can't help but noticing."

"But I thought I ought to cover myself chastely while we ate. I didn't want the sight of my breasts sticking out at you across the table to distract you from your appreciation of my cooking's finer features."

He laughed. "Very thoughtful of you."

"Here. You sit in this chair."

They were midway through the meal before Judy decided on the approach that she wanted to take. He didn't say much as he ate, and that was fine with her. It allowed her some breathing space to figure things out. Her forehead was throbbing with excitement. Some of her initial burst of fear had returned, now that she saw him in front of her again. There was such a cold, brooding strength about this man, she thought. He was more than a little frightening even when he was just quietly sitting and eating hamburgers. Odd how at first glance he seemed like a nice, Ivy-League young chap, and how as you continued to watch him, he turned into a devil.

But her mind was made up. She wasn't going to turn from her course.

"Jim?" she said suddenly.

"Mmm?"

"Jim, have you ever been in Sacramento?"

He looked at her strangely, but she could see him making an attempt to mask his feelings. "Why do you ask that, Judy?"

"You remind me of somebody else who lives in Sacramento," she said.

"Who?"

"Fellow name of Lloyd Holbrook. Runs a finance agency up there."

His lips tightened into thin white lines. A muscle writhed, suddenly uncontrollable, in one of his lean cheeks.

"Lloyd Holbrook," he said in a very quiet voice. "I remind you of a fellow named Lloyd Holbrook."

"That's right," she persisted. "You could practically be his brother."

"Very curious."

"And another thing, Jim. You and this Holbrook fellow—you both drive the same sort of car. Brand new maroon Buicks. Isn't that odd? A really funny coincidence. When I came up from the beach and saw your car parked outside my place, I thought it was Lloyd Holbrook's car. And then I saw you. But you said you were Jim Norton."

He was silent for a long moment. His eyes drilled into hers like augers. But Judy steeled herself and met his glance without flinching. She was not afraid of his eyes. She had killed people, too.

At length he said, "What kind of gimmick do you think you're working?"

"I heard the news broadcast a little while ago. It said that police are looking for a man named Lloyd Holbrook who killed two people in Sacramento. He's driving a car like yours and he's got a physical description that happens to match yours. So I was wondering, Jim. Are you really from Seattle? Do you really have a wife in New York? Is your name really Jim Norton?"

He shoveled a chunk of hamburger into his mouth, chewed it thoroughly, swallowed it. Then he said, "You're either a very brave girl or a very stupid girl, Judy. I can't make up my mind which."

"Maybe a little of both," she said. "Maybe neither. Let's level with each other, Lloyd. You are Lloyd, aren't you? You tell me why you killed those people. Then I'll tell you a few little secrets about myself. And then we'll figure out where we go from here."

He moistened his thin lips. "Why did you stir all this up? What's in it for you?"

"I'll tell you afterward. Are you Holbrook?"

"Yes. Of course. What did you think?"

"I just wanted to hear you say it yourself," she said. "Be honest with me, Lloyd. And I'll be honest with you. You'll be surprised when you learn about me."

"I suppose you're really Adolf Hitler wearing a clever, plastic disguise."

She laughed. "Not quite. Why'd you kill them, Lloyd? Murder interests me. Why did you kill your wife?"

"Several reasons. Reason number one was that I was tired of her and she wouldn't give me a divorce. Reason number two was that she had been unfaithful to me. Reason number three was that I wanted to make a clean break with the life I'd been living, and I needed her out of the way."

"And this other one, this Paul Kremer? He was her lover, I suppose?"

"No. He just happened to be a bystander. A witness. He blundered in at the critical moment, so I had to kill him too. I don't even know who he was, really. But at a time like that you don't stop to ask questions. He had to die, that was all."

"How did you kill them?"

"With a knife," he said. "The messy way. But the quiet way. A knife is quiet."

"There are quiet ways that aren't even messy," Judy remarked casually.

"Such as?"

"Finish your dinner and then I'll let you in on the scoop," she said.

He stared levelly at her. "You're a strange one, you know? Sitting here asking me a million questions. Why aren't you screaming for your life? Why aren't you trying to telephone the police?"

"How do you know I haven't?"

"I don't," he said. "I ought to be clearing out of here and not making conversation."

"Well, I haven't called the police. Take it on faith, I haven't. And after you've read something I'm going to give you to read, you'll understand why I haven't."

"Maybe I'm crazy too," he said. "But I'll stay. I'll take it on faith."

He cleaned off his plate.

Then Judy rose and went to her dresser drawer, and took out her black-covered murder notebook, and gave it to him to read.

CHAPTER ELEVEN

She sat quietly, watching him leaf through the pages. He didn't skim. He read every word, carefully, sometimes going back to read a sentence twice. His expression was absolutely unreadable.

It was a strange sensation, sitting there watching someone else reading her secret book, her book of books, the book of her life. Judy knew that there had been some reason why she had kept that murder diary, and now she knew: it was so she could show it to Lloyd Holbrook.

He had finished reading about the way she killed Charley Donoway, now. He was past that account, with its flat description of the way she had rabbit-chopped him and dragged him face down into the sea. And now he was looking at her account of the second murder.

Her accidental murder, she liked to call it.

Judy let the details drift back into her mind. It had happened early in the spring, right after Charley Donoway's decomposed body had been found. Murder had been on Judy's mind, then—the pleasant temptation to try it again, to even up the score some more.

But she hadn't really planned to kill this particular man. Except that circumstances dictated it that way, and she let events break as they chose.

It had all happened early one morning. A bright, warm morning in April, and Judy came on the beach for her daily constitutional. In the nude, of course.

A swim. Cold water glancing exhilaratingly against her bare breasts, her thighs.

Then a sunbath. Stretched out nude in the brightness, drying off, letting the sunlight steal across her body and caress it. She was totally relaxed, fully exposed, shameless. It was about seven in the morning. The world was silent.

And a shadow fell across her face.

Judy's eyes flickered open. A man was standing above her. He had come up on her so silently that she had not heard him approach at all—or perhaps she had slipped into a light doze a few minutes ago; she could not be sure. Anyway, there he was.

He was about forty, maybe forty-five. Thin, medium height, graying hair. Rimless eyeglasses. He wore knee boots, khaki pants, an Eisenhower jacket. He carried some kind of satchel over his shoulder. He was staring at her in a bug-eyed way, as though absolutely flabbergasted to find a naked girl on the beach. He was flushed, excited by the sight of her bare heavy breasts, her ripe, luscious thighs, her unconcealed femaleness.

Judy wondered how long he had been standing there, ogling her.

"Hi," she said.

"Oh. You're awake."

"Looks that way. You're afraid of me, aren't you?" she asked.

"I—I don't mean to intrude—your privacy—" He backed away from her, looking shy and flustered now that she had come to life.

Judy snorted. "Listen, if my privacy meant anything to me I wouldn't be stretched out here bare-rear on the beach, would I? Don't run away. Stay here and talk. It gets lonely here."

He scratched his chin nervously. "You aren't embarrassed—naked like that?"

"Nope. Is my body so ugly that you want me to cover it up?"

"No—no—"

"Okay, then. Stay here. Look all you like. Wherever you like. It's free. It'll probably do you some good. Who are you, anyway?"

He gave her a mild smile. "Emory Blaisdell," he said. "I'm from the University of California. A zoologist. I'm on a field trip, collecting shoreline crustacea. I've been walking along the beach since four in the morning. I don't know how many miles I've walked, and you're the first person I've met. And—"

"And you didn't expect to find any nude Crustacea lying around, eh?"

"No."

"You from the Berkeley campus, maybe?"

"Yes," he said. "You aren't a student there?"

"No. But—well, never mind. I had a relative who taught there for a while. You probably didn't know him. Forget it. Sit down and make yourself comfortable. Is that box of yours full of crabs?"

He grinned shyly. "Yes, as a matter-of-fact. And—and—"

"Hey, you're shaking," she said.

"I can't help it."

"You feeling all right?"

"Fine," he said. "Only—only—your body—listen, my wife left me eight years ago. I—I haven't had a woman since then. And the sight of you—your body—your naked body—" He paused. "Oh, God," he blurted. "I can't control myself!"

That was when he fell on her.

It was pathetic, Judy thought. This poor, crab-hunting kook of a professor, so mild-mannered and scholarly, unable to control his sex impulses when he stumbled across a naked blonde on a deserted beach. He was really going ape all of a sudden, a total crack-up.

He was down on top of her, gasping and grunting and moaning like the madman that in effect he had just become. His hands clawed at her breasts, gripping the sensual hills of taut flesh as though his life depended on being able to cop a feel. He was trying to work his knees between her thighs.

"Please," he begged. "Please—don't fight me, don't resist—"

"Cut it out, professor. Down, boy! Down!"

But he was beyond the point of reason. He was wild, lust-maddened, determined to carry through on his sudden assault.

Judy felt his hands all over her, gripping her soft flesh ... breasts, buttocks, thighs ... they thrashed about on the sand ... his lips hunted for hers....

But she was an expert on how to handle a rapist, by this time. All these years of living by herself on the seashore, toughening herself with morning swims, building up techniques of defense—they hadn't been just amusements. She was able to defend herself.

Especially against a bespectacled, middle-aged man of no particular physical strength.

When it became apparent that Professor Blaisdell was going to cling to her until he got what he wanted from her, Judy went into action. Her slim body tensed to repel the invasion.

She parted her legs, but not for his sake. She brought her knee up sharply and gave it to him where it would produce the fastest effect. It did. He pulled back from her, crying out in sudden anguish.

Judy rammed her fist into the pit of his stomach. She caught his arm and twisted. She flipped him upward and in a short sharp pivot and threw him entirely off her, some distance away on the sand. He landed heavily. He didn't get up again. He didn't even move.

Judy rose to her feet, her breasts heaving from her exertions, her skin tingling. She walked over to him and stood above him, glowing in golden nakedness as the sunlight bathed her slender form.

"Professor?" she said. "Hey, Professor!"

No answer.

She looked down. His neck was bent at a funny angle. His head was twisted around. His glasses had come off, and one lens was broken.

His face looked strangely gray.

"Professor?"

He remained still. Judy touched his shoulder. He was motionless. She shook him a little, and his head rocked back and forth in a weird limp, see-sawing motion, as though it was likely to fall right off his head if she shook too hard.

He had broken his neck when she flipped him off her, Judy realized.

And he was dead. She had killed him without even really meaning to. It hadn't been murder, exactly; more like manslaughter. But he was dead. No jury would convict her, if she could prove the truth of what had actually been happening—that he had found her sunbathing and had attempted to force her to have sex with him.

But of course, she couldn't prove that. There were no witnesses.

And she didn't want to get involved in any police investigation, regardless of how good a case she might be able to make out. If the police dug around, they might learn that she had known the late Charley Donoway, and that could lead to some uncomfortable discoveries. So Judy realized that she was going to have to dispose of Professor Blaisdell's body, just as if she had premeditated his murder.

And she had to do it fast. It was past seven in the morning, now, and she couldn't count on many more minutes of complete solitude on the beach.

She grabbed him by the arms and dragged him toward the water. Then, just as she had done the November before with Charley Donoway,

Judy waded out into the ocean and swam for the deep water, towing the corpse behind her. It was a fight to get far from shore, because his heavy boots and water-logged jacket were weighing him down. But Judy struggled nudely on, because she knew it was idiocy to dump him just off shore.

Out in the far sea, she let go of him and he slipped immediately below the surface. Those thick leather boots would keep him down, Judy knew. This was one body that they would never find.

She treaded water for a while, making sure he didn't reappear. He didn't. Then she swam toward shore, stepped out onto the sand, her breasts heaving as she gasped for breath. That had been work!

And she wasn't finished, yet.

She walked up the beach, scuffing out the trail that had been made when she dragged the body toward the water. Nobody else was likely to recognize that as the trail of a dragged corpse, but she knew what it was, and she felt better after she had obliterated it.

His collecting case was lying near her beach blanket. So were his shattered glasses. Judy held the case at arm's length and opened it. About a dozen live crabs came quickly scrabbling out and went scuttering away across the sand toward freedom.

"You didn't even say thank you," Judy called laughingly after them.

She dropped the eyeglass frames and the broken lens into the attaché case, and put her beachrobe on over her nakedness. She would dispose of the collecting case later, at a safe distance from the area. No doubt somebody would miss Professor Blaisdell sooner or later, and somebody would guess that he had drowned while on a collecting trip. She wouldn't be involved.

Poor Professor Blaisdell.

Judy hadn't really intended to kill him. But now that she had, she was able to take some satisfaction in the deed. In a way, it was as if she had killed that other gentle rapist, the one who had taken her home from the bar that night she had been so drunk seven years before. This evened the score for that one.

Two dead, now. She felt pleased with herself.

And when Joe Carter came down the pike, looking for a little action a few months later, Judy decided on the spur of the moment to make him number three.

Lloyd Holbrook closed the notebook and looked up at Judy, who was staring at him across the room in frozen intensity.

"This is quite a book," he said. "What do you do, write fiction for a living?"

"There's no fiction in that book."

"You really killed those three guys?"

She nodded. "I really did. You must have been listening to the radio a little, the last few days. Haven't you heard anything about a guy who was supposed to have drowned himself around here? A guy named Carter, they found his automobile and his clothing down the road?"

"Yeah—yeah, I think I do remember."

"He's number three in my book. It happened just the way I said. We made love on the beach, and then we went swimming and I drowned him. And drove his car down to that parking lot."

Holbrook frowned. "You're strong enough to grab a man in the water and make him drown? And that other stuff, the karate, the judo—"

"You wrestled with me," Judy reminded him. "You know for yourself how strong I am. You know I've got muscles under all this pretty flesh. And if you go swimming with me tomorrow morning, you'll find out how good a swimmer I am, too."

He was silent a long moment.

"Yeah," he said finally. "Yeah. I do believe it. You did kill them. You're the strongest girl I've ever known. And the weirdest. That bit you pulled with your teeth—sure. Sure. Okay, I take it back, Judy. This notebook isn't fiction. I see that now."

"Thanks."

"Why'd you kill them, though?" She smiled.

"You want me to tell you the whole story of my life?"

"Is that necessary?"

"To understand, yes. But I'll make it quick. You want to hear?"

"Keep it short."

"All right," Judy said. "I've had three bad breaks in my dealings with men. Like three kicks in the teeth. When I was sixteen years old and still a virgin, my older brother raped me."

"Damn!"

"Then I went into a bar a couple of years later and had too much to drink, and a nice kindly fellow rescued me when I was about to get heaved out. He took me to his apartment and raped me too."

"Nice."

"And then a lot later I fell in love with a guy and my whole life revolved around him. And after a few months, just when I was hoping he'd ask me to marry him, he told me to pack and get out of his apartment on one night's notice. He was the first of the three men I killed. The other two were strangers."

"And that's why you kill?" Holbrook said. "To get even with the men who fouled you up?"

"That's why," Judy said.

They stared at each other. Then he said, "I never met anybody like you."

"I never met anybody like you either," she replied. "We're two of a kind, Lloyd. We're made for each other. We're both killers. We stand away from the rest of the world. We're tough. And sexy. We make a good team."

His smile was hard to interpret. "Maybe you've got something there, baby."

"Listen," she said. "Tomorrow morning, come down to the beach with me. We'll take a swim at dawn together. Then we'll clear out. In my car, because they'll he watching for yours. You can hide in the trunk when we go through the roadblocks. We'll scoot right across the border into Mexico, and nobody'll bother us ever again. We'll just have each other."

"Sounds interesting."

"I'll get you safely across. Without my help, they'll nab you. But I can swing it. I'm a pretty resourceful girl. It's all there in the notebook. You know I've got guts. And you've made me twice. You know what I've got to offer him in that department."

"Yeah," he said. "I sure do."

"Let's go to bed," Judy suggested. "It's almost ten o'clock. We'll get up at five, all right? And we can be on the road by seven, eight o'clock. I want you to love me tonight, though. Love me right now. I'm a hungry girl, Lloyd. I've got a big appetite for loving."

He stood up. "Okay," he said. "Fair enough. You took care of my appetite. Now I'll see what I can do about yours."

He went with her into the bedroom.

CHAPTER TWELVE

They stripped quickly. For Judy, it was just a matter of whipping her muu-muu over her head and presenting her jiggling nudity to him. Holbrook required more time, but not much more, to get his clothing off.

Then they dropped down together on the mattress.

Although they had made love twice already that afternoon, and with great passion both times, Holbrook was ready to serve her needs again, less than five hours after the last round. That confirmed Judy's opinion that this was really an extraordinary man.

Her hand went to him, seized him and guided him toward her.

There were no fancy frills to their lovemaking this time. No biting, no spanking, no upside-down tomfoolery. Neither of them seemed to be in the mood for anything like that. His body covered hers, he slid to her, and they began to move in the rhythms of passion. Judy responded quickly, eagerly.

His long, lean body lunged against hers. He crushed down against her breasts, hammered himself against her. And pleasure was theirs. Rapidly.

It arrived in a double burst of fulfillment. He didn't try to hold himself back, this time. He just went surging ahead, pushing her to the brink of completion and then over it, all in one frenzied rush.

"Good night," she said.

"Yeah. Good night."

They rolled apart and lay side by side on the mattress. But it was a long time before Judy fell asleep. She had a great deal to think about.

The nearness of him—his big powerful body naked alongside hers. Having him like this every night. Yes. Yes! It was what she wanted.

She would not permit herself to fall in love with him. She would remember, at all times, the lessons that life had taught her. Cruel lessons. Bitter lessons. So she would go along with him for the ride, and get what happiness she could from him. When the time came for parting, she would part and never look back with regrets. When you limited your objectives that way in advance, you also limited the scope of possible pain.

To live with him in Mexico....

Nights of rapture. Days of delight. Find a seashore like this, live in a remote cliffside cabin. The Pacific washed Mexico's shores just as it did those of California.

Judy smiled. After a while, she slept.

The alarm clock in her brain woke her at five the next morning. She rolled over, ready to wake Holbrook up, assuming that, like most people, he would be sleeping. He wasn't. He was sitting up, puffing on a cigarette and watching her with interest.

"You look very young when you sleep," he said. "All the toughness goes out of your face, and you're just a pretty girl with no clothes on and big boobs lying there. You look about nineteen, asleep."

"How long have you been up?"

"Maybe fifteen minutes. One of your cats walked on my face. Woke me."

She stood up, letting the blanket drop away from her, revealing her body in all its naked glory. "Let's go down to the beach for a swim," she said. "Then we'll start packing to go."

"All right," he said.

She covered her nudity with her beachrobe, and gave him the blanket to wrap over himself. They left the cottage and made their way to the sea. Gray mists of dawn still swirled over the woods.

They clambered down the stone steps. It would be her last time on the beach, and Judy felt a little sorrowful about that.

She shrugged out of her robe and stood proudly naked on the sand. Holbrook looked a little hesitant at first about denuding himself out in the open, but after a moment, he let the blanket drop. "Follow me!" she cried.

She ran down to the sea, sprinting with vigor that was almost immoral at such an early hour. She felt the melons of her breasts pounding up and down as she ran. She felt wonderfully alive as the sea breezes whistled around her nakedness.

Holbrook ran right behind her.

She hit the water fast, dove and swam outward. He followed her. She tried to get away from him, but this was one man she couldn't show off for. He kept pace with her, stroke for stroke, remaining just behind her and to her left, a couple of feet back of her kicking legs.

Judy tried to put on a spurt of speed. No use. She drove herself forward, giving it all she had, and hoped to open up a gap of ten to twenty yards between herself and him. But when she paused, gasping, and looked over her shoulder, he was right behind her, as always.

He grinned. "This cold water really wakes you up," he said.

Judy nodded and cut diagonally across him, moving fast, once again trying to show him that she could outswim him.

It became a contest. Back, forth, back, forth—stroke after stroke after stroke. Her slender arms bit into the water. Her breasts ached from the strain of so much swimming. Her thighs throbbed. Kick. Kick. Kick.

Serenely, as though unaware that anything out of the ordinary was going on, Holbrook swam right behind her. The corded muscles in his arms and shoulders rippled magnificently. Judy sensed that he had reserves of strength behind his reserves; that he could swim, if he had to, for twelve or fifteen hours without showing fatigue.

Stroke. Stroke. Stroke. She set a grim pace, but he matched it. She swung around, headed straight out toward sea, far out, farther than she had ever dared to go before. She knew she couldn't lose, either way. If he gave up and turned back, she was the winner of their little contest. If she got tired before he did, she knew that he would laugh in triumph and then help her get to shore. So she kept on going straight out.

He stayed with her.

And suddenly, Judy realized that she had pushed herself beyond her own limits. She was very, very tired. Her heart was pounding wildly.

Her jaws throbbed. Her eyes were having trouble focusing.

She halted bobbing white and naked on the huge sea. The shore was terribly far away.

"I'm—I'm tired," she gasped. "You win!" She sucked breath into her lungs. "I quit. Lloyd, hold onto me ... help me toward shore."

He came up to her. He bobbed alongside her, seemingly unwinded, and reached out. He squeezed the firm globes of her breasts. He cupped the satiny hills of her buttocks. She stared at him in exhaustion as he toyed with her.

Then he said, "You're staying out here, Judy. I'm going to Mexico alone."

"What?"

"You think I want to travel with a kooky killer girl? You're dangerous, baby. You might get into a killing mood any old time. I stayed up all night because I couldn't take the chance. This is the end of the line for you."

"No!"

"You got to go. You know so much about me, I got to eliminate you. Can't trust taking you with me, can't trust leaving you behind. Only one thing left."

In terror, Judy felt his hands clenching the soft flesh of her shoulders. She struggled for strength, but she had none left. In order to show her powers, she had gone right to the breaking point ... but he hadn't.

"No," she whimpered. "We belong together!"

"Afraid not," he said. "You kooky killer. It's a real pity, wasting you like this. You got a lot to be said for you. Especially in bed. But I can't take the risk. So long, beautiful."

He squeezed her breasts once more, as though saying farewell to the sensual glory of her body.

Then he shoved her under the surface. Down.

Down.

Down.

THE END

Easy Money

ROBERT SILVERBERG

CHAPTER ONE

Charley picked the girl up in a roadhouse in Delaware, not far from the Pennsylvania line. She was waiting on tables there. He took one long look at her and knew that she was exactly the kind of girl he was looking for, for his little blackmail project.

She was slender, even lean, but her body was full in the places that counted, with firm, high breasts and flaring hips and buttocks that jutted out nicely against the sheer fabric of her white waitress's uniform. Her hair was dark and long, her eyes were bright and smiling, her lips were full and kissable.

She looked bedable.

But Charley had more in mind than just a bedable girl. He needed a girl whose looks were very special, and this one seemed to fill the bill right down to the last specification. What he was looking for was a girl who could seem mature and womanly wearing one kind of outfit, and young and immature dressed another way. He wanted someone who could seem adult while she was picking up suckers and taking them to bed, but who would look like a teenager when the time came to make the blackmail squeeze.

This girl looked right.

Charley couldn't really tell how old she was. Past sixteen and under thirty, that was all he could be sure of. The lush thrusts of her breasts, the ripeness of her buttocks, gave her a set of feminine charms that could easily be played up by the right kind of clothing. On the other hand, those saucy eyes, that perky smile, that long hair when allowed to dangle in a girlish pony-tail. Sure. She'd do.

Charley leaned back, gave her the eye as she brought the menu over. He was a big, rangy man, almost thirty now, who earned his living in a variety of ways, none of them legal and none of them very taxing on the energy.

The girl smiled at him. Just a waitress smile, he thought, a mechanical thing. But Charley smiled back and put some oomph into it. His eyes flicked down the front of her uniform.

"Good evening," she said. "Would you like to order a drink?"

"I'd love to," Charley said. His eyes drank her in. "Make it a martini, very dry."

"Olive or lemon peel?"

"Lemon," he said. He grinned at her. "Mind if I make a personal remark, miss?"

"Depends on how personal."

"I just wanted to say that I've been driving for five straight hours since I left New York, and you're the nicest thing I've seen in all that time. It's a real pleasure to come in off the road and find a girl like you in a place like this."

She smirked at him. "I bet you tell that to all the waitresses."

"Scout's honor, I don't." He glanced around at the nearly empty roadhouse. "Business is pretty slow tonight, huh?"

"About normal for a Tuesday."

He eyed her fingers. No trace of a wedding ring. Good, he thought.

"What time do you get through here?" he asked.

"We aren't supposed to make dates with customers while we're on duty."

"I won't squeal," he said. "What time?"

"Nine."

It was eight o'clock now. Charley said, "Got anything going after work?"

"Nope. Why?"

"Just wondering. I thought maybe you'd like to go for a drive. Ride around the neighborhood a little, show me the sights. You a local girl?"

"From Philadelphia," she said. "I've only been here six months."

"That's probably long enough."

"Listen, you better let me go get you your drink. The manager doesn't like it if I stand around talking at the tables."

"Okay. But don't be gone long."

She gave him another smile, a warm, real one this time, and hurried away. Charley watched the motions of her buttocks against her tight uniform. He liked what he saw. He liked the sound of her voice, the smile in her eyes, the thrust of her breasts. He liked everything about this girl. Charley began to foresee a big future for himself and her, a future spangled with dollar signs.

The girl came back a few minutes later carrying a martini in the middle of a tray. As she put it down, one of her breasts pressed against Charley's shoulder. What he felt was firm and resilient and exciting—exciting simply as flesh, and exciting because he knew that the gesture had been deliberate.

She straightened up. "See if that's dry enough for you. Otherwise I'll bring you another one."

He tasted it. "It's fine."

"Good."

"I'm Charley Simmons. You?"

"Janey Vaughn."

"Hi, Janey. Do we have a date for nine o'clock?" Charley asked.

Her eyes were twinkling. "We sure do, Charley. Would you care to order now?"

He hadn't been planning to have an elaborate meal when he walked into the place, nor even a cocktail. A hamburger and a beer were all he had on his mind. But the sight of the girl had made him feel like splurging, and so he had ordered the martini. He was in the same mood when the time came to decide on dinner. He ordered the most expensive thing on the menu, sirloin steak, five bucks. Janey's eyes widened a little as he gave her the order. Obviously they sold a lot of hamburgers and not very many sirloin steaks in this place. But he figured it was a good investment. For one thing, he was hungry. For another, he wanted to show this girl that he was a big spender. For a third thing, he figured that she was going to bring him lots and lots of money in the very near future, so why stint himself now? He would splurge.

The steak wasn't bad. Charley had had better steaks in the past, and he expected to have much better ones in the future. But it was edible. That was about all you could ask, when you stopped off at an unknown roadhouse in the middle of nowhere.

He ate slowly, using up the time. By quarter of nine, he was finished. The girl brought him his check.

"I still got fifteen more minutes," she said.

"I know. I'll wait."

"You want another cup of coffee while you're waiting, Charley?"

"Why not?"

She brought the coffee pot and left it on the table. He handed her a ten-dollar bill, and she went to get change. The total tab was a little over six bucks. He left her a dollar and a half as her tip. He pushed the money toward her, and she looked at it in an embarrassed way, as though to say you didn't take tips from a guy you've made a date with for nine o'clock.

But she took the money anyway.

"I'll be back in ten minutes," she said. "I can't come to the table and get you. You follow me out when you see me go by, and I'll meet you in front."

"Sure thing," Charley said.

He poured some more coffee for himself and sipped it slowly, wondering what the girl looked like under that shapeless uniform. Two nice round boobs, he thought, and long sleek legs, and a cute little rear end. His throat tightened. He hadn't had a woman for a while, and he was hungry for one. Especially one who was built like this chick.

The minutes crawled away. Charley finished his coffee. It got to be nine o'clock, and then five after nine. And then the girl came out. She crossed the dining room, smiled a bedroom smile at him, and went out the front door.

She looked a lot different now that she had shed her uniform. In its place, she was wearing a green sweater and a tight short skirt. The sweater clung to the lush contours of her breasts, molding and outlining them in an eye-opening way. The skirt glided over the curves of her buttocks in an equally agreeable fashion.

The change was dramatic. The girl seemed five or six years older than she had been when in her waitress costume.

Perfect, Charley thought. Exactly what he needed for his dodge—a girl who could shift her age back and forth like that with a few tricks of make-up and dress.

He got up, followed her out of the roadhouse.

She was waiting by the porch steps. It was a cool, crisp night in late November, with more of autumn in the air than of winter. The stars were out, and the moon was nearly full.

"My car's over there," Charley said.

"That one?"

"That's right," he said, grinning. It was a big, shiny 'ol Imperial that he had picked up under complicated circumstances a few months before. The previous owner had dropped a big World Series bet and was trying to raise cash in any way possible. Charley had been glad to relieve him of his car for a fifth of its market price, in a quick straight cash transaction. It was an impressive hunk of merchandise. Charley felt like a stockbroker or a senator when he sat in it, instead of like the chiseling drifter that he knew he really was.

They got in. He started the car with a mighty rumble, and pulled it out of the roadhouse parking lot. "Where to?" he asked.

"I don't know," she said. "Do you have a motel room somewhere around here?"

"I didn't bother," he said. "I was figuring I'd just have dinner and hit the road again. I'm bound for Florida to pass the winter. Suppose we just drive around for a while."

"Okay," she said. "I've never been in a car like this anyway. I want to see what it's like."

"Sure. Why not?"

He showed her what the car was like. He took her over to the highway and ran a few test sprints for her, gunning the big car up to sixty and seventy and eighty miles an hour. On the return trip he nudged it to ninety-five on a straight-away stretch, and he sneaked a glance at her while he drove, just to see how she was reacting.

She seemed to be loving it. There wasn't a trace of fear on her face. She seemed almost ecstatic as the miles rushed past.

Good, Charley thought. He needed a girl who liked to take chances, a girl who got a thrill out of moving fast.

He turned off the highway onto a country road and said, "You want to try driving it, Janey?"

"Sure. Why not?"

He got out, let her get behind the wheel. She started the car with a jerk, but after a moment she got the hang of controlling the monster, and it went purring smoothly along. She drove for about five miles, then pulled the car off at the side of the road.

"Nice," she said. "Real nice."

"I like a car that's got some zoom," Charley said.

"Let's get out. Get some fresh air."

"Okay."

They were in a lonely, deserted area, where the only sign of civilization was a billboard a few hundred feet up the road. They stood by the side of the road, looking toward a woodsy stretch of pines and spruces. The air seemed very mild even for this time of year.

Charley turned to her. She slid easily into his arms, and his mouth went to hers. She had a cooperative mouth, soft and warm and willing for him, and as he slid his lips against hers he felt her responding pressure from the opposite direction. She knew how to kiss, obviously, and just as obviously she didn't have any inhibitions about kissing a man she had met an hour and a half ago, and kissing him pretty passionately at that.

Charley brought his hand up and cupped that over one of her breasts. She didn't push the hand away. Through the fabric of her sweater he could feel a firm, ripe globe of flesh. No falsies on her, he thought. Just good honest boobs there.

The kiss became more torrid as he caressed her breast. She moved her entire body at him, pushing to a close contact. Charley let his other hand slide down her back to her buttocks. Her skirt was thin, and the panties beneath offered no obstacle. He felt solid, resilient flesh there. Good, he thought. Charley was a big bottom man. He loved to look at a nice pink pair of buttocks. But he liked boobs too. Charley wasn't single-minded about such things.

Neither was she, that seemed. She left no doubts at all about herself when she slipped her hand between her body and his, and touched him. Apparently she liked what she found, because Charley didn't overlook her little hiss of excitement and pleasure.

They stood that way for a long moment, bodies clasped tight. Then he said, "There's a lot of room for two in the back seat."

"All right, Charley."

He opened the door. She got into the car, and he joined her on the back seat. She acted as though she knew something about how to love on the back seats of automobiles. Charley wasn't surprised. He didn't imagine that she was any virgin.

She kicked off her shoes and stretched out full length, resting her head against the arm rest of the far door. She arranged herself on the seat, letting one leg dangle down, leaving some room for him. Charley bent forward to kiss her.

Their kiss was a long, eager, enthusiastic one, just as passionate as the one outside the car. But this time Charley ran his hand down the front of her body and under the hem of her skirt, and then over stocking-clad legs to the place where her stockings ended, and then along the smooth, tempting bare flesh.

His hand was busy. She began to gasp.

Meanwhile his other hand was groping around under her sweater, looking for the clasp of her brassiere. He found that. Opening a girl's bra with one hand had always struck him as something of a trick, but she helped him, shrugging her shoulders together to give him plenty of slack on the strap.

The cups dropped away. Charley slipped his hand around to the front and felt firm, cool globes of taut flesh, very nice indeed. He couldn't see them, because she still had her sweater on, but he could feel them, and he liked what he felt. They were mighty fine boobs, he thought. The nipples were small and warm against his fingertips as he touched them.

They were both breathing hard, now. The girl shifted her position on the seat of the car and pulled her skirt up so that the material bunched around her waist. Charley looked at her and saw long, tapering, exciting legs.

She made a little panting, gasping sound of pleasure. He went on playing with her, one hand maneuvering around her legs, the other one gliding back and forth from one jutting breast to the other, unable to decide which he preferred.

She said, "If you want me I'm ready."

"Sure thing, baby."

Smiling, Charley pulled his hand away from her legs and began to roll her panties down. She arched her back, lifting her buttocks away from the upholstery of the seat to make matters easier for him. He got the panties past her knees and she reached down to pull them the rest of the way. They dropped to the floor of the car.

The moonlight filtering into the car gave Charley a good view of her. Her skirt was pulled up so high that he could see her navel.

Nice, he thought. Very nice.

Long legs. Soft flesh. Slim waist. Her skin was creamy and inviting. The straps of her garter belt cut downward across her.

He pushed her sweater up to her arms. The hills of her breasts sprang into view. They were as easy on the eye as they had been to the touch. They looked as though they had been carved out of marble, two firm, white mounds of sensuous flesh, rising steeply, set close together with a deep valley. Charley grinned. He had pulled himself an ace this time.

Her hand went to his trousers. She obviously wasn't afraid of seeming too forward. That was a point in her favor for Charley. He hated fake modesty. He hated that when a girl who had lost her virginity ten years ago suddenly came on big with the shy maiden routine. If a girl did things, Charley wanted her to do them with enthusiasm.

Janey seemed very enthusiastic.

Her hand went away. Charley moved forward and she adjusted her position on the seat for his convenience. She was ready to go.

Charley took her.

He was aware of warmth and softness, and he kept on the way he was going, and she responded to him. He got his hands underneath her, cupping her buttocks, gripping the taut springy flesh.

His lips went to hers for a deep kiss. Through his shirt he could feel the globes of her breasts with their tense little tips. Her body was moving eagerly now, and her eyes were closed, her nostrils wide as she sucked air into her lungs.

Charley worked diligently. He pulled his lips from hers as the gasping began, and his head went down alongside hers, his cheek to her cheek, his face on the upholstery, his big body alive with ever mounting frenzy and excitement.

He knew when she was about to achieve her fullest pleasure. She was fast to get there, he thought. Another point in her favor. Charley didn't like slow women much. If he had to, he could satisfy them, but he preferred the kind who got turned on right away.

Like this one.

She was turned on fit to beat the band, all of a sudden. Her slender, nearly nude body flew around wildly on the seat of the car, in constant motion, breasts jiggling and leaping around.

"Oh, yes," she cried. "Yes, go, man, go!"

Charley went.

He went right to the top of the stratosphere, and she went right along with him. In another moment they were both flying high. There was a pounding in his eardrums and a throbbing in his chest and a thunder in his brain, and then there were jolts of pleasure, the hammer blows of ecstasy repeated again and again and again, and her trembling body shook and shivered and went through moment after moment of fulfillment.

Their bodies sought to wring the utmost from the moment of ecstasy. For one long timeless instant they worked with furious abandon.

Then they subsided.

Sweat rolled down Charley's husky body. He shifted his weight, trying to brace himself, not wanting to hurt her.

After a long moment he broke the silence.

He said. "How would you like to go to Florida with me, Janey?"

CHAPTER TWO

She had suspected that something like that was in the offering. She didn't know why she had thought so, but somehow she had expected that. Just as she had expected, when she first saw the big handsome man come into the roadhouse, that she would end up sleeping with him before the night was over.

She didn't answer right away. She pulled her skirt down, and twisted her body to a more comfortable position. Love on the back seat of a car was fun, in a way, but you needed to be double-jointed to enjoy yourself properly, Janey had always thought.

Not that she had done badly just now. Even with all the weird angles her body had been bent at, she had had herself a ball.

She pulled her bra back into place and yanked her sweater down. She smoothed her skirt down again over her legs. Her panties were still on the floor of the car, but she didn't bother with those. She sat up, leaned back. Charley was getting his clothing adjusted, and he was looking at her steadily, waiting for the answer to his question.

She said, "For how long?"

"All winter."

"What would I do down there?"

"More or less what you just did now," he said. "Only under more comfortable circumstances."

She said, "You got a job down there?"

"I've got a deal waiting for me."

She let that pass without questioning it. He was probably in some kind of illegal or semi-legal racket, but that didn't worry her too much. There was something flashy about him and about his expensive car. He didn't look very old, maybe twenty-seven, twenty-eight years old, and you didn't ordinarily get to drive a car like that at that age unless you had some special gimmick going for you.

Janey looked him in the eye. "We'd live together down there, huh?"

"That's the general idea," he said.

"In a hotel?"

"We'll get an apartment," he said. "In Miami, near the beach. It's better than working in a roadhouse in Delaware, believe me. You won't need to wait on tables down there."

"What'll we live on?"

"You leave that to me, Janey."

"How soon do we leave?"

"What's wrong with tonight?" he asked.

Janey thought that one over. Drop everything, go running off to Florida with a guy she hardly knew? Well, why not?

Why not?

She thought about the loose ends in her life. There weren't many. She wasn't seeing any guy in particular these days, just going out now and then, as the mood struck her, for casual pickups like this fellow Charley Simmons. She lived alone, in a boarding-house room on the edge of town, nothing that she'd miss leaving behind. She didn't have much in the way of personal possessions. It would all fit into a suitcase or two.

Her rent would be due in three days. Leaving tonight would mean skipping out on that. On the other hand, the restaurant owed her for four days' pay. She wouldn't be able to collect it if she left tonight. One thing would just about balance out the other, she thought. Let the landlady sue the restaurant.

She said, "Why don't we stay at my place tonight and leave first thing in the morning?"

"I'd rather not. I want to get moving."

"What's the matter, Charley?" she asked. "Are the cops on your trail?"

"It isn't that at all. I'm not in any trouble. But I'm itching to get on my way. Why stick around a drum-bum town like this an hour longer than you have to? It's half past ten, now. How long would it take you to pack, anyhow?"

"Maybe an hour."

"Okay. We can go over to your place, freshen up a little, get you packed. We'll be on the road before midnight. Drive for maybe six, seven hours, find a motel room in the morning. Sleep while everybody else is on the road. Then get going again. We can be in Miami day after tomorrow, maybe."

She looked at him closely. "What's the catch in all this, Charley?"

"No catch. You're a good-looking girl and I want company down there. That's the whole deal."

"There's got to be more."

"Well," he said, "just a little. I figure you can help me out down there. The kind of work I'm in, a pretty girl is useful. What do you say? We have a deal, or don't we have a deal?"

"One string attached," she said.

"Name it."

"Any time I want out," she said, "I'm entitled to it, just by telling you so. And if I decide to walk out on you, you've got to pay my bus fare back North. That's the only condition I'm tying on."

"Okay. Fair enough."

"We'll leave tonight, then," she said. "You got yourself a deal."

He grinned and leaned forward to kiss her. His hands went to her breasts. She had big breasts, but he had bigger hands, and he gave them a good squeeze. The kiss wasn't as fiery as their earlier ones, but that managed to stir a throb of excitement for her anyway.

Then he straightened up. "Come on," he said. "Let's get over to your place."

They got into the front seat of the car again. Charley drove, Janey directed him. She pondered this whole deal that had come up.

It sounded pretty good, she thought. Whatever the angles were, she was sure she could manage them. Anything was better than slinging hash in this roadhouse. She was averaging about sixty bucks a week, including tips. Big deal. And winter was coming on, now. Why spend the winter living in this nowhere town when she could be down basking on the beach at Miami?

Anyway, Janey was a restless girl. She had done a lot of wandering in her twenty-three years. Only once since she had left home at seventeen had she settled down for any length of time, and that had been the year and a half, from nineteen to twenty-plus, that she had been married. Marriage had bored her after a while. The idea of putting up with the same guy, night after night began to get to be pretty sickening, especially when she didn't love her husband, as she discovered after she had been married to him for a little while.

So the marriage had conked out. On and off, Janey had lived with other guys, before and after—maybe two, three months at best—then she felt footloose and took off for greener pastures. She had come to

Delaware because a friend of hers offered her a job. The friend had gotten married and left town almost immediately, leaving Janey stranded with a lousy job in a lousy town. That had been in April. Now it was November.

Time to be moving along, Janey thought.

And this Charley Simmons, with his Florida proposition, provided as good an excuse for her to pick up and go as anything.

They cut across town into the street of old frame houses where she lived. The street was quiet and most of the lights were out. Around here, the sidewalks were rolled up pretty early on a week-day night.

"Here we are," she said. "Be it ever so humble, et cetera, et cetera."

They went in, and up the creaking stairs to her room on the second floor. Janey switched on the light. The place was pretty untidy. She hadn't made the bed all week, or even emptied the ash trays.

"It isn't much of an advertisement for my neatness as a housekeeper," she said. "But I haven't had much incentive, living alone."

"That's okay. I'm not the neatest guy in the world. I think we'll get along."

"I think so too, Charley."

She went to the closet and hauled her suitcase out. Janey believed in traveling light, not cluttering yourself up with property. Personal possessions were evil, she thought. You thought they belonged to you, but really you belonged to them. What good was surrounding yourself with a lot of things? They crippled you when you wanted to get moving again. She would never have been able to make this spur-of-the-moment decision to travel with him if she were all encumbered with solid possessions.

She said, "It's not going to take me long to pack. Why don't we take showers before we leave, too? Make use of the facilities. I feel kind of sweaty."

"Good idea," he said. "Let's go take a shower together, right now."

"Uh-uh! My landlady would flip if she ever saw us going in there with each other!"

"She's probably fast asleep."

"Doesn't matter. She's a nice old dame and I don't want to shock her sensitive soul. You go take a shower and I'll start packing. Then I'll take a shower when you get back," she said.

"Okay."

He began to undress. Even though they had already made love, Janey felt a little odd about watching him strip in front of her. They were still really strangers, after all. The half hour of frenzied loving on the back of the car hadn't changed that. And though she had never objected to nudity as a preface to making love, this casual undressing of his was something else entirely, almost a domestic thing, like a husband taking off his clothes while the wife went about the chores of packing.

But she kept an eye on him as he peeled. She wanted to see what kind of merchandise she was getting. He was a good lover, she knew that much, but she really didn't know what his body was like.

She liked what she saw.

He was a big guy, about six feet three, weighing well over two hundred pounds. There was some extra beef on him, but not much, considering how big he was. His muscles were big and well-developed, and she figured that the little paunch he was sprouting around his middle would begin to vanish under the Florida sun.

He was a powerful-looking guy, she thought. And masculine. Very much so. Almost startlingly so. No wonder he had been so good when he loved her.

"Here," she said, tossing him a robe. "That isn't much, but that'll keep you decent. The shower's just down the hall, the first open door on your left. Make sure you test the water before you get under it. Gets pretty scalding sometimes when you don't expect it."

He looked pretty comical wearing her robe. It came down only to the middle of his upper legs, and he had to hunch his shoulders inward to keep from bursting the seams. But he was covered, at least. He winked in a good-natured way and went out, carrying a towel and soap.

Janey got down to the business of packing.

It was a quicker job than she had thought. Just open the drawers, stuff the things in. Luckily, she hadn't sent a laundry bundle away yet this week. She didn't have so much clothing that she could afford to pull out of town leaving some of it behind. But all the dirty laundry was still in her closet. She stuffed it into the corner of her suitcase. She'd take care of it in Florida, she figured. Let him pay the laundry bill.

She was almost through packing by the time he returned from the shower, smelling fresh and faintly soapy. He wriggled out of her robe and said, "It's your turn now, baby. How's the packing?"

"Just about done," she said. "Just this stack of panties and I'm finished."

She loaded the last items into the suitcase and closed the lid. It didn't quite make it.

He said, "You want me to sit on it for you?"

"Do something, anyway. Get it closed. I'm going to take my shower."

She began to undress. He concentrated on closing the suitcase, and he managed to force the clasp shut by the time Janey had taken off her sweater. She unhooked her bra and started to remove her skirt.

He was looking at her.

She smiled, felt a faint tension in her muscles as his eyes came to rest on her bare breasts, and stepped out of her skirt. A moment later her panties followed, and then her stockings and garter belt.

She was nude.

He was drinking her in with his eyes. She could see his glance shifting from her breasts to her hips, her hips to her legs, her legs back to her breasts.

"What's the matter?" she asked. "Do I have three boobs or something?"

"You mind if I stare?"

"You're looking at me like you've never seen a naked girl before."

"I haven't seen too many that look like you," he said.

"You like, huh?"

He nodded. "Mucho. You don't get a very good idea of what a girl looks like when you're wrestling around in a parked car. The view's a lot better the way that is right now."

Janey smiled. She liked to be looked at by men. Especially when she was nude. She was tall and slender, with ramrod-straight posture, and she drew air into her lungs, making her voluptuous breasts swell outward. She was proud of her body, proud of the way she could make a man light up and glow the way Charley Simmons was doing right now.

She turned, picked up her bathrobe. She could practically feel the intensity of his gaze on her bare buttocks as she stood with her back to him. She started to get into the robe.

"Wait a second," he said.

He moved behind her. He was still naked himself. He took the robe from her hand and put that down. At first she thought he was going to love her again, but she realized all he wanted was a kiss. He really was in a hurry to hit the road, then.

He spun her around and she went into his arms. The tips of her bare breasts grazed his hairy chest, and then her breasts were being crushed against him as he gave her a bear-hug. She felt his body firmly against hers, his hands gliding down her back to the ripe mounds of her buttocks, fingertips digging at the lush flesh. Then he released her.

He gave her a quick pat on the buttocks. "Go take your shower, now. I'll wait."

She put her robe on and went down the hall. The shower room was still steamy from his shower. Janey turned the water on and got in. She gave herself a brisk rubdown, getting the sweat of a long day's work off her, as well as the sweat of the back seat of Charley Simmons's car.

When she emerged, she was pink and clean and well-scrubbed. The heavy globes of her breasts were glistening. She swept her dark hair back and returned to the room. Charley was dressed and waiting for her. Janey had left a blouse and slacks out to wear as traveling clothes, and she put them on.

"Ready?" he asked.

"As ready as I'll ever be," she said.

He took the suitcase. Janey glanced around the room for the last time, and then they went out. As they started down the stairs, she warned him not to make any noise. She didn't want the landlady to find them sneaking out like this.

It was just before midnight. The air was crisp and mild, the stars brilliant. He loaded her suitcase into the trunk of the car.

"Away we go," he said.

She winked. "Florida bound."

They got into the car. He was behind the wheel. Janey stretched out comfortably. There was plenty of leg room in the spacious Imperial. The engine came thrumming to life, and they went zooming away from the curb.

He said, "I figure we'll stay in Florida till the end of the peak season. Say, around the middle of March."

"Where to then?"

"California," he said. "That's where I'd like to go next."

"I've never been out there."

"We'll drive across the country, baby. We'll do the real tourist bit. The Grand Canyon, Yosemite, Las Vegas—you name it, well go there."

"Sounds great, Charley!"

"It's going to be," he said.

After they had driven about a dozen miles in silence she said, "Aren't you going to tell me a little about yourself? I mean, now that we're on the road together, I ought to get some autobiography."

"Sure," he said. "Charles Simmons, white, male, aged twenty-nine. Born New York City. No convictions except in traffic court. High school diploma, no college. Variety of jobs. Unmarried."

"Never been married at all?"

"Never," he said. "You?"

"Once. It didn't work."

"It hardly ever does," he said. "I don't understand why people get married so much."

"For the loving?" Janey suggested.

"You don't need a license for that, do you? At least, I never thought I did."

"Me neither."

"You're a good kid," he said. "How old are you, anyway, Janey?"

"It isn't polite to ask a woman her age."

"I'm not a polite guy," he said. "The next time we make love, do you want me to be polite?"

"No, sirree!" she said, laughing. "You just be rough and tough and mean. Even belch a little, if you like. I'm twenty-three."

"It's hard to guess your age," he said. "Do people ever think you're younger?"

"Sure," Janey said. "Depends on how I dress. Sometimes when I'm wearing shorts and a polo shirt people come around, salesmen, they knock at the door and ask if my mother's home."

"I sort of figured that would happen. They take you for a teenager, huh?"

"Sometimes. But when I'm dressed up it's a lot different. You didn't think I was any teenager tonight, did you?"

"No," he said. "I sure didn't."

"What kind of work do you do, Charley?"

"Whatever pays."

"Digging ditches? Cleaning out septic tanks?"

"Correction," he said. "I do whatever pays and whatever's pleasant to do."

"Such as?"

"Well, I've been a race track tout, and a gigolo, and a couple of other things, I guess. Mostly kind of shady things. But I've never been arrested for anything and I've never spent a night in jail."

"I have," Janey said.

He swung around and looked at her in surprise. "You have?"

Janey giggled, remembering it. "I sure have," she said. "For indecent exposure."

"Sounds interesting."

"A lot of other people thought so too. That happened when I was married. That was about three years ago. The second summer of my marriage, the last summer. The marriage was breaking up then. We were fighting all the time. My husband was a kind of boring guy, square as anything. We went on this picnic, him and me, two other couples. We went to a state park."

"What happened?"

"I got drunk," Janey said. "Dick and me, we had a big argument right there at the picnic, and I must have had eight or nine cans of beer, and he kept telling me to shut up, to stop singing and making so much noise, because it was embarrassing him. So I decided to embarrass him real good and proper."

"Oh-oh," Charley said.

The memory floated through her brain: the blazing sun overhead, the crowd of people picnicking by the lake, the yellow bathing suit she was wearing. "I had on a two-piece bathing suit," she said. "It wasn't really a bikini, because it was cut pretty wide, not skimpy at all. Just a bare midriff, you know. And when Dick began coming on with this shushing bit, I said I'd take my bathing suit off if he didn't stop annoying me. He said he'd divorce me if I did. So I took the top of my bathing suit off."

"And the cops hustled you away?"

"Like hell they did. I stood there with my boobs bare and walked up and down, and there must have been a thousand people there. Everybody stared, but nobody did anything. The place got very quiet. Dick tried to grab me and pull me away, but I threw my bathing suit top at him and ran away. He chased me up and down the beach. You can picture that, my boobs bouncing, all these people with their mouths wide open, little kiddies pointing and asking questions out loud."

"Must have been some show," Charley said.

"I guess that was. But Dick got disgusted and started to leave. So I went a step further. I took my bathing suit bottom off, too. I ran around without a stitch on. That was when the park police grabbed me. A couple of them had been watching, looking at my boobs, but I guess now they figured I had gone too far. So they hustled me away into the wagon, me stark naked, all the cops grabbing free holds as they dragged me off."

"Did the cops take advantage of you down at the station house?" he asked.

"Uh-uh. They all took a good look first, and then they put a blanket over me. They booked me for indecent exposure and drunk and disorderly, and since I didn't have any money on me, or anything else except skin, they tossed me in the jug overnight. Naked. And then in the morning one of the other people we had been with at the picnic came down and bailed me out. I was fined twenty-five bucks. And my husband divorced me, just like he said he would."

"That must have looked good in court," he said. "Grounds of divorce that you showed off wantonly in front of strangers."

"Oh, that wasn't it," she said. "I was unfaithful to him, and he knew I was. I loved all his friends. I did that just to make him angry."

"The poor jerk."

"He deserved it."

"You sound like you're a wild one, girlie."

Janey laughed. "I guess I am. Do you like them wild, Charley?"

"You bet I do."

"Then I think we're going to get along," she said.

He reached his right hand toward her as he drove, and snaked that around her shoulders, going under her arm to cup her right breast. She enjoyed the feel of his big hand holding her there. The car hummed along southward down the highway at a steady seventy miles an hour.

When they had been driving about two and a half hours, he pulled off into a service station and they changed drivers. She got behind the wheel, starting off cautiously at first but then pushed the speed up close to seventy as she got the feel of the car. She drove for an hour and a half, and then he took over again. By this time they had left Delaware behind and were slicing across Maryland toward Virginia.

About six in the morning, Charley said, "How about stopping?"

"Good idea. I'm getting pretty sleepy."

"So am I."

He turned off the highway. A row of motels greeted them, each one with its VACANCY sign lit. Charley passed two or three of them by, pulling into one that seemed to strike his fancy.

The night clerk checked them in, without any folderol about looking at marriage certificates. Charley paid for the room in advance, ten bucks. It was a nice, neat, modern room, with a double bed and pretty furniture and a gaily tiled shower.

They got undressed quickly.

Charley glanced at the big, bouncy bed. "Looks pretty comfortable," he said.

"More comfortable than the back seat of a car," Janey agreed.

He turned out the light. She closed the blinds. Dawn was breaking outside, but they weren't going to let that bother them. Nude, Janey slipped onto the bed. He was already there, waiting for her.

He didn't plan to go to sleep right away.

Neither did she.

She let him take her. He was big and burly, and her breasts, her nipples hard and rigid against his lips, his hand gliding to her, warming her, stroking her.

Janey put her head against the bouncy foam rubber pillow and drew his weight against her.

She let him take her. He was big and burly, and she shivered with delight as he began, and then their bodies began to work with rhythmic motion, and Janey felt the excitement of passion grow and swell for her. She thought back on the last few hours and how suddenly things could happen. At eight o'clock last night she had been slinging hash in a Delaware roadhouse, and now here she was between the cool clean sheets of a Virginia motel bed, being loved by a big husky stranger who had stepped into her life out of nowhere to take her off to Florida for the winter.

Her body moved. Trembled. Shook.

Her nipples responded. Her muscles tensed.

She tightened her arms around his body. She dug her fingers at the thick, ridged muscles of his broad, strong back. Her body still moved.

Ecstasy rose for her and overwhelmed her.

And after the wild tide of passion there was sleep, deep and dreamless.

CHAPTER THREE

They were somewhere in South Carolina when Charley decided to let her in on the nature of the deal he was going to be working in Florida.

The day before, he had been deliberately vague about the nature of the deal. But he didn't need to be any more, now that he knew Janey better. He had been traveling with her for two days now, and had been to bed with her four or five times, and he knew that she was his kind of girl from the word go. They were simpatico.

And he also knew that she wouldn't be offended or moralistic about what he had in mind. He knew that because she had told him, yesterday along about sundown as they were hitting the road, that for a few months after the breakup of her marriage she had been a professional.

"I didn't like that much," she told him. "That wasn't the love part that bothered me. Love is fun, and I don't mind sleeping around. But I didn't like the work. I didn't like hunting up men and paying off cops and having to put up with five or six guys every time, never knowing what kind of kook I'd catch."

"Why'd you quit?" he had asked her.

"I wasn't making much money, for one thing," she said. "Maybe a hundred fifty a week, which sounds like a lot, but not when you have to earn that way. And the risks were too big. So I tried some other line of work."

She had worked as an artist's model for a while, posing in the nude, she told him. And as a waitress in a variety of cheap restaurants. And as a clerk in a department store. A lot of dull jobs.

She had the right qualifications for Charley's job, though. She had the looks and she had the temperament. She didn't mind showing her body off and she didn't mind sleeping with strangers—for the right price.

So as they motored southward through South Carolina Charley finally gave her the pitch.

"Basically," he said, "what it is is a blackmail operation."

"Blackmail?"

"Or extortion. Or something like that. I call it easy money."

"Tell me more."

"I'll fill you in on the background first," Charley said. "This time of year, Florida is full up to the brim with vacationers. A lot of them are married folks, but a lot of them are singles, too—men in their thirties and forties and fifties who come down to Florida looking for adventure. A lot of them have more money than brains. They're square rectangles."

"But looking for girls."

"Exactly. These aren't really sophisticated guys, mind you. The sophisticated ones are down in the Caribbean, down in the real islands. The guys who go to Florida these days are the hicks. But they're rich hicks, even though they're dopes. Even a dope can make a lot of money if he's got something to offer that people want to buy. What we're going to do down there, Janey, is let you get into romances with these boys. One at a time, I mean."

"What am I supposed to do?"

"Look good and let them pick you up. Put on a low-neckline dress and show them enough frontage to knock their eyes out. Put your hair up. Go to their hotel rooms with them and give them a good time."

"For free?"

"Sure," Charley said. "That's the whole gimmick. You aren't supposed to be a tramp. You're just a nice clean-cut girl down in Florida on a vacation, looking for adventure same as these guys. So you have your adventure with them in their hotel room, and then you smile and bat your long eyelashes and thank them for the pleasure, and you put your clothes on and leave."

"Then what?"

"Then we hit them with the squeeze. You let your hair down into a nice pony-tail. You scrub all the make-up off your face. You dress in a little-girl kind of outfit that doesn't cling tight to your boobs. Then you pay another visit to your boy friend in the hotel room, only this time you take your big brother along."

"You?"

"Me. And we explain the situation. We tell them that a terrible mistake has been made, that a seventeen-year-old virgin has been seduced and ruined."

"Me?"

"You," Charley said. "A clear case of statutory rape. A dirty old man picking up an innocent young vacationing girl and banging her. We intend to go to the police right away. Unless, of course, we can come to some kind of arrangement that will recompense you in some way for the terrible thing that's happened to you."

"A cash arrangement, of course."

"Of course," Charley said. "Five, hundred bucks, I think. That's a good price for a seduction. Then we move on to some other hotel and try the whole thing again. We ought to be able to score every week. Five hundred smackers a week, and the rest of the time we're relaxing on the beach."

Janey said; "What happens with the money?"

"We split it."

"Who gets what?"

"Fifty-fifty," he said. "Could anything be fairer than that?"

"I've got to prostitute myself, though," she said. "I'm the one who provides the bed action."

"But I'm the muscle who enforces collection," Charley pointed out. "Fair is fair. We each play an essential part in the operation. I can't work the deal unless you go to bed with these guys, of course. But you can't collect without me. They'll laugh in your face if you come on with the virgin act all by yourself. We need each other. So a fifty-fifty split is perfect."

"All right," she said. "Fifty-fifty."

"We ought to be able to clear four or five thousand bucks apiece by the end of the season," Charley said. "Then we head for California and enjoy ourselves. Maybe work the dodge a few times out there to cover expenses. In the fall, back to Florida for the new season."

"Now I see why you kept asking me if people make mistakes about my age," Janey said. "I've got to dress up first and catch them, and then I've got to look like a shy little girl afterward."

"Keerect."

"I think I can do it."

"I'm sure you can. I never doubted it."

"But answer me this," she said. "How did you know, when you picked me up that night, that I'd go along? Just because I let you love me in the car, that didn't mean I'd necessarily want to go for something like this."

"I had a hunch," Charley said.

"You could have been wrong. What would you have done if when you finally sprung the pitch on me, I'd said no and slapped you in the face for even daring to suggest such a shocking thing?"

He shrugged. "We had a deal. Any time you wanted out, you could get out, and I'd pay your bus fare back north. If that's how it worked out, that's how it worked out, that's what would have happened, Janey."

"But you guessed I'd play along?"

"I had a hunch."

"Your hunch was right," she said. "I think it's a terrific idea. Will it work?"

"Sure it will," he said. "We'll be rolling in cash. With your body and my brains—we'll rack 'em up, Janey, we'll rack 'em up."

The weather was warm and balmy as they pulled into Florida. It was still early in the season, with Thanksgiving still a week away. But Charley wanted to get a jump on the season. The vacationers would start thronging to Miami Beach the first week in December, and they would keep on coming in droves, until by the week before Christmas the place would be packed six deep. Then there would be a gradual dip after the first of the year, and a second spurt in February.

The Miami cops couldn't possibly keep up with all the swindlers, bunco men, and extortionists who descended on the city during the winter months. They had their hands full. Florida vacationers, like the dumb bunnies who go to Honolulu to get leis, are the biggest marks in the country—mostly rubes from the Middle West and from small towns, all gaga over the palm trees and the bikinis on the beach. They were ripe for plucking. Charley meant to do his share, with Janey's help.

They kept heading southward, and by nightfall they were in Dade County.

"We won't try to stay in Miami Beach," Charley said. "No sense running up the overhead for nothing."

"You're the boss."

"We'll get ourselves a little apartment in Miami, nothing special. And we can drive out to the hotels to work our routine."

They found a place that evening. It was no palace. It was a two-room apartment in a cheap boarding house, a little fancier than the place Janey had been living in back in Delaware, but not much. The rent was fifteen bucks a week. Charley had come south with just a couple of hundred dollars to his name, so he wasn't eager to make like the last of the big spenders until there was some money coming in.

"We'll get a better place in a month or two," Charley promised her "As soon as the dough starts rolling this way, baby."

"I don't mind living here, Charley. It's okay," Janey said.

"You deserve a lot better."

She laughed. "That landlord was a scream, wasn't he? Didn't care a hoot whether we were man and wife, brother and sister, just a couple of good friends, anything. All he was worried about was were we both white."

"They're very sensitive about that down here. Maybe they've got a law about letting a man and woman of different races share an apartment."

"Wouldn't the Supreme Court throw something like that out, Charley?"

"The Supreme Court doesn't live in Miami. They've got to know about something before they can do anything about it," Charley said.

"I felt like telling him that my great-grandmother was mulatto. What would he have done, do you think?"

"Rented the apartment to someone else," Charley said. He walked to the window and looked out. Not much of a view, just a row of rickety houses across the street. But nearby lay that glittering sand bar known as Miami Beach, and Miami Beach was full of fools and their money, soon to be parted, Charley hoped.

Janey had begun unpacking.

Charley said, "I want to run a little rehearsal tonight. I want you to try on your costumes for me. First the pickup one, and then the little-girl one. Okay?"

"Sure, Charley."

She fished clothing out of the drawer. He settled down in the wobbly armchair that had come with the apartment, and watched her as she changed.

She peeled off the slacks and blouse that she had been traveling in. Then she took off her bra, too, revealing the ripe, luscious globes of her high-rising breasts. After some rooting around in her dresser, she pulled out a strapless bra and put that on. That was like carrying coals to Newcastle, making her already sumptuous breasts look even more impressive than they were to begin with, thrusting them up high and close together.

Then she slipped into a wine-colored dress that scooped practically navel-deep in front. The dress showed off the loveliness of her full breasts the way a fine setting shows off a valuable gem.

She tossed him a torrid, sizzling bedroom look, leaning forward a little to let the heavy globes tumble into prominent display.

Charley applauded. "Great! Terrific!"

Her voice was low and almost comically suggestive as she murmured throatily, "Hello, handsome. Want to show a girl a good time?"

"Sure thing, baby. Come to papa."

She crossed the room toward him, hips swiveling, batting her eyes in a parody of sensuality. She melted into his arms, her lips seeking his, her kiss the bite of a treacherous serpent escaped from a cage. He held her tight. His hand crept across her body, fastening at the thrusting globe of her left breast. Her breath was warm his fingers enjoyed her yielding, resilient, satin-smooth flesh.

They kissed, fiercely, passionately. She pulled her lips from his, and, panting, ran them across his jaw to his ear, nibbling his earlobe. her breath was warm against his cheek. Her body was trembling with desire. Right now she was the incarnation of sin, she was walking passion. Her body twisted and turned in his arms, gliding voluptuously from side to side, rubbing against him the way a friendly cat might.

"Oh, baby," she whispered hoarsely. "Please, baby, show me what you can do."

He guided her toward the bed, keeping his hand to her breast. He sat her down. She looked at him, eyes turning to little slits of desire, nostrils flaring with lust, her whole expression steaming and tropical.

"Let's go," she said.

Charley grinned. "Later. We aren't through with the rehearsal yet."

"I've got a yen that needs to be satisfied, Charley. I need you bad."

"You fell for your own act, huh? You got yourself all worked up?"

"I'm easily excited, Charley."

"So I've noticed."

"You don't seem to mind."

"No," he said. "I don't. But I'm not going to love you just yet. I want you to show me the other part of the routine, now. The injured virgin act. Change into some different clothes and let's have a look."

She got out of the low-cut dress, out of the strapless bra. Charley eyed her with pleasure as she bent over the things in the dresser drawer, selecting her new costume. Her breasts, dangling forward, swayed to and fro like bells.

She put on a different bra, one that did absolutely nothing for her— a loose-fitting thing that covered her breasts without supporting them. Over that she wore a baggy white blouse. She pulled a pair of weather-beaten blue jeans over her legs.

"You look great to me," Charley said.

"Wait. I'm not finished."

She went into the bathroom. A couple of minutes went by. Charley began to wonder whether this deal would work out at all. Having seen her in her low-cut dress, with those magnificent boobs of hers jutting like firm melons, he knew that was going to be hard for him to fool himself into thinking that she was only a teenager.

Then she came out.

"Well?" she said.

"I'll be a monkey's grandma," Charley gasped in astonishment. "If it isn't Lolita herself!"

"In person," Janey said. Her voice was suddenly high, with an adolescent whine to it. "I think I'm very grown up for my age, don't you? Seventeen last week, that's what I am. I'm allowed to smoke two cigarettes a day and to stay out with boys until midnight on Saturdays."

The effect was amazing. She had wiped her face clear of make-up, and she had gathered her lustrous dark hair behind her head in a long pony-tail. That was all that she had done in the way of actual physical changes. All the rest was sheer acting.

Her eyes were wide open in a cutely innocent way. Her face wore a dumb-bunny grin. She held herself in such a way as to minimize the thrust of her bosom. The shirt and bra she was wearing did the rest, so that she looked almost skinny, not at all remotely like the voluptuous creature whose glorious breasts Charley had been caressing so avidly five minutes ago.

She looked seventeen—at most.

"I'll do, huh?" she asked, still grinning. She was obviously pleased with herself, and she had good reason to be, Charley thought.

"You look terrific," he said. "You'll wow 'em, baby."

"Come rob the cradle now."

"I feel creepy about loving you now." he said. "You look so damn young."

"But I'm not," she said, dropping her voice out of its bobbysocks register into the low, husky, exotic tone she had been using before. "You may think I'm only a child, my dear, but I've been around, I assure you. I've been made, relayed, and parlayed. I've made love all the usual ways and know a variety of mild perversions. This adolescent garb you see me in is but a mask. Take me, lover! Take me!"

She ended up on her knees by him with her arms flung wide like somebody out of a silent movie. Charley guffawed with pleasure. She was colossal, he thought. He couldn't have gotten a better girl for this job if he had tried Central Casting, She got to her feet.

She began to strip.

The fake teenageness dropped away from her as her clothing did. Oft came the girlish shirt, off came the loose-fitting baggy bra, and the high rises of her breasts returned to view, the nipples dark red and standing up tall in the agitation of her eager desires.

Off came the weather-beaten, faded pair of blue jeans, next.

Off came the panties.

She stood before him nude and desirable, her body fully mature, a woman's ripe and opulent figure. Only the lack of make-up on her face seemed to rob her of years. She swept away her barrette, and what had been a pony-tail turned into a cloud of dark, exciting hair.

"Get your clothes off," she said to him in a low, vibrantly throbbing voice.

Charley didn't need a second invitation. The rehearsal was over, and now was the time to get down to business. He stood up and began to peel. Janey helped. In a moment, he was as naked as she was.

They ran for the bed.

That was a dead heat. They landed on the mattress, laughing and gasping, and the bed creaked in protest. They didn't pay any attention. Her body was soft and warm and willing against his. He caressed the hard-tipped breasts, ran his hands over the sleek front, caressed the silkiness of her legs, setting her afire with his caresses.

"Lie back," she told him. "Let me run this show, Charley."

He grinned at her. She pushed him down against the pillow. A moment later she was actively running the show, no doubt about that. Charley's breathing grew ragged as she bent forward, the big bells of her breasts dangling downward, the warm nipples touching him.

Her lips worked.

Her hands grasped at him.

Charley hissed with delight as she began to move her head, her hands still grasping him and playing a symphony of lust. Charley was particularly fond of having women love him this way. And what made him specially gratified right now was that he hadn't suggested that. Janey had decided to act of her own accord. That meant she was anxious to please him. That meant she was interested in making him happy.

Charley liked that idea.

For moment after long moment she paid homage to him, and Charley happily accepted the tribute from her. Then she raised her head. Her lips were parted and shiny. Her face was a mask of desire.

She crawled toward him until they were touching. Her hand helped him, guided him.

Then she began.

Slowly at first, again and again, her body in constant rippling action. Charley's eyes were still open, and he saw the heavy globes of her breasts swaying, saw the glittering beadlets of sweat that were bursting out all over her as she grew more passionate.

Her gyrations grew more violent. Her body trembled and shook. Charley reached out, caught the big globes of her breasts in his hands, squeezed them tight. He felt the nipples like little pebbles against his palms as he held her.

She was gasping, crying with pleasure now. Charley found ecstasy rising like the temperature on a blazing summer day. He closed his eyes. He gripped her breasts even more tightly.

"Now," she cried in a lust-distorted voice. "Now, lover! Everything!"

He gave her everything.

His head swam, his brain reeling with lust, and he knew the ecstasy of her, the invisible pleasure gripping him, and an explosion of passion rocked him, and another, and another, and somewhere far away he was dimly aware that she was crying out, a high wordless wail of delight, and the sizzling flame of fulfillment enveloped them both.

Afterward, she lay quietly against him, her breasts warm and exciting against his chest.

He put his arms around her. He pressed his face into the depths of her black hair, and breathed deeply. She was fragrant, sweet as new wine.

She sighed and made a little purring sound of pleasure.

Then all was still.

CHAPTER FOUR

At the beginning of the following week, Janey began her new career.

She was edgy about it. Blackmail was more illegal than anything she had ever done before. She had hustled, sure, but that wasn't much of a crime. If they chose to enforce the law, they hauled you in and fined you a few bucks and told you not to sin again, and the next day you were right back on the streets. But extortion was different. Extortion was a real crime. They could put you away for a few years for extortion.

But she had promised Charley she'd go through with it. The way he lined it out to her, it seemed pretty foolproof, anyhow. The trick was to pick a mark who was so scared of a scandal that he wouldn't raise a fuss, but would simply hand over the blackmail money and allow the whole business to drop quietly. That sounded like it ought to go off without trouble.

For the first couple of days in Florida, they didn't make any attempt at getting started. Charley didn't appear to be in any hurry.

They went out to the beach instead. Janey had a chance to wear a couple of her bikinis that she hadn't worn in two years. They were real riot-starters, little strips of fabric that covered her breasts and bottom and most of her buttocks and nothing else. A girl could get lots of sunshine in an outfit like that.

The beaches were crowded. But Charley had been right: the clientele here was pretty square. There weren't many young people in their twenties. Most of the folks on the beach were middle-aged, married couples in their fifties and sixties, and even older. Also a big family trade, men and women in their thirties and forties with small children. The college kids weren't here, because it was the season for pre-Christmas exams. And the hipsters weren't here, because Miami Beach was an out place to go in the winter.

A square crowd, all right, Janey decided. Full of likely marks.

The two of them lolled in the sun, and swam, and wandered up and down the row of towering, garish hotels, just feeling things out. Charley had his eyes wary for unattached males. "You've got to find somebody who's dopey but who wants adventure," he said. "If he's too timid, he'll never let you get near him."

Janey nodded. She had already spotted a couple of men who were likely prospects. But she didn't call them to Charley's attention. She was nervous about this whole routine, and she realized that she was stalling, trying to delay the opening gambit as long as possible.

But then the stalling ended.

Charley said, "Tonight's the night. We make our first score."

He drove her from the boarding house to Miami Beach and parked the car about a block from the elegant Boardwalk Plaza Hotel. They had earlier decided that they would try to make the first pickup in the hotel cocktail lounge, the next one on the beach, the next perhaps in a hotel lobby. You had to vary the routine a little each time if you didn't want to buy trouble.

The posh Imperial looked right in tune on the street where Charley parked it. There were massive Cadillacs and gleaming Continentals and even some foreign sports cars around. This was the Gold Coast; there was plenty of money lying around down here.

They got out of the car. Janey was dressed fit to kill, but she felt nervous despite her finery. Her newly tanned breasts rose magnificently out of her scoop-necked dress. Her body was scrubbed and polished, ready for love with an unknown man.

She told herself sternly to snap out of it, get rid of the edginess. She had been a ten-buck-a-trick streetwalker, hadn't she? So what was she kicking about now? This was a lot more dough than that.

She flashed an impish smile. "Let's synchronize watches, captain."

"Right. It's quarter after eight, now," Charley said. "Figure that you'll pick up your mark by, say, nine o'clock at latest."

"In only forty-five minutes?"

"It shouldn't take you that long," he said. "You'd be surprised how many hungry males are sitting around in there waiting for you to come along and fleece them. Pickup by nine, up to his room no later than half past, spend an hour there and make a lady-like escape—I'd say you ought to be back here by ten-thirty."

"To the car?"

"That's right. I'll be waiting for you."

"Okay," she said.

He smiled. "Good luck, baby."

Janey winked at him. "I think we'll be in the money tonight."

"I know so," he said.

She went teetering along toward the hotel on her high heels. It was a warmish, muggy night. Even the fronds of the palm trees that were all over the place looked droopy. But everything would be air-conditioned once she got past the front door of the enormous gold-and-blue palace that was the Boardwalk Plaza Hotel.

A few strollers paused to stare at her as she went by. Good, she thought. She didn't doubt that she was attractive in this outfit. A single girl walking around down here dressed in such a flamboyant garb was bound to attract attention. She knew that she looked like a high-quality B-girl. The men would come flocking.

Her nerves twinged a little. But as she got closer and closer to the hotel, she felt more and more confident that everything was going to work out.

She walked into the hotel lobby.

It was a swanky place, all plate glass and thick carpets and tropical vegetation growing out of porcelain pots. It was crowded, too, mostly with fat, dumpy middle-aged women who were standing around swathed in voluminous mink stoles and draped with acres of sheath dresses—maneuvered back and forth, carrying glittering jewelry. Their harried, paunchy-looking husbands stood by.

There wouldn't be any action in the lobby, Janey knew. A glowing green sign to her left said COCKTAIL LOUNGE, and she steered her course that away, ignoring the genial leers of the bellhops standing around in the lobby. The bellhops knew that she wasn't here for her health.

She entered the lounge.

It was crowded and noisy. Waitresses hurried with trays of drinks. Most of the people in the cocktail lounge were couples, though there were some little knots of businessmen, three and four to a table. Nothing to be gained from them, Janey thought. But here and there she saw a single man drinking alone and hopefully eyeing the waitresses.

Janey stood at the entrance for a moment, looking over the crop. It was very important for her to guess right the first time, she knew. This was a fashionable place, and the management didn't want B-girls buzzing around from patron to patron—at least not free-lancers who weren't kicking in with a cut. She would have to pick a winner the first time, or else clear out and try some other hotel along the tourist strip.

Charley had warned her not to go looking for the handsomest man available. It wasn't just simple jealousy that had prompted that advice. A slick-looking man, Charley had pointed out, was likely to be sophisticated and wise in the ways of the world. He probably wouldn't fall for the extortion stunt in the first place, and might make lots of trouble when the squeeze was applied.

Look for a schnook, Charley had told her.

So she looked for a schnook. And she found one. She spotted the mark sitting at the far side of the cocktail lounge, all by his lonesome. He was made to order for a swindle, Janey thought.

She headed toward him.

He was about fifty, she thought. Maybe fifty-five. A short, broad-shouldered man, it was quite likely that the breadth of his shoulders was due more to the cut of his jacket than to the build of his body. He was baldheaded and deeply tanned, his head so shiny it looked like it had been polished. He was wearing a trim gray suit that looked more expensive the closer Janey got to it. There was a glittering ring on his finger. He was plump and paunchy, obviously a successful man.

He had a look of money about him.

But he also looked like a schnook.

She could tell from the way he was eyeing a waitress that he was hungry for love. The waitress happened to be a cute blonde kid with a honey tan, and the tight black sheath she was wearing outlined the contours of what seemed to be a very nifty pair of boobs. She was standing about two tables away from Janey's mark, talking to a youngish couple nearby.

The schnook was gazing at her with obvious desire. His mouth was open, his eyes were glassy. It was possible to trace a direct line from his eyes to the jutting thrust of the waitress's profiled bust. But his mouth was quirked at the corners as though in self-disgust, as though he was inwardly chewing himself out for not having the nerve to make a pass.

Janey got close.

Close enough for him to notice.

She got in the line of sight, cutting off his view of the waitress. His head turned as though on a mechanical swivel. His eyes flickered greedily behind his horn-rimmed glasses. Janey flashed a smile at him.

It was a million-volt smile, and she could see him sizzle. His mouth opened and closed a couple of times. He was gaping like a fish yanked up into a rowboat.

Under the deep mahogany of his tan, Janey could see a blush beginning to sprout.

She walked over to his table.

"Are you waiting for anybody?" she asked, her voice a throb of lustfulness.

He goggled at her. "N-no—that is—I mean—"

She got him off the hook. "Mind if I sit down, then? You look lonely, and I feel lonely. Let's get to know each other."

He still didn't seem to believe that this was really happening to him. But he hopped to his feet—he was short, maybe five feet six-and started to bustle around to pull her chair out for her. Janey let him do that. She settled down comfortably and waited for him to get seated again.

She leaned forward, giving him plenty of breast action. He was funny to watch as he struggled to keep his eyes from diving into her cleavage.

He said, "Can I get you a drink, miss—miss—?"

"Janey Vaughn," she said. "And yes, I'd love a drink. A gimlet, I think."

He wigwagged to the blonde waitress. "Two gimlets," he blurted. "No, make that a Scotch on the rocks for me, a gimlet for the lady." He stared hungrily at Janey, practically drooling at her. "I'm Morton Kolb," he said. "I'm from New York. This is the first vacation I've taken since my wife died."

"Oh, I'm so sorry," Janey said.

"Last March, it was. From cancer. It just ate her up, like fire. We got the diagnosis in December and by March she was gone. Twenty-four years married, and now she's in the ground half a year."

Janey looked sympathetic. "You must feel strange down here without her."

Morton Kolb nodded. He was brightening, relaxing with each moment. All he had been waiting for, it seemed, was a chance to talk about himself. "We came down here every winter for maybe twenty years. Since right after the war, we were coming here. I wanted to go to the islands, Puerto Rico, Virgin Islands, but Esther said no, you had to fly to get there and she wouldn't fly. Not ever. We always took the train down from New York. Now she's dead and I still don't fly. I took the train. I've been here two weeks, but it isn't the same, a vacation without her."

"I can understand," Janey said warmly. "I know just how it is."

The drinks arrived. He gulped his down in a hurry, looking more at ease afterward. Janey sipped at hers. His eyes flicked toward her bosom again, then quickly headed for more demure territory.

He said, "Are you here on a vacation?"

Janey nodded. "Been saving all year for it. I just get here a couple of days ago."

"Alone?"

"That's right," Janey said. "All by my lonesome."

"It seems a shame, a pretty girl like you, not having a fellow down here."

"Well, you know how it is, these younger men," Janey said. "They give you a fast line but they get you in trouble. A girl's got to be careful. I prefer more mature men, myself. Men who've seen something of the world, men who know what they're doing. What kind of work do you do, Mr. Kolb?"

"Morton."

"Morton," she said.

"I'm a stockbroker."

"That sounds interesting."

"Not really," he said with a rueful smile. "I'm with a small house. We specialize in over-the-counter stocks. I make a lot of money, but what good is money if you aren't happy?"

"True," Janey said sagely. "Very true. Do you have children?"

"Two of them," he said. "Both disappointments to me, I'm afraid."

"That's too bad."

"There's a boy, he's twenty years old. Lazy, doesn't want to work, asking for money all the time. Waiting for me to drop dead so he'll get it all. And a girl, she's eighteen. We don't get along. She's got a lot of rich friends, she's so stuckup she won't even talk to her own father. She doesn't think I'm cultured enough. All I'm good for is making money. Would you like another drink, Miss Vaughn?"

"Call me Janey. And yes, I would."

She had another. So did he. But she was drinking gimlets, which consisted mostly of lime juice. He was drinking Scotch on the rocks, which consisted mostly of Scotch. He was getting lit up. Evidently he had been here drinking and mooning at the waitresses for half an hour or more before Janey had come along.

They talked for a little while. He seemed restless, straining at the bit. He wanted her to go to bed with him, obviously, but he didn't seem to know how to bring the subject up. So she brought that up for him.

She said in a soft, low voice, "Why don't we go somewhere where it's a little more private?"

"Well—ah—"

"I've had enough to drink, Morton. And I'd love to talk to you. But it's no noisy and crowded in here, don't you think?"

"Ah—well—"

"We could go to your room, maybe."

A glow of pleasure spread over him. His eyes seemed to give off sparks.

"Wonderful idea," he said. "Wonderful, wonderful, wonderful!"

So they went to his room.

His room was on the sixteenth floor of the hotel. It was big, enormous, even, with a large bed and a gleaming picture window and a terrace overlooking the beach and the Atlantic, and a television set and a white telephone and all the other little gadgets that you see in the movies but never in a real-life hotel room. This was quite a place. Janey wondered how much it set him back. Thirty, forty, fifty dollars a day, maybe.

They went in and he locked the door and they looked at each other across twenty feet of empty space, and she said, "I've always felt more at ease with older men. I don't know why. I guess it's because my father died when I was very young."

"I'm sorry to hear that."

"So I've been looking for substitute fathers all my life," Janey went on glibly. "Don't get me wrong, though. I'm not in the habit of going up to hotel rooms with strangers all the time."

"Of course not."

"It's just that when I meet a man, and I'm powerfully drawn to him, and something clicks for me right away—do you follow what I mean, Morton?"

"Of course I do," he said. He looked like a fat cat licking his chops, a roly-poly potbellied baldheaded fat cat.

"Such a powerful attraction," she said. "Immediately—instantly—"

"Yes. Yes."

She flung herself into his arms. "Love me," she said in a voice throbbing with passion. "Make me happy, Morton! We need each other. We've both been so lonely."

Their embrace struck Janey as a pretty funny one. She was an inch or so taller than he was to begin with, and her high heels made her tower over him. And he was nervous, hesitant, almost shy, so that it was she who had her arms around him rather than vice versa.

But his hesitation ebbed away as his passions rose.

She thrust her breasts against him and put her lips to his mouth.

His arms encircled her, and he kissed her. Not a deep kiss, but a pretty passionate one all the same, Janey thought.

She wasn't enthusiastic about the idea of going to bed with a man more than old enough to be her father. But he was obviously loaded with dough. And he was a softie. He could be pushed around.

He could be blackmailed.

They broke the clinch. "Let me make myself more comfortable," Janey said.

"Yes. Yes."

"You, too. Take your jacket off. Loosen your tie. Relax, and enjoy yourself."

He followed her with his eyes as she first kicked off her shoes, then unzipped her dress and stepped out of that. She wore no slip beneath. He got a look at her heavy, bulging breasts all but bursting out of the top of her strapless bra, and once again his face turned that deep, burnished red under the tan.

He was excited.

He wanted her.

But he also felt guilty about what he was doing.

He said, "I haven't been with a woman since—since my wife got sick."

"Life goes on, Morton. You can't lock yourself away from the world."

"I used to cheat on her sometimes. I'd hire girls, you know, that kind of girl. I'd call them up, fifty dollars, whatever that was. They'd go to bed with me. I got to tell you, my wife wasn't much in bed. I loved her with all my heart, but love never meant anything to her. So I had to take these other girls. But since the day she got sick, I haven't been with a woman. Almost a year now."

"That isn't fair to you," Janey said. "You ought to let yourself have some enjoyment. You're still a young man, Morton."

"Fifty-three."

"You think that's old?" Janey laughed and whipped her bra off. The bare hills of her breasts tumbled into view, red marks cutting across the white flesh where the brassiere had compressed her.

"You're beautiful," he whispered. "Gorgeous. But you aren't a bad girl. I know that. You aren't like those others."

"No," she said. "I wouldn't think of taking money. I won't kid you and say I'm pure. Morton, but I don't sell myself. When I meet a man, and I really and truly like him, I can give myself to him, but the emotion's got to be there. The emotion's got to be real."

"Yes. Yes, of course," he said, nodding vigorously.

What malarkey, Janey thought. But that seemed to be working.

Hurriedly, she peeled away the rest of her clothing, the panties and the stockings and the garter belt. She stood nude before him. He was pathetically eager for her now, huffing and puffing, his bald dome gleaming with the sweat of desire.

He was undressing now, too. Janey had gone to bed with some middle-aged men in her brief career as a streetwalker, and she was prepared for all kinds of ugliness. But Morton Kolb seemed to have taken pretty good care of himself. He was big around the middle, sure, but he didn't have the varicose veins or the operation scars or the other mutilations that men of his age and general build might be expected to have. His legs were slender, out of proportion to the stocky top of him, as though once long ago he had been slim and graceful.

He stood there naked in from of her and said in a shamefaced way, "I almost hate to say this, but—but there's a way I like to love—"

"Tell me about that," Janey said, wondering what kind of weird kink he was going to spring.

He reddened again. "My wife never went for this. That's why I had to hire girls who'd do things my way. What I do is a kind of spanking. I don't really hurt the girl, but that's something I enjoy, that makes me get excited. Without that I don't have much fun."

"Of course," she said. "Anything you like, Morton. I want you to be happy with me."

"Move over here, then."

He sat down on the edge of the bed. She went to him, and he indicated by gestures that he wanted her to do: to be down across his knees with her buttocks upward.

She had had some experience with this sort of thing before. One of the men who had hired her, one night, had insisted on spanking her, and then she had had to spank him. He had been completely unable to love without those preliminaries.

So she sprawled out across Morton Kolb's skinny, bony knees. She could hear his hoarse breathing.

"So lovely," he murmured. "So beautiful—your skin, so white, so pale—"

He put his hands tenderly to her buttocks, rubbing his soft palms over the cool, fleshy globes, caressing them, stroking them, exploring them. He was snorting with excitement now. For two or three minutes he played with her, running the tips of his fingers along, toying with her dimples, cupping the firm flesh.

Then he lifted his hand.

And brought that down.

Crack! There was more strength in his pudgy frame than Janey had expected. She let out an involuntary howl of astonished pain as his palm slapped against the bare flesh of her buttocks. The blow stung. She shifted in discomfort.

Whack!

Thawack!

Again and again he brought the spanking hand down. Janey's buttocks began to glow. She imagined how the pale flesh was turning an angry red. The pain was spreading through her whole body now, making her throat tighten and tears start from her eyes.

He kept that up. He was gasping, grunting, moving around as he spanked her. And he was getting terrifically excited, she could tell. Turning her head, she looked up and saw him drenched with sweat, his head and shoulders bright red. She wondered what would happen if he had a stroke and dropped dead while he was whaling her. You couldn't blackmail a dead man, Janey thought ominously.

But he had had enough of that particular game now, anyway.

"Okay," he gasped. "Turn over, now. I'm ready."

He certainly was. Janey slipped over onto her back. Her buttocks were glowing. She lay back, head against the pillow. Morton Kolb crouched beside her, his chunky body inflamed with lust.

Then he fell at her.

She adjusted to him, and he took her, quickly, like a man possessed. Janey was more repelled than excited. She couldn't really adjust to the idea of loving a man who didn't attract her in any way. But she gave herself to him, and put on an act. He was so keyed up by his excitement that he couldn't possibly notice whether or not she was faking, anyway.

So she moved and turned and twisted and shook. She gasped and grunted and sobbed and panted.

She worked very busily, hurrying him on to the fulfillment of his excited passions.

That didn't take long. A man who hasn't had any loving for a year isn't likely to have much self-control when he finally gets onto a bed with a breasty and cooperative chick like Janey.

No more than two or three minutes went by, at the very most, and then Kolb heaved a long sigh of satisfaction and shook himself and shivered a couple of times and had his pleasure from her. Janey made the moment a gaudy one by turning on all the gasps and cries of ecstasy at her command.

He lay there, panting, sweating. He rested a long while before he could speak.

He said finally, "Will you stay all night with me? I don't want to let go of you.”

"No, I've got to get going.”

"But it's early.”

"This has got to be this way, Morton. I couldn't stay all night with you. I—I'd feel so cheap.”

"But you've already loved me,” he said. "If we just stay close on the bed—”

"No,” she said. "I made up my mind long ago that I'd never spend a night with a man, not a whole night. Not until I was married. Maybe that's just a crazy quirk of mine, but—”

He swallowed her story. He didn't really have much choice about that. He sat up and modestly put a towel around his waist and watched her dress.

Janey dressed quickly. It was twenty-five past ten. Charley was waiting for her.

She kissed Morton Kolb good-bye. She promised that she'd see him again soon, and she wrote down his room number on a piece of paper.

She wasn't lying, either. He was going to see her again, all right.

A lot sooner than he was figuring.

CHAPTER FIVE

Charley Simmons had passed a peaceful, relaxing evening.

He had watched Janey toddle off to the hotel to do her bit. Then he had gone into another hotel just up the block to have a couple of drinks and while away the evening until she returned. He didn't doubt that everything would go smoothly. Janey had a good little head on her shoulders. She'd make out all right.

He had a couple of martinis, and watched television in the bar, and ogled a few girls who went by hunting for company. He didn't try to make any pickups. For the time being, Janey was woman enough for his needs. Maybe later in the winter, he'd step out a little on her as the mood took him. After all, she'd be getting plenty of outside love during the blackmail bit, so why shouldn't he have some variety too?

The evening ticked away. Around ten o'clock he went back to the car and got in.

Half an hour more went by. Then Janey appeared.

He knew at once that she had scored. She didn't have the neat, well-groomed look that she had had when he had last seen her. She looked rumpled now, her make-up smeared, her eye shadow blotchy, her hair askew.

She looked as if she had been had. He honked the horn. She waved to him and came up alongside.

"Well?" he asked.

She grinned and made a little circle with her thumb and forefinger. "That worked fine," she said. "I picked up a mark and we went to his room."

"Get in the car," Charley said. "What kind of guy was he?"

"Stockbroker from New York, name of Morton Kolb."

"Old? Young?"

"In his fifties. A widower since March. Very lonely. Very hungry for some loving."

Charley started the car. "I hope you took care of him properly."

"I sure did," she said. "So properly that my seat's a little sore now."

"What did he do?"

"He's a spanker," Janey said. "He gave my bottom a good tanning. But that wasn't so bad. And the main event was over fast. He didn't have much staying power. We've got this made, Charley. This guy's a natural. He's got loads of dough, but he's easy to push around. A schnook. A little baldheaded schnook."

"If you're right, we're in the chips, baby."

"Sure we are. I know we are." She grabbed his arm, squeezed the muscle hard. "The old cash register is going to ring and ring tonight."

They were back in Miami now, hurrying toward their own apartment. Janey rushed quickly through her transformation from seductive siren to seduced teenager. All her clothes had been laid out in advance, before they had set out on the evening's business.

Off came the wine-colored dress with the stunningly low neckline. Off came the fancy tan brassiere that thrust her breasts upward and forward. Off came the sophisticated-looking hairdo that she had adopted.

Charley watched with pleasure as she got into the new outfit.

A cheap yellow sweater, tight against her body, the kind of thing that a teenager proud of her newly sprouted breasts would wear. An ordinary plaid skirt. Bobby socks, loafers, a wide leather belt.

She bunched her hair into a pony-tail and put on a different colored lipstick, an unsophisticated orange color that a high school girl would be likely to go for. She made a mental change of gears so that she would be wearing a more innocent, less worldly expression.

The transformation was complete.

In the space of ten minutes Janey had blotted ten years from her apparent age.

"How do I look, Charley?" she asked, swinging round to give him the view.

"Like a perfect bobby soxer," he told her. "Like Lolita herself."

"In person."

"You bet. Ready to go?"

"Yeah," Janey said. "Just let me find the bubble gum and we can take off."

By quarter after eleven, they were on their way again, and by half past Charley was pulling the car into a parking spot outside the Boardwalk Plaza Hotel. They walked toward the hotel. Charley was dressed reasonably well, in a summer suit and Italian shoes. He looked like a vacationer. Janey looked more like a fugitive from a dragstrip movie, he thought.

They went in. As they passed a clump of bellhops near the entrance, Janey giggled.

"What's so funny?" Charley asked.

"The bellhops," she said. "The last time I came through here, in my low-cut dress, they were all giving me the eye. Now they take a quick look and that's it. I'm just another dumb kid to them now."

"Means the costume's a success," he said.

They walked to the elevator.

"Sixteen," Janey said.

The car zoomed them up, up, up. They emerged into a brightly-lit, deeply carpeted corridor. Charley said, "Remember, now, let me take care of this. You just stand around and look injured, and don't speak until spoken to."

"I hear and obey," Janey said.

"Which room is it?"

"Right over there."

Charley knocked. There was no response, so he knocked again, after a moment, rapping harder.

A sleepy voice from within said, "Who is it?"

"Mr. Kolb?"

"That's right. What is it?"

"Important message for you, Mr. Kolb."

"Just a minute, just a minute."

Silence again. "He's putting on his bathrobe," Janey whispered. "He must have gone to sleep."

Charley nodded. The door opened. He found himself facing a short, potbellied, middle-aged man wearing a purple bathrobe over bright green pajamas. He looked sleepy and bewildered at the invasion.

Charley didn't give him a chance. He pushed the door open before Morton Kolb could do anything, striding into the room. Janey followed him. Kolb stepped back a couple of paces, his face blank with confusion.

"May I ask—"

Charley cut him off. He pointed to Janey and said, "You ever see this girl before?" His tone was belligerent and loud.

"Why, no," Kolb said. "I never—that is—I mean—no, it can't be!"

"Hello, Morton," Janey purred.

Charley shot an angry glance at her. He didn't want her to say anything.

"It can be, Kolb," Charley said. "It is."

"Janey?" Kolb blurted.

Charley said, "It's Janey, all right. Only she was all dressed up before, but now she's wearing her everyday clothes. I made her change. A girl her age doesn't have any business dressing up the way she liked to. That's downright indecent. That's a crying shame."

Morton Kolb looked more and more baffled and distressed. He stared at Charley, then at Janey, then back to Charley again. He looked terribly pale beneath his tan.

"A girl her age?" Kolb repeated slowly, frowning.

"Just—how—old—is—she?"

"She'll be seventeen next month," Charley snapped, his eyes blazing with pretended anger. "Seventeen, Mr. Kolb!"

Kolb seemed to pull himself together a little. "This is some kind of joke you're pulling on me, huh? This is the kid sister of the girl who— who was here earlier. She has to be."

"She's my kid sister," Charley said. "And she's the same girl you put your lousy paws all over. I heard the whole story, the spanking bit, all of that. Show him the birthmark, Sis."

Janey had a small round birthmark on the inside of her left leg. Kolb had noticed that. Now she hiked her dress up to her hips and thrust her leg forward, sullenly demonstrating the mark again.

"You see that?" Charley demanded. "She's the same girl, you can't deny that now. And not even seventeen years old. You ought to be ashamed of yourself. Of all the disgusting things, Kolb. Picking up a girl who's underage, making her amuse you in your perverted way—"

"No," Kolb said in a husky, shaken voice. "I didn't pick her up. She picked me up. I was sitting down there in the bar, minding my own business, and she walked in, said hello to me, started flirting."

"However that happened," Charley said, "the fact still remains that you seduced a girl in her teens."

"No. I tell you, I'm a victim in all this. She suggested coming up here! She led the way! She got undressed first. And anyway, how was I supposed to know how old she was? She looked like she was in her twenties. You saw her when she was all dressed up, mister. You must have known that she looks older than she is."

"But she's just a kid. There's a law against that kind of stuff, Kolb."

"How was I supposed to know? She didn't carry a badge saying she was too young."

"It doesn't matter," Charley said stubbornly. "It doesn't matter at all. The law is supposed to protect young girls against themselves, too. It doesn't matter who picked who up. It don't matter that she was willing. She's a dumb kid and she doesn't know what's right and what isn't, sometimes. You went to bed with her, and that makes you guilty of statutory rape."

The stockbroker's jaw sagged. He stared expressionlessly at Charley. He looked at Janey again, as though unable to believe the evidence of his eyes. After a moment he said bleakly, "Statutory rape?"

"You heard me. They can put you away a long time for that. And the story makes a noisy splash in the papers. Especially when that's a fat old man who sleeps with a pretty young girl."

"She wasn't any virgin. She told me so!"

"The law protects girls who aren't virgins too," Charley said. "Just so long as she's underage. I feel like busting your face in for you, Kolb. The only reason I don't do so is on account of your age. You're a dirty old pervert and I hope you rot in jail."

The stockbroker gasped. "Are you going to turn me in to the police?"

"Why not? Your kind ought to be locked up."

"But—but, no, I never dreamed—I've got a teenage daughter myself, I wouldn't knowingly touch a girl underage I—I—"

Charley said, "My heart bleeds for you."

"It would ruin me if you turned me in. I can't afford a scandal. Not at my age, not in my kind of work. I've got to be above reproach. Look, be reasonable, whoever you are. I had no intention of seducing your sister, and I certainly would never have gone near her if I had any inkling how old she really was. She took advantage of me, not the other way around. I beg you. Don't turn me in to the police. It's not right."

"Well," Charley said, "maybe I will, maybe I won't."

"What do you mean?"

He shrugged. "It all depends on you."

"I don't understand you," Kolb said.

"All right, I'll spell things out," Charley said. "My sister here, she needs an education fund, something to set her straight, keep her from doing the crazy things she does. You can help contribute to that fund, if you don't want a fuss with the police."

Charley nodded smugly. "Meaning that I don't want my kid sister's good name to get ruined by being smeared all over the front pages. So I'm willing to let you get off easy."

"How easy?"

"Well, suppose you give me five hundred bucks in cash, and then get yourself out of town by tomorrow, and I'll forget all about the whole thing. And otherwise I go to the cops right now and tell them that you're the slimy old creep who seduced my underage sister."

Kolb's face became rigid. "Five hundred dollars is a lot of money."

"Not for you it isn't. You've got plenty. Anyway, that's not such a bad price for a round in bed with a girl built like her."

Kolb didn't make an answer for a long moment.

He stared sadly at both of them. Charley waited, his arms folded. This was the key moment, he knew. Kolb might call their bluff, decide to risk exposure. That would end it all, since for obvious reasons Charley couldn't actually go to the cops yelling statutory rape, not with Janey actually five years past the age of consent.

Would Kolb outmaneuver them, though? Charley waited.

And the short balding stockbroker said after a while, "I'm not carrying that kind of cash on me. Will you take traveler's checks?"

"Let's see them."

Kolb went to his luggage and took out a little black folder of traveler's checks. They looked okay to Charley, the familiar American Express kind. He riffled through the book. They were fifty-dollar checks, and there were a lot of them. Janey sure hadn't picked any pauper for her first mark.

Charley handed the book back to Morton Kolb. "All right," he said. "Sign them and I'll take them."

Kolb nodded nervously. He sat down at the little desk near the window and took out his pen. Slowly, reluctantly, he began to countersign the neatly printed traveler's checks. One, two, three, four… ten.

As he signed each, he tore it from the book. Finally he gathered up the whole stack of them and handed them in silence to Charley. Charley examined them, carefully comparing Kolb's new signature with the earlier signature on the checks. They matched.

"Everything okay?" Kolb asked edgily.

"Fine," Charley said. "Tomorrow you check out of here, you follow me? Take yourself to Sarasota or St. Petersburg or San Juan or any where you damn please, but don't stay around this town."

"All right."

"And in the future, be more careful when you sleep with pretty girls," Charley added. "Ask for a birth certificate before you do anything incriminating. That could get awfully expensive otherwise."

Kolb nodded. He was trembling now. "All right. All right. Would you go, please? Both of you. I—I've given you your money. Now leave me alone. Please? Please go away?"

Nodding in return, Charley said, "Sure, Mr. Kolb. Let's go, Sis."

They went out of the room. They walked down the hall to the elevator. Charley rang for the car.

"It worked!" Janey said in wonder.

"Of course it worked. What did you expect?"

"We made five hundred bucks?"

"On the nose. Two and a half bills apiece." He looked at his watch. "It's a little past midnight now. The whole caper took maybe four hours tops. That's better than sixty bucks an hour for each of us."

"I didn't even get sixty bucks a week at that roadhouse," Janey said.

The elevator came. They got in, and Charley shot her a warning glance to change the subject. Elevator boys have ears.

When they reached the lobby, Janey said, "I feel kind of sorry for him, though."

"Why?"

"He was a good sort. He's lonely, he misses his wife, his kids don't like him."

"So what? Everybody's got some kind of trouble," Charley said. "At least he's got money. More money than he knows what to do with. So he gave some to a charitable cause: us. It isn't as though he didn't get something in return. What's the matter, don't you think that's worth five hundred bucks to love you?"

"I've been known to settle for less," Janey said with a sly grin.

"You take what the market can bear."

"Where are we going to go to celebrate?"

"Home," Charley said. "I got a special kind of celebration planned."

"Can't we go somewhere and have a drink first?" Janey asked. "Champagne cocktails for two at the hotel bar right here?"

Charley laughed. "Look at how you're dressed! They won't let you in. They'll say you aren't old enough to drink there."

Janey grinned. "I guess you're right."

"We'll stop in a package store, though. We'll pick up a little something to brighten the night."

He bought a bottle of champagne. Not the domestic kind that the liquor store proprietor offered him, but the real thing, French champagne, a bottle of Piper Heidsieck that set him back nine bucks. Half of it would come from Janey's share, Charley figured thriftily.

Charley paid for the champagne with a traveler's check. The liquor store man looked at it suspiciously and said, "You've signed it already, Mr. Kolb. You're supposed to wait until you're in the presence of the person you're giving the check to before you sign it."

"I'm not Kolb," Charley said. "Kolb gave the check to me. In return for services rendered. I'm just passing it along, on account of how the banks are closed this time of night."

"Oh. Oh, sure. I get it."

He gave Charley forty-one bucks change from the traveler's check. They went out again and Charley drove them quickly to the apartment.

"Put the champagne in the icebox," Charley said. "Then go take yourself a good shower."

"Why? Do I smell bad?"

"You been in bed with another man tonight," he said. "You think I want you without you at least cleaning yourself up first?"

"I guess you're right," she admitted.

He watched her undress. Her slim form disappeared into the bathroom. He eyed the pert pink buttocks, the tapering legs. Then the door closed. Charley smiled in satisfaction. He had really found himself a doozie, he thought. Pure luck, too.

Carefully he counted out the money. He built two stacks of four traveler's checks each. On top he put the change from the liquor store, twenty dollars and fifty cents in each pile. He put the remaining traveler's check aside.

Janey came out of the bathroom a few minutes later, looking well-scrubbed and delicious. She stood nude in front of him, her breasts rising and falling gently. Her nipples were a pale pinkish color right now. But he knew that they'd turn a dark red pretty soon, when he got his hands on her boobs and stirred her up and made her blood begin to pound fast.

He pointed to the money. "Here," he said. "Yours and mine. I'll have to cash this last traveler's check tomorrow and we'll split it."

She riffled through the pile. "There's about five bucks short," she said.

"Your share of the champagne."

"We going Dutch treat on the celebration?" she asked.

"Fair is fair. I've been paying the expenses all the way down out of Delaware," Charley said. "Time we began splitting fifty-fifty."

"All right," she said. "If that's the way you want it to be."

"Fair is fair," Charley said.

"You think the champagne's ready yet?"

"Give it another five, ten minutes. I'll go take a shower first. If there's anything I hate, it's warm champagne."

She eyed him skeptically. "You an expert on champagne, or something?"

"I've had enough of it to know that it tastes better cold," he told her, as he began to undress.

"How come you forgot the caviar, then?"

"All the caviar stores were closed. Liquor stores stay open later around here."

"I've never had caviar. It's just eggs, isn't it? What's so special about fish eggs?"

"They taste good," Charley said. "Especially with champagne as a chaser. Don't go anywhere, kid. I'll be right back and we'll celebrate."

He stepped into the shower and gave himself a good rub-a-dub. The champagne had been a fine idea, Charley told himself. He was in a bubbly mood after tonight's successful caper, so why not splurge a little?

Five hundred cookies, and easy money. There was no reason why they couldn't pull the same kind of deal seven nights a week. Thirty-five hundred bucks a week? That sounded too fantastic to be real.

But of course Charley didn't plan to try it that often. He knew the story about going to the well with the pitcher once too often. And killing the goose that laid the golden eggs. It was a risky operation, this extortion bit, even if it had seemed easy tonight. The more frequently they tried it, the more likely it was that something would eventually go awry. There was no sense being greedy about it, Charley figured. If they worked the deal once a week, that would give them plenty of cash. They could spend the rest of their time loafing around.

He dried off and got out of the shower room. Janey was sitting in their combination living room-kitchen, and she was still nude.

She said, "We got problems."

"What kind of problems?"

"No corkscrew, honey."

Charley laughed. "Since when do you need a corkscrew to open a bottle of champagne?"

"Don't you?"

"I see you've led a sheltered life," he said. "Go get the glasses and I'll give you a little demonstration on how the upper crust lives."

She fetched two water tumblers from the closet. They had rented the place complete with furniture and some miscellaneous pots, pans, dishes, and glasses.

"They aren't champagne glasses," she said. "I'm sorry, it's the best I can do."

"We'll manage," Charley told her. He got the champagne bottle from the icebox. It was nice and cold now. He glanced at her naked body, at the pinkness of her, all that luscious flesh, the swelling breasts and firm legs and trim, succulent buttocks. His. All his.

Except for a few hours each week when he had to share her. But he didn't mind that. Not at the going price, anyway, he thought.

He picked up the champagne bottle and unwrapped the metal foil covering the cork. Then he unwound the twisted wire casing.

"Notice," he said. "The cork sticks out of the bottle. You grasp it thusly. Then you begin to turn the bottle. Always hold the cork and turn the bottle. If you try to hold the bottle and turn the cork, it'll pop out good and hard and maybe blow a hole in the ceiling."

The cork came out with a little popping sound. Janey held the glasses up, and Charley filled them. Then he put the open champagne bottle back into the refrigerator until they were ready for refills.

They stood nude in the middle of the room, gravely clinking glasses.

"To us," Charley said.

They sipped. Janey's eyes lit up. "Hey, it's good stuff!"

"The best," Charley said.

They clinked glasses again. "To Morton Kolb and his five hundred bucks," Janey said. They drank again. "To your kid sister," Janey said.

"Yeah," Charley said. "Here's to incest."

"That isn't nice."

"Sure that is."

"What is?"

"Incest," he said. "With the right kind of sister, I mean."

"What's the right kind of sister?"

"The kind that isn't really related to you," Charley said.

"I'll drink to that."

"So will I."

"My glass is empty," she said.

"That's easily fixed."

He went to the refrigerator and got the champagne. He filled both their glasses again.

They toasted some more. He pointed and said, "Here's to that."

She pointed to him and said, "Here to that."

They giggled. He toasted her breasts and her buttocks next. She toasted him in specific anatomic detail. He filled the glasses again.

Before they knew it, the champagne was nearly all gone. There was about one glass left in the bottle for each of them, Charley figured.

"Let's save the rest for morning," he suggested.

"A champagne breakfast. Good idea!"

He put the bottle away. He felt just a little high, not much, but enough. Reaching out, he scooped Janey off her feet, picking her up with one arm slung under her buttocks and the other around her shoulder.

He carried her into the bedroom. He dumped her down onto the unmade bed.

Her eyes were bright and shiny. Bedroom eyes, he thought. And a bedroom body.

"Over here," she said huskily.

"Careful, now. Remember that you're only seventeen and you mustn't do anything naughty."

"But you can," she said.

"Be delighted to."

He flopped down next to her on the bed. He filled his hands with the bounty of her breasts, enjoying the touch of the hard nipples against his palms. Her mouth was eagerly receptive to his kiss. She tasted of champagne. He couldn't imagine a better taste for a woman's lips to have.

Charley rolled over closer to her, and found warmth, the eagerness of her. He took her.

His body began the familiar rhythm, and she moved with him. Her nails dug at his back and her arms clutched him tightly as she gave herself to him as wildly as was possible. Charley showed his appreciation.

Their bodies trembled on the brink of the abyss of ecstasy.

Then they tumbled in, and fell down, down, bodies pressed, arms around each other, lips glued, down to the roaring volcano of bliss at the very bottom.

CHAPTER SIX

It was more than a week before Janey tried to pull a new caper.

It was an easy, loafing sort of week. Every morning they went out to the beach, swam, sun-bathed, dozed. They both began to get deep, rich tans. It was the beginning of December, now, and Janey got a big kick out of being able to swim and sun-bathe and snooze in the sun at a time when most of the country was shivering under the first icy blasts of the approaching winter.

It was a good life, Janey thought.

In the afternoons, they wandered around Miami Beach, sightseeing, watching the amusing antics of the tourists, listening to some of the old codgers on the public street benches loudly arguing politics. Most of them were big Goldwater fans, but there were plenty who weren't, and the shouting got pretty fierce at times. And then they went shopping. Janey had never seen stores like these. They only seemed to sell luxury goods, gay, fashionable, dashing merchandise.

She had a couple of hundred dollars to burn. It didn't take her long.

Forty bucks bought her two French bikinis. When she modeled them for Charley he shook his head and said, "There can't be fifty cents worth of material in both of them put together."

"That's why they're so expensive," she said. "The more daring they are, the higher the price."

These were on the fantastic side. They were just one notch away from indecent exposure—a strip of cloth across the breasts, and a triangular thing below that covered some front and most of the buttock flesh, but left a good many square inches exposed.

Thirty bucks bought Janey a pair of airy, open Italian shoes, high-heeled and sophisticated.

Fifty bucks bought her a new low-cut evening dress, even more revealing than the wine-colored one, even more a body-hugger and a breast-barer. She bought a new bra to go with it: nine bucks.

Three-fifty got her a pair of bikini panties to wear as underwear in the warm weather. Thirteen dollars produced a sleek little handbag. Nine dollars gave her a reasonable quantity of new stockings.

That took care of her wardrobe, and it also took care of almost $150 of her first night's earnings. She had almost a hundred dollars left, but there were a lot of other things she still wanted to buy, frilly female things of a sort that she had had to deny herself while she was living on low wages—earrings and perfume and bracelet and necklaces and whatnot. The hundred dollars that she had left after her initial shopping spree wouldn't take her very far into her list of necessary luxuries.

"I think it's time we pulled another caper, Charley," she said.

"Fine with me. It's been more than a week."

"What about tonight?"

"No," he said. "Let's wait till tomorrow and make the pickup on the beach. We ought to vary our M.O. so the police don't get wise."

"Vary our what?"

"Our M.O.," Charley said. "Our modus operandi. That's Latin for our 'way of operating.' What's the matter with you, you ignorant or something?"

"I never learned any Latin," she said.

"How about Greek?"

"That neither. I'm not an educated girl, Charles. I lack the higher graces."

"You've got an educated body, though. You've got all the lower graces."

"Wouldn't you prefer it if I knew Latin and Greek instead?"

"No," he said, and reached for her.

The next day was a Thursday, bright and hot, without a cloud in the sky. The humidity was low, and the air was crisp, but the sun hung up there like a giant torch blazing just overhead. Even at nine in the morning the temperature was up in the middle eighties, and it looked like it was going to get well past that before it was time for lunch. Crazy kind of December weather, Janey thought.

They drove out to the beach, going a mile uptown from the Broadway Plaza Hotel, their last scene of action. This time they chose the strip of beach that belonged to the Tropical Beach Hotel. In theory, only paying guests of the hotel, and friends of paying guests, were supposed to use the beach. But nobody paid very much attention to the theory.

Janey was wearing one of her new bikinis. Might as well make use of the investment, she thought. Over it she had thrown a beach robe, just for the sake of decency until she got on the beach. Charley parked the car and they crossed the street to the beach entrance.

"We'll go in separately," Charley said. "I'll keep my distance from you on the beach. I'll be watching you but don't you watch me."

"Okay," Janey said.

"Go on in. I'll wait a few minutes."

He hung back. She went through the gate and out onto the beach. It was about ten in the morning, but because of the heat the beach was already filling up. There were the usual family groups, and some fat women in bikinis almost as revealing as hers. There ought to be a law against women like that wearing bikinis, Janey thought. She wondered what would happen if she had come out on the beach wearing one of those new topless bathing suits. Probably start a riot, she thought Get herself arrested for indecent exposure. She didn't need that. She'd been there once already, and once was enough.

Janey found herself a vacant piece of beach. She unrolled the blanket she had brought along, spread it out, sat down on it.

Then she took out the sun-tan cream. In this bikini, she'd be exposing parts of her body that hadn't had a chance to get a tan before. Carefully she oiled the tops of her breasts. The bikini bared them almost to the nipples. The rosy upper circle of the aureole was just visible. Then she oiled the line along the top of the bikini pants, and oiled the chunk of buttocks that was newly exposed.

With that job done, she stretched out flat to get some sun and take stock of the situation.

She kept her eyes open, looking for unattached males. The first one that she saw was Charley. He came rambling across the beach, a big, husky, hairy man in purple trunks, took a casual glance at her, and kept on going. He settled down next to a palm tree about a hundred feet away from her.

Charley wasn't what she was after right now. She kept on looking.

She saw some middle-aged men who looked very much like last week's victim, Morton Kolb. But she wasn't in the mood for another middle-aged man right now. One of those was enough, for the time being, whatever Charley said. She wanted to pick up somebody with a little more life and oomph this time.

She looked around.

And she saw her man.

He was sitting about seventy feet away from her, on the opposite side from Charley. He was alone. He was reasonably young, that is, about forty years old. More important, he was reasonably good-looking.

He was a shortish, lean-bodied man with dark curly hair that was going gray at the temples. His body was trim and muscular, and he had a heavy tan and a little clipped mustache. It was the little clipped mustache that led Janey to think that this guy was a good prospect. It meant that he was a vain man. He had a prissy, fastidious look about him. Most likely he kept to a diet, got plenty of exercise, sun-bathed and swam—a man who was fussy about his appearance, Janey thought.

A man like that, she figured, was weak at the core. He would be a pushover for Charley's extortion demand.

And he was looking in her direction.

He wasn't exactly ogling her. He was just staring with considerable interest.

Janey rolled over, so that instead of lying on her stomach she was lying on her side, facing him. She propped her arm up on her elbow and used it to support her head. The heavy globes of her breasts strained against the bikini halter in that position, making the view all the more spectacular.

Mr. Clipped Mustache's eyes lit up a little.

Janey smiled at him. She put a twinkle into the smile.

He smiled back. Warmly.

The chemistry was working, Janey thought. She watched him take a deep breath, sucking air into his lungs to push his ribs out and make him look more muscular. He squared his shoulders.

He was showing off for her, Janey thought. Next thing, he'd get up and turn a few handsprings, she figured in amusement.

The bait had been cast and the hook had been taken. The victim was free to wriggle, but his fate was sealed now.

Janey rolled over again and lay on her back, looking up at the sky. She didn't want to flirt with him too obviously. He had seen her and he knew that there was something there for him if he cared to follow up that exchange of smiles. Now let him stew about her for a little while, Janey thought.

She closed her eyes and let the sun take her.

The sun's warm fingers caressed her body. They stroked her almost bare breasts, they passed over her legs, they penetrated her body, warming her, exciting her.

Janey counted off about five minutes. Enough time to let Mr. Clipped Mustache work up his nerve for a proposition, she thought.

She sat up and looked in his direction. He was staring at her in an earnest, contemplative way. Janey smiled at him again, making the smile another dazzler.

Then she got to her feet, facing him and bending forward as she did so, so that the heavy globes of her breasts swayed down and out, threatening to burst the flimsy fabric of the halter. She was quite an eyeful, and Janey knew that. Slowly, she straightened up.

She began to stroll toward the water.

She didn't spare the voltage as she walked. That was a kind of exaggerated parody of a stripper's stride, with plenty of hip action and a provocative waggle of the buttocks with every step. This was her turn to fill her lungs with air and make her chest expand.

Janey knew that a lot of eyes were on her as she made her sizzling, solitary promenade toward the water. Little boys were staring at her, and love-hungry fifteen-year-olds, and wistful husbands, and jealous wives, and paunchy old men who sighed for their youth. But, though she didn't look in his direction, she was pretty certain that Mr. Clipped Mustache was staring too.

She reached the edge of the beach. She waded out into ankle-deep water and stood there, letting the warm surf swirl up around her legs. That felt good. She stepped out a little further.

Then she allowed herself to look around. Mr. Clipped Mustache had gotten to his feet and was ambling down toward the ocean himself. He was a short, compact man, she saw, with weight-lifter's muscles. He wore tight red trunks that outlined his body with explicit clarity. An exhibitionist, Janey thought.

But he was interested, at any rate. He was coming after her for sure.

She turned and waded out into deeper water. Then she launched herself forward and began to swim, heading straight out for the open sea. Far away, there was a row of buoys that marked the borderline beyond which the hotel guests weren't supposed to go. Janey made for it. She wondered vaguely about sharks. She had heard some people talking before on the beach; they were having a lot of trouble with sharks along the beaches this season at Florida.

She swam powerfully. She was a good swimmer, though she hadn't had much chance to keep in practice lately. Stroke after stroke after stroke, slicing through the water, breasts enjoying the flow of coolness across them.

Then she paused and looked back. He was following her.

He was trying to be casual about that, as though wanting to swim after her without seeming to swim after her, just happening to head in her general direction. He was swimming effortlessly, but making pretty good time. Janey grinned and started to swim again. The white bobbing line of buoys was just ahead. The water was deep here. Were there large ugly beasts moving silently through the depths below her kicking legs, she wondered uncomfortably?

"Miss!" yelled Clipped Mustache. "Miss!"

Janey turned. "You calling me?"

"Yes. I wouldn't swim so far out there!"

Janey let herself tread water. He came swimming up to her.

"Why shouldn't I?" she asked.

"Sharks," he said "There's been some nasty shark trouble lately. You oughtn't to come all the way out here to swim."

"Oh, I don't know," Janey said. "Why would any shark want to bite me?"

"I could tell you," he said. "I saw you on the beach. You looked good enough to bite."

"Depends on your point of view. What looks good to a man might not attract a shark at all."

"We can discuss this further," he said. "But let's go closer to shore, shall we? Only last week a boy was attacked right by the line here."

"He get hurt?"

"Sixteen stitches. Shall we swim in? My name's Mark Avery."

"Janey Vaughn."

"Pleased to meet you, Janey." He flashed her a white, toothy grin. Then he began to swim in toward shore. Janey kept pace with him.

He was good looking, she thought, but in a phony, synthetic way—capped teeth, most likely, and a carefully built-up body, and maybe a nose job too. Probably he had left the gray at his temples only because he thought it made him look distinguished, which in a way it did. He was the sort of man who would attract a certain kind of girl. Not Janey. Ordinarily she would have fended him off without stopping to think about it.

But she wasn't looking for love, just now. She was looking for loving—and for cash.

They reached the shallow water. When they got to a point where they could stand, they waded in. Janey's upper half emerged from the water, her breasts all but bursting out of her halter. Mark Avery gave them a quick look, and then a not so quick look.

He said, "Are you here with anyone, Janey?"

"All by my lonesome."

"Care to join a bachelor's blanket, then?"

"Sounds like a good idea, Mark."

"You're a good swimmer," he said.

"So are you."

"Intercollegiate champ at Ohio State," he said. "Not exactly last year, you understand, but in my time I was pretty good in the sprints."

"Are you from Ohio?"

"Wisconsin," he said. "Fond du Lac."

"You've come a long way for a vacation, haven't you?" she asked.

"If you've ever spent one winter in Wisconsin, you'll know why," he said as they left the water. "Where are you from?"

"New Jersey," she said at random. "Trenton."

"Hey, really? I once knew a girl from Trenton. In fact, you might say I was in love with her. Maybe you know her. She's probably just a couple of years older than you are. Her name's Martina Holt."

"Sorry. Never heard of her."

"You haven't? The Holts are a pretty big family in Trenton, I thought."

"I'm from the south end of town," Janey said. "Practically the suburbs."

She stretched out on his blanket. He got down next to her. "That's quite a bikini you almost have on," he said.

"It's pretty cute. I was going to get the topless kind but I didn't have the nerve."

"This one is pretty near topless," he said.

"The extra couple of inches makes all the difference," she replied.

"Are you here on a vacation?"

"Uh-huh. Till next week. I've been down here about a week so far. Then it's back to the old grind. Stenography. I saved two years to come down here. And it's been pretty lonely so far, let me tell you. A girl comes down by herself, can't find the right kind of man to keep her company. Just these fat old lechers here. I've been at my wit's end for company."

"Maybe I can help out," he said. "Would you care to have dinner with me tonight?"

"I'd love to."

"We'll spend the morning on the beach. Then we can go for a drive, cool off during the hot part of the day. I've got a Jaguar you'll like to ride in. Drove all the way from Wisconsin in it. Are you staying at the hotel here?"

"No," Janey said evasively. "I'm down the beach a little way. Look, would you do me a favor? My sun-tan oil just about washed away while we were swimming. If you'll rub a little on my back—"

"A pleasure," he said.

"Thanks so much."

He went to work. His hand traveled over her smooth skin, oiling her, and she could hear his breathing rate pick up as the touch of her skin excited him. When he had oiled the area between her shoulder blades, she told him to go lower, and he went as low as the bathing suit would let him, oiling her back right down to the dimples that marked the beginning of the swelling globes of her buttocks. Then she had him oil the sides of her back, and she turned so that his fingers passed under her arms, and touched the flesh that was the edge of her breast.

He was hooked, all right. He was practically snorting and pawing at the ground by the time he put the cap back on the tube of sun-tan oil.

They sun-bathed side by side for a while. Janey looked around, caught sight of Charley looking at her. She winked at him. He made an annoyed-looking face, as though telling her to ignore him.

When it began getting hot and the beach started getting really crowded, Mark Avery said, "You want to go for a drive now?"

"Love it."

"Let's take off, then."

She put her beach robe on over her bikini. He wrapped a towel around his shoulders. They left the beach and crossed into the hotel parking lot. He got the car keys, and they entered a sleek, low red Jaguar that had dollar signs painted all over it in invisible paint.

"Lovely," she said.

"I'm rather fond of it," he told her.

They zoomed away. He was a reckless driver, but there was something exhilarating about his recklessness. As they drove, he did most of the talking, which was exactly the way Janey wanted it to be. The less she had to say about herself, the less chance there was that she might slip up and give something away that was better off hidden.

He was thirty-eight years old, he told her, and he was in the real estate business in Wisconsin, but actually he had inherited a pile of money from his father and didn't devote much of his time to the cares of business. He had been married, he told her, but it hadn't lasted. The divorce had come through last summer.

He talked on and on. He was his own favorite topic of conversation. Janey was a good listener, throwing in a word or two whenever it seemed necessary to keep the flow of wordage going. Eventually he swung in a big arc and doubled back toward the hotel.

And then he made the pass for which Janey had been waiting so patiently.

"I've got an idea," he said.

"Do tell."

"It's too hot to go back on the beach for a couple of hours yet. Why don't we go up to my room? We can order lunch from Room Service, something light and cool, and relax for a while, and then about two, three o'clock we can go down and swim some more. Then I'll take you back to your hotel and I'll pick you up again at dinner time. How's that?"

"Fine," he said.

So they went to his room. It was cool and airy, even bigger and sweller than Morton Kolb's room had been last week. He picked up the Room Service menu and studied it. Then he gave it to her.

"Whatever you like," he said.

"What about the open-face caviar sandwich?" she said. "I love caviar so much!"

It was the most expensive thing on the menu, four dollars, twice as much as any other sandwich. But he didn't bat an eye at the price.

"Good idea," he said. "I think I'll have one also. And a bottle of nice cold wine to go with it. White wine. Chablis, I think. Very good. I'll put the order in. How soon do you want to eat?"

"It's—umm—twelve-thirty now," Janey said. "I feel like taking a shower first, getting all the sand and stickum off. Why don't you ask them to bring the food up around half past one?"

"Will do." He gestured toward the bathroom. "The shower's right in there. Make yourself at home."

Modestly, she kept her beach robe on until the bathroom door was safely closed. Then she slipped it off, got out of her bikini, and took a quick shower, scrubbing away the sand that had clung to her oiled skin.

She wasn't modest at all when she came out. She didn't bother to put the beach robe back on. Or the bikini.

She stepped from the bathroom in the nude, her full-breasted lush body on complete display for him. Mark Avery was standing by the window, lighting a cigarette, and he glanced up at her and smiled, and then did a double take as the fact of her nudity sank in.

"This is so much more comfortable this way, I think," Janey said.

"How beautiful you are!"

"Take your trunks off, Mark. That isn't polite to stand around wearing clothing when a lady's undressed."

He grinned. His nostrils widened in desire. He seemed to tense like an athlete about to begin running a race. Quickly, he rolled down his red trunks and stepped out of them. His body was lean and firm, with a single narrow stripe of white across the middle. Janey, with two bands of white at breasts and buttocks, smiled at him and walked toward him.

They met near the bed. He grabbed her in a stagy, Hollywood way, pulling her to him dramatically and pressing his lips against hers. His hand cupped the heavy globes of her bare breast. She was aware of the need of his lust.

They tumbled down toward the bed.

In silence they grappled, body moving against body, his hands roaming her, his lips going over every square inch of her body, resting now on the deep socket of her navel, going now to the hard rock of her left nipple, then to the satiny surface of her leg. He was snorting like a stallion as he caressed her sleek body.

In short order they were both panting and gasping in anticipation of ecstasy. Then he pulled his surprise. Without a word, he rolled her over so that she lay face down on the bed Then he fell at her.

She felt hands grasping her. Tugging at her tender flesh.

"Hey, what are you doing?"

"Please, darling. This is very important to me," he murmured.

"You're hurting me!"

"That'll just be for a moment. This is the way I most enjoy myself!"

Her heart pounded. She had never done anything like this before, not even when she was selling herself. Of all her luck, she thought. First the spanking bit, and now this. Why did she only pick up the quirky ones, she wondered?

But the spanking had been relatively harmless. This was agony.

He went at her like a madman, slipping his hands onto the round, dangling globes of her breasts, and holding her, drawing her toward him.

There was a moment of fire.

And then there were his hoarse gasps of wild ecstasy. Janey felt him shudder, move against her, with sudden burgeoning pain. And then, just as suddenly, that was over. They both slumped forward on the bed. The pain wasn't so bad, now. Just a kind of dull throbbing.

He was covering her with kisses. Her back, her neck, her ears, her cheeks, everywhere that he could reach. She lay on her side with her back to him.

He whispered, "Did I hurt you badly?"

"I'll live."

"I'm sorry if I took you by surprise. I didn't know if you'd agree to that or not, and this means so much to me, loving this way. I'll never forget this afternoon, Janey. Never in my life."

He cupped her breasts and kissed the nape of her neck. She was silent. The pain was ebbing away, but she suspected she was going to be uncomfortable for a few days afterward.

But he'd pay through the nose for his twisted little moment of pleasure, she thought. That was a comforting bit of knowledge.

There was a knock at the door.

"Room Service," a bellhop called.

Janey smiled. Mark Avery rose from the bed, got his bathrobe on. Nude, she stretched out voluptuously on the bed like a big panther.

He'd pay, all right. Five hundred bucks in cash for the pleasure.

Plus a caviar sandwich.

CHAPTER SEVEN

Charley watched her leave the beach with the short guy in the red suit. He didn't exactly approve of Janey's choice of victim, this time. This guy looked like a kook, with his well-developed weight-lifting muscles and his tight shorts and his little clipped mustache. Charley wished that she would stick to the middle-aged guys. They were safer. Somebody who looked like this was too unpredictable. Charley thought.

The arrangement he had made with Janey was that he would wait on the beach until she got back. If she didn't show up by six o'clock or so, he was to go back to the apartment, and she'd take a cab back. It was just about noon now, so there was plenty of time to go.

Charley relaxed.

He stretched out in the warm sunlight and dreamed sweet dreams of money.

After a while, he opened his eyes and glanced around. And he noticed a very interesting sight no more than a dozen yards away. Two girls had appeared and put down their blanket near him. The girl on the far side was a brunette in a bikini, sleeping with her back toward him, and he couldn't tell anything about her. But the one nearer him—

She was worth looking at.

She was a blonde, and a big one, in all possible directions. Her legs were long—she looked like a six-footer, Charley thought—and her skin was tanned the lovely deep honey color that only a blonde's skin can get. Her golden hair glowed like spun metal in the noon sunlight. She was wearing a bikini that was almost as skimpy as the one Janey had on, and he could see the firm side of one buttock half exposed by the suit.

She had opened the straps of her halter so that her back could get an even tan. And she was giving Charley the eye. He smiled at her. She smiled back. That was where matters stood for maybe three minutes.

Then, lazily, she lifted herself off the blanket. Not far. Maybe three inches. That was far enough so that Charley got a good side view of her nearer breast, round and pale, clearly visible in the curve of her arm. Then she turned, ever so slightly. The nipple, which had been hidden under the swell of the breast as she lay face down, peeked into sight.

Charley got a real good view. He could only see one of her breasts, but he saw that all, a firm, massive round of flesh, a mammoth boob indeed. The nipple was red and tall.

The view lasted perhaps thirty seconds. Charley was the only person on the beach in a position to take advantage of that, and he let his eyes rest on the delicious sight as long as he could. Then she shifted position again, turning the other way and lying down so that once again her breasts were covered by her body. But before she turned her face away from him, she winked.

Charley contemplated the situation for a long moment.

He didn't feel that he had any particular responsibility toward Janey. They weren't man and wife. The deal under which he had brought her down here hadn't said anything about fidelity.

He didn't particularly want to make Janey jealous, because, after all, she was his meal ticket. She was uniquely qualified for the kind of stuff they were pulling, because of her knack for looking like a teenager at the right moment. It would be impossible for him to work the routine, say, with this busty blonde over here. He'd only get a horse laugh in the face if he tried to claim she was underage. But Janey looked convincing, and with Janey the gambit could work. So he needed her.

But she was off pleasuring a mark right now, and he figured there wasn't any reason why he couldn't make some time while she was gone. At least set up a deal for himself, a little amusement on the side.

After a while he got up and ambled across the short distance separating him from the blonde. He dropped down on the sand next to her and said, "You ought to be more careful when you turn over, miss. You might get arrested for indecent exposure."

She turned her head toward him, again displaying a bare breast, this time for a fraction of a second. She grinned and said, "Are you going to report me?"

"I doubt that."

"Some men find the sight of a woman's body repulsive," she said.

"I like girls," he said. "Honest, I do."

Her eyes sparkled. "What's your name?"

"Charley Simmons."

"Zelda Morton. This is my sister Doreen who's asleep over here."

"One blonde sister and one brunette?"

"Different mothers," Zelda said. "Same father. We're half sisters. Should I wake her up and let you say hello to her?"

"Not till I get to know you a little better," Charley said. "Where you from, Zelda?"

"New York City."

"That's a nice place to be away from at this time of year. What do you do?"

"Television. I'm an actress."

"Doreen too?"

"She's with a public relations company. How about you, big boy?"

"I'm retired," he said. "I clip coupons for a living these days."

"How'd you make your pile?"

"Selling falsies," Charley said. "I built a better falsie and all the women in the country bought a dozen. I was a millionaire when I was twenty-two years old."

"I can tell you one girl who didn't give you any business," Zelda said.

"So I noticed. Well, you can't sell 'em all."

"You're putting me on, aren't you?"

"How'd you guess?"

"Funny man. What do you really do for a living?"

"I'm a blackmailer," Charley said.

"How exciting! Does it pay well?"

"So-so," he said.

"You could blackmail us, if you like," Zelda said. "We sleep together. We find each other very attractive, Doreen and I."

"Sure," he said. "I bet you do. You're such a tremendous Lesbian that you showed your body off to the nearest man on the beach."

"Maybe I'm bisexual." she said.

"Hey, that sounds like fun!"

"That sure is," Zelda said. "Why don't you come up to our room for an orgy and find out?"

"What room is it?"

"Room 1114. Right here in the Tropical Beach. I'll wake Doreen up and we'll all go right now."

Charley couldn't tell whether she was pulling his leg or not, with this talk of sister-sister Lesbianism and orgies and whatever.

He said, "I can't go right now. Can I take a rain check until tomorrow?"

"What's the hitch today?"

"I'm waiting for someone to meet me here on the beach. I can't leave."

"Male or female?"

"Female, as a matter-of-fact. My—ah—sister," Charley said.

Zelda grinned at him. "Is she pretty?"

"I think so."

"Do you sleep with her?"

"None of your business," he said.

"That's a serious thing when a man sleeps with his sister," she told him. "Much more serious than a girl sleeping with her sister, I think."

"You're a real kook, aren't you?" Charley said.

"You started it. With your business about being a falsie millionaire."

"Just a false millionaire," he said. "Do we have a date for tomorrow?"

"Sure," she said. "Room 1114. You and me and Doreen."

"The three of us?"

"What else? Get there around one in the afternoon, okay? We'll be waiting for you."

"Will do," Charley said.

She winked at him. Then, just for encouragement, she pried herself up from the blanket and gave him a quick look at both breasts at once, two huge round globes of firm flesh, before she pulled her halter on.

"I'm going for a swim," she announced. "We'll see you tomorrow. Don't be late."

Charley stayed on the beach when Zelda and Doreen left, a few hours later. Janey still wasn't back. It had turned out that he would have had time after all to hop up to Zelda's room for a little action, but he hadn't had any way of knowing that. If Janey had come back and found him gone, there would have been trouble.

There was always tomorrow, he thought. He'd find some way to get rid of Janey—send her off on a shopping expedition. And then he'd have a ball with Zelda. With Doreen too, if she really was part of the deal, it was hard to tell whether anything Zelda said made sense.

The afternoon ticked away. Three o'clock, four o'clock, five o'clock. Charley was just about deciding to leave the beach and go back to the apartment to wait for Janey, when she showed up. She was alone.

She looked annoyed.

"What happened?" Charley asked. "Didn't you make out with him?"

"I made out all right," Janey said. "If you want to call what he did making out."

"I don't get you."

"He's got certain peculiarities."

"You mean he's a spanker, too?" Charley asked.

Janey shook her head. "Uh-uh. Not that again. He just has odd ways of loving."

"Like—?"

Janey told him.

"He talked you into that?"

"He didn't exactly talk to me," Janey said. "That was more like a rape. I didn't know what was going on until too late."

"Did he hurt you?"

"I'll live. But make him bleed in the checkbook, Charley. There ought to be an extra high price for that kind of thing."

"What arrangements did you make with him?"

"He's supposed to take me out for dinner at seven o'clock. I'm meeting him in the lobby of the hotel here for drinks first."

Charley got to his feet and began rolling up his beach blanket. He said, "Let's get back to the apartment, then. We'll get you into costume and pay a visit to him. What's his name?"

"Mark Avery."

"Sissy name. Mark."

"Hit him good, Charley. Hold him up for a thousand bucks. He deserves to pay big for that."

"You poor kid," Charley said. "You ever do that sort of stuff before?"

"Never. And never again. I hope."

He shook his head. "I don't understand what makes some guys tick. I just don't figure them at all. They get on a bed with a beautiful girl and they've got to pull a stunt like that."

"Did you ever make out like that with a woman, Charley?" Janey asked.

"Me?" He laughed. "Baby, I'm not perfect, but I'm not peculiar either. The good old way is good enough for me. Always has been. Come on, let's go."

They left the beach and went back to the Imperial. Charley's mind was not really on Janey or her problems with the new mark. He was thinking about Zelda and Doreen, and the possible delights they would have to offer when he went to their hotel room.

But that was tomorrow, and there was money to earn tonight. Big money, at that.

He took a shower and got into some decent clothes while Janey dolled herself up in her Lolita outfit. Then they drove back to the Tropical Beach Hotel, going in the main way this time instead of going to the beach entrance at the side.

The elevator swooshed them up to the floor where Mark Avery's room was. The time quarter to seven. Charley knocked.

"Who is it?" a voice called from within.

Charley nudged Janey. She said, "It's Janey, Mark."

"You're early."

"I know. I thought I'd come right on up to your room."

"I'm not quite ready."

"I don't mind," Janey said. "Let me come in. I'll wait for you,"

"Okay."

The door opened. Charley grabbed the doorknob and pushed it inward, and got the wedge of his foot in there too, and followed on into the room, with Janey right behind him. Mark Avery was wearing black slacks and a white shirt, and there was a white dinner jacket laid out on the bed. He blinked and goggled at Charley in surprise.

"What is this?" he snapped. "Who are you?"

"Janey's brother. I came to tell you a thing or two, you stinking little creep."

Avery stared at Janey. His eyes went wide at her looks in the teenager costume.

"What's going on?" he asked her. "Janey, who is he? Why aren't you dressed for dinner?"

"He's my brother," Janey said in her high-pitched little-girl voice.

"I feel like mopping up the floor with you," Charley muttered. "Of all the stuff to pull. Abusing a seventeen-year-old girl!"

"Seventeen?"

"That's right. Seventeen years old and you've got to try your perverted acts with her. Don't you have any decency? No, I guess you don't. She told me the whole story. How you raped her and all."

Avery seemed to be trembling. "Listen, you expect me to believe that she's only s-seventeen?"

"Take a look at her."

"I never dreamed—I had no way of knowing—"

"Well get the book thrown at you, Avery. Statutory rape, just for a beginning. And then there's the little matter of your abusive technique. I don't know what the penalty is for that in this state—maybe ten years, maybe twenty, something like that. To take a teenage girl and do that—they ought to put you away for life, you filthy stinking slob!"

Avery shrank back against the dresser. He said, "Look here, I didn't know how young she was. She acted like a sophisticated woman."

"She does that, sometimes. But she's really just a wild kid. That doesn't excuse you, though. There's no excuse for a guy like you."

"Have—have you called the police yet?"

"Not yet. I wanted to get a look at you first, see what kind of creep you were."

Avery's tongue furtively flickered out to moisten his lips. He seemed to be on the edge of a nervous collapse. He said, "Maybe we can keep the police out of this. There's no need to bring them in."

"You want me just to forget that you touched my sister?"

"I'll make this worth your while," Avery said. "If I've done something wrong, I'm prepared to offer some—some compensation to the injured party. But if I go to jail, what good does that do your sister? Let me pay you something instead. You can use the money for—for anything, for sending her to college, whatever you like. That's much more constructive, isn't it? Isn't it?"

Charley slowly folded his arms. "What kind of compensation you got in mind?" he asked quietly.

Avery shrugged. "Two hundred dollars?"

"Don't make me laugh."

"Two hundred's a lot of money," Avery said.

Charley turned to Janey. "Come on, Sis. Let's go file a complaint against this pervert."

"Wait! Let's make it three hundred!"

"You got yourself a six thousand dollar automobile, mister," Charley said. "You got yourself a thirty buck a day room in this hotel. And then you take an innocent little girl and scar her personality for life, and you're only willing to pay three hundred bucks for that? You make me want to spit in your face."

A muscle flickered in Mark Avery's cheek. "All right," he said. "How much do you want?"

"A thousand dollars," Charley said.

Avery seemed to sag. "A thousand dollars?"

"You repeat real good. Let's get out of here, Sis. There's a stench in here that I don't like."

"No," Avery said. "Don't go yet. Will you take five hundred?"

"A thousand," Charley said. He had settled for five hundred from Morton Kolb, but this guy seemed to be even wealthier. Besides, he had done a filthy thing with Janey, and Charley figured he ought to pay double for that, if not more.

Avery sat down on the bed and put his head in his hands. All the fight was gone from him. The heavy tan, the built-up muscles—they were nothing but a facade. He had no nerve at all

"I didn't mean any harm," he whimpered. "I had no way of knowing—"

"Okay, okay. Spare us the tears."

"I don't have a thousand dollars in cash on me," Avery said. "Can we work out an arrangement?"

"Such as?"

"I'll give you two hundred in cash and the rest by check."

"Which you stop payment on the moment I'm out the door. Uh-uh."

"What else can I do? How can I pay you?"

"The hotel will cash a check for you," Charley said. "Phone the manager. Work something out."

"That's a lot of money to ask them for."

"Phone them," Charley said.

Avery phoned. It took him a while to get the manager. It took him a longer while to persuade the manager to cash a check of that size. But finally he wangled an agreement. Avery's credit was pretty good at the Tropical Beach, it appeared.

He put down the phone, finally.

"They'll have the money ready in half an hour," he said in a hoarse voice.

CHAPTER EIGHT

Back at the apartment, they divided the money.

No traveler's checks to bother about, this time. Just good old crisp greenbacks, straight from Washington, D. C. to the pockets of Charley Simmons and Janey Vaughn, with a minor detour along the way.

"Fifty for you, fifty for me, fifty for you, fifty for me, there we are," Charley finished. "Five hundred clams apiece."

"I can't believe it, Charley."

"You don't need to believe it. Just enjoy it. You oughta open a bank account now."

"You think so?"

"That's a lot of cash to carry around loose."

Janey grinned. "I expect to unload some of it tomorrow in the stores."

"You aren't going to spend the whole five hundred, are you?"

"A good chunk of it. I need some clothes. I don't have enough clothes."

"Right now it looks like you got too many," Charley said. "On you, I mean."

"But I've been poor so long. I want to dress up fancy, Charley. I'm going to get myself all the things I've always wanted. An ounce of 'Joy' and a pair of gold Florentine finish earrings, and a couple of low-necked dresses, and a cashmere sweater, and—"

"I take it back," Charley said. "You don't need no bank account. What you need's a business manager to watch your money for you."

"There's no sense not spending it once you've got it, Charley. That's what it's for, isn't it?"

"Sure," he said. "But what do you do when it's all gone?"

"Go out and get some more. Look how fast we got ourselves fifteen hundred bucks down here. There were whole years I didn't make that much money, and here we have this inside of two weeks."

"It's not always that easy to get it."

Her eyes glittered. "I think it is," she said. "Once you learn the trick. You've got to know the ropes, that's all. Anyway, I've denied myself all kinds of goodies for too long. There's time to start saving money next week or the week after. Tomorrow I'm going to splurge."

"What time are you going on this shopping expedition of yours?"

"Oh, I don't know. The afternoon, I guess. I hadn't thought about it."

"Go around half past twelve, one o'clock," Charley said.

"Why?"

"Because you'll be by yourself anyway then. I got an appointment."

"Oh? With who?"

"An old friend of mine. A guy I used to know at the track, at Hialeah. I met him on the beach this afternoon while I was waiting for you to come back. He invited me to go over to his place and have a couple of drinks with him tomorrow."

"Okay," Janey said. "You go visit your pal, and I'll go visit the stores. And we'll all live happily ever after."

"Sure thing," Charley said. He gathered up his share of the night's haul and tucked it into his wallet. Then he stood up and began to peel away his clothing.

Janey stripped too.

When they were both nude, he reached for her, yanked her firm, taut-globed body against his, pulled her lips to his mouth.

"We're gonna have a celebration again now," he said. "I forgot to pick up the champagne, but that don't really matter, does that?"

"No," she said. "We can get along without the champagne, baby."

They tumbled down onto the bed. His hand went to the warmth of her. Her nipples began to rise and swell as he touched her.

He said, "I'm gonna make you forget all about what that guy did this afternoon. I'm gonna remind you what the real thing is like."

She sighed. The next moment her arms were around him. He moved, and she returned a counterassault of her own. And then they began to work, slowly at first, then more rapidly, racing with headlong frenzy toward the blazing culmination of their breathless passion.

After lunch the next day, Charley drove over to the Tropical Beach Hotel. He was a little queasy about revisiting the scene of the crime, because if he ran into Mark Avery there might be a sticky scene. He had told Avery to check out and leave Miami Beach, and most likely Avery was gone, since he had seemed so scared stiff of that statutory rape and the other rap. But there was always that one chance in a hundred that he had firmed up and called the cops to tell them about the extortion bit. In that case, it might just be that the cops were waiting in the Tropical Beach lobby to pick up anyone who matched Charley's description.

But he decided to risk it. The invitation from Zelda was too good to pass up. Anyway, there were ninety-nine chances out of a hundred that the sniveling little Avery had taken his weight-lifter muscles and clipped mustache out of Miami Beach on the first plane of the morning, afraid that Charley would pocket the thousand dollars and then report him for his misdeed anyway.

He didn't run into any cops in the hotel lobby, nor did he see Mark Avery, nor were there any hitches of any other kind. He went straight through to the bank of elevators and rode up to the eleventh floor.

It was exactly one o'clock when Charley knocked on the door of Room 1114.

"Coming, lover!" sang out Zelda's rich contralto voice.

She opened the door. All she was wearing was a kind of terry-cloth beach robe that came down to her legs. Her lower portion was exposed. She was pretty exposed above that point too, because she had left the terry-cloth robe unbelted and that hung wide open. Charley had an excellent view of the round, heavy, jutting mounds of her breasts, and of other things too. She had the blue eyes and the honey-tanned skin that went with a real blonde.

He stepped in. She closed the door.

"You're right on time," she said.

"I like to be punctual when beautiful women are involved."

Zelda smiled. In a deliberately provocative way she drew the front of her robe together and tied the belt. That hid her breasts from view, but not much else.

When she turned, he could see the lower halves of her buttocks exposed where the skimpy robe ended. She walked across the room and stooped to pick up something from the floor, bending forward so that the robe rode up on her hips and put the entire area of her buttocks on display.

That wasn't very subtle, Charley thought. But that was certainly plenty effective. She had ripe, firm buttocks, milky-white in contrast to the deeper tan elsewhere.

Straightening up, she said, "Doreen's taking a shower. She'll be out any minute. Relax and have yourself a drink. The bar's over there."

Charley followed her pointing finger. Along the top of the dresser were arrayed various liquor bottles. It was quite an assortment. Charley sauntered over and saw Scotch, bourbon, rye, gin, vodka, light and dark rum. Plus an ice bucket and a few bottles of miscellaneous mixers.

"You're all stocked up, aren't you?" he asked.

Zelda grinned. "We like to be hospitable to our guests. Fix yourself a drink."

"Can I fix you one first?"

"I've got one," Zelda said. She indicated a highball sitting on a low table next to an arm chair. She flopped down in the chair and picked up the drink. The hem of her robe rose four inches, baring her from the navel down. She seemed unconcerned about her semi-nudity.

Standing by the dresser, Charley glanced at her in the mirror, letting his glance ride over the reflection of her body from ankles to calves to knees to upper legs to bare middle. His hand shook a little as he reached for the bourbon bottle. He still couldn't figure this deal out. Zelda hadn't been kidding when she said that Doreen would be on hand too. Was he supposed to love them both? Or just make Zelda while Doreen stood by and cheered? Or what?

He dropped two ice cubes in his glass and lowered himself into another armchair just across the television set from Zelda. Zelda had pulled her legs up onto the chair with her knees flexed and just far enough apart to make the view both highly shameless and highly distracting. Charley figured there was no sense being prudish, so he took a good long look at the merchandise that was being so casually put on display.

There was a pounding in his chest as excitement rose for him. For the last couple of weeks he had been with a brunette, Janey. But blondes had a special fascination all their own. And he had always like variety in his love life.

He hoped that Janey had an entertaining shopping trip this afternoon.

He was pretty sure that he was in for an entertaining time.

The bathroom door opened. Doreen came out. All she was wearing was a towel wrapped around her middle, sarong-fashion, leaving her breasts bare. Charley looked at her. She was a tall, willowy brunette, built a lot like Janey, but with smaller breasts and narrower hips. Doreen wasn't a voluptuous girl like her blonde sister or half-sister

Zelda. But she was anything but unattractive.

She took five paces into the room before she appeared to realize that there was a man present. Then she looked at Charley and smiled and said, "Oh, our company is here! Hello, company."

"Hello," Charley said.

Zelda said, "Charley Simmons, my half-sister Doreen Morton. Charley's the man I met on the beach yesterday while you were asleep."

"Pleased," Doreen said.

"Mutual," Charley said.

Doreen crossed diagonally in front of him and went to the bar to fix a drink for herself. He eyed the reflection to her breasts in the mirror. Small high pointed breasts they were. A nice contrast to Zelda's opulent fleshiness, Charley thought.

As Doreen busied herself with the drinks, Zelda snaked out a foot. She hooked a toe into the towel Doreen was wearing, and yanked. The knot in the towel opened and the towel dropped to the floor.

Doreen was nude underneath. She went right on mixing her drink without bothering to cover herself. Her buttocks were slender and very pink. Charley studied her from top to toe. He liked what he saw.

When she had put her drink together, the dark-haired girl, still completely nude, walked back across the room and sat down on the edge of the bed. She took a sip of the drink. Her nudity was apparently a matter of no concern at all to her. In a pleasantly conversational voice she said, "I hear that you're a blackmailer by profession, Mr. Simmons. Is that right?"

"Sure," he said, figuring that the best way to make it seem like a joke was to go along with the gag. "Sure, I'm a blackmailer. Though in the trade we prefer to refer to ourselves as extortionists."

"How exciting," Doreen said.

"And I hear that you and Zelda make love with each other," Charley said.

Doreen smiled. "That's right. We're very fond of each other. That's only half-incest because we're only half-sisters. But we also like men. Don't we, Zelda?"

"Naturally," Zelda said.

Charley frowned. Were they pulling his leg or not? He said, "Which do you find better? A man, or each other?"

"That depends," Doreen said.

"On our mood," said Zelda. "And on how good the man is. Are you a good lover, Charley?"

"I like to think I am," he said.

"Why don't you get undressed, then?" Zelda suggested. "After all, here are the two of us sitting around without clothes, and you're fully dressed. That isn't really proper."

"I guess that isn't," Charley said. He put his drink down, got to his feet, and began to undress. The two girls watched him with keen interest.

This was the craziest situation he had ever been in in his life. These two kooks were completely deadpan, and they seemed to be inviting him to a genuine orgy. But they didn't look depraved. Just two nice clean-cut kids from New York who liked their fun on the wild side.

All the same, he felt odd about that. Their nakedness, when they were so casual about that, was weird to him. And the idea of just undressing in front of two strange girls—

No sense being inhibited, he thought. He took off his shirt and his shoes, dropped his trousers, paused for a sip of his drink, and slipped out of his shorts.

"Very nice," Zelda commented.

"I think so too," said Doreen.

Charley said, "Now you're the only one who's wearing anything, Zelda."

"So I am, so I am." The blonde girl smiled, rose, shrugged off her bathrobe. For the first time Charley saw her completely nude. She was a stunning sight, six feet of utterly magnificent woman, heavy-breasted and heavy-hipped and heavy-legged, but yet not fat. Just big. A love goddess modeled along the lines of a movie star. Charley didn't make the comparison out loud. He figured that Zelda had heard that often enough by now to be pretty sick of that.

Now all three of them were naked. A cozy little cocktail party.

Zelda said, "How do you feel about Lesbians, Charley?"

"I've never really thought much about them, I guess," he said.

"Does that disgust you?" Doreen asked. "The thought of one woman going to bed with another?"

"Not really. That strikes me as kind of interesting, in a way."

"Have you ever seen two Lesbians loving?" Zelda asked.

"No. Never."

"Do you want to?"

Charley hesitated. "Are you two going to stage a show for me?"

"That's what we had in mind," Doreen admitted. "Of course, if you find the idea repugnant—"

"I don't think he does," Zelda said. "Look at him. Look how excited he's getting."

Doreen looked. Charley didn't need to look. He knew what was going on, knew that his state of excitement was becoming obvious. He reddened.

Zelda said, "What we thought was, we'd put on a show for you, and then you could love us afterward. How does that strike you?"

"I'm not able to love you both at the same time," Charley pointed out.

"Oh, we can work things out," Zelda said. "Don't worry about that."

"We've done this kind of thing before," said Doreen. "We've had experience at this."

Charley took a long gulp of his drink. Weirder and weirder, he thought. To fall into the clutches of two exhibitionistic Lesbo sisters, to get himself invited to a wingding of an orgy—

Well, why not?

"Sure," he said. "I'm game."

"Let's all have another drink first," Zelda said. "Then we'll begin."

Charley acted as bartender. He mixed a fresh drink for Zelda, then one for Doreen, carrying them to the girls. That seemed to him as though they were starting to shed their casual attitude. Now that the fun and conversation was over, they were getting excited, getting steamed up. Doreen's nipples rose tall from her small pale breasts. Zelda's big boobs were starting to go up and down with increasing rapidity.

They had their drinks. Quickly.

Then Zelda got to her feet, stretching voluptuously, her huge breasts swaying. She smiled warmly at Charley and said, "Any time you feel like joining us on the bed, go right ahead and pile on. Let's go, Doreen."

The blonde-haired sister rose and walked toward the bed, where Doreen awaited her.

The orgy was about to begin.

Charley detected a moment of self-consciousness as both girls stretched out on the bed. But only for a moment. They smiled at each other, and that was though an invisible curtain had come down, locking them off into a private room of their own without an audience.

Doreen reached out a hand, found the heavy globe of Zelda's right breast. Doreen's slender fingers cupped the breast, and a dark red nipple peeped through. Zelda began to gasp and move on the bed.

Charley leaned forward on the edge of his chair. His heart began to thump. There was something terrifically exciting about the sight of these two women, the blonde one and the dark, the voluptuous one and the slender, beginning to move on the bed, to entangle themselves in one another's arms, to twist and turn and gyrate.

They were kissing, now. Body pressed against body, lips meeting—a passionate kiss, Charley figured—hands clasped to breasts. Muscles tightening. Bodies beginning to produce the rhythms of passion.

A cold sweat burst out on him. The temptation was great, almost overpowering, to go over there and throw himself at those two nude forms, pull them apart, quench the fire of his lusts with one or the other. But he waited. He wanted to see the whole show first.

Things were getting more interesting over there. Doreen was flat on her back and Zelda was attending her diligently. Charley heard muffled gasping sounds of pleasure from Doreen. He stood up to get a better view of her face, and saw that her expression was distorted with excitement, the eyes tight shut, the nostrils wide, the mouth pulled down in a twisted slash.

Then the positions changed. Doreen was working, Zelda giving herself up to pleasure. Zelda lay on her side, her firm ripe buttocks pointing toward Charley.

Doreen was very, very busy.

That went on and on for an endless time. Harsh, hoarse ragged sounds of ecstatic breathing filled the room. Charley had always wondered how Lezies performed, and now he was finding out. And how he was finding out!

And now Doreen was lying with Zelda, as though she were a man.

"That's good!" Zelda was shouting. "Yes, yes, I'm close, I'm close!"

The scene grew wilder. Body worked against active body. Big firm breasts pushed against small hard ones. Nipples touched.

Then there was a long hissing cry of ecstasy. Charley couldn't tell which of the sisters had produced that. Perhaps both at once, he thought. They were all wrapped up, working at a frantic pace, working hard toward the summit of bliss. A moment later they seemed to get there, both of them at the same moment, and they subsided.

They lay limply in each other's arms, breathing hard, bodies dappled with sweat. Their nude forms seemed fantastically attractive to Charley Simmons.

He couldn't be a spectator any longer. He was bursting with desire. Now was the time for him to join the fun.

Charley walked toward the bed. He stood over them for a moment, looking down. Their eyes were closed. Doreen had her hands to Zelda's big breasts. Zelda's hands were resting quietly on Doreen's breasts. The scene was very peaceful. Like babes in the wood, Charley thought. He ached with desire.

He put his hand to Doreen's buttocks. They were cool, satiny to the touch. He ran his fingers along her back. She stirred. Her eyes fluttered open. She smiled at him.

"Okay, big boy. I'm ready for you."

Zelda lifted her head. "And so am I."

"Who goes first?" Charley asked.

"I do," Doreen said. "I'm the older one."

"I do," said Zelda. "I'm better."

"Says who?"

"Says me."

"Let's flip for this, girls," Charley said. He pivoted around and picked up an ash tray that had the hotel's monogram on its upper surface. "Heads or tails," he said. "You call the turn, Zelda."

He threw the ash tray into the air. The disk spun as it rose toward the ceiling.

"Tails," Zelda said.

Charley caught the ash tray and pressed it against the back of his left hand. The monogram side was uppermost. He grinned at Doreen. "Looks like you're the lucky one," he said.

"I'll get my turn," Zelda said.

The two sisters pulled him down onto the bed. Charley was lost in a tangle of arms and legs, of warm bodies, of breasts and buttocks. He felt a hard nipple against his lips, and he moved his mouth to take advantage of the offering. From the bulk of the breast that the nipple was attached to, Charley guessed that must belong to Zelda. He groped out with his other hand and encountered smooth cool buttocks. Doreen's, he figured. He couldn't see a thing. The girls had him surrounded.

Suddenly he was aware of some very special action. A moment later, whoever had been obscuring his view moved, and as the body moved a way, letting him see again, he discovered that Doreen had begun her turn, had started to enjoy the passionate rhythms of love.

Charley worked with her. Once again he wasn't able to see what he was doing, because Zelda had wrapped her big arms around his neck, and all he could see was the generous swell of her breasts. That was all right. He didn't need to see in order to keep these girls happy. His body kept up a steady pace, satisfying Doreen. Meanwhile he pushed his face forward against the warmth of Zelda, loving her the best way he could at the moment.

Zelda seemed to enjoy his attentions. She gasped and cried and thrashed around. He got his hands to the heavy globes of her buttocks, cupping the firm flesh. In her ecstasy she tightened her throttlehold on his neck, nearly choking him, but he shifted to a new position where he could breathe again.

He didn't have much idea of how Doreen was getting along, since his view of her was completely blocked by Zelda. But he had the idea that Doreen was doing all right. She was still working, and he could sense the thrills of delight that went shuddering over her every few seconds.

In another couple of moments he had each sister gasping with delight. Doreen was the first one to reach her full ecstasy. She went into a wild frenzy, gripping him tightly, her body rolling and thrashing. She took her pleasure from him, and at the same exciting instant Charley took his, too.

And then Zelda let out a hoarse whoop of pleasure and clamped her arms tight around him once again. Charley closed his eyes and sucked in air. After a breathless moment she relaxed.

All three of them lay still. They were curled in a tangled knot on the bed. Charley felt exhausted, depleted. They were a pretty wild team, these two.

They rested.

He fell into a light doze. He knew that he still owed Zelda a round— the way he had pleasured her didn't really count as the full thing—but first he wanted to get this strength back. Mercifully, Zelda wasn't in any hurry for her turn.

Charley dropped deeper and deeper into sleep. He didn't have any idea how long he was out, but he was awakened after what could have been ten minutes or five hours by the steady creaking of the bedsprings.

Zelda and Doreen were loving again.

He was lying diagonally across the bed, and they had settled down on the far corner. They were in each other's arms, and their bodies were busy, breasts pushing breasts, nipples touching with steady passion.

Charley propped himself up and watched. There was a creepy fascination to that. These two long-legged girls loving each other a few feet from him—all that sleek flesh.

Excitement swelled for him afresh.

Doreen and Zelda weren't paying any attention to him at all. They were off in that private world of theirs again, the world where nothing existed except the body of the other. Charley watched them, and waited until they were right at the peak of excitement.

Then, as they gasped through the intensity of their ecstasy, Charley moved again.

"My turn," he said to Zelda. "And yours."

He fell at her breasty blonde body. She was still dazed from her experience with Doreen. Charley took her so rapidly that that must have seemed to her like one continuous fling, different only in nature.

His body whipped into action. She was a big, strong, healthy girl, and she took his assault without any trouble. The giant cushions of her breasts were good to rest against. Her powerful arms held him in a wild embrace.

While he was loving Zelda, Doreen lay curled around them both. There didn't seem to be much passion left for Doreen, at least not at the moment. The brunette was content just to touch them. She had her hands resting lightly on Charley as though helping him with her sister.

The moment of pleasure was not long in arriving. For Charley, for Zelda.

They rested once again.

"Have a drink," Doreen said. "That'll pep you up, Charley."

"Sure," he said. "Sure."

They had drinks. Then they scampered into the shower, all three of them, and got under the nozzle together. That was the wildest shower Charley had ever taken in his life. The girls were prankish and playful, soaping him and running their hands all over him, Zelda letting him run his soapy hands over the swelling hillocks of her breasts and buttocks, cold cascades of water coming down over all three of them all the time.

After the shower, they went back to bed.

More loving was on the schedule.

Charley wasn't sure which girl he was loving at any one time. Everything was getting blurred, now. Reality was dissolving. He thought vaguely of Janey and wondered what time it was. Then she drifted out of his mind again and he busied himself with the small hard globe of Doreen's nearer breast.

The fun and frolic went on and on.

That went right on to the point of exhaustion—and kept going past that point. Charley drove his weary body to new heights of achievement. But there had to be a limit somewhere, and the limit was reached. He reached that while he was trying to love Zelda for the third or fourth time around. He just couldn't do that. Even with the skillful help from both girls, he couldn't manage. There was nothing to be ashamed of, he knew, not after what he had been through this afternoon. He was only human, after all.

With a goofy smile on his face, Charley lay back, pillowing himself against the thrusting mounds of Zelda's fantastic breasts. He patted the cool firmness of Doreen's nearby buttocks. Then he closed his eyes.

He dropped off into the bottomless well of exhausted sleep.

CHAPTER NINE

Janey had a busy day. And an expensive one, in the bargain.

She had pretty near run through the five hundred dollars that was her share of last night's take. She had distributed her money with gay abandon. It had been a heady, exhilarating feeling to toss twenty-dollar bills around like pennies. It was a wild and joyous thing to do, like stripping naked and getting loved by a whole regiment of movie stars in Times Square.

Now the apartment was festooned with the afternoon's haul. Dresses and jewelry and perfume, handbags and shoes, another bikini or two, frills and laces—Janey had bought as though all the stores for women were being shut down by government decree the next day. She couldn't wait for Charley to get home so she could show everything off to him, model her new clothes, prance around in her shortie nightgown and her practically off-the-bosom cocktail sheath and all the rest.

But where was he?

Janey had returned from her shopping spree at half past five. The apartment had been empty. Now, after everything was unpacked, it was well after six, and still no sign of him. He had said that he was going to spend the afternoon with an old pal from his Hialeah days. All right, that was the afternoon. But the afternoon was over. Was he going to leave her stranded for the evening? They hadn't made any arrangements, but Janey had figured they'd go out together for dinner tonight, by way of celebrating last night's thousand-dollar kitty.

Seven o'clock came.

And went.

Janey was getting hungry, and more and more irritated with each passing minute. She waited until half past seven, feeling like a suburban housewife whose hubby has failed to show up for dinner. Angrily, she went into the kitchenette, opened a couple of cans, slung together a quick dinner for herself. She had counted on something much fancier than that for tonight.

Eight o'clock. Eight thirty. Nine.

Now Janey began to worry. At first she had simply thought he was out getting boozed up with his cronies, but it struck her now that it might be more serious than that. What if he had been arrested? Chilling thought! She could picture it clearly: Charley stepping out of his car on a busy street, cops closing in on him from all sides, handcuffs clicking into place on his wrists.

A tough voice saying, "All right, Simmons, come quietly. You're wanted on an extortion charge. We'll pick up that girl friend of yours later on."

Was that it, Janey wondered? Had Mark Avery filed a complaint? Morton Kolb, maybe? Had they been trying to track them all week?

Would they arrest her next?

She didn't think that Charley would give away the address of their apartment. So she was safe, for the time being. But for how long?

Of course, she realized, she was probably imagining the whole thing. It wasn't too likely that the police had picked him up. Maybe he had been run over by a car, she thought. Splat! A dead man in the middle of the boulevard. Janey shuddered. She couldn't exactly say that she loved Charley Simmons, at least not yet, but she was fond of him. He was a good guy and he was swell in the hay, and he had shown her how to make more money than she had ever dreamed of raking in. She didn't want him to be dead. It was half past nine, now.

Janey's thoughts swung to another tack. Maybe, she thought, he was with another girl. Maybe his "old friend" was female. And he was off in some Gold Coast apartment now, on a bed with a busty wench, banging her for the third or fourth time today, swilling down booze and blearily thinking about going home to Janey.

The idea made Janey seethe with inner fury.

She didn't know why it should. They weren't married, were they? They just shacked up together. He was entitled to step out on the side.

But that wasn't fair. What did another girl have to offer that she didn't?

The least he could do was stay faithful. Here she was, she thought, putting up with all sorts of creeps and sadists for the sake of earning money for him, and he was off having a good time with some other wench, letting her sit home alone at night. Standing her up.

Ten o'clock.

Ten-thirty.

Eleven.

Not knowing whether to be angry or worried, Janey began to undress for bed. She wasn't going to wait up till all hours for him. She got out of her clothing and took a quick shower. Then, just before getting into bed, she unwrapped one of her new necklaces and put it on.

She liked the effect, nude with a necklace dangling over her bare breasts. Too bad Charley wasn't here to see that, she thought. That curve of gold, arching across the rosy-tipped mounds of her bosom, would turn him on. Janey sighed in annoyance. She took the necklace off and put it back in its box.

She began to get into bed. Then the door opened and Charley walked in.

He looked rumpled and seedy and tired, and Janey could smell the liquor on him from across the room. He stood by the door, blinking at her, smiling a feeble smile. Janey, nude and angry, glared back at him.

"Hi," he said.

"You know what time it is?"

"Pretty late, I guess."

"It's almost half past eleven," Janey said. "I thought you were just going away for the afternoon."

"I was," Charley said. He shambled into the room, sat down heavily on a chair, and began to pull his shoes off. "I guess we got kind of tanked up, and I lost track of the time. I closed my eyes for just a second, you see, and next thing I knew it was ten o'clock at night."

"I see," Janey said sourly.

"Look, I'm sorry, kid. It wasn't my fault, really. It could have happened to anyone. An old friend, good liquor, you have a little too much, you doze off—you know how it is."

"Sure," she said. "I know. What's your old friend's name, by the way?"

The question seemed to catch him off balance for a moment "Uhh—Harry," he said.

Janey nodded. "Harry didn't have any girl friends along, did he?"

"What is this, twenty questions?"

"Okay, okay."

She turned and went back toward the bedroom. He stood up and began to pull his clothing off.

"How'd your shopping go today?"

"I spent a pile and I got some nice things. I'd model them for you, but you're probably too sleepy to appreciate them now."

"Show them to me in the morning."

"Sure," she said.

She got into bed and watched him moving around the room, putting his clothes away. Her anger was down to a low simmer, now. Maybe he really had dozed off at his friend's place, she thought. In any case, it wasn't really her business, though it had been inconsiderate of him to leave her alone all evening.

He joined her on the bed.

"You smell like a distillery," she told him.

"We did a lot of serious constructive drinking today," Charley said.

"I bet you did."

"Listen, Janey, I'm sorry. I didn't mean to stay out so late."

"All right already."

"I'll make it up to you tomorrow. We'll go out for a fancy dinner. Anywhere you like. We'll have steaks and cold mashed potatoes and wine and all the trimmings. Okay?"

"Okay."

"Forgive me?"

"Just don't let it happen again," she said. "If you want to go off for the night, say so and I'll make arrangements of my own. But don't just leave me dangling like this. I thought you got killed by a car. Or maybe got picked up by the cops."

"No such luck," he said. "I just had a quiet afternoon hoisting the booze with my old friend Harry." He yawned. "And then a nice nap."

"Okay," she said. "Kiss me and I'll accept your apologies."

His arms curved around her. His lips went to hers. Janey moved against him, her nipples already responding to her passion. After the tension of the long, lonely evening of waiting, she wanted him to take her now, love her, send her off to dreamland.

But there was something casual and offhand about his kiss. He didn't seem excited by the nearness of her nude body. The nipples at his chest failed to draw any notice from him.

His mouth covered hers, briefly. Then he pulled away. That wasn't even a deep kiss.

They lay there quietly in the dark.

"Good night," he said.

"That all? Just good night?"

"I'm tired, Janey."

"You've been sleeping all afternoon. You ought to be wide awake now."

"Look—"

"Raring to go."

"Well, I'm not," he said

"Maybe I can fix that," Janey murmured.

Her body sidled against his. She took one of his hands and put that against the ripe globes of her breasts. He cupped them, but without enthusiasm. Janey let her hand steal over the front of his big body.

He wasn't at all ready for love. He was like an impotent old man of ninety.

"What's the matter?" she said.

"Nothing. I'm tired."

"That tired?"

"That happens sometimes," he said.

"Maybe I can do something about that," Janey said.

Her hand caressed him. But she failed to produce any effect. She had never known him to be like this before. He was always ready for love, night after night, two or three times a night, even.

And now—nothing.

"Let's go to sleep, Janey."

"No. I want you to love me."

"In the morning."

"Now."

"I can't. I'm tired."

"Tired from what?"

"Look, Janey—"

She hissed in annoyance. Taking her hand from him, she pressed her face against him. She moved her lips.

No response.

The caress failed to produce any reaction from him. Now she was certain something was wrong. This above all turned him on, she knew. But this sure wasn't doing any turning on tonight, somehow.

She said, "Harry had a girl for you, didn't he?"

"Come on, Janey. Cut this out!"

"That's the only explanation. This is the first night you haven't loved me since we started traveling together, Charley."

"All right," he growled. "So there was a girl. What of that?"

"You must have had quite a time with her, huh? Once wouldn't exhaust you like that."

"Stop this, Janey. I don't ask you to account to me for where you go when I'm not with you."

"How many times, Charley?"

"There were two of them," he said.

"Huh?"

"As long as you have to know, I'll tell you. I don't have any old friends named Harry. While you were up in the hotel room with that creep yesterday, I got picked up by two girls on the beach. Sisters. A blonde and a brunette, Zelda and Doreen. They invited me to visit them and have some fun today."

"Okay, Charley. I don't want to hear the gory details," Janey said.

"You listen, now. It turned out that they're gay, and when they're not sleeping with men they love each other. So we had a party. I don't know how many times. But finally I fell asleep and when I woke up it was ten o'clock, so I got dressed and cleared out and came home."

Janey bit her hp. "You had yourself a high old time, huh?"

"I did."

"I'm not enough to keep you happy?"

"There was nothing personal to this. This was just a little amusement. Hell, you get enough loving on the side, don't you?"

"Sure," she said. "I sleep with baldheaded old men who spank me, and then I sleep with creepy guys who try disgusting things. Big thrill."

"Can we just drop the whole subject now? I don't plan to see those two girls again. It's you I'm interested in, Janey. You're my partner. You're my girl."

"You aren't much good to me tonight," she said.

"Tomorrow's another night. Just let me rest, will you?"

There was nothing to be gained by badgering him. Janey dropped the subject and let him go to sleep. He dropped off in a few minutes. Janey, in a tense and bitter mood, stayed awake for a while.

Jealousy curdled her thoughts. He had gone off and had an orgy, had he? All right. If he wanted to slip off and have fun on the side, she would too. There were plenty of non-creepy men around here that she could get some pleasure from, she told herself. She'd get even with him for tonight. Letting her stew in this dismal apartment all evening, then not being able to love her when he came home—

She slept, finally.

In the morning, a lot of the tension was gone. She was in a relaxed and even cheerful mood. They slept late, past eleven o'clock, and when they woke Charley said, "How about modeling your new things for me now?"

"Okay," she said. "What do you want to see?"

She began with the jewelry. Nude except for her necklace and bracelet and earrings, she paraded before him, turning and pirouetting to show off the rising hills of her breasts, the firm mounds of her buttocks. His eyes gleamed as he looked her over. The night of sleep had done him some good, she thought.

"You aren't looking at the jewelry," she said.

"There's all that pink stuff underneath," he told her. "Very distracting."

"Then I'll cover up," she said.

She took the new panties and bras out of their boxes and tried them on for him. She pulled her new stockings on over her long, shapely legs. She modeled her new cocktail sheath and her new dresses.

He lay there, watching her, appreciating the show.

"You really spent a mint, huh?" he asked her.

"Easy come, easy go. Money's just green pieces of paper. These things will last me a long time."

She took everything off, got down to scratch again, and tried on her new bikinis for him. He grinned in approval.

Then he said, "I like that all fine. But what I like most of all is what goes underneath the clothing."

"You mean that, Charley?"

"Get over here, baby."

Nude, she went toward him. He gathered her to him. Their lips met, and her breasts pushed against him.

He was still showing some of the after-effects of yesterday's orgy, Janey realized. He wasn't his old swaggering virile self. She got the impression that he was forcing himself, pushing for a love session that he could just as well do without.

But he was making the effort. That was what counted. He had slipped yesterday, but now he was going out of his way to even things up. She was still annoyed with him about yesterday, but not as much as she had been at bedtime.

She moved against him. His response was not very wild at first, but she didn't mind that. All of last night's frustrations were still simmering for her, and she was eager, hungry to have him rid her of them in one wild burst of passion right now.

Charley's enthusiasm grew as he worked. She was aware of that, and her own pleasure was increased. She trembled and hissed and clung to him fervidly.

Charley was snorting and gasping and bellowing like a water buffalo. There was nothing subtle about his technique, Janey thought. He was direct and un-subtle. His idea of pleasuring a woman was to get hold of her and work away.

There was nothing really wrong with that, Janey figured. So long as he could deliver the goods. And Charley could. He had never failed to give her pleasure in bed.

And he wasn't failing now.

Higher and higher she soared, her head spinning, her whole body tingling. Sensual delights radiated over her. She closed her eyes and let the thunder of ecstasy rumble through her.

When that was over, she lay back, alongside Charley. There was an odd sensation of tension still with her. That was strange, Janey thought. Love had always relaxed her in the past. What was the trouble now?

She thought about it and decided that she was still bothered with Charley about last night. That was it. Annoyed with him about staying out so late without telling her where he was going. Annoyed, too, about that wild orgy that he claimed he had taken part in.

Had he really? Two Lesbian sisters loving each other and then him?

There was no reason in the world why he should have made up such a fantastic thing, Janey thought. So he had really done that. Somehow he had made her feel rejected and unwanted. She didn't enjoy the sensation. She had thought that she meant something to Charley—meant something other than dollars and cents, that is.

Apparently not.

As she lay there by his side after their session, Janey began to rethink their whole relationship. She started to see that it was dangerous to get emotionally involved with Charley. Very dangerous indeed. She had been just on the edge of falling in love with him.

But you didn't want to fall in love with a man who was capable of going off and casually having himself an orgy with a pair of Lesbians.

Charley was a guy to live with, yes. To ball now and then, yes. Above all, a business partner. So long as she kept things on that basis, Janey thought, everything would be all right. But when she started getting delusions that there was more to their relationship than that, she knew she would be asking for trouble.

Charley said, "What are you thinking about so hard, baby?"

"Things."

"Like what?"

"Like where we're going to go for dinner tonight," Janey said.

"The best place in town. Whichever it is. You'll dress up in your new finery and we'll have ourselves a ball. We'll shoot the works."

"Dutch treat, I suppose?"

"Come on, Janey, don't be sarcastic!"

"We went Dutch treat on the champagne," Janey pointed out.

"Not tonight," he said. "Tonight's going to be my treat, And nothing spared."

He rolled toward her. His hands sought her breasts, cupped them, trapped them playfully. He played with the rosy little nubs of puckered flesh that jutted out.

He said, "Everything okay again now?"

"Sure, Charley. Sure."

But she couldn't forget about those two Lesbian girls and the things Charley had told her he had done with them yesterday.

CHAPTER TEN

They went out and had dinner that night at the Chateau Mazarin, the finest French restaurant west of Paris, south of New York, and east of New Orleans. Janey wore the sleekest and most daring of her new dresses. She donned her necklace and her gold bracelet. She put a dab of "Joy" between her breasts. At umpty-ump dollars per ounce, you didn't smear perfume on like eau de cologne.

Charley dressed up too, in his best suit and a sharp tie. They made an impressive-looking couple as the big Imperial pulled up in front of the Mazarin's striped-awninged front and they got out.

The doorman smiled graciously at them. Charley smiled back, every bit as graciously, and, arm in arm, he and Janey went into the restaurant.

"Do you think my neckline's too low?" Janey whispered anxiously.

"It looks great."

"I know that. But does it look too much like I'm an exhibitionist?"

"Low necklines are very fashionable in this set," Charley assured her. "Stop worrying about things. You look gorgeous, Janey."

"I don't want to be out of place," she said.

A slick-looking maitre d' loomed up before them. Charley said glibly, "Reservation for C. Simmons, table for two."

"Of course, m'sieur. Would you come this way?"

Janey's eyes widened as she saw the interior of the restaurant. The walls were hung with mirrors, and between the mirrors there glistened marble columns, and red velvet hangings. Impeccably dressed waiters and busboys stood about. There were tables of goodies scattered through the room, groaning with cheeses and hors d'oeuvres and desserts and appetizers. At one of the tables a towering waiter was engaged in making some flaming dish, his long arms weaving through the air as he dumped brandy into the pot and touched off leaping blue flames.

The maitre d' led them to a banquette along one mirrored wall, and sat them side by side, facing outward so that they could watch the goings-on.

Janey was relieved to see that she wasn't over dressed for this place. Diagonally across from her was a woman whose neckline was just as low as her own—a big blonde, well along into her forties, with mountainous heavy breasts overflowing her black dress. It wasn't exactly a pretty sight, Janey thought, but the woman seemed fashionable and relaxed, as though she had no doubts at all about the tightness of her costume. Good, Janey thought. She didn't want to seem out of place.

A tuxedoed waiter asked softly, "Wouldn't m'sieu and madame care for cocktails before dinner?"

"I think so," Charley said. He glanced at Janey and said, "What would you like?"

She felt flustered. She knew she ought to ask for some kind of sophisticated fancy-restaurant sort of cocktail, but she couldn't think of any. The only thing that came into her head was Scotch on the rocks. So she ordered that.

The waiter gave her a peculiar glance, as though she had asked for milk or maybe tomato juice.

Charley said, "I'll have a gimlet."

The waiter moved away. Janey said, "Why did he look at me like that?"

"I guess it's what you ordered. Scotch on the rocks isn't what he figured you for."

Her cheeks reddened. "What should I have ordered, then?"

"Something lady-like. A glass of sherry, maybe. Or sweet vermouth on the rocks with a twist of lemon peel in it," Charley said.

"My mind wouldn't work. I tried to think of those things and I couldn't."

"Should I call him back? You can get some sherry instead?"

"No," Janey said. "That would only make it worse. I don't want to start a fuss."

She felt very small, very ignorant, very unsophisticated. But it wasn't her fault, she told herself. She had never had a chance to eat in places like this. She'd learn. Give her some time.

The drinks arrived.

Charley said, "We'd like to look at the menu now."

"Of course, m'sieur."

The menu was about a yard long and sumptuously engraved. Just about everything on it was in French except the prices. The prices were in dollars and cents, and they were fantastic. Janey's eyes bulged as she looked at them. Everything was a la carte—everything. "Potage"—that was soup, she remembered—soup was a buck or a buck-fifty, depending on which kind you ordered. The appetizers ranged all the way from a dollar fifty for something with an incomprehensible name all the way up to seven dollars for caviar. How much caviar did they give you for seven bucks, Janey wondered?

And the main dishes—six dollars, seven, seven-fifty! Even a salad was a dollar. Coffee was seventy-five cents, she saw. Her head swam. Her idea of a really fancy meal was a five-dollar dinner that included everything from soup to dessert. Here you couldn't even get a main dish for five bucks, and all the rest was extra.

She glanced at Charley and said, "You eat at places like this very often?"

"Not really. Why?"

"I was just wondering. Looks pretty flossy. The prices, I mean."

"Don't worry. It's Mark Avery's money we're spending tonight."

"And I can't figure out what half the menu means," Janey said.

"What's troubling you?"

"Can you translate some of these things for me?" she asked. "What's— escargots?"

"Snails," he said. "They cook them in a kind of garlic and butter sauce."

Janey shivered. "Forget that one. How about coquille St. Jacques?"

"Beats me," Charley said. "Why don't you order it and find out?"

"It might turn out to be frog's heads," she said. "I'd rather not experiment."

Between them, they managed to puzzle out enough things to make a meal from. Charley knew a lot more about the meaning of the things on the menu than she did, but he didn't really know much, she discovered. He was best at translating the easy things. But about two items out of three on the menu stumped him.

And though he didn't mind pronouncing things out loud to her, he was wary about trying his French out on the waiter. Instead of naming things, he simply said, "We'll have this… and this… and this…." while pointing at items on the menu.

The waiter smiled as though he was used to American ignorance. "Very good, sir."

"And let me see the wine list."

"Certainly, sir."

They had played it safe and ordered filet mignon for the main dish, and cold mashed potatoes—that, at least, presented no translation problems. Charley leafed through the wine list, which was no simple card but an elaborate leather-bound book of about twenty pages. He frowned deeply.

"Let's see," he said. "With steak, you want red wine. Something good. A Burgundy, I think."

Janey peered over his shoulder. "Here we are. Red Burgundy. But there are twenty of them!"

"Well, pick one."

"Just in the dark?"

"Why not?"

"And look at the prices! Six, seven dollars a bottle!" Janey exclaimed.

"That's nothing. Here's one down here for fifteen smackers."

"Should we order it?"

"It would be wasted on us," Charley said. "Let's pick one in the middle here. Number 112. Chambertain. That sounds like a good solid wine."

It was. It was a sturdy red wine with plenty of oomph, and they toasted each other with it, grinning in mutual satisfaction. They hadn't really done badly in the ordering department, considering their abysmal ignorance of French restaurants. They had had oysters casino for their appetizer—a successful guess at the French on Charley's part—and then vichyssoise, which required no guessing, and the filet mignon, rare, with mushrooms and cold mashed potatoes. The big bottle of wine left them relaxed and happy, washing away their self-consciousness, and by the time they came to the end of the meal Charley was able to tell the waiter grandly, "Well have cheese for dessert, and some cognac with our coffee, please."

"Very good, sir."

Janey leaned back against the soft upholstery. "I'm stuffed fit to burst."

"So am I. But it was good, wasn't it?"

"I never knew food could taste like that."

"Some people eat in restaurants like this every night," Charley said.

"I bet they're fat as pigs."

"Probably they are. And rich as kings, too."

"I wouldn't want to eat some place like this very often," Janey said. "The thrill would wear off."

"I don't know," he said. "I can think of some other things where the thrill doesn't wear off when you keep on doing them. Unless you're a hog about them and do them six times a night."

Janey laughed. "I suppose. But it's different with eating."

She closed her eyes a moment, then carefully opened them and let them focus. All the drinking was making her woozy. The Scotch, the wine, now the cognac—it was quite a load to take on.

But when the check arrived it sobered her instantly. She stared at it in astonishment. It was for thirty-nine dollars!

"I never thought two people could possibly spend that much on dinner," she gasped.

Charley smiled unhappily. "It seems kind of high, doesn't it?"

"Add it up. Maybe they made a mistake."

"I don't think so. Six bucks for four drinks, seven for wine, fourteen for the steaks—heck, that's twenty-seven right there. And then the soup, the dessert, the salad, whatnot—sure. Thirty-nine bucks."

"Plus tip."

"Plus tip," he agreed. "Let's see—I guess six bucks is right. Makes forty-five."

"I used to work practically a whole week for that kind of money," Janey said. "And here we are eating it up in two hours."

"Funny how things change, ain't it?" Charley said. He took out his wallet and dropped one of the crisp fifty-dollar bills into the tray. The waiter scooped it up and carried it off, returning after a while with Charley's eleven dollars of change. Charley pocketed a five-dollar bill. "Not much left out of a fifty, is there?" he said ruefully.

The waiters and busboys and maitre d' bowed them out of the restaurant. Janey felt a warm glow of satiation as they emerged into the street. She had been wined and dined like a princess tonight. Here she was, wearing an eighty-buck dress and a twenty-buck bra, with a ninety-buck necklace around her throat and her share of a forty-five buck dinner in her stomach, getting into a plushly elegant Imperial limousine. She had come a long way from that Delaware hash house, she thought. A long, long way.

"You know what I want to do now?" Janey asked.

"Can't guess."

"First I want to go for a drive. Get on some highway and drive at eighty miles an hour. I want to feel the wind rushing past."

"And then?"

"Then I want to go home and take off every stitch of clothing I'm wearing."

"And then?"

"Then," she said, "I want to get some exercise. To burn up all these calories I ate tonight."

They did just what she said. First they drove, whooshing through the moonlit night at eighty and sometimes eight-five miles an hour, and the breeze coursing through the car's open windows helped to cool Janey, who was flushed and perspired from all her eating and drinking.

Then Charley turned the car homeward. It was something of a comedown to step out of the big, handsome automobile and enter their miserable little furnished flat. It was like Cinderella's coach turning into a pumpkin again at midnight.

But this particular Cinderella didn't mind too much. The place of residence could always be improved later on. A few more jobs at five hundred or a thousand cookies per throw and they'd get themselves a more imposing apartment somewhere. There was time for all that. Things were moving quite fast enough as it was.

They went in.

Janey removed her clothing. Everything but the necklace. She stood in the middle of the room wearing the strip of gold that curved down over the high-rising hillocks of her breasts, and she smiled at Charley and held out her arms toward him invitingly.

"Come here," she said.

He went to her. He cupped her breasts, slipping his hands up under the necklace. Kissing her, he ran his hands around her body, to the taut globes of her buttocks. Then he led her to the bed.

"Take the armor off," he said.

"Don't you want me to wear my necklace while you love me, Charley?"

"That's got sharp edges. Anyway, I like my women naked in bed."

She giggled. Then she unclipped the gold necklace and put that aside.

They got onto the bed. His arms encircled her.

And then they put the topper on the evening, sealing that with a celebration of love that was the ideal finish for a night of luxurious carousing.

It was a couple of weeks after that before Janey went after the next mark.

She felt reluctant to do so. She wasn't in immediate need of cash—she had done all the shopping she wanted to do, for the time being—and the Mark Avery experience had been such a bruising one that she was in no hurry to subject herself to the whims of the next victim. And, so long as Charley had plenty of cash in his pocket, he didn't push her.

But the days went by, and the cash supply dwindled. They went to the beach a lot, toasting in the sun. They drove out to the race track a couple of times, Charley losing fifty bucks the first time, winning thirty bucks the second. They went sightseeing. They ate dinner out often, though not on the same extravagant scale as that night at the Chateau Mazarin. One way and another, they got all the benefits of a Miami vacation. And as the old year ebbed toward Christmas, the town began to fill up with vacationers.

Charley started to nudge her, now.

"Time for another hit," he said.

"Wait a couple of days."

"What for?"

"I'm not in the mood."

"Hey, come on! I'm down to a couple of hundred bucks. It's expensive loafing around down here."

"All right," she said. "All right. You don't need to nag me."

She made up her mind to go through with it. Like a visit to the dentist, she thought, except that you got a payoff at the end. She knew she couldn't duck Charley much longer. This was what they were down here for, after all. There were risks, sure—risks of arrest, risks that the operation would blow up in their faces, risks that she might get seriously hurt by one of her "lovers." But there were risks in any kind of business venture. And the potential profits here were high.

So Janey dressed up again and went out on the prowl. She picked up a middle-aged Milwaukee businessman at the Morley Plaza Hotel, went with him to his room, and submitted to about ten minutes of his sweaty, grunting lust. Then she rang in Charley.

He asked for a thousand dollars, on the theory that what he had been able to wangle out of Mark Avery he might be able to milk from the next sucker too. But the Milwaukee businessman wasn't Mark

Avery. He didn't have that kind of money. He turned pink and purple, and paced up and down, and talked about jumping out the window to avoid the embarrassment of arrest or the pain of blackmail.

"Don't do that," Charley said. "What would it get you? You've got dough or you wouldn't have come here. What's the sense of killing yourself?"

After long haggling, he settled for four hundred dollars as the price of his freedom. Not bad, not good. It brought their take so far to nineteen bills during the month, but they had hoped for more.

"We'll make it up next time," Janey said.

"How about tomorrow?"

"Too soon. Remember, you wanted to space these jobs, didn't you?"

"I guess. All right, next Wednesday, then."

"So soon?"

"We got expenses, baby. You want to have more fancy dinners? We got to take in more than four hundred bucks a throw, then."

Charley bugged her all week. He was changing, Janey sensed. He was getting hungrier for the dollar. At the beginning, he had talked about not being greedy, about not killing the goose that laid the golden eggs. But now all he could think about was how soon she could get out there and pick up another sucker.

It was that night at the restaurant, Janey thought. That touch of luxury. It had wowed him as much as it had her, apparently. The thrill of being able to plunk forty-five bucks down on a tin tray and walk out without giving it a second thought. He wanted money, now. Lots of it. And the way he could get it was through her.

A week later, they played the game again. This time, their involuntary playmate was an accountant from Chicago. They shook him down for six hundred dollars. That rounded things off, making up for the four hundred that the other one had given them.

They had dinner at Mazarin again to celebrate. This time, Janey ordered caviar for her appetizer. Why shouldn't she? Mark Avery had taught her that she liked the stuff. And it was only seven bucks. Seven, and she had earned twenty-five hundred from her four suckers.

The check came to fifty-two dollars that night, including tip.

As they drove home, Charley said, "The last time I took you here it was weeks before I could get you to go out and work again. Is it gonna be the same way now?"

"Don't worry."

"It's New Year's. The height of the season. We ought to be able to pick ourselves a good one."

"All right," Janey said.

"Day after tomorrow?"

"That would be two this week, Charley."

"The season isn't going to last forever."

"I'll see. I'll think about it."

"What's the matter?" he asked. "Don't you like making money?"

"Some of these old guys, they're no fun to make love with," she said. "You ought to try an old bag sometime and see what she's like."

"So pick yourself a young one next time, then," Charley said.

"All right," Janey replied. "I will."

CHAPTER ELEVEN

Janey stood in front of the mirror, combing her hair, admiring the youthful beauty of her full-breasted body. Tonight she was going out on the prowl again. Before she saw this room again, she figured, they'd be another five hundred or a thousand bucks ahead.

It was a real sweet setup, Janey thought. Despite the risks and the nuisance involved. It was one of the niftiest, coolest cons anybody had ever thought up.

Behind her Charley said, "Hurry it up, Janey. It's after eight o'clock. We want to catch our mark before it gets too late."

She didn't look around at him. "Don't rush me," Janey said evenly. "I hate being rushed, Charley. You ought to know that by now."

Deliberately and slowly she finished doing her hair, and reached for the filmy underthings lying spread out on the bed. She smiled in pleasure at the sight of her nakedness in the mirror. Her body, she knew, was her biggest asset in life, lean but full in the places that counted, with firm high breasts and flaring hips.

It was almost as if she had been specially designed for the racket Charley had dreamed up for her. She had the body of a girl in the first ripeness of youth. When she wore her sweater-and-bobbysocks outfit and kept her hair pulled back in an adolescent-style pony-tail, she could easily pass for only sixteen or seventeen. And she knew how to turn on that dewy-eyed, virginal look, too.

"Come on," Charley said impatiently, as she fumbled with her buttons.

She glared at him. "I tell you, I don't like to be rushed."

"It's getting late."

"You're bugging me, Charley. Don't bug me, or I'll get sore at you. Remember, I can do this act without you, but you're nowhere without me."

"Is that a hint?"

"It ain't nothing. I'm just telling you not to get on my nerves," Janey said. "I got to look cool for this performance tonight, you dope."

He sighed in loud irritation at her slowness, but nothing else was said until she was finished dressing. Right now Janey looked nothing at all like a teenager, with her hair done up in a fancy coiffure, her eyes darkened by make-up, her dress cut low in front to show the ripe, tanned hills of her firm breasts.

This was going to be the fifth time in their eight weeks down here that they had worked the gambit. So far they were four for four, and you can't have a more perfect batting average than that. It was easy enough to make the suckers come across, Janey thought. Most of them were down here alone to get away from their wives for a while, or else newly divorced or widowed, and the last thing in the world they wanted was to get hauled up on a statutory rape charge.

Of course, if somebody ever called their bluff—

Janey didn't like to think about that.

"Okay," she said to the impatiently fuming Charley. "I'm ready now."

"Damn near about time."

"Remember what I said about getting me riled up?" she said.

"Okay, okay. I'll lay off. You're pretty darned touchy tonight, though."

Janey shrugged. "I always am," she said. "Just before an engagement."

They went downstairs, and out of the house, and into the car. Charley started the engine and they went off, toward the strip of glamorous hotels.

Who was it going to be tonight, Janey wondered?

Someone good looking and reasonably young, she had promised herself. Why not? The youngest and best-looking of the other four had been the one they had gotten the biggest payoff from. So why not have pleasure and profit mixed? She thought about her four victims. The first one, Morton Kolb, the baldheaded, potbellied stockbroker from New York. Then the playboy type from Wisconsin, Mark Avery, with his red Jaguar and his little clipped mustache. After that the gray-haired businessman from Milwaukee, and the accountant from Chicago. Four out of four. They had all coughed up the cash without too much of a squawk. They were all deathly afraid of getting dragged into court on the statutory rape charge. That one was murder.

Charley parked the car across the street from the swanky, elegant Palms Hotel. He said, "It's quarter to nine now. You ought to be able to get back here by eleven or so."

"I'll do my best, general."

"I'll be waiting for you."

She went into the hotel. It was as garish and as flashy as all the other Miami Beach hostelries, all tile mosaic and glitter, fountains in the lobby, birds cluttering in cages overhead, that sort of thing.

Janey headed straight for the cocktail lounge. That was the usual place to make a pickup, wasn't it? It was as good a place as any to begin her night's quest. She didn't think it would take her very long to find her victim.

It didn't.

He was sitting at the far end of the bar, nursing what looked, at a distance, to be a martini. Janey studied him critically. He seemed to be pretty young—in his late twenties or early thirties at best—but his forehead was very high, and most likely he was sensitive about losing his hair. The best kinds, for the purpose of this sort of operation, were the sensitive ones, Janey had learned. They were easy to pick up, and they were vulnerable to Charley's pressure afterward.

This fellow wore sports clothes; he was tanned and broad-shouldered and pretty muscular, and he looked reasonably handsome except for the unfortunate thinning of his hair. Was he a singleton, or was he just waiting for wife or girl friend to join him? Janey couldn't tell that at a glance, of course. She would simply have to take her chances.

Most important, he looked well-heeled. He had that money look about him.

Janey walked over to him.

There was a seat at the bar that was empty, just to the right of him. Janey smiled sweetly, leaning ever so slightly forward to give him an ever so tempting peek at her bosom, and said. "Do you mind if I sit down here, or is it taken?"

"Go right ahead," he said. "You're welcome to it. More than welcome, matter-of-fact." His voice was deep and musical-sounding.

Janey wriggled into the seat, making sure to give him another good look at her bosom as she did so. The brassiere that she was wearing moulded her figure with seductive cunning, thrusting her ripe breasts upward and out and putting them on display. And she had a classy figure, no doubt about it.

The bartender, a swarthy, Spanish-looking man, was busy mixing drinks about a dozen stools away. Janey smiled warmly at the man next to her and said softly, "Do they make a good martini here? Some of these hotels give you a so-called martini made out of one-third gin, one-third vermouth, and one-third ice water, all for only ninety cents."

"This one isn't bad," he said. "I asked for extra dry. He gave me proportions of five to two, unless I miss my guess."

"Oh, a connoisseur, eh?"

He shrugged self-effacingly. "Oh, you get to tell the proportions by the way the drink hits your tongue," he said.

"I've never studied the subject that closely," said Janey.

"You ought to. It's quite interesting to develop your abilities. It's always a plus mark when you sharpen a bodily ability."

"I suppose it is," Janey agreed.

He smiled at her. His eyes flicked to her bosom for an instant, then to her face. "Would you like to start learning now?"

"I'd love to."

He waved to the bartender. "Carlos!"

"Momento, amigo!"

"The lady wants an extra-dry martini. The same kind you gave me."

"Si, Señor Martin."

Janey felt the warm glow of triumph, knowing that she had made her catch. And the feeling deepened as the man put a dollar bill down on the bar to pay for her drink. That was the first and essential step, getting him to buy her a drink. It meant he wasn't expecting any other girl tonight. The rest, Janey knew, would follow smoothly enough.

"Oh, no, you mustn't," Janey said as he paid for her martini.

"Don't worry about it, Miss, Miss—"

"Vaughn. Janey Vaughn."

"Janey. It's a nice name."

"Thank you," Janey said demurely.

The martini arrived. Janey sipped it without forming much of an opinion about it.

They talked for a little while.

His name, he said, was Ron Martin. He was an architect by profession, and he lived in Philadelphia, and he had come down to this resort city for a couple of weeks of fun and relaxation. He was, of course, unmarried. But that part was all right, Janey thought. If he came from Philadelphia, he would certainly prefer to pay up rather than to get involved in a scandal that might hit the local papers and ruin his architectural business. Janey knew Philadelphia. She knew how narrow-minded the people were, there, when it came to the private lives of professional men.

"And what about you?" he said.

Janey gave him a line that she made up on the spur of the moment. She told him that she was a local girl, that her father was dead and her mother quite poor, that a Hollywood producer had once met her and promised her a screen test if she went to Hollywood, but she had never been able to afford the fare across the country.

Ron Martin ate it all up, nodding sympathetically at every turn of the tale.

"Those Hollywood guys. They're all alike," he said. "They're just out for easy pickings."

"I didn't find that out until it was too late, though. I was only a kid. I had stars in my eyes, and he knew it."

"Took advantage of you?"

"Sure did."

"How old were you?"

"Just eighteen then," she said, not meeting his eye. "Some guys have no decency at all."

"You're so right," she said.

She kept her eye on the clock as she talked, and as the time ticked away, Janey began letting it be known less and less subtly that she was interested in going to bed with him.

Finally she said—she had had two martinis and he had had three, but every time he turned his head she had dumped a little of her drink into a nearby glass of water so that she could remain sober and in control of the situation—"It's getting pretty crowded in here, isn't it, Ron?"

"It is."

"And I think I've had about enough to drink, at least for now. How about you and me clearing out of here?" Janey suggested.

"Fine idea," he said. "Where to? A late movie? A stroll by the beach?"

"Don't pull my leg," she said. She grinned conspiratorially at him. "How about—upstairs?"

"How about that," he said.

And off they went.

His room was on the sixteenth floor, with the usual terrace and with the usual big picture window overlooking the ocean. It had the usual jumbo-sized bed, too. In these hotels, you just couldn't get a single bed. If you didn't like a lot of room when you slept, you were out of luck unless you found some company in bed.

He drew the blinds, shutting off the view, though there was nobody out there sixteen stories up over the ocean to peek. Then he pulled her to him for a passionate kiss. His mouth covered hers. His kiss was deep.

This was the best part of the whole routine, Janey thought.

She began to get excited. She hadn't had much fun with the middle-aged businessman or with the stockbroker from New York or with the accountant from Chicago, because they were clumsy, aging men who had no finesse with women. And she certainly hadn't had fun from the violent embrace of Mark Avery.

But this man held her as though he knew what a woman was for.

He caressed her tenderly, and then, slowly and almost reverently, he began to undress her. He was obviously delighted at the lush loveliness of her. Her dress came away, and then the bra, and the panties. She wore only stockings and garter belt, and she stepped back to give him the full view.

"Lovely," he murmured. "Absolutely lovely."

"Hurry," she said, her heart pounding with anticipation "Get your clothes off, Ron!"

He rapidly peeled his garments away. He was solidly built, muscular without an ounce of fat on him. For the first time in this routine Janey felt real and genuine desire for the man she was going to fleece. She was aware of warmth, of gathering need.

They moved toward the big bed.

The bed had plenty of bounce and supported them nicely. Their bodies twined. His hands went to her breasts, not gripping them roughly the way Charley might do, but cupping them delicately, the fingers spiralling inward to center on the nipples, which were now rigid with lust.

Then his hands trailed over her body, back and forth across her waist, then to the smooth satiny skin of her legs, round and round, coyly, tantalizingly, teasing her, playing with her.

His hands encountered her warmth.

His hands aroused her desire.

Janey gasped and panted. Her body twisted and turned in his arms. He was covering her with kisses now, expertly moving from place to place, now her earlobe, now the nape of her neck, now the excited little nipples.

He was a superb lover, Janey thought. He made every nerve in her body tingle.

"Take me," she whispered, when she could stand the waiting no more.

His firm, lean body moved to hers.

He took her.

She clung to him, gasping and panting, as he carried her toward the brink of satisfaction. There weren't many times in her life that she had been loved this way, Janey thought. This architect fellow really made a fine art of loving.

Her head whirled.

Her body knew frantic abandon as the ecstasy of ecstasies drew near.

Too bad this was only a con game, Janey thought. Too bad.

A sunburst of passion, a nova of bliss, blazed through her brain. Time and the universe were blotted out, and jolt after jolt of stunning ecstasy hit her, and then Janey lay still, resting in the arms of the man who was going to be the victim of extortion.

CHAPTER TWELVE

They were quiet a long time. Janey kept her eye on the clock by the side of the bed, while her delighted body gradually slid back to normal from the dizzying heights of pleasure.

At twenty minutes to eleven she gasped and said, "I'd better get going, Ron!"

"So soon? Stay all night."

"No," she said. "If I'm not home by eleven or so my mother gets terribly worried, and these days her heart isn't so good—"

"Do you have to go?"

"Yes. I have to."

"I thought you'd stay all night. The night's only beginning for us, Janey."

"I'm sorry."

"Not half as sorry as I am," he said.

His eyes followed her longingly as she got out of bed, a slim, nude, full-breasted figure, and began to gather up the clothes that he had slipped from her body an hour before. She dressed rapidly, now, three times as fast as she had dressed earlier this evening. Charley was waiting for her. There was business that had to be transacted.

As she donned her clothes and tidied her hair, he said, "This certainly was wonderful having you here like this—"

"I liked that too," Janey said, and she knew that she meant what she said.

"Will I see you again?"

"Of course."

"When?"

"How long do you expect to be in town?" she asked.

"Another week," he said.

"I'll meet you in the cocktail lounge at eight o'clock tomorrow night," Janey promised

"I'll be looking forward to that."

"Me too," she said.

"But you won't be able to stay all night tomorrow either, will you?" he asked.

She shrugged. "Maybe I can work something out. Tell my mother I'm visiting a friend."

It was ten minutes to eleven when she finished saying good-bye to him and left him in his room. Hurrying to the elevator, she rode downstairs and walked quickly across to the place where Charley had parked the car.

He was waiting for her.

He looked unhappy, the way he always did when she came back from one of these sessions. He can't help feeling jealous, Janey thought. Even though he wasn't the first fellow she had made out with, not by a long shot, he hated that when she was cooped up with anyone else. Only the thought of the five hundred bucks involved made him swallow his jealousy.

"Well?" he said roughly.

"All is well," she said. "I picked up an architect from Philly. He was looking for companionship. I gave that to him." She didn't add that she had found thrilling physical pleasure in his arms. She doubted that Charley would appreciate that detail.

"You sure took your time about things," he grunted.

"I said I'd be back here by eleven, and here I am. So what are you moaning about? Come on, get this heap moving Charley."

"Okay. Okay."

They hurried back to the apartment. Janey sped through the transformation. Out of her Cinderella-goes-to-the-ball clothes, into her working costume, the teenager rig that was so effective.

By twenty of twelve, they were on their way again, back to the hotel. Janey had magically peeled the years away with a simple change of clothes.

Up to the sixteenth floor. Down the corridor to Ron Martin's room. She and Charley exchanged a glance. He looked nervous. He didn't usually look nervous when it was time to cash in.

"Go ahead—knock!" Janey urged him.

Charley nodded. He took a deep breath, rapped twice on the door.

"Who's there?" the architect's deep voice called from within.

"Mr. Martin?" Charley said. "There's a message for you."

"I'm coming."

The door opened. Charley and Janey burst into the room, pushing past the puzzled-looking Martin. Martin was wearing only a silk dressing gown. He stared at Janey, frowning as though he couldn't believe the evidence of his eyes.

"You ever see this girl before?" Charley demanded in a tough voice.

"You're kidding," Martin said. "She looks just like—like someone I know."

"She is someone you know," Charley said.

He ran through the whole routine. It was a familiar spiel by now. He let Martin know that Janey was only seventeen, that he was her outraged brother, that he intended to bring the authorities in to deal with this dastardly case of statutory rape.

Ron Martin was bewildered and confused at first. Then he got angry, and insisted Charley was pulling his leg, that the girl who was here was some younger sister of the one he had gone to bed with. The birthmark on the leg bit settled that point.

The architect slowly shook his head as the truth got to him.

"She really is," he said. "Can you beat that? She really is!"

With that point taken care of, Charley began to touch on the most important theme: the blackmail. He worked round to the fact that he wanted to keep his sister's name out of the court records and out of the newspapers. He might accept some kind of payment, he let it be known.

"How much?" Martin asked.

"Give me five hundred bucks, cash down," Charley said. "And then get yourself out of town by tomorrow. You do that, I'll forget that you're the louse who seduced my kid sister."

Instead of answering, Martin began to laugh. His eyes twinkled with mirth. They had never gotten this kind of reaction from a mark before.

"What's so funny?" Charley growled.

"Nothing, really," the architect said. "Except that this is such a good dodge I wish I had thought of it myself."

Janey and Charley exchanged glances. This guy didn't seem as doltish as the others.

"Huh?" Charley said. "What are you talking about? What kind of dodge?"

Martin folded his arms. He looked relaxed, cool as a cucumber. "I mean, this business of sending the girl into a hotel to pick up wealthy strangers, and then dressing her up as a teenager to milk some dough. It's a lovely idea! Lovely! And I don't mind telling you, you pretty near fooled me, too."

Charley's face darkened. He took a step forward.

"Listen, mac. I don't know what you're chattering about, but I want five hundred bucks for what you did to my sister, and I want it—"

"Fast," Martin finished for him. "Listen yourself, mac," he said. "It's a good story, and you put it over well, and she sure looks the part. Only a little common sense tears the whole thing to pieces. If your kid sister's as young and as innocent as she looks and as you say she is, where'd she learn to be so good on a bed? That 'teenager' knows some pretty grown-up stunts, let me tell you. And she puts on a pretty sophisticated line in a bar, too, coming on with talk about the proportions of martinis. So I'm not swallowing your story. Tell it to the cops if you want. See where it gets you, huh?"

Charley was absolutely silent. Janey looked at him in surprise. This was the first time anyone had called their bluff.

They couldn't go to the cops, of course. Martin wasn't guilty of a thing except going to bed with her, and there was no law against that, not when she was five years past the age of consent. If he flatly refused to pay up, they couldn't do a thing.

Charley said uncertainly, "I want that five hundred bucks, or—"

"Or you'll go to the cops. So go to the cops, if you want to," Martin said. "Try telling them she's seventeen, and prove it. You got a birth certificate or something?" Martin laughed. "Suppose you two get the devil out of here, now, before I call the cops and have you both run in for extortion. It's been very pleasant talking to you, and it was very nice to get an hour in bed with your sister, or whoever she is. Now beat it. Scram."

Janey saw the anger flare up in Charley.

"Why, you lousy—"

He came rumbling forward. He was three or four inches taller than Martin, and maybe thirty pounds heavier. He brought one big fist up, but before he could do anything Martin's right hand came slipping in between Charley's fists and landed a blow in the middle.

Charley grunted and stopped advancing. Martin came in to attack him.

In short order Charley was cut to ribbons. He had weaved in and out, round about the confused Charley, all the weight and size on his side, but Martin fought with what was practically professional skill. His fists landing damaging blows on face, chest, midsection.

Charley's lip was split and bloody, his eye puffed, his cheek bruised— all within a moment. He hadn't landed a single blow himself.

Janey stood frozen, unable to do a thing, as Martin mercilessly battered Charley to a pulp and finally grabbed him by the shoulder and shoved him, tottering dizzily, out into the hall.

Martin slammed the door.

Janey said, "Let me out of here. You hurt him!"

"He asked for it."

"Let me out," she said. "Why are you keeping me in here?"

Martin stepped forward, grinning, and his hand shot out and dug into her shoulder. He said, "You've got a pretty good racket here, kiddo. It's too bad you picked the wrong customer to deal with. How old are you—I mean, really?"

"None of your lousy business."

"How old are you?"

"None of your lousy business."

Martin's open hand sailed through the air and collided with Janey's cheek. The impact of the blow nearly tore her head off.

"For the third time," he said. "Don't make me knock all your teeth out. How old?"

"I'm—I'm almost twenty-three," she said, stammering with fright.

"That's about what I thought. Though you make a very convincing teenager in this outfit, I must say. Okay. We leave for New York first thing tomorrow morning."

"New York? We leave?"

He nodded smilingly. "I was just handing you a line, about me being from Philadelphia and being an architect. I'm from New York. Down here on vacation. I'm not an architect, either. I'm—I'm in a number of businesses. And now I've got a new one."

"I don't understand you."

"You will, soon enough. You have any family here? Are you married to that goon I beat up?"

"I was just living with him," Janey said faintly. "I don't have any family."

"Okay, then. You're coming with me. I'll set you up in my place in New York and we'll run this statutory rape gimmick for all its worth."

"No—no," Janey murmured. "Charlie and I—we were partners ..."

"He's a nothing."

"I don't want to go away with you."

The so-called architect's face was suddenly menacing. "You'll leave with me or I'll fix you so you aren't good for anything after this. You hear?"

Thoughts pinwheeled wildly through Janey's head. She was afraid of this strange man, afraid of his strength, his cruelty. But he offered the mystery and adventure of New York, of money. Why hang around with—he said it—a nothing like Charley, when she could go to New York? She wavered half afraid, half tempted.

Suddenly the door burst open. Charley stood there a battered, bloody, disheveled figure. There was a knife in his hand. He had gone back to the car to get the knife, Janey thought.

"Okay, you wise guy," Charley muttered in a low, hate-filled voice. "You're pretty handy with your fists, ain'tcha? And you got cute ideas about my girl? Well, after I've carved you a little maybe you'll have different ideas."

He came forward, kicking the door shut behind him. Martin, unarmed, retreated into a corner of the room. He had gone very pale. Charley was like a hulking gorilla, moving slowly toward him with the knife.

"Nobody gets to beat me up like that," Charley grunted. "I'm gonna cut your ears off first. And then—"

"Keep away from me, you ape!"

Janey watched, dry throated. In another moment Charley would reach him, would cut him up, and then the two of them would be free to leave. Suddenly she remembered the way Martin had talked to her in the bar, that smooth, slick way, and the way he had been later, loving her so excitingly. And she thought about Charley and his two Lesbian girl friends, thought about Charley fumbling his way through that French menu.

The decision took only a second to make.

Janey grabbed up the ornamental vase that was sitting on top of the television set, and smashed it down on Charley's skull.

He dropped like a felled oak. She looked down, seeing the blood welling out of his hair.

"Janey," he whimpered. "Janey—you hit me—"

His voice died away. He was out cold. Martin snatched the knife from his nerveless fingers and put it in his pocket.

"I didn't think you were going to do that," Martin said in a hoarse voice. "I thought for sure that ape was going to cut me up."

Janey smiled. There was a strange, bright, new look about her. She looked down at the bloody, unconscious Charley.

To hell with him, she thought.

"We leave for New York first thing tomorrow," she said.

THE END

THE EROTIC NOVELS OF ROBERT SILVERBERG

As by Loren Beauchamp
Love Nest (Midwood, 1958)
Another Night, Another Love (Midwood, 1959)
Connie (Midwood, 1959)
Unwilling Sinner (Midwood, 1959)
Meg (Midwood, 1960; reprinted as *All the Best Beds* as by Don Elliott, 1967)
Nurse Carolyn (Midwood, 1960; reprinted as *Registered Nympho* as by Don Elliott, 1967)
And When She Was Bad (Midwood, 1961)
Sin on Wheels (Midwood, 1961; reprinted as *Orgy on Wheels* as by Don Elliott, 1967)
The Fires Within (Midwood, 1961)
Campus Sex Club (Midwood, 1962)
Sin a la Carte (Midwood, 1962)
Strange Delights (Midwood, 1962)
Wayward Widow (Midwood, 1962; reprinted as *Free Sample*, 1968)
The Wife Traders (Boudoir, 1963)

As by Dr. Walter C. Brown
The Single Girl (Monarch, 1961)

As by David Challon
Campus Love Club (Bedside, 1959; reprinted as *Campus Sex Club* as by Loren Beauchamp, 1962)
French Sin Port (Bedside, 1959; reprinted as *Rouge of the Riviera* as by Don Elliott, 1967)
Suburban Sin Club (Bedside, 1959; abridged & reprinted as *The Wife Traders* as by Loren Beauchamp, 1963)
Thirst for Love (Bedside, 1959; reprinted as *Wayward Widow* as by Loren Beauchamp, 1962)
Man Mad (Chariot, 1960)
Suburban Affair (Bedside, 1960)

Campus Hellcat and Other Stories (Bedside, 1960)

As by John Dexter
Stripper! (Nightstand, 1960; reprinted as *One Bed Too Many* by Jeremy Dunn)
Sex Thieves (Nightstand, 1961; reprinted as *Wife in Name Only* by Jeremy Dunn, 1974)
Sin Festival (Nightstand, 1961; reprinted as *The Goddess Makers* by Jeremy Dunn, 1974)
The Bra Peddlers (Nightstand, 1961; reprinted as *The Venus Affair* by Jeremy Dunn, 1974)
The Lust Plotters (Nightstand, 1962)
Passion Bum (Nightstand, 1962)

As Walter Drummond
Philosopher of Evil: The Life & Works of the Marquis de Sade (nf; Regency, 1962)
How to Spend Money (nf; Regency, 1963)

As by Dan Eliot
Dial O-R-G-Y (Ember, 1963)
Flesh Flames (Ember, 1963)
Lust Lover (Pillar, 1963)
Nympho (Ember, 1963)
Sin Doll (Ember, 1963)
Sin Hellion (Ember, 1963)
Sin Mates (Pillar, 1963)

Don Elliott (all published by Greenleaf under various imprints)
Love Addict (1959)
Gang Girl (1959)
Naked Holiday (1960)
The Flesh Peddlers (1960; reprinted as *The Flesh Merchants*, 1973)
The Lecher (1960)
Mistress of Sin (1960; reprinted as *Depravity Town*, 1973)

Party Girl (1960)
  Sin on Wheels (1960; reprinted as *The Instructor*, 1973)
Passion Trap (1960; reprinted as *Carnal Cage*, 1973)
Sex Jungle (1960; reprinted as *Jungle Street*, 1973)
Convention Girl (1960; reprinted as *The Man Collector*, 1973)
Summertime Affair (1960)
Woman Chaser (1960)
Backstreet Sinner (1961; reprinted as *The Bed and the Beautiful*, 1973)
Expense Account Sinners (1961; reprinted as *Keep the Clients Happy*, 1973)
Lust Goddess (1961; reprinted as *The Temptress*, 1973)
Lust Queen (1961; reprinted as *The Decadent*, 1974)
The Lust Seekers (1961; reprinted as *Till Love Do Us Part*, 1974)
Sin Club (1961; reprinted as *The Lady from Soho*, 1974)
Sin Cruise (1961; reprinted as *Fifteen Nights of Love*, 1973)
The Sinful Ones (1961; reprinted as *Every Night in Rome*, 1974)
Wild Divorcee (1961; reprinted as *Nowhere Girl*, 1973)
Streets of Sin (1961; reprinted as *The Untamed*, 1974)
Hotrod Sinners (1962)
Kept Man (1962)
Lust Captive (1962; reprinted as *The Game Susan Played*, 1974)
Lust Cat (1962)
Lust Cult (1962; reprinted as *None But the Wicked*, 1974)
Lust for Two (1962)
Lust Lord (1962)
Lust Market (1962)
No Lust Tonight (1962)
The Orgy Boys (1962)
Passion Thieves (1962)
Roadhouse Girl (1962; reprinted as *No Pleasure So Painful*, 1974)

Sex Fury (1962)
Sexteen (1962)
Shame House (1962)
Sin Bait (1962)
Sin Kin (1962)
Sin Quest (1962)
Sin Sick (1962)
Three Sinners (1962; reprinted as *A Change for the Bedder*, 1974)
Wild Flesh (1962)
Lust Crew (1963)
Passion Patsy (1963)
Sex Bait (1963)
Sex Bum (1963)
Sin Crazed (1963)
Sin Made (1963)
Sin Servant (1963)
Beatnik Wanton (1964)
Black Market Shame (1964)
Flesh Bride (1964)
Flesh Lesson (1964)
Flesh Melody (1964)
Flesh Pawns (1964)
Flesh Prize (1964)
The Flesh Seekers (1964)
Flesh Taker (1964)
Gutter Road (1964)
Lust Burns (1964)
Lust League (1964)
Lust Set (1964)
Lust Spree (1964)
Orgy Isle (1964)
Orgy Maid (1964)
Passion Pair (1964)
Passion Partners (1964)
Passion Trio (1964)
Pickup (1964)
Shameless (1964)
Sin Bin (1964)
Sin Circuit (1964)
Sin Partners (1964)
Sin Service (1964)
Sin Sold (1964)
Switch Trap (1964)
Wanton Web (1964)
Alternate Wife (1965)
Carnal Carnival (1965)
Escape to Sindom (1965)

Flesh Bigamist (1965)
Flesh Boarder (1965)
Flesh Cry (1965)
Flesh Man (1965)
Good Girl, Bad Girl (1965)
Lust Doomed (1965)
Lust Finale (1965)
Naked She Died (1965)
The Nite Lusters (1965)
Nudie Packet (1965)
Of Shame Reborn (1965)
Only the Depraved (1965)
Orgy Slaves (1965)
Passion Killer (1965)
Passion Peeper (1965)
Passion Pusher (1965; cover listed as
    by Don Holliday)
The Shame Protector (1965)
Shame Scheme (1965)
Sin for Solace (1965)
Sin Kill (1965)
Sin Spin (1965)
The Sin Switch (1965)
Sin Warped (1965)
The Sins of Seena (1965)
Teaser (1965)
Would-Be Sinner (1965)
The Young Wantons (1965)
All on Sunday (1966)
Big Blast (1966)
Campus Traders (1966)
Cousin Lover (1966)
Diary of Desire (1966)
Every Bed Her Own (1966)
The Gay Girls (1966)
Initiates (1966)
Lust Demon (1966)
One Night Stand (1966)
Pain Lusters (1966)
The Passion Barons (1966; reprint of
    Streets of Sin by Mark Ryan, 1959)
Take My Wife (1966)
The Virtuous Ones (1966)
All the Best Beds (1967)
Carnal Counselor (1967; ghost-
    written, author unknown)
Diary of a Dyke (1967)
Flesh Fever (1967)

Flesh Tryst (1967)
Orgy on Wheels (1967)
Registered Nympho (1967)
Rogue of the Riviera (1967)
Those Who Lust (1967)
The Wanton West (1967)

As by Marlene Longman
Sin Girls (Nightstand, 1960;
    reprinted as *The Tormented*, 1973)

As by Dan Malcolm
The Mystery of the Judge's Mistress
    (*Guilty*, March 1962)

As by Ray McKenzie
The Wild Party (Chariot, 1960)

As by Gordon Mitchell
Immoral Wife (Midwood, 1959;
    reprinted as *Henry's Wife*, 1961)

As by Mark Ryan
Company Girl (Bedside, 1959)
Streets of Sin (Bedside, 1959;
    reprinted as *The Passion Barons*
    as by Don Elliott, 1966)
Twisted Love, (Bedside, 1959;
    reprinted as *Strange Delights* as
    by Loren Beauchamp, 1962)
Savage Love (Bedside, 1960)
Illicit Affair and Other Stories
    (Bedside, 1961)

As by Stan Vincent
The Hot Beat (Magnet, 1960)

As by L. H. Walker
The Lascivious Abbott (Greenleaf,
    1967; introduction by L. T.
    Woodward)

As by L. T. Woodward, M. D.
Sex Fiend (Monarch, 1961)
Sex and Hypnosis (Monarch, 1961)
Sex in Our Schools (Monarch, 1962)
Virgin Wives (Monarch, 1962)
The Deceivers (Beacon, 1962)

90% of What You Know About Sex is
  Wrong (Parliament, 1962)
Sex and the Armed Forces
  (Monarch, 1963)
The History of Surgery (Monarch,
  1963)
You and Your Sex Life (Monarch,
  1963)
Twilight Women (Lancer, 1963)
Masochism (Monarch, 1964)
Sex and the Divorced Woman
  (Lancer, 1964)
Sophisticated Sex Techniques in
  Marriage (Lancer, 1967)
I Am a Nymphomaniac (Belmont,
  1967)

THE SCIENCE FICTION WORKS OF ROBERT SILVERBERG

Novels

Revolt on Alpha C (Thomas Crowell,
  1955; Scholastic, 1959)
The 13th Immortal (Ace, 1956)
Master of Life and Death (Ace, 1957)
The Shrouded Planet (with Randall
  Garrett, as Robert Randall;
  Gnome. 1957; Dell. 1963)
Invaders from Earth (Ace, 1958)
Lest We Forget Thee, Earth (as
  Calvin M. Knox; Ace, 1958)
Stepsons of Terra (Ace, 1958)
Aliens from Space (as David
  Osborne; Avalon, 1958)
Invisible Barriers (as David
  Osborne; Avalon, 1958)
Starhaven (as Ivar Jorgenson;
  Avalon, 1958; Ace, 1959)
Starman's Quest (Gnome, 1958)
The Plot Against Earth (as Calvin
  M. Knox; Ace, 1959)
The Dawning Light (with Randall
  Garrett, as Robert Randall;
  Gnome, 1959; Dell, 1963)
The Planet Killers (Ace, 1959)
Lost Race of Mars (Scholastic, 1960)

Collision Course (Avalon, 1961; Ace,
  1961)
The Seed of Earth (Ace, 1962)
Recalled to Life (Lancer, 1962;
  revised version, Doubleday, 1972)
Blood on the Mink (written in 1959,
  first published in 1962 as "Too
  Much Blood on the Mink" in
  Trapped magazine, re-published
  by Hard Case Crime, 2012)
The Silent Invaders (Ace, 1963)
Time of the Great Freeze (Holt,
  Rinehart and Winston, 1964; Dell,
  1966)
Regan's Planet (Pyramid, 1964)
One of Our Asteroids is Missing (as
  Calvin M. Knox; Ace, 1964)
Conquerors from the Darkness
  (Holt, Rinehart and Winston, 1965;
  Dell, 1968)
The Gate of Worlds (Holt, Rinehart
  and Winston, 1967; Magnum,
  1980)
Planet of Death (Holt, Rinehart and
  Winston, 1967)
Thorns (Ballantine, 1967)
Those Who Watch (Signet, 1967)
The Time Hoppers (Doubleday, 1967;
  Avon, 1968)
To Open the Sky (Ballantine, 1967)
World's Fair 1992 (Follett, 1970; Ace,
  1982)
The Man in the Maze (Avon, 1968)
Hawksbill Station (Doubleday, 1968;
  Avon, 1970)
The Masks of Time (Ballantine,
  1968)
Nightwings (Avon, 1969)
Downward to the Earth (serialized
  in Galaxy, 1970; Signet, 1971)
Across a Billion Years (Dial, 1969;
  Magnum, 1979)
Three Survived (Holt, Rinehart and
  Winston, 1969)
To Live Again (Doubleday, 1969;
  Dell, 1971)
Up the Line (Ballantine, 1969)
Tower of Glass (serialized in Galaxy,

1970; Charles Scribner's Sons,
1970; Bantam, 1971)
Son of Man (Ballantine, 1971)
The Second Trip (Signet, 1971)
The World Inside (Doubleday, 1971;
Signet, 1972)
A Time of Changes (serialized in
Galaxy, 1971; Signet, 1971)
The Book of Skulls (Charles
Scribner's Sons, 1971; Signet,
1972)
Dying Inside (serialized in *Galaxy*,
1972; Charles Scribner's Sons,
1972; Ballantine,
1972)
The Stochastic Man (Harper & Row,
1975; Fawcett, 1976)
Shadrach in the Furnace (Bobbs-
Merrill, 1976; Pocket, 1978)
Homefaring (Phantasia, 1983)
Lord of Darkness (Arbor House,
1983; Bantam, 1984)
Gilgamesh the King (Arbor House,
1984; Bantam, 1985)
Sailing to Byzantium (Underwood-
Miller, 1985; Tor, 1989)
Tom O'Bedlam (Donald I. Fine, 1985;
Warner, 1986)
Star of Gypsies (Donald I. Fine,
1986; Popular Questar, 1988)
At Winter's End (Warner, 1988;
Warner, 1989)
Project Pendulum (Walker, 1989;
Bantam, 1989)
Letters From Atlantis (Atheneum,
1990; Popular Questar, 1992)
The New Springtime (Warner, 1990;
Warner, 1991)
To the Land of the Living (Gollancz,
1989; Warner, 1990)
Nightfall (expansion of the 1941
novelette "Nightfall" by Isaac
Asimov; Doubleday; 1990; Bantam,
1991)

Thebes of the Hundred Gates
(Axolotl/Pulphouse, 1991; Bantam,
1992)
The Face of the Waters (Bantam,
1991; Bantam, 1992)
Child of Time (expansion and
revision of the 1958 novelette
"Lastborn" by Isaac Asimov;
Gollancz, 1991; US edition, The
Ugly Little Boy, Doubleday, 1992)
Kingdoms of the Wall
(HarperCollins, 1992; Bantam,
1993)
The Positronic Man (based on the
1976 novelette The Bicentennial
Man by Isaac Asimov; Gollancz,
1992)
Hot Sky at Midnight (Bantam, 1994;
HarperCollins, 1994)
Starborne (Bantam, 1996; Voyager,
1996)
The Alien Years (HarperCollins,
1998; Harper Voyager, 1999)
The Longest Way Home (Gollancz,
2002; Harper Voyager, 2003)
Roma Eterna (Eos, 2003; Harper
Voyager, 2004)
The Last Song of Orpheus
(Subterranean, 2010)

Majipoor Chronicles

Lord Valentine's Castle (Harper &
Row, 1980; Bantam, 1981)
Majipoor Chronicles (Arbor House,
1982; Bantam, 1983)
Valentine Pontifex (Arbor House,
1983; Bantam, 1984)
The Mountains of Majipoor
(Bantam, 1995; Bantam, 1996)
Sorcerers of Majipoor (Macmillan
UK, 1997; HarperPrism, 1997)
Lord Prestimion (Harper, 1999; Eos,
2000)
King of Dreams (Voyager, 2001; Eos,
2001)
Tales of Majipoor (Gollancz, 2013;
Roc, 2013)

Short story collections

Next Stop, the Stars (Ace, 1962)
Godling, Go Home (Belmont, 1964)
Needle in a Timestack (Ballantine, 1966)
The Calibrated Alligator (Holt, Rinehart and Winston, 1969)
Dimension Thirteen (Ballantine, 1969)
The Cube Root of Uncertainty (Macmillan, 1970; Collier, 1971)
Parsecs and Parables (Doubleday, 1973)
Moonferns & Starsongs (Ballantine, 1971)
The Reality Trip and Other Implausibilities (Ballantine, 1972)
Valley Beyond Time (Dell, 1973)
Earth's Other Shadow (Signet, 1973)
Unfamiliar Territory (Charles Scribner's Sons, 1973; Berkley, 1978)
The Feast of St. Dionysus: Five Science Fiction Stories (Charles Scribner's Sons, 1975; Berkley, 1979)
Sunrise on Mercury (Thomas Nelson, 1975; Pan, 1986)
Capricorn Games (Random House, 1976; Starblaze, 1979)
The Best of Robert Silverberg (Pocket, 1976)
The Shores of Tomorrow (Thomas Nelson, 1976)
World of a Thousand Colors (Arbor House, 1982; Bantam, 1984)
The Conglomeroid Cocktail Party (Arbor House, 1984; Bantam, 1985)
Beyond the Safe Zone (Donald I. Fine, 1986; Warner, 1987)
The Collected Stories of Robert Silverberg Volume 1: Secret Sharers (Bantam, 1992)
Pluto in the Morning Light: The Collected Stories Volume 1 (Grafton, 1992)
The Secret Sharer: The Collected Stories Volume 2 (Grafton, 1993)
Beyond the Safe Zone: The Collected Stories Volume 3 (Grafton, 1994)
The Road to Nightfall: The Collected Stories Volume 4 (Grafton, 1996)
Ringing the Changes: The Collected Stories Volume 5 (Grafton, 1997)
Lion Time in Timbuctoo: The Collected Stories Volume 6 (Grafton, 2000)
Phases of the Moon (Subterranean Press, 2004),
In the Beginning: Tales from the Pulp Era (Subterranean Press, 2006)
To Be Continued: The Collected Stories Volume 1 (Subterranean Press, 2006)
To the Dark Star: The Collected Stories Volume 2 (Subterranean Press, 2007)
A Little Intelligence (with Randall Garrett; Crippen & Landru, 2009)
Something Wild Is Loose: The Collected Stories Volume 3 (Subterranean Press, 2008)
Trips: The Collected Stories Volume 4 (Subterranean Press, 2009)
The Palace at Midnight: The Collected Stories Volume 5 (Subterranean Press, 2010)
Multiples: The Collected Stories Volume 6 (Subterranean Press, 2011)
We Are for the Dark: The Collected Stories Volume 7 (Subterranean Press, 2012)
Hot Times in Magma City: The Collected Stories Volume 8 (Subterranean Press, 2013)
The Millennium Express: The Collected Stories Volume 9 (Subterranean Press, 2014)

NON-FICTION

Treasures Beneath the Sea (Whitman, 1960)

Sir Winston Churchill (as by Edgar Black; Monarch, 1961)

First American Into Space (Monarch Books, 1961)

Lost Cities and Vanished Civilizations (Chilton, 1962)

The Fabulous Rockefellers (1963)

Sunken History: The Story of Underwater Archaeology (1963)

How to spend money (as by Walter Drummond; 1963)

Fifteen Battles That Changed the World (1963)

Empires in the Dust: Ancient Civilizations Brought to Light (1963)

Home of the Red Man: Indian North America Before Columbus (1963)

The History of Surgery (1963, as L. T. Woodward)

The Great Doctors (1964)

Man Before Adam: The Story of Man in Search of His Origins (1964)

Akhnaten: The Rebel Pharaoh (1964)

1066 (1964, as Franklin Hamilton)

The Loneliest Continent: The Story of Antarctic Discovery (1964, as Walker Chapman)

The Man Who Found Nineveh: The Story of Austen Henry Layard (1964)

Great Adventures in Archaeology (1964)

Socrates (1965)

Scientists And Scoundrels: A Book of Hoaxes (1965)

Men Who Mastered the Atom (1965)

Niels Bohr: The Man Who Mapped the Atom (1965)

The Old Ones: Indians of the American Southwest (1965)

The Great Wall of China (1965)

The World of Coral (1965)

The Crusades (1965, as Franklin Hamilton)

Antarctic Conquest: The Great Explorers in Their Own Words (1966, as Walker Chapman)

The Long Rampart: The Story of the Great Wall of China (1966)

Rivers: A Book to Begin On (1966, as Lee Sebastian)

Forgotten by Time: A Book of Living Fossils (1966)

Frontiers in Archeology (1966)

Kublai Khan: Lord of Xanadu (1966, as Walker Chapman)

Leaders Of Labor (1966, as Roy Cook)

Bridges (1966)

To the Rock of Darius: The Story of Henry Rawlinson (1966)

The Hopefuls: Ten Presidential Campaigns (1966, as Lloyd Robinson)

The Morning of Mankind: Prehistoric Man in Europe (1967)

The Golden Dream: Seekers of El Dorado (1967, as Walker Chapman)

The Auk, the Dodo and the Oryx (1967)

The World of the Rain Forests (1967)

The Dawn of Medicine (1967)

The Adventures of Nat Palmer (1967)

Challenge for a Throne: The Wars of the Roses (1967, as Franklin Hamilton)

Men Against Time: Salvage Archeology in the United States (1967)

Light for the World: Edison and the Power Industry (1967)

The Search for Eldorado (1967, as Walker Chapman)

Sophisticated Sex Techniques in Marriage (1967, as L. T. Woodward)

Mound Builders of Ancient America: The Archeology of a Myth (New York Graphic Society, 1968); reprint (Ohio University Press, 1986) - Silverberg's fourth-most widely held work in WorldCat libraries

The World of the Ocean Depths (1968)

The Stolen Election: Hayes vs. Tilden, 1876 (1968, as Lloyd Robinson)

Four Men Who Changed the Universe (1968)

Sam Houston (1968, as Paul Hollander)

The South Pole: A Book to Begin On (1968, as Lee Sebastian)

Stormy Voyager (1968)

Ghost Towns of the American West (1968)

Vanishing Giants: The Story of the Sequoias (1969)

Wonders of Ancient Chinese Science (1969)

The Challenge of Climate: Man and His Environment (1969)

Bruce of the Blue Nile (1969)

The World of Space (1969)

If I Forget Thee, O Jerusalem (1970)

The Seven Wonders of the Ancient World (1970)

Mammoths, Mastodons and Man (1970)

The Mound Builders (1970)

The Pueblo Revolt (1970)

Clocks for the Ages: How Scientists Date the Past (1971)

To The Western Shore: Growth of the United States 1776-1853 (1971)

Before The Sphinx: Early Egypt (1971)

Into Space: A Young Person's Guide to Space (1971, with Arthur C. Clarke)

The Realm of Prester John (1972)

The Longest Voyage: Circumnavigation in the Age Of Discovery (1972)

John Muir, Prophet Among the Glaciers (1972)

The World Within the Ocean Wave (1972)

The World Within the Tide Pool (1972)

Drug Themes in Science Fiction (1974)

Reflections and Refractions: Thoughts on Science Fiction, Science and Other Matters (1997)

Musings and Meditations (2011)